HOUSE OF FROST AND FEATHERS

HOUSE OF FROST AND FEATHERS

A NOVEL

LAUREN WIESEBRON

[Add permissions here - style as cred.]

This is a work of fiction. Names, characters, places, and incidents are products of the author's imagination or are used fictitiously and are not to be construed as real. Any resemblance to actual events, locales, organizations, or persons, living or dead, is entirely coincidental.

HarperCollins books may be purchased for educational, business, or sales promotional use. For information, please email the Special Markets Department at SPsales@harpercollins.com.

Originally published as *House of Frost and Feathers* in the United States in 2025 by Harper Voyager, an imprint of HarperCollins.

FIRST HARPER VOYAGER PAPERBACK PUBLISHED 2025.

Designed by Alison Bloomer

Library of Congress Cataloging-in-Publication Data has been applied for.

ISBN 978-0-06-337149-1

$PrintCode

DEDICATION TK

HOUSE OF FROST AND FEATHERS

ONE

he sleeping plague was still nine months away, but the frenzied anticipation had already begun. Marisha passed a family as she hurried to her interview. The mother and children wore large vials of stoppered yellow water around their necks, surely believing the liquid had otherworldly protective powers. Probably diluted tea, or worse.

Marisha tried to turn a blind eye to the signs of shabbiness that had overcome Severny as the plague year approached. Doors boarded up, garbage strewn in the snow, and everywhere people hurried in the streets without making eye contact with each other. The only places where the throngs seemed to congregate were around those sham kolduni hawking their most potent hale water for warding off the sleeping plague. Marisha turned her face away from one such street corner, her chest tightening uncontrollably.

Ow! She clutched her head. She had been so keen on avoiding the crowd gathered around a koldun brandishing a glowing bottle, that she had run into a lamppost. Fantastic, now she would have to be interviewed with a great big bruise across her forehead. The corners of her lips flitted up as she imagined explaining, 'I was attacked by a lamppost.' Then she remembered how important the interview was for her immediate future and her smile vanished.

Despite countless letters sent and hours spent knocking on doors of the remaining open businesses, the interview for the clerk position was the only opportunity she had been able to secure. Openings that accepted female applicants were rare in the best of times. And now, with kolduni stirring up superstitions about inviting the plague along with strangers into one's home, even advertisements for governesses had disappeared.

Without a salary and a place to live, she would have no choice but to accept whatever repulsive husband Aunt Lyubov drummed up for her. A spike of fear at the prospect momentarily displaced her attention from the painful aftershock radiating from her forehead.

A poster was stuck to the lamppost. It was too colourful for winter: bright blue letters against a large block of orange. Marisha leaned in closer. The block of orange was a drawing of a house, and the blue letters read, 'Applicants Wanted'. Then beneath it was written 'Baba Zima, Koldunya,' and 'Must be a young lady of quality; intelligent, ambitious, and willing to travel. Generous compensation.'

She quelled the small spark of hope that had lit up at the sight of the phrase, 'Applicants Wanted'. Working for a koldunya was unthinkable. Kolduni did nothing to help ease people's troubles, all they did was ease the desperate of their money. They couldn't ward away the sleeping plague.

They couldn't change someone's fate.

Marisha had been standing still for too long, she'd be late. She hurried along to her interview, pushing the garishly orange drawing of the house from her mind. It was easy to spot the company offering the clerkship. A lump formed in Marisha's throat as she did her best not to count the people waiting in line at the door. She tried to rearrange her hair to cover the bruise that was surely blooming across her forehead. The lump in her throat grew bigger and bigger the closer she made it to the door.

THE INTERVIEW WENT TERRIBLY. MARISHA knew it; the portly man interviewing her knew it too. He barely glanced her way when he dismissed her and started tidying the papers on his desk. Perhaps determined to show she did not care about the interview's outcome, she asked the man if he had seen an orange house in the city. He looked surprised, as though he had already expected her to have left the room.

'I heard there's an orange house come to the Poets' Square. But I haven't seen it.' The man frowned at Marisha. 'Why do you ask? It may truly be Baba Zima's house, and she's not to be trifled with.' The man had said 'Baba Zima' as though it were a name of great significance. He looked at her differently now, with curiosity and a bit of fear, while a moment ago she had been something to glaze over. This merchant seemed to think that if she wanted to visit Baba Zima to buy a remedy, she was willing to take a big risk. She would not get a job out of him, but at least she knew better than to be afraid of a koldunya.

Marisha left the building and trudged through the muddy snow towards the square, doing her best to ignore the ball of dread in her stomach at the thought of the interview and the scant handful of rubles in her pocket. There, wedged in between the other ordinary brick houses, stood an orange house. Painted shingles in shades of peach and carrot covered it from sidewalk to chimney, reminding Marisha of fish scales or bird feathers.

Was she really going to do this? Was she really going to ask a koldunya for a job? Marisha's forehead throbbed, reminding her that two hours ago she had been smacked by a lamppost, and shortly after that she had lost the only job prospect she had found in two weeks. Without a job, she would have no choice but to slink back to her aunt's house in defeat–which would be unbearably humiliating in itself–and how long would it take Aunt Lyubov to bundle her off as a wife for Gregor Pavlovitch Otresin or someone equally loathsome? She recalled Gregor's meaty hands, the cruel glint in his eye—No!

Marisha looked for a door but couldn't find one. Instead, she knocked on a window at the height of her forehead. She knocked timidly at first, then louder as her knocking went unanswered. The window opened and a woman leaned her head out and shouted, 'If you're a supplicant, it's too late, we closed at seven.' The window slammed shut.

Marisha knocked again, her jitters melting into annoyance. The window opened again and the woman shouted, 'We open at nine o'clock tomorrow, come back then.'

Marisha shouted back, 'I'm not a supplicant.' She would rather drink unsweetened tea for a month than buy something from a koldunya. 'I—I saw the advertisement. For a job.'

The window slammed shut. Marisha wondered if she should leave. Then, the house shuddered. Marisha watched with wide eyes as the house creakily lifted on two fat stilts that unfolded like legs. The stilts were tipped with what Marisha could only describe as wooden talons. The house rose until its bottom edge was just above Marisha's head and she could see down the next street. Incredibly, the talons moved with dexterity and the house turned on itself. The stilts folded back up and the house touched the ground again. The side now facing Marisha had a door.

Marisha's eyebrows were frozen halfway up her forehead.

She caught a whiff of smoke and squinted at the life-like talons. They must be some ingenious steam powered contraption intended to fool poor supplicants into handing over their rubles.

The door opened. Out stepped a tall middle-aged woman with an imposing frame. Marisha immediately noticed the orange shawl wrapped around her shoulders: it was embroidered in shades of orange thread that matched the house. Then Marisha met the woman's piercing gaze. The woman's beady black eyes seemed to sparkle with cold intelligence, just like a predatory bird's would. 'You,' the woman, surely Baba Zima, said. Her voice boomed across the square. 'You want to be a koldunya's assistant?'

Marisha nodded, not trusting herself to speak. She knew what the koldunya must see: just a sturdy young woman with a thin face and light brown hair pulled back. Aunt Lyubov often said that Marisha should smile more, for when she did not smile, she appeared cross. She had worn boots with a thick heel to appear taller, but still had to tilt her head up to look at the statuesque koldunya.

'The advertisement said to come in the morning. The morning's long over.'

Her stomach sank. 'So, the position's been filled?'

Baba Zima huffed, crossed her arms, and narrowed her eyes. 'To my eternal annoyance, no. Come in, if you wish.'

She then whirled around and though she did not touch the door, it began to slam shut behind her. Marisha had to rush forward and wedge her arm between the door and doorjamb to keep it from shutting. The door pressed down on her arm with a weight that seemed disproportionate to its thickness, and she had to use all her strength to push it open wide enough to slip into the house. She got through, but the door caught the bottom of her skirt's hem, and pull as she might on the door's handle, it did not open. If she tugged any more, the dress would rip. Marisha looked up, furious that Baba Zima stood a few feet from the landing, watching her struggle, her face impassive.

Baba Zima said, 'Won't you come further into the house?'

'I would, but your door has caught my dress.'

Baba Zima shrugged and turned around, walking away from Marisha further down the hall. Marisha gritted her teeth, the starukha's mean trick making her seethe. And for what purpose–to scare her off? She took a deep breath. Baba Zima wouldn't be rid of her so easily. Marisha yanked on the fabric caught in the door, and after two tries it ripped away. She smoothed her skirt, doing her best to pretend that the rip wasn't there (just like the bruise on her forehead) and hurried after the koldunya.

Maybe it was because she was flustered, but it seemed to her that she was rushing after the koldunya for quite a while. Baba Zima's footsteps echoed ahead, the edge of her bright orange shawl disappeared around a corner. Marisha trotted faster, craning her neck as she passed a second, then a third staircase. A shiver of unease ran down Marisha's spine. How could this house be so big? She had seen it stand up on its hydraulic legs and turn around, surely they should have reached the other end by now?

Thankfully, the koldunya stepped through an open large, blue-painted door. Marisha stopped on the other side of the threshold and looked, tingling with curiosity. The room seemed like an ordinary oven room, the heart of any home in Chernozemlya. Except that the blue-and-white tiled oven dome was needlessly enormous. It almost reached the ceiling, and its door was big enough for Marisha to crawl through. The comforting aroma of baking rye bread was almost enough to mask a woodsy scent that reminded her of autumn mushroom hunts and walking on fallen pine needles. She noticed the pink and green paisley curtains framing the window and the large rectangular table before Baba Zima turned around and stopped, causing Marisha to almost crash into her. They stood nose to nose. 'So,' Baba Zima said, 'You're here because you want to work for a koldunya. It's an assistant's position, mind you. For my apprentice, Olena.'

Marisha nodded. Baba Zima looked at her with beady eyes, apparently waiting for her to say something else. Marisha cleared her throat and said, 'I'm sure whatever it is, I can do it. If it's a position to assist your apprentice, should I speak with her?'

'No. Luckily for you, she's busy at the moment.' A corner of Baba Zima's mouth lifted. 'You wish to learn remedies, do you? I am one of the most powerful kolduni in all Chernozemlya as you cannot fail to have noticed.' She gestured expansively to the surrounding house. The koldunya smirked. 'Perhaps you have a secret ambition to find a cure for the sleeping plague?'

Ha! If Marisha believed a plague cure existed, a koldunya's house would be the last place she would look for it. Marisha was careful to keep her expression blank. Still, she couldn't stop a stab of longing as she said, 'Everyone wants a cure for the sleeping plague.'

Baba Zima's smirk widened. 'Including you? You don't strike me as harbouring such ambitions. What makes you suitable?'

Marisha squared her shoulders, 'I went to a preparatory, a good one—'

'Strange to see a lady who finished preparatory school wishing to enter the world of koldunry. Shouldn't you be getting married to a rich muzhik?' The woman's mouth curled.

Marisha's fingers tensed. 'My marital ambitions are none of your business. What *is* your business, is that I am interested in this position.'

'But why?'

Marisha heated with anger as she recalled the long line of people waiting to interview for the clerkship position. But she knew better than to point out to the koldunya that opportunities for employment were few and far between with the upcoming sleeping plague. Instead, she said, 'It would be an amazing opportunity to heal people, and–all the other things kolduni do for people.' The words sounded artificial even to her own ears. 'I won't deny being curious.'

Baba Zima finished studying Marisha. 'No.'

Marisha's heart sank. 'But I'm sure I can do—'

'No.'

A bell tinkled somewhere in the room and the koldunya muttered to herself, completely ignoring Marisha, 'What now?'

She marched to a narrow door in the corner next to the oven and it opened. Behind the door hovered a guinea pig flapping duck wings.

Marisha's mouth dropped open. Her gaze stayed glued on the impossible creature tucking its wings close to its furry body and dropping a letter from its teeth onto the small table next to the door. She barely blinked when the creature neatly bit the seam of the letter open and pulled out a piece of paper for the koldunya. Baba Zima leaned over to read it, her bent pose looking slightly ridiculous and making Marisha wonder if the letter was harmful in some way. If not, why wouldn't the koldunya just pick it up? Baba Zima said, 'Kchort, so soon?' She straightened and looked at Marisha again.

Marisha tore her gaze away from the guinea pig-duck to meet the koldunya's beady black eyes. Baba Zima held herself strangely, arms slightly pulled away from her sides, fingers splayed as though ready to grab something out of the air. The alacrity of her gaze and her tense stance reminded Marisha of the storied raven, the last and most vicious of the three bird wives to carry off and marry a king, leaving poor Prince Ivan behind. Marisha was better prepared to meet the koldunya's piercing gaze this time and did not shrink back, though she wanted to. Instead, she returned the unwelcome stare. Marisha was surprised to see the koldunya raise her eyebrows slightly.

Baba Zima barked, 'Tell me, what can you do?'

Hope flared in Marisha's chest and she spouted, 'I can read and write, my calligraphy is excellent. I know French, music, geography—'

'Useless!' Baba Zima winced. 'Do you know how to sweep and scour and chop?'

Marisha stiffened. 'Yes, I do.'

'But you don't like doing it. Ha! And you don't care for sorcery, that much was clear from the moment you shoved your way through my door. You probably study those idiotic philosophy treatises, don't you? Olena would *love* that. As much fun as it would be to see her rage at you, you're very straightforward–not really the best trait for a koldunya's assistant. Besides, you're too old. I need someone with a soft, malleable mind, who can learn.'

'I'm not that old.'

'You look practically a spinster.'

Marisha sputtered. She was only twenty-one! The koldunya ignored her. 'I need a young girl who has not learned so much she can still unlearn.'

'You said I don't know anything useful to you, so what would I need to unlearn?'

Baba Zima pressed her mouth into a wrinkled prune. She said, 'You seem to be bright enough. And Golgolin did not frighten you as he did all those other simpering fools. To think, squealing at a guinea pig-fowl.' She gestured at the unbelievable half-guinea-pig-half-duck perched on the back of a chair and preening its fur. The koldunya continued her musings, 'An assistant with a bit of a backbone might last longer with Olena. And, heh, it might even be good to have one who's not slobbering to lick up the scraps of my incantations.'

Baba Zima paused and opened her hand. Marisha did not know what she wanted and the koldunya made the insistent gesture again, lifting her own hand up near her face. Marisha lifted her right hand so that it was level with koldunya's eyes. The koldunya brought her head so close to Marisha's hand that her nose almost touched it.

'Slender fingers,' she said. Baba Zima suddenly bent Marisha's pinky finger back. Marisha winced and Baba Zima declared, 'Flexible.' The koldunya dropped Marisha's finger like it was a hot coal.

She glanced at the bruise on Marisha's forehead and her mouth quirked, 'Stubborn.'

Baba Zima straightened out and gave Marisha a slight nod. She said, 'If you assist my apprentice for a year, I will teach you. I will teach you how to cure ailments, both real and imagined. And many other things besides. Useful things. Not like geography or French. The contract's over there.' The koldunya pointed at the table next to the oven. Strange, Marisha did not remember seeing it there before, but there it was, a creamy piece of paper with heft and small print. When the koldunya did not hand it to her, Marisha walked over to the table and picked it up herself.

Marisha glossed over the formal language to glean the contract's bones: she would be an assistant to Baba Zima until either Marisha wanted to leave or Baba Zima dismissed her.

She frowned. 'The salary will only begin to be paid after a

year's work?'

'There is a high attrition rate among assistants. I usually require three years of work before the salary is collected, but since the plague year is beginning soon, *and* your main duties would be assisting Olena . . .' Baba Zima raised her shoulders. 'I'm willing to cut the trial period down.'

Marisha quelled the stab of trepidation by continuing to peruse the contract. The position could be terminated at the least infraction or disobedience, or if she did not progress quickly enough, or if she did not show the necessary 'koldunic quality', whatever that meant. She would also be subjected to a quarterly review period. And, strangest of all, she would be required to keep secrets and tell lies.

But the money was more than enough. Marisha's fingers trembled with excitement as she lowered the contract. With this money, in only a few years, she could start rebuilding her family's fortune, even buy back her parents' dacha. Her mind jumped to a memory of running with Dima to the sprawling cherry tree that dominated the garden. They would race to the top, though Dima would help her up the first branch. Her heart constricted. She still loved her brother, despite it all.

The koldunya interrupted Marisha's thoughts. 'If you want the position, it's now or never.'

'Shouldn't I meet your apprentice before you hire me?'

'I don't think that would be wise.'

That answer should have sent Marisha running for the door. But Marisha stayed where she was. Though she hated the possibility of being turned out without pay, she would be housed and fed and if she lasted for a year the money would be worth it. She wouldn't have to return to Aunt Lyubov and the dreaded marriage that would follow. Her less-practical self warred against aligning with her cousins' beliefs in koldunic power. It was because of koldunry and their damned superstitions that Marisha's aunts and cousins had forked their fingers at her to ward off the evil eye. But just because she agreed to work for a koldunya did not mean she had to abandon the principles of reasonable philosophy. Baba Zima was clearly an infamous koldunya, and if Marisha could expose her as a fraud, then maybe people would stop pouring their money into koldunry's false promises for a plague cure.

She could feel herself stretching her moral strictures to justify taking the job. But whatever way she looked at the problem, the bottom line remained: she needed the salary, she needed a place to live. She stole a glance at the impossible creature perched on the back of a chair, now preening its wings with sharp teeth. Her pulse trilled. What else was hiding in this house?

'I'll do it.'

Baba Zima twitched her lips and said, 'Very well. We leave now.'

'Could I return to the boarding house for my things?' Marisha asked. 'It wouldn't take more than an hour.'

Baba Zima pursed her lips and gave Marisha a pointed look, standing between Marisha and the table where the contract lay, as though it was something to be guarded. 'You could leave,' Baba Zima said. 'But I cannot guarantee we will still be here when you return.'

Marisha did not have much, but her few belongings were precious. She thought about what she had in her bag: her wallet, her emergency kerchief, and the letter from Dima that still cut her with every reading. But the childhood notes her father had written her, and, worst of all, the owl her mother had knitted before she was born—all at the boarding house. She did not have much to remember her sleeping parents by, but those had given her comfort at the preparatory and during the lonely time when Dima was gone and her aunts tried to marry her off to anyone who was willing.

Marisha imagined returning to the square, loaded down with her meagre belongings, and the pit that would form in her stomach at finding an empty spot in the drab row of houses. 'It's fine.' Marisha said, voice thick. 'I don't have anything at the boarding house I truly need.'

The koldunya grinned at her like they shared a private joke and stepped to the side. She pointed to the pen lying on the table.

Marisha blinked and told herself that she simply had not noticed the pen lying on the table earlier. She dipped the pen in ink and signed. She felt lightheaded, like stepping out into the cold and only then realising the inside air had been stuffy.

The woman raised her hands and called out, 'Poshol! Poshol! Away we go!'

The house rose slowly and lurched. Marisha stuck her hand out to the wall to steady herself. She contemplated the possibility that the house's chicken legs were magical, not mechanical, and that the koldunya could teach her something beyond pretending a dramatic song could banish the evil eye. But that was absurd. Her gaze was drawn to the large rectangular tabletop tilting the opposite direction the house did, thanks to a hinge that connected it to the heavy wooden foot rooted in the floor: a clever way to keep the table's surface level as the house swayed.

The row of narrow houses bobbed outside the window as the orange house walked down the moonlit street. The house left the city centre as the koldunya led Marisha up flight after flight of stairs. Marisha struggled to categorise the realities of the house: the mundane practicality of the swinging tabletop against the five flights of stairs that should not, could not, fit in a two-story house. The koldunya pointed Marisha to the last flight of rickety ladder-like wooden stairs, and said the assistants lived up top. Wake-up was an hour before dawn the next morning. Marisha would learn of her duties then.

Baba Zima left quickly, taking the kerosene lamp with her. Marisha's resolve faltered in the cold and dark stillness. And lest she collapse in a heap on the floor, she felt for the banister with her hand and fumbled her way up the stairs.

She had to use her shoulder to open the door. The room was a small, low-ceilinged attic. The full moon shined through the curtain corners of the only window, small and cramped in the wall opposite the door. Marisha threw the curtains open and light poured into the room, illuminating two blanket-covered lumps huddled on pallets and a set of drawers in a corner. There was no extra pallet on the floor. Marisha concluded they had not expected to collect another assistant today.

Though it was much warmer in the attic than she would have expected, she was relieved to find several woollen blankets at the bottom of the last drawer. She knew she should sleep, but her heart still thundered in her chest and an army of thoughts jostled for her attention. She threw two blankets around her shoulders and sank into the chair next to the window. They now traversed a stark and beautiful snowy landscape that gleamed blue in the moonlight. The trees were black outlines against the grey night and the moon cast their long shadows onto the untouched snow. A strange and empty calm suffused her. She felt like they had left the whole world behind along with the city. The motion of the house was no longer jerky. Marisha wondered sleepily if it had found a moving road.

TWO

arisha woke to a still, dark room and a twitter of whispers and muffled footfalls. She raised her head. Her neck was stiff from falling asleep in the chair. She let out a soft groan to signal she was awake. The whispers stopped.

One of them lit a candle and crept over. 'Who are you? How did you sneak in without Baba Zima noticing?'

The other one nudged her companion and said, 'She couldn't.' The two of them huddled against each other, reminding her of the coltlike younger girls at the preparatory. All big eyes and long legs. Shepherding them around their first week had made her feel wise indeed. Except now she was the new one. She was much too old to be the new one.

Marisha yawned to cover her discomfort. 'I'm the new assistant.'

The first girl, the tall one with rumpled blonde hair, said, 'Are you really? Baba Zima said Olena had not found anyone suitable yesterday.'

Marisha shrugged. 'Well, I signed the contract. And here I am.'

The other girl padded back to her pallet, leaving the candle. Marisha pointed to her, and though she thought she already knew the answer, she asked, 'Is she Olena?'

'Damp earth, no. She's Anka-ny Simonevna, and I'm Dunya Igorovna.'

'I'm Marisha Elyasevna.'

'Nice to meet you, Marisha!' Dunya clapped her hands together, her halo of messy curls quivering. Marisha smiled despite the early hour. Dunya's good mood was infectious. Marisha glanced over at Anka-ny, curious at her Sibirskaya-sounding name. The girl's eyes were large and hooded with sleepiness as she brushed her long, black hair.

Marisha remembered her previous question. 'But Olena, is she all right? Not as mad as the starukha?'

Dunya's eyebrows shot up. 'Don't ever call her a starukha! Address her as Baba Zima, always. Even when she's not around.' She looked behind her fearfully as though someone listened.

'And Olena?' Marisha frowned, remembering how Baba Zima had not wanted them to meet the previous night. How bad could the apprentice be? Marisha quelled visions of her aunt reciting a litany of her faults and smiling at how it made her blood boil.

Dunya's head tilted to the side and she said, 'She's a bit–sharp. Be careful around her, and whatever you do, don't comment on her, you know, appearance.' Dunya covered half of her face with her right hand.

'We'll be late,' Anka-ny said. Dunya looked back in alarm and ran to her pallet to dress. Marisha's stomach began to clench with nerves. What she had heard so far about Olena was not exactly reassuring.

Anka-ny had finished her own braid and motioned Marisha to come closer. She produced a brush from one of her pockets, undid Marisha's braid, and pulled it through her hair. No one had brushed Marisha's hair since she left preparatory school. The girl was not gentle, and Marisha tried to jerk out the way but Anka-ny followed her movement. Luckily Marisha's hair was not as long as Anka-ny's. She had cut at least a foot off after leaving her aunt's house. She had been practical enough to know that waist-length hair was a waste of time for a working woman, but vain enough to feel a loss at seeing the pile of brown hair on the floor. Marisha caught a glimpse of Anka-ny's face in concentration and realised she looked very young, younger than she had thought. And now that she got a closer look, Dunya, though she was tall, did not look much older.

'How old are you?' Marisha asked.

'Thirteen,' Anka-ny answered with much composure, 'I've been here almost two years.'

'I'm fifteen. And you?' Dunya called from her pallet.

Marisha hesitated. She was silly to even consider lying. 'Twenty-one.'

'Twenty-one?' Dunya repeated.

'Yes.' Marisha said, trying not to cringe.

Perhaps deciding that her disbelief was embarrassing enough, Dunya asked for no further clarification. The silence stretched uncomfortably until Anka-ny finished Marisha's braid and stood in front of her again. 'There. Nothing to do about your clothes, but there's a basin at the bottom of the steps to wash your hands and face.' They descended all the flights of stairs, Marisha counted five in all, and Dunya chattered the whole way down about their visit to Severny.

Marisha had not noticed the previous evening that the ground floor hallway was lined with crystal wall sconces in the rounded bell shape of lily of the valley. They were faintly lit but not by candles—how surprising when gas lighting could only be found in Severny. The oven room was dark. The only light glowed through the oven door, red and faint. Marisha walked over to grab the nearby poker hanging from a hook when Dunya cried, 'Stop! Only Baba Zima stokes it.'

'So, we don't cook?'

'The Hands do most of the cooking. You can take burning coals for the samovar, but under no circumstance are you allowed to stoke it with the poker.'

What an odd restriction. And 'the Hands'? An unkind nickname for a servant? Anka-ny walked to the side of the room that faced the outside and threw the large green-and-pink paisley curtains open. 'We're not there yet,' she said.

Marisha had completely forgotten the house was moving. Unlike last night when the house lurched from side to side as it walked down the street, its current motion was signalled only by a light rocking of the tabletop. Marisha joined Anka-ny at the window, straining her eyes for a clue that the house was ambulating through the snow. The moon had long since set and only a bit of greying at the horizon indicated that dawn was imminent. Marisha focused on feeling the house's motion. It barely swayed at all, and if Marisha were not keeping her eyes trained on the far-off stand of dark grey pines slowly passing them by, she would have thought she imagined the feeling of motion altogether. Marisha suddenly felt dizzy. She tightened her hold on the windowsill, as though to guard herself against the house bucking her out.

Marisha asked, 'How is the house even moving?'

Anka-ny said, 'It has legs.'

Marisha thought of the house's chicken legs as she had seen

them yesterday, thicker than her own torso, articulated like an elbow and capped by flexible four-toed feet. She had seen them with her own eyes. But, if those same feet walked in the snow, the house would buck, the shelves would rattle, and she would need to keep her arms stretched out in case a particularly jerky movement sent her flying.

'The house isn't walking,' Marisha said.

'It's skiing,' Anka-ny said, without batting an eyelid.

'What? How? Does it have—' Marisha searched for the word she heard in a philosophy café, 'Hydraulics?'

Dunya and Anka-ny shared a puzzled look. Dunya said, 'The house comes from the other world.'

The other world? Yesterday such an explanation would have made her scoff, but today . . . Marisha looked back out the window at the snow-blanketed pine trees passing by and grappled with the idea that the other world was not just a place that her aunt referenced in prayers, but somewhere things–real physical things–could come from. It seemed impossible–but yesterday she would have said *this* was impossible. Yet the gradually lightening landscape and the gentle sway of the house proved that it wasn't. A skiing house. Pinging between *How could it be?* And *I perceive that it is* made her feel like a stream of water sloshing against a glass wall.

'You get used to it,' Dunya said. 'It gets a bit wobbly when walking around towns, but when travelling between them, it's as smooth as anything.' She tilted her head to the side, 'What made you want to become a koldunya's assistant now?'

Usually, Marisha appreciated looking older than her years, but under Dunya's stare she felt as withered as an oat husk. Marisha answered briskly, 'It sounded interesting, and I could use the money. How about you? How long have you been here for?'

Dunya said, 'A bit over six months. My family wanted to introduce me into society, but I have four other sisters: one older, three younger, and, well, I'm quite clumsy and not very pretty.' She ran her hand over her hair, smiling apologetically. It was the colour that mothers affectionately called 'rusi', not quite brown or blonde, and with a silver sheen that brought birch bark to mind rather than honey. Marisha thought Dunya's parents were fools. Dunya continued, 'So my parents didn't know what to do with me. I suggested reading or flower arranging as an occupation, but they said no. Not respectable enough. But they thought apothecarist was a good idea. Especially with a talented koldunya. I suppose they thought the connection would be a good one come the plague year.'

'And, you like it?'

'It's all right, I'm afraid I'm not very good at it. Especially the mixing and measuring.' Dunya's shoulders slumped. 'I'm terrified she will kick me out. I'm surprised it hasn't happened yet.'

'She won't,' called Anka-ny from the other side of the room. 'You're too good a saleswoman, all the supplicants love you. Baba Zima has gotten much better prices since you've been here.'

Dunya shot Anka-ny a grateful look.

'I hope I can keep up,' Marisha said. And as soon as she spoke, she wished she hadn't.

'Don't worry,' Dunya said, 'You can't be worse than me. And I'm still here. Besides the workload and some people being less than, well, pleasant, it's really not that bad.'

'Your family promised to keep Baba Zima supplied with copper.' A soft, low, female voice carried across the room from the stairs' landing outside the door. 'Baba Zima would not want to lose such a valuable resource. That's why she's so . . . pleasant with you.'

Dunya coloured. A woman stepped out of the doorway into the room. Marisha's eyes were immediately drawn to her face. She had a bright red birthmark that blossomed from her right eye and covered much of her forehead, nose, cheek, chin, and neck. The skin was pebbled and purple on her nose and lower cheek. Her back was ramrod straight and her black hair was braided and pinned up into a bun. Not one hair was out of place. Marisha tried to keep her gaze on the woman's eyes, but it kept straying to the birthmark.

She stopped in front of Marisha. Marisha focused on keeping her expression neutral, while her mind tried to parse out the woman's features on the smooth left side of her face: a long, narrow, slightly downturned eye and a high cheekbone. Could she come from one of those nomadic Buryat tribes in the icy North? The two were the same height but the other woman, obviously Olena, still managed to look down her nose at Marisha.

'And who are you?' Olena asked quietly.

'Marisha Elyasevna.' She squared her shoulders and returned the apprentice's stare. When Marisha arrived at the preparatory school nine years ago, Grusha Pavlevna made fun of her dirt-smudged dress, and Marisha, still reeling from her father's fate, hadn't done anything except try to hide her burning cheeks and eyes. Marisha only got relief from Grusha's torment when the girl left the preparatory a year later. Marisha could not let herself be intimidated now. She touched her fingers to her thighs to keep them from shaking.

'Marisha . . . And what are you doing here? A stowaway, perhaps one of the rejected applicants from yesterday. Except I don't remember you.' Olena tilted her chin to the side. 'Leaving *no* impression is not much better than a bad one.'

Marisha did not let her stance falter. 'I'm not a stowaway.

Baba Zima hired me yesterday.'

'She hired you?'

'To be your assistant.' Marisha could not keep the tiniest smile from her lips. The expression of surprise and dismay on Olena's face was so satisfying.

'No, she didn't.'

'I signed the contract.'

Olena leaned in, perhaps a handbreadth away from Marisha's face. 'Kchort, she cannot be serious.'

Marisha raised an eyebrow.

Olena's hand darted from beneath her tightly wrapped grey shawl and grabbed Marisha's wrist. She pulled Marisha out of the oven room and down an interminably long corridor. Marisha wondered again if it was her unfamiliarity with the house that made it seem so much bigger than it should be. Olena's grip hurt and Marisha twisted away.

'What is the meaning of this?' Olena said as she exploded through a door.

Marisha froze. Baba Zima sat at a round table, drinking tea, but she drank it from a teacup proffered by a disembodied hand. Another hand floated by her shoulder like a flying spider. A huge ivory satin-glove floating-hand spider. Blood pounded in Marisha's ears.

'Ah, Olena,' Baba Zima said, 'I see you've met your new assistant.'

'As I recall, I didn't hire anyone yesterday.'

'No, you didn't. Nor the day before, and nor the day before that. Frankly, it was getting a bit tiresome. It almost seemed like you didn't want to hire anyone at all. So, I took matters into my own hands.' The hand at Baba Zima's shoulder waved at Marisha. Marisha swallowed and tried to look nonchalant, or at least less like she wanted to scream.

'But I don't know anything about her. Except that she's old. What do you do?'

It took Marisha a moment to realise the question was directed at her. Remembering how well received her list of accomplishments had been by Baba Zima, she said, 'Loads of things. As you noticed, I'm older, and so have a lot of experience.'

Olena scoffed. 'Look at her fingernails, her skills must amount to flirting and French.'

Marisha did speak excellent French. Why was that such a bad thing among kolduni?

'You'll just have to teach her,' Baba Zima said in a calm voice. She took a long sip from the teacup lifted by the floating hand.

'But I need someone to assist me! Not some air-headed daughter of a muzhik who has never lifted a finger in her life.'

Marisha started to protest when she noticed something. Olena's shawl came untucked as she waved her arms to emphasise her statements about Marisha's incompetence. She was missing her left hand. Her left arm ended a bit below the elbow, in a stump maybe three inches long, knobbly and rounded at the end. Marisha must have been so focused on not staring at the apprentice's red and purple face that she hadn't noticed her missing hand. Marisha looked away quickly. How had someone with only one hand, and a Buryat no less, ended up the apprentice of a koldunya?

Maybe Baba Zima had saved Olena from a superstitious mother. Marisha remembered how her cousin had once pointed out a woman whose baby had been born without a foot. She told her that a koldun had told the woman her baby was cursed by her vanity, and the woman was rumoured to have drowned it shortly after. Marisha had looked down upon the woman with horror and pity for her backwards ways, but she knew such fates were common enough.

Olena spoke again. 'I cannot use her.' Marisha's sympathy for Olena evaporated. She couldn't be dismissed on the first day!

'Too bad, because I'm not hiring anyone else.'

Marisha breathed a sigh of relief. Thank goodness for Baba Zima's unflappable tenor.

Olena's voice took on a pleading quality. 'But Matrionka, don't you want us to find a cure to the sleeping plague?'

What? The apprentice was wasting her time with that impossible task? The kolduni of Chernozemlya had laboured to find a cure for decades, but every ten years the plague year arrived and thousands and thousands of people fell asleep no matter what the kolduni did. A few lucky souls woke up after a month, unchanged. Most woke up after a year and a day, shadows of their former selves. And a small number of deep sleepers, most unfortunate of all, stayed asleep long after the plague year had passed.

Hellhorses, she really was in a house of delusional tregetours.

Olena said, 'And there's the Grand Prince's reward—'

'As you ceaselessly remind me.' Baba Zima rolled her eyes. 'We have rubles aplenty. Many of which you have squandered on this project.'

'The books will help me know the source of the plague, I'm sure of it. And it's not only the reward, but the undying recognition of the people.'

'If I wanted to be adored, I would have been a saint, not a koldunya.'

Olena's eyes lost their shine. She delicately touched a finger to her mottled cheek. 'So you don't care if someone else finds a cure?'

'Me? Never.'

Olena tilted her chin. 'Good, because Baba Elizaveta wrote to me yesterday that Anatoli is boasting he's found a sure lead.'

Baba Zima's eyebrows shot up. The teaspoon slipped from the floating hand's grasp and clattered to the table. 'How dare he! That boorish trumpet, if he thinks he can quack without a challenge, no!' Then her shoulders relaxed and she made a small motion with her fingers. The gloved hand picked up a spoon and hovered it in front of her face at eye level. Baba Zima twitched her fingers and the hand moved the spoon one way and the other as though to cover and uncover Olena from her sight. 'You're very pleased with yourself, aren't you?'

Olena shrugged.

The other floating hand brought the teacup to Baba Zima's lips and she took a long sip. 'Anatoli won't find a cure,' Baba Zima said.

'If you say so.'

'You think he'll find a cure.'

'I only think how insufferable he would be if he did find it. And how unbearable it would be knowing that if he found the cure, we could have found it first.'

'Aren't you a crafty crinkle.' Baba Zima narrowed her eyes. 'Anatoli can eat his incantations for all the good it will do.'

'Yes! To beat him, I'll need the best resources possible. I haven't asked for anything these twelve years. Just let me find someone else, I promise I won't dither anymore.'

Baba Zima fixed her beady eyes on Olena. 'You asked for an assistant. And here she is.'

'But—'

'No. I'm sure the quality of the assistant won't increase *your* probability of finding a cure.'

'But Matrionka, a bad assistant can create so much more work than she relieves. If you'd really not let me make my own choice, I'd rather do this alone.' Olena crossed her arms, grabbing her stump above the elbow. It was hard for Marisha not to stare at it.

'My dear buttered blin, you are my sole apprentice for a reason. I trust in you and your abilities. But, if you're to take over my bolshina one day you need to prove to me that you can train someone. You're a good koldunya, but your people skills—' The hand floating above Baba Zima's shoulder made a tilting floppy motion. 'Could be improved.'

'You use Dunya to interface with the supplicants.'

'Yes, but when I talk to people they don't run away crying.'

Olena's birthmark flushed purple. 'I can't help what I look like.' Her self-assurance crumpled momentarily and Marisha realised Olena was younger than she had first thought, maybe only a few years older than herself.

'My dear, it's neither your face nor your arm that puts people off, it's your personality. Now, Marisha's first review is in three months, so we'll talk about her performance then. And until then, she will assist you, so you had best find some way to make her useful.'

Olena swept away and Marisha was unsure what to do. The hand at Baba Zima's shoulder made a shooing motion. Marisha sighed and turned to run after Olena.

'What can you do?' Olena asked when Marisha caught up. 'Have you worked before?'

'I went to a preparatory.'

'Of course you did.' Olena rolled her eyes.

'I'm a quick study. I'll learn to speak in incantations and wave my hands over supplicants–whatever's necessary.'

Olena stopped and stared at her. Marisha cringed internally, wondering what she had said wrong. She hoped her comment about waving her hands was not offensive to Olena.

'This is very serious,' Olena said, 'I'm labouring to find a cure for the sleeping plague. If you don't take it seriously, you should leave now.'

'No, of course I take it seriously, I'm here, aren't I? I mean, I've never seen anything like this–the house, those hands, that . . . guinea pig duck.'

Olena snorted. 'Relics of the other world. Only a fool would deny those. But I'm referring to koldunic arts, so if you think that warding the evil eye takes nothing more than waving your hands around—'

'Of course not! Why would I be here if I did?'

'Why indeed. I should have known Baba Zima would use this opportunity to torture me with a philosophy-loving stone-brain.'

Marisha gritted her teeth. 'As Baba Zima reminded you, I'm here for at least three months, so you'd best find some use for me.'

'No. It is *you* who must make yourself useful.'

THREE

lena found a spotless white dress for Marisha. It was too short in the sleeve.

'Now, as your first task you can clean the scalding pans. We need them after breakfast to make cypress bud essence.'

Olena led Marisha to another room where a table was obscured by a large pile of cast iron pans. Marisha stared at them open-mouthed. 'You want me to clean these.'

'Obviously. Any complaints?'

Marisha shook her head. Olena waved goodbye with a wicked grin. At the sight of the empty washbasin, Marisha realised Olena had not told her where to fetch water. She shuffled over to the table and took a closer look at the pans. They were caked with some awful residue. She drew back, disgusted, and groaned. Olena was obviously testing her. Marisha grabbed a bucket from the corner and opened the door to the hallway. It would take more than some filthy pans to chase her out of the house.

She only walked a few steps down the hallway when she saw something scurry across the wall. The pair of gloved hands. Marisha dropped the bucket and cringed, then steeled herself and leaned in for a closer look. They really were a pair of fawn-brown leather gloves, puffed out as though filled with hot air–or flesh–but resting on the wall, twiddling thumbs, unattached to anybody.

'There you are,' Dunya called out, hurrying to Marisha's side. 'Sorry it took me so long to find you, but Olena wouldn't leave and she never told us exactly what she's having you do. But she mentioned cypress essence, so–what's wrong?' She followed Marisha's gaze and put an arm around Marisha's shoulder. 'Oh, I should have known Olena wouldn't explain! Those are a pair of Baba Zima's Hands.'

'Yes. I saw some earlier. But Dunya . . . What are they?'

'Um. Well, they're Hands. They help around the house. Though they're practically useless for following direct orders, unless you're Baba Zima. But the kitchen Hands like to help if you're polite.' Dunya motioned for the Hands to come forward. They leapt off the wall and hovered in front of the bucket. 'You should let them carry the bucket. They like doing that.'

'I'm sure they do,' Marisha said faintly. She added disembodied hand servants to her list of impossible possible things about the house and forced herself to lift the bucket in the direction of the Hands. One of them landed on the bucket close enough to her own hand that she dropped the handle in surprise. The Hand was warm. Very warm.

'You're quite lucky. The kitchen Hands are usually cooking. Now follow them to the door and they'll give the buckets back to you. If the snow is out of reach, you'll have to help. They can't go more than a few dozen feet from the house, you see. I don't know why.' She tilted her head to the side. 'But I guess I'm glad they can't.'

'And how many of these Hands are there?' Marisha asked, trying to keep her voice even.

'Well, there's the kitchen Hands, and there are Baba Zima's Hands. They're always with her except when she sees supplicants. Unless she wants to scare them. I'm surprised she didn't have them with her last night when she interviewed you. I've seen some red Hands, but I don't know what they do.'

'So why doesn't Olena make herself a pair? Or even one.'

'They're from the other world, you can't just *make* more. Baba Zima says you'd lose a year off your life just from visiting, dark earth knows what would happen to you if you actually tried to bring something back.' Dunya shivered. 'That's one way you know Baba Zima is so powerful.'

Dunya walked with Marisha and the Hands down the hallway to a back door. They both watched as one of the Hands held the bucket and the other used a spade to pile snow inside. The Hands lifted the bucket back together. Marisha and Dunya stood out of the way as the Hands floated by, carrying the bucket. Marisha was astonished. On the one hand, she was strangely comforted by what Dunya had said about the Hands being from the other world: it meant that Baba Zima's power were not limitless. But on the other, she felt completely unmoored. She would never have imagined disembodied hands that filled buckets with snow. What else was there in this house that she could not imagine?

'Dunya,' Marisha said as her gaze were glued to the Hands scooping snow into the buckets. 'Baba Zima said that this house protects its inhabitants from the plague.'

'Yes.'

'Any idea how?'

Marisha glanced over at Dunya. The younger girl leaned against the doorway, watching the Hands. She shrugged. 'I don't know. The house is a bit of a mystery. But if Baba Zima says it's true, then it is.'

'And you're not the least bit curious?'

Dunya turned her head and grinned at Marisha. 'Oh, I am curious. But within moderation. Otherwise, I'd never get anything done.'

In the washroom, the Hands threw the snow into a cauldron by the well-stoked stove. Marisha could not keep her eyes off the Hands as they floated through the air with the bucket, whizzing back with more snow a few minutes later. The snow was soon melted and the Hands followed her to the washroom, carrying the cauldron of warm water. But the help stopped there. The Hands emptied the cauldron and left. Marisha looked at the huge pile of dirty pans and sighed.

It seemed to take hours to clean them all. She scrubbed the same pan over and over again while her stomach growled. She hadn't eaten anything since her tea yesterday afternoon and was hungry enough to almost regret not checking whether the gunky residue on the pans was edible. Finally, the sloppy pile transformed into a neat stack. *Just like magic*, Marisha thought to herself as she wiped her hands on a rag. Now that her task was done, she hoped she could find Dunya to take pity on her hunger.

Marisha remembered that the washroom was near the kitchen, only a few doors away from the oven room. She tried a few doors before meandering down a recognisable stretch of hallway, and almost walked past the oven room before pausing in surprise at the open door. Everyone was there, seated around the large rectangular table. The smell of kasha and buckwheat pancakes wafted to Marisha's nose, making her knees weak. There was a vacant seat between Anka-ny and Olena.

'Breakfast is at eight-thirty. You're late,' Baba Zima proclaimed.

Marisha bobbed. 'I didn't know.'

Baba Zima sniffed. 'I see that you'll be in charge of the laundry this afternoon.'

Marisha looked down at the white dress. It was indeed covered in grease spots and other unidentifiable blemishes. Marisha nodded but couldn't bring herself to care about Baba Zima's slight with the overladen table in sight.

The table was set with a feast: large loaves of black rye bread, steaming blini, porcelain dishes of sour cream and butter studded with roe, mushrooms in dill brine, pickled tomatoes with bursting skins, glistening jams in jewel hues. There was even a small dish of black salt. One of the kitchen Hands set a bowl of hot kasha on Marisha's plate and a cup of strong black tea next to it. She could have grabbed the Hand out of the air and kissed it. She mixed a heaping spoonful of sour cherry preserves into her cup. She sipped it, savouring how the sweet and sour cherry aroma smoothed the tea's tannic bite. Marisha sipped again before attacking the kasha. It was nutty and had the right amount of salt. It took much self-control to remember her manners and take small bites of the kasha. She mixed another spoonful of cherry preserves into her tea. She had earned it.

'We have many salves to make, Severny near cleaned us out. Anka-ny, you will assist Olena with the moulding of charms. Excellent work Olena, on your incantation for banishing fevered air. And Dunya, you will be copying the incantations. I don't care if you must work into the night, your progress would have made Baba Serafima weep. Pass the butter?'

The other women shovelled food into their mouths. Marisha forced herself to eat slowly and taste the tang of the sour cream she swirled into her kasha. She had not had such a rich breakfast since she had left her aunt's house, and even then, the sour cream had not been so thick. Though she wasn't used to eating at a slightly swinging tabletop, Marisha appreciated the feature. What a shame it would be for all this food to slide off the table!

The ivory Hands buttered Baba Zima's dark rye bread. One of them even lifted the slice to her lips. Marisha did not know whether to be amazed or disgusted. Did Baba Zima do nothing for herself?

Marisha took advantage of the activity of the breakfast table to take a closer look at Baba Zima. She was not as old as Marisha had initially thought, probably in her mid-forties; rather, her authoritative manner lent her the dignity and dominance that Marisha associated with older matrons. She was what Marisha's aunts would call a handsome woman: by no means beautiful, but with commanding features. She had a long face with a square jaw and the corners of her mouth seemed to naturally curve upward, giving Marisha the impression that she was constantly amused at some private joke. Her nose and mouth were broad, making her eyes seem small and deep-set. Her movements were brusque, and even while sitting at the breakfast table with the Hands feeding her bits of buttered bread, it seemed impossible for her to stay still: she emphasised a point with her arms and her head swivelled about her neck as she chewed, gaze darting around the table and at invisible points of interest around the room. It was only when her gaze snapped onto Marisha that a predatory stillness tensed her body.

'So, Marisha, how are you enjoying your first day?'

'Um, the work is . . . stimulating. The food is delicious,' Marisha tore her attention from spooning a cottage cheese dumpling onto her now empty plate and racked her brain for another positive thing to say. 'The house is absolutely incredible.' Baba Zima's eyes lit up and Marisha felt triumphant at hitting the right thing.

'It is, isn't it?' Baba Zima said. 'This house is a coveted jewel, one of the few that exist, as rare as the waters of life and death among koldunic circles.'

'And how did you come to have it?' Marisha asked, leaning forward, not having to feign her interest.

Baba Zima paused like a grandmother about to tell the third refrain of a story and said, 'It was brought up to the earth hundreds of years ago by a fierce koldunya who was so wise, springs bubbled beneath her feet. She was the first holder of the house's *bolshina*: the authority–the power–to be the house's mistress, and the bolshina passed from koldunya to koldunya until it reached my mistress, my dear matrionka, Baba Serafima.' Baba Zima's eyes misted over. 'Baba Serafima was an incredible koldunya, so perceptive she could know your deepest desires with a look. Or at least, that's what it felt like to me. And, unlike Olena, I was not Baba Serafima's only apprentice. She had two others, Olga and Anatoli. It was a very different house, not as friendly and relaxed as now, what with three apprentices competing for the same bolshina.'

Olena smiled and Marisha wondered if it was out of satisfaction at being Baba Zima's only apprentice, or because she appreciated the humour of Baba Zima calling the household 'friendly and relaxed'. Probably the former.

'And then what happened?' Marisha asked.

Baba Zima frowned slightly, as though she was not used to her assistants interrupting her well-practised story. Baba Zima's voice snagged on her words as she continued.

'Twenty years ago, when the bolshina became too much for her and she wanted to retire, Baba Serafima picked me to pass it along to. Hmph, of course she did, I was the best! Anatoli was so put off, he challenged my matrionka's decision. That drooling woodlouse, he could never admit I had a stronger connection to the other world than he did. And so, Baba Serafima went back on her decision and administered a test to Anatoli and me. It almost destroyed me, but I bested him and even *he* could not protest that I had earned the bolshina fair and square. Though he tried,' she added.

Baba Zima fell silent after that, brooding. Marisha frowned. Something had not felt quite right about the koldunya's story, and it was not just that the end lacked the same theatrical smoothness as the beginning. But Marisha could not put her finger on what it was that had felt off.

Marisha asked Baba Zima what she had asked Dunya earlier, 'And how does the house protect its inhabitants from the plague?'

'Quite the burning question,' Baba Zima said, chuckling. 'The house comes from the other world, it doesn't follow the same rules as those that bind us to on the dark earth. Surely, even you must have noticed already.' Baba Zima raised an eyebrow at Marisha. The koldunya was framed on one side by the pink and green paisley curtains, and on the other by the enormous domed oven. Quite ordinary on their own. Except that the tabletop swung slightly from the house's locomotion. And then there were the Hands cutting Baba Zima's toast. 'The house doesn't only protect us from the plague, but from all outside curses and ailments. So long as the house's mistress cares for the house, so long as she is strong enough to hold the bolshina, then the house will care for her. Of course, the house can't do anything to that which we bring inside.' Baba Zima smirked at Marisha. 'But at least we're safe from the plague.'

Marisha sat back and took a sip of her strong black tea. Baba Zima's explanation wasn't a real explanation, but what else should she have expected from a koldunya? The familiar warmth from her cradled cup alleviated some of Marisha's uneasiness at being among strangers in this impossible house. She closed her eyes. This was almost all right.

The rye bread was closest to Olena. Marisha asked, 'Can you cut me a piece?' And she remembered Olena's missing left hand and sat up straight.

'I–I mean, um–I can do it.'

Olena shot her a look like daggers. Her birthmark stood out red against her otherwise pale skin. Everyone around the table stopped eating.

'Well, Olena?' Baba Zima said with a small and malicious smile directed to Marisha. 'Can you?'

Olena smirked and grabbed the bread knife with her right hand. She sawed the bread through while anchoring it with her stump. Olena dropped the slice on Marisha's plate.

Olena leaned her elbow on the table and held the knife so that it pointed up into the air. 'Anyone else?'

Anka-ny and Dunya vigorously shook their heads. Baba Zima sipped her tea. Her look of glee at Olena's display sickened Marisha. Olena left the table, shoving her chair back so hard it clattered. Marisha looked down at her plate, cheeks flushed, and silently cursing herself for saying the wrong thing.

After several long uncomfortably silent seconds, Baba Zima stood up. 'Back to work!'

Dunya and Anka-ny stood up too. Marisha gazed sadly at her unfinished tea.

'You,' Baba Zima said to Marisha, 'Have you finished with the scouring?'

Marisha nodded.

'In that case, if I'm happy with your work I'll let you help with some meadowsweet steeping before laundry.'

Marisha had a moment to spot Dunya's worried face before trailing Baba Zima to the washroom. She clapped a hand over her mouth when Baba Zima threw open the door. The pans were not in the neat pile Marisha had left, but scattered and smeared.

Baba Zima put her hands on her hips. 'This is what you call washed?'

'They were washed when I left here!'

Baba Zima held up a hand. 'Then you did not do a very good job,' she said softly, 'did you?'

Marisha did not say anything. She was afraid if she opened her mouth she would scream.

'These had better be washed by the end of the day. And the laundry done as well. If not, well, Forny Oblast will be your last stop. Is that understood?'

Marisha nodded, numb.

Baba Zima gave her a tight-lipped smile and pushed past her. Marisha stood in front of the pile of pans in disbelief. She forced herself to walk over, pick up the first pan and place it into the now-sullied water. As Marisha worked through the pile, she wondered whether Olena had done this out of spite or if maybe Baba Zima was playing an elaborate but cruel game with her. Then, she saw an addition to the pile, and knew the identity of her tormentor with grim certainty. She threw the bread knife into the washbasin, grey water splattering more stains on her once-white apron.

FOUR

arisha scrubbed the pans more vigorously than she had the first time. Strangely enough, she felt relieved. Olena's lack of enthusiasm about Marisha's hiring had been bound to bubble over in a nasty way. If resoiling pans was the extent of Olena's cruelty, Marisha knew she could withstand whatever the apprentice threw at her. After all, washing dishes was a small grievance next to being forced to marry Gregor Otresin. But the knowledge that she could endure this did not rid her of that hollow feeling below her ribcage. She chided herself for hoping things would be different in this magical skiing house, that work could be enjoyable. Friendly, even. The thought made her pause her scrubbing. At least Dunya was kind. But she remembered Olena's furious expression after her faux pas at the breakfast table and her stomach churned.

When she was done her lower back ached and the drudgery of cleaning the pans a second time made her feel abraded, as if she had scrubbed herself with the metal wool. Though she had vowed to herself upon restarting the task that it would take a lot more than a few dirty pans to scare her away, her feet dragged when she looked for Baba Zima to inspect her work.

Baba Zima declared her work passable and took Marisha to

the laundry room herself. The ivory Hands accompanied Baba Zima, hovering next to her wrists or at shoulder level as though they were attached to invisible limbs. Baba Zima shifted her eyes and the Hands shot through the doorway. They returned with buckets of steaming water. She demonstrated the proper way of doing laundry by using the Hands. And while the Hands grabbed a sheet and scrubbed it with lye against a washboard, Marisha wondered why they could not do all the work. But when Baba Zima left, the Hands followed her out.

Baskets piled with sheets and tablecloths crowded on the floor. She avoided calculating the volume and threw a pile of tablecloths into the tub. She remembered her own stained dress and thought to wash a replacement with the first load of tablecloths for her to change into later.

'Don't put a white in with the colours,' Anka-ny said from the doorway.

Marisha looked down. The water swam with the colourful tablecloths. 'What?'

'The colours will bleed. Wash the whites with the whites and the colours with the colours. And make sure to add some lye to the water when washing the whites, it will make the white brighter.'

Marisha nodded. Her arms and neck were sore, her hands were red and already chapped from washing the pans. She leaned forward and fished out the dress.

Anka-ny stepped to her side. 'Let me help you.'

'Oh, it's fine,' Marisha said. It was embarrassing enough that Anka-ny thought she needed her help. 'Don't you have things you need to do?'

'I finished with grinding the linseed oil. I don't mind.'

'Oh. Well, you don't need to help me,' Marisha's protests

died as the younger girl bent over the washboard and grabbed a handful of tablecloth. 'But thanks.'

Marisha could not see Anka-ny's expression as she bent over the washboard. She looked instead at Anka-ny's glossy black braid draped over her shoulder and wondered if the house had travelled far to find this serious Sibirskaya girl. The silence stretched. Marisha pushed away her dark mood and said with forceful cheer, 'So how is it that Baba Zima needed to hire me with two perfectly capable assistants already at Olena's disposal?'

Anka-ny said, 'Olena declined to take Dunya and I didn't want to work on her plague cure project.'

'Really? I don't understand how one can refuse. It's been such an illustrious honour so far.' Marisha wrinkled her nose and grinned at Anka-ny as she lifted a soiled tablecloth.

Anka-ny smiled back and looked down at the water. Her smile disappeared. 'My aunt and sister were cursed by the plague during the last cycle. They woke up after a year. My aunt–before the plague, she was a weaver. She was always quick to laugh, always ready with a story at her lips and another three in her pocket. But now—' Anka-ny shrugged. 'She mostly sits in a corner next to the oven, unravelling skeins and winding them up again.' Anka-ny paused, her gaze fixed somewhere beyond the wall. 'With my sister–it was like she was missing something vital. She grew more silent by the day until she stopped talking altogether. There's no cure for them.'

Marisha looked down, her forced levity dissipated. 'I'm sorry.' Her stomach twisted and she considered for a moment sharing her own family history. But she dismissed the impulse almost immediately.

Anka-ny nodded in acknowledgement, grabbed the paddle

and stirred the sodden cloth in the tub. 'Olena tolerates me, but still. Maybe you'll do better.'

Anka-ny reached her hands into the water and pulled out a tablecloth. Marisha grabbed the other end and they both twisted until the torrent of dripping water slowed. She thought back to Olena's pleading with Baba Zima to pick her own assistant. She imagined her own subsequent conversation with Olena might have gone better if she had tried harder to convince Olena that she wanted the assistant job.

'We'll see how long I last.'

'Do you want to stay so badly?' Anka-ny said with the first traces of curiosity Marisha had detected in her voice.

Marisha said, 'Yes.' And she realised for the first time she meant it. Marisha thought of the sad, grey squalor of Severny, and the soul-crushing possibility that she could have been forced to return to her aunt's. But instead she was here, in an impossibly ambulatory house. The thought strengthened her like hot cabbage soup on a cold day. She wanted to be here.

Anka-ny helped her finish the load. Marisha was grateful for the help, but ashamed she needed it. She insisted on finishing the rest by herself. By the time she was done, she had long since missed lunch. Afterwards, Baba Zima ordered her to take the basket of sheets up to the attic room. Marisha lugged the heavy basket up the stairs, pausing frequently to straighten her aching back and arms. 'A magical house with magical feet,' she muttered to herself. 'But could it contrive to have magical moving stairs?' Marisha waited, but the stairs stayed disappointingly still. 'Not even a measly shortcut?' She said aloud. 'Seems to me like a house from the other world that doesn't even have a shortcut from the bottom to the top shouldn't be allowed to be called magical at all.'

A few treads later and Marisha opened the door that should have led to the attic landing, but instead opened on a very familiar staircase in a hallway with very familiar green and pink paisley curtains. She was back on the ground floor, by the oven room. Marisha would have kicked the basket of laundry to the floor if she had the strength. Instead, torn between incredulity and fear, she sank onto the bottom tread and leaned her head against the rail. A weak chuckle escaped her at the house's joke. 'I guess I deserved that. I'm sorry,' she whispered to the wood. She couldn't believe she was talking to a house.

Of course there was no response, and a few minutes later, as she lugged the laundry up the five flights of stairs, she wondered if she had just imagined the whole thing. But the screaming muscles and aching back belied that feeling and Marisha did not dare complain out loud again–not even to provoke the house into confirming that it had, indeed, somehow magically transported her to the bottom of the stairs as punishment. And she was relieved that the door at the end of the five flights opened onto the rickety staircase that led to the attic. She tugged the basket up the wooden ladder stairs, one tread at a time.

But as she finally made it to the top and heaved the basket through the door, she found the contents of her bag strewn across her pallet. Her small coins, her kerchief, and, unfolded and placed on top of the envelope, the letter from Dima. The last letter he had ever sent her, five years ago.

Marisha's heart pounded as she ran to her pallet. Someone had not only rifled through her most private possessions but had wanted her to know about it. It had to be Olena. If either Dunya or Anka-ny had snooped, they'd be secretive. All this because Olena was upset Baba Zima had hired Marisha without her consent? Or was this continuing punishment for what she had said at the breakfast table?

She remembered that the letter alluded to her parents and groaned. Someone in the house now knew her secret.

Marisha sank down into the chair next to the window. She trembled all over. Her fingers smoothed out the crumpled paper as best she could. She could recite it from memory.

My dearest Maryonushka,

This is the hardest letter I've ever had to write. My ink keeps drying as I delay penning the words that I must. I wish I did not have to tell you.

Maryonushka, we're destitute. I invested heavily in a mine which had the terrible luck of collapsing, taking our small fortune with it, including your inheritance. I was careless. I thought our fortune would take care of itself. I know what you may say: it's not really my fault, it was our father's business and I was too young to know–but that's not true. I should have known better. My only solace is that our parents do not know what a wretch their son is. But you'll pay for my mistake and it breaks my heart.

An older brother is supposed to look after and provide for his sister and I have done neither. But, I will labour to be more worthy. I am leaving on a journey, a sea voyage, where I will find riches in the Spice Islands to rebuild our fortune. There is enough left to keep our parents in the sanitorium. There's also enough for you to spend a season at court when you're ready. Of course, you'll dazzle them all. It comforts me to think of it.

I miss you so much, my dear Maryonushka. Remember when we used to climb the cherry tree and spit the stones at passing grown-ups? You were so little and scared to jump down from the branch that I jumped down first and caught you. I caught you every time.

I'm so sorry.
Dima.

Marisha leaned her head back and blinked the tears from her eyes, the mix of anger and love hitting her as hard as when she first received the letter five years ago. He had let himself become a martyr. They had lost their fortune, yes, but he acted as though he had caused the mine to collapse himself. No. He ran away. And what's worse, he had couched his act in love for her. No one knew where he'd gone, not the lawyer, nor her aunts and uncles. He had just left her alone, and had thought only of himself and his shame and not the terrible position running away had put her in. She had been fifteen, and with the preparatory drawing to a close, she had no choice but to go to her aunts and uncles who offered brittle smiles to her face and forked fingers to her back.

And of course she would not marry well. That hope had been shattered years before, along with the hope that her parents would wake from the plague after a year and a day as most other sleepers did: bewildered, personality diluted, but awake nonetheless. Her family was thrice cursed, really. The first curse was that the plague had struck Marisha's mother less than a week before Marisha's first birthday. And, ten years later, the unimaginable happened. Marisha clenched her fists, remembering the condemnation in the visiting koldun's cold eyes when he confirmed her father had fallen to the sleeping plague. And third curse and worst of all, neither parent ever woke up.

She smiled bitterly. Everyone was afraid of becoming a deep sleeper. Marisha was afraid too–she didn't want to sleep for the rest of her life! But almost worse than the terror of the plague itself was being subjected to the horrible, irrational belief that the deep sleeper's fate tainted those closest to them. That was the reason for the damning rituals: no funeral rites for deep sleepers, for fear that the misfortune of a deep sleeper would latch onto a mourner. There was no peace, they all said, for a deep sleeper's spirit in the other world. And worse than having her aunt and cousins flick their fingers at Marisha to ward off the evil eye, was the simple truth that no one would want to align themselves with someone whose parents were both plague victims in subsequent cycles–and were still sleeping.

After receiving Dima's letter, she endured eighteen months of her aunts trying to fob her on every muzhik's third or fourth son that passed their way. She had always wanted a great love story like that of her parents: her mother falling for her father when he was only a cloth merchant's apprentice. Marisha's aunt told her that the affair had brought great shame to the family: he was poor and unconnected, even rumoured to have picked pockets in his youth. But for some reason, their father, who had been stern and unshaking in his opinions, had allowed the match! And even Aunt Lyubov's tight-lipped disapproval could not hide the fact that the couple had been happy. On some level, though they did not say it, the aunts thought that the sleeping plague was retribution for the couple's unbelievable good fortune.

The suitors only irritated Marisha, and luckily, they were never interested in her for long. Not when they learned she had no dowry and her father had been asleep for five years and her mother for well over a decade. But Gregor Pavolvitch Otresin did not lose interest in her, even after Marisha had dropped the hint about her parents herself. He was rude, more than twice her age, and had a glint in his eye that scared her. And still her aunts encouraged the match. But she refused Gregor, and her aunts' outraged reaction only reinforced her decision: she had to leave.

Marisha wiped her face with her sleeve. She had to keep this job to stay independent. Going back to her aunts was not an option, and if she had to stay in this strange house to do so . . . Her hand tightened its grip around the windowsill. She felt like she was being watched, as though the house knew that Marisha felt uneasy at being there. It was a similar feeling to meeting a stray dog or seeing a bear in the woods. Papa always said that if she met wild animals, she must not show weakness or fear lest the animal sense it as an attack. Marisha slammed her hands down on the windowsill and pushed herself away from the view of the snow spreading out like a bolt of linen in all directions. The house didn't like her? Too bad. It couldn't buck her out. And neither could Olena. At least by trying to get Marisha to leave through bullying, Olena had made it clear she couldn't force Marisha to leave by command. She smiled. She was glad Olena had shown she wanted her gone. It meant that by staying she would not only be accumulating the means to survive and maybe even buy back her parents' dacha, but she would also be stopping Olena from getting her way.

Marisha had three months to make herself useful, and by the damp dark earth, she would do so.

FIVE

nfortunately, Marisha did not get a chance to make herself useful to Olena over the following days. Baba Zima kept her busy with chores and announced that she would need all assistants to help with the supplicants when they arrived at Forny Oblast.

Marisha was pleased that she had survived the last four days without any further catastrophes. Olena, thankfully, left her alone. The house had not played any more tricks on her, except for one incident on the third day. Marisha had been told to get coltsfoot from one of the stillrooms where dried herbs hung from the ceiling. She had visited it earlier in the day with Anka-ny and had managed to find it again despite the house's illogical layout (how could the same number of stairs lead to the second floor on one side of the corridor but to the third floor on the other?). But when she tried to open the door, it wouldn't budge. Marisha pulled on the cool metal handle and banged into the door several times, trying to dislodge it.

She was giving the door handle one last heave before giving up when Dunya came up the stairs.

'What's going on?' she asked.

'The door,' Marisha said through gritted teeth, trying to force it open. 'It's stuck.'

'Let me see,' Dunya said. Marisha stood aside, and Dunya turned the handle. The door swung open gently without even making a creak.

Marisha's mouth fell open. 'It was stuck a moment ago!' The door swung open wider.

'I'm sure it was,' Dunya said soothingly. She put her hands on her hips and faced the door. 'Now, you be nice to Marisha. She's doing her best. She's the good sort, you'll see.' Marisha tried not to show how astonished she was that Dunya had reprimanded a door as though it could understand her. Dunya did not seem to be the least bit embarrassed by addressing an inanimate object.

Dunya closed the door and gestured to Marisha to try. Marisha turned the handle and the door opened onto the stillroom, just as easily as it had for Dunya. Unbelievable. She glanced at Dunya, who looked back at her with sympathy. 'It may take a bit of time, but the house will warm to you.'

'How long did it take to warm to you?' Marisha asked.

Dunya put a hand on the wall. 'Not that long,' Dunya admitted. 'Don't worry, it will happen for you. You'll see.' But Marisha had the distinct feeling that, without Dunya's intervention, the door would not have opened for her no matter how much she cajoled.

Now they had reached Forny Oblast at last. The house's smooth movements slowed as they approached the edge of the town. It was early morning and the moon cast pointed shadows from the surrounding roofs. Dunya and Marisha watched from the same window as the house turned toward the main square. Marisha longed to open the window and let in the cold air. She was used to taking long, daily walks, and being cooped in the house for five days was enough to make her jittery.

It looked like the chicken-legged house was aiming for the

end of a row of houses. Except they were getting too close. The corner of one of the houses bobbed dangerously into view.

'We're going to crash!' Marisha braced herself against the wall.

'Don't worry. The house makes room.'

And indeed, the house did not crash, but seemed to squeeze in next to the other two houses. It turned around to settle on the ground, its door facing the street.

'We're here,' Dunya called and jumped away from the window, running down the hall to announce what must have been clear to everyone. Marisha smiled to herself. Despite the difficulty of the past few days, Dunya's infectious optimism lifted her spirits as well.

Baba Zima entered wearing a heavy cinnamon-coloured dress and a blue shawl patterned with black eyelids. And on her head was the most ridiculous hat Marisha had ever seen: red silk and turban-like, with three large peacock feathers sticking out near her left temple.

'Love the hat,' Olena said from the doorway.

Baba Zima did not take the comment as sarcastic. 'My dear buttered blin, you say that about all my millinery choices and yet I never tire of hearing it.' And she smiled at Olena with actual warmth, eliciting a mirror response from her apprentice.

Baba Zima's kohl-rimmed eyes alighted on Marisha. 'You will watch and hand me what I require. And silently, is that clear?' Marisha nodded.

Baba Zima did not need to announce their arrival. People would notice the orange house and the line of supplicants would stretch out to the town square. Or at least, that's what Baba Zima said.

'And now,' Baba Zima declared, 'the fun begins.'

The bell tinkled somewhere in the house and Baba Zima sailed through to the receiving room. Marisha loved this room. Roses sprouted from the walls and carried candles in their centres. The roses were real. Marisha had examined them closely when she had replaced candle stubs and trimmed the wicks the day before. The other features of the room were a wooden table in the centre and a large chest with tiny drawers against the back wall. Each of the drawers had a small handle embossed with a different plant or animal. Marisha had also polished the handles. That was a job she had enjoyed, the tiny metal reliefs were so detailed, so perfect. But none of the drawers opened when she pulled.

Baba Zima sat down at the table and Marisha stood by the chest of drawers. Dunya entered the room followed by the first supplicant, a woman wearing a bright, yellow knit sweater and holding hands with a girl around nine years old.

Marisha caught the tail end of their conversation. 'You have three sons as well?' Dunya said, her warm cheer putting the woman at ease. 'That's so lucky, I always wished to have a brother, but no luck. Only sisters.'

The woman in the yellow sweater bobbed her head to Baba Zima who gestured for her to sit. The daughter remained standing by her mother's side. She bowed her head, obviously frightened. Dunya went out to fetch the teacups for the samovar.

The woman in yellow's easy manner vanished along with Dunya. 'What a pleasant girl.'

'Yes, yes,' Baba Zima said, 'Very pleasant. Not the brightest, but not all of us can be. So. This is your daughter.'

The woman nodded. 'Yes, Baba. I'm afraid she's cursed.'

Baba Zima looked at the child who cowered by her mother. 'Go on.'

The woman licked her lips. 'A few months ago, I left Tonya alone and she had got into the yarn basket. She unraveled *all* the skeins and tangled them around her wrists. We had to cut her hands out! She never would have done such a thing before! And how one loses a full pail of milk, I don't know.'

Marisha listened to the woman's story and was surprised at Baba Zima's patience, and what's more, by how intently the koldunya listened. She did interrupt once to redirect the woman's story with a well-placed question. Dunya returned with the teapot and she poured Baba Zima a cup of tea as the woman finished her tale. The woman waited nervously. Her daughter had stayed silent through the whole story, no doubt instructed not to speak. Baba Zima held the teacup between her fingertips and sipped her tea.

The woman asked, 'Baba, do you know what's wrong with her?'

Baba Zima studied the still-silent Tonya. 'Of course. Someone has cast the evil eye on her.'

The woman pulled her daughter close and they shared a terrified glance. 'I knew it! Who would do such a terrible thing?'

'Whoever it was and whether it was on purpose or not, the result is the same. Have you been boastful?' Baba Zima addressed the girl for the first time.

'My Tonya, never!'

Baba Zima raised her eyebrows. The woman looked down. Tonya's gaze darted between them, but she said nothing. Baba Zima said, 'No matter, even if we don't know how she attracted the evil eye, I can remove it.'

Baba Zima gestured for Marisha to come and open her book. It was threaded through with bookmarks of various colours. 'Crimson,' Baba Zima said, 'I think the third one.' Marisha proffered the requested page under Baba Zima's nose. 'Yes,' Baba Zima confirmed.

She told Marisha to get a vial of hale water from Olena. Marisha lingered for a moment, watching how Baba Zima took the child onto her lap and chanted softly. The child cowered at first but relaxed as Baba Zima touched her hand and forehead with the tips of her fingers.

Marisha hurried down the hall and up the stairs where she found Olena sitting by herself in her workroom. She held the guinea pig-fowl in her lap and scratched the fur around its wings. Olena had her head bent down towards it and spoke in a voice free from all sharpness. 'Now that's a good Golgolin. How did you get such a knot in your fur? You're the most adorable guinea pig-fowl there ever was and don't let anyone else tell you otherwise.'

Golgolin made snuffling noises. It had not yet allowed Marisha to stroke it even though she had tempted it with treats. Marisha was almost too surprised to be jealous.

But as soon as Olena noticed Marisha she pushed the creature off her lap and stood up. Marisha gave Olena an abbreviated version of the supplicant's story and Olena poured the water from the appropriate pitcher into a vial and mixed in a drop from another vial in the row above the bench. She studied her collection of pungent salves and herbs and selected a packet. Marisha took the packet and hurried out of the room. She wanted to look over her shoulder to see if Olena picked up the guinea pig-fowl again.

Back in the receiving room, Baba Zima gestured for the supplicant to take the water and the bundle of herbs from Marisha, and declaimed some words invoking the protection of hearth spirits. She also told the woman to twist a circle of yarn around a pin and leave it in her daughter's pocket to prevent the evil eye from sticking. The woman thanked Baba Zima profusely.

Once the woman left Marisha asked, 'The woman believed the incantation and water would help her daughter. But will they? I don't doubt the spirit forces,' she hastily amended, 'But . . . the girl tangling yarn and losing a pail of milk . . . how do you even know that stems from the evil eye?'

'As a koldunya, I have the power of *knowing*. But it takes some finesse to *know* what the problem is.' A corner of Baba Zima's mouth lifted. 'As for the supplicant, she believes my cure will work, so it will. It's much harder to ply my art if the supplicant is sceptical. What I'm not used to is sceptical assistants.'

Marisha bowed her head. 'I just thought if you asked the spirits for help, it would be more, well, visible. Like how this house is visibly . . . other.'

'What did you expect? A flash of light? A wind strong enough to knock the house's knees together? Hmm.' Baba Zima tilted her head at Marisha like she was seeing her for the first time. Marisha did her best to keep her face blank. Then she grinned at Marisha, 'Don't worry. There's always at least one rotten egg among the supplicants. Your wish may come to pass.'

As Baba Zima predicted, the rest of the morning was uneventful–except for one incident. The supplicants came and went and Marisha paid attention, but she was more taken with how attentive Baba Zima was, and how closely she listened to their problems. Then, mid-morning, a supplicant barrelled into the receiving room ahead of an uncharacteristacally silent Dunya, swinging his arms a little as though he were used to people hurrying out of his way. He wore good leather boots and a clean, blue wool kaftan. Marisha immediately did not like him. Baba Zima did not seem to be bothered by his lack of deference. She sat, insouciant, sipping scalding tea from almost translucent china. Dunya did not return to the queue of supplicants, but rather stood in the doorway, wariness all over her face.

'Madame koldunya,' he said, 'They say that your power knows no bounds.'

'I wouldn't go so far, but it's barely an exaggeration, yes.' She finished taking another sip and fixed the man with her gaze. For all his posturing, his shoulders dropped a fraction. She said, 'What do you want?'

The man sat down in the chair on the other side of the table without being invited. 'I have lost something. Or rather, someone stole from me. An employee. And I would like to recover my lost item.'

'And what was this item?'

He hesitated. 'A family heirloom. A necklace of great value. It was part of my wife's dowry.'

'I see,' she narrowed her eyes at him. 'And your wife couldn't come with you to ask for it? That would have made finding it a lot easier, since she likely knew it better than you.'

The man snorted. 'She couldn't come. Besides, the dowry belongs to me. She never even wore it.'

Baba Zima said, 'Oh. But you did?'

The man shook his head brusquely as though he hadn't heard her well. 'What?'

'No? Not much of a link then.' She paused, studying the man. She called to Marisha, 'The bowl.'

Marisha froze for an instant, then rushed forward. There was a bowl on the ledge. Marisha placed it on the table in front of Baba Zima. Baba Zima said. 'Now, water. The green pitcher is fine. That's enough.' Marisha put the green pitcher back on the ledge next to the blue one. She hadn't spilled. She didn't know why she was so nervous, except that the man set her on edge.

'You,' Baba Zima said to the man, 'Dip your hands in the bowl. Go on, it's just water.' The man looked like he was going to object, but after a moment he quickly submerged his hand. The slight indentation between his eyes smoothed as he felt that it was, in fact, just water. Then a frown of bewilderment and irritation appeared. He withdrew his hand. 'Don't you have a towel?' Baba Zima ignored him and leaned over the bowl, looking. The man held his slightly dripping hand out as though he didn't know what to do with it. 'You,' he said to Marisha, 'bring me a towel.' Marisha was startled, then taken aback. She started to walk forward, though she immediately questioned her compliance.

Baba Zima raised her head from the bowl. 'Leave it,' she said to Marisha, and then snapped her gaze onto the supplicant. 'I can procure your lost necklace for you, but it will cost you.'

He smirked. 'I can pay. Money isn't an issue.'

'I can see that. But no, it will cost you a tooth.'

His eyes widened. He sat back, incredulity making him squint at Baba Zima. 'A tooth?'

'Yes. A pre-molar should do nicely. One of my assistants would be more than happy to divest you of one. Should only take a few quick yanks.' She frowned slightly. 'Though perhaps it will take all of them to keep you from squirming.'

He shook his head and clapped his hands down onto the table. 'I'm not giving you one of my teeth! Is this really the best you can do?' He guffawed and leaned back. 'Maybe you're just like those other frauds. All talking to the spirits, but no results.'

Baba Zima raised her eyebrows. 'You're the one who wants this necklace so badly.' She stood up. 'To recover a lost item, you need to offer something in return that is dear to you. Now, I know you find great pleasure in doling out pain.' Baba Zima tsked at the man as he sputtered in protest, his face turning red.

'No, no. No need to be modest. I hardly needed to look in the bowl to confirm it. You are well-versed in doling it out, but not so practised in receiving it. It's time for you to address that shortcoming.' Baba Zima shook her head as though she were disappointed in the man. 'A tooth is a small price to pay. It's certainly worth a lot more out of your mouth than in–especially considering who the necklace is attached to. Don't you agree?'

His face turned the colour of pickled beets and he leapt to his feet. He bellowed, 'You can't talk to me like that, witch! You think that you can keep her from me? Tell me where she is!' Marisha's heart pounded. He took a few steps closer to Baba Zima's table until he leaned over it, like he was about to lunge at Baba Zima.

Baba Zima grew still. She towered and seemed to crackle with power. 'Be quiet.' Her voice boomed and echoed around the room, drowning out the man's sputters. Marisha heard clattering down the stairs. Olena appeared in the doorway to the hall and stayed there, watching her mistress.

Baba Zima continued speaking, her deep voice booming around the room, 'Know your place, you stupid man. You think you could fool the spirits in hiding your true intent? You think you could fool *me*?' The windowpanes swung inwards and flattened against the wall, over the curtains, making Marisha jump at the sudden movement. Marisha pulled on one of the handles to close it, but it wouldn't budge. Then all the air in the room seemed to woosh out of the window, tugging on Marisha's hair and clothes, and the candles in the rose sconces blew out. The wooden edge of the windowpane pulled out of her fingers and slammed shut. She gasped for breath. The room had gone dark and cold and she couldn't breathe. Her fingers closed on the rough fabric of the curtains, her heart hammering. The man made a choking, gurgling sound. He clutched at his throat and coughed. Something plinked on the ground and rolled to Marisha's feet. It was a bloody tooth.

Baba Zima shrank back to normal. The window cracked open, and warmth and light seemed to return to the room. The candles sputtered back into life. Marisha felt like she could breathe normally again. Still, her heart galloped as she gulped deep breaths, unsure if she had imagined the air growing thinner. Her awareness shrank down to the bloody tooth lying on the floor at her feet. The man froze, hunched, his eyes wide with fear, riveted by Baba Zima, and his hands covering his mouth. A line of blood trickled down his chin.

Baba Zima said, 'Leave. Before you lose something else.'

The man scarpered away as fast as he could. Baba Zima breathed heavily and sat back down behind her table. No one spoke until Baba Zima held out her teacup. 'More tea. Dunya, bring in the next supplicant. If there are any left. That idiot is sure to make a ruckus.' Her gaze alighted on Olena. 'Did I disturb you?'

'I heard your voice. Sounded serious.'

'It was. Do you mind taking care of that tooth? I trust you'll know where to put it. Don't touch it.'

Olena raised her eyebrows. 'What do you take me for?' She grabbed a rag from the table and knelt at the ground by Marisha's feet, scooping the tooth into it.

Baba Zima smiled at Olena and she finally seemed to relax. 'Thank you.' Olena's lips turned up at the corners. She turned and left.

Baba Zima's gaze moved on to Marisha and her warmth drained from her gaze into steely amusement. 'I'm surprised to see you still standing.'

Marisha did not answer. Her throat still felt tight and dry

and she did not trust herself to speak. But Baba Zima was looking at her with expectation and Marisha forced herself to open her mouth. 'How did you—' Marisha started. Her voice came out a squeak.

Baba Zima grinned devilishly. 'How did I know he tried to hide that his wife ran off?

Marisha had meant to ask how Baba Zima had made him lose a tooth, but she lost her nerve. So, she swallowed and said, 'You mean, no one told you that his wife left him?' Her voice was still shaky.

'Think, girl–we arrived last night! You think I have nothing better to do than to groom informants in every village in Chernozemlya?' Baba Zima frowned at Marisha. 'My connection to the spirit world allows me to know things. I know what to look out for, what questions to ask. Come on, even you must have intuited that he was a sack of shit.'

Marisha said, 'I knew something was wrong, but what it was exactly . . .'

'People are the same everywhere.' Baba Zima said, 'When you spend so much time listening to their problems, it becomes a lot easier to spot those who have bad intentions and want to swindle you. Even without help from the spirits, all you need is practice.'

'And . . . you made him lose a tooth?'

Baba Zima grinned. 'It was loose already. Didn't you see his cheek bulging?'

Marisha felt a small measure of relief–and was surprised to also feel an edge of disappointment. She continued, 'Still. The way the air left the room, the window—'

Baba Zima's grin widened, 'Can't explain everything away, can you? There's nothing like a good demonstration to really put the fear in someone.' Marisha figured that Baba Zima meant the man, but the way that she was looking at her, she couldn't help but think that Baba Zima had meant to scare her a little too.

SIX

aba Zima said that they would take a tea break after the next supplicant. Marisha shifted from side to side. Her feet hurt terribly after running up and down the stairs all morning, fetching remedies from Olena when they were necessary. She thought that surely there must be a better way to bring the bottles from upstairs to downstairs. But she wasn't about to ask the house to help her.

The current supplicant, a woman with a newborn daughter, had been given an incantation and some water to calm the baby from crying all night, and lingered after Baba Zima dismissed her.

'Is there anything else I can do for you?' Baba Zima said imperiously.

The woman glanced nervously over to Marisha before licking her lips. 'Well, it's just, I was wondering–I, I heard that you could help . . . with a protection spell. Against the plague.'

Marisha looked expectantly at Baba Zima. Surely the koldunya would reprimand the woman for listening to gossip, but instead she said, 'Young woman, there are methods to protect against the plague, but these are dangerous. A shield spell is the only reliable way. Do you know what that is?'

Marisha had heard of these so-called shield spells. For a

great sum of money, a koldun would perform a ritual that would protect someone from the plague. But it was impossible to know whether the spell had worked in advance of the plague's arrival, which, in Marisha's opinion, was the perfect set-up to defraud the public. And that did not stop the desperate from clamouring for them, as was evident here.

The young mother looked down. 'I–I had heard—'

Baba Zima's hands flew up in dismissal. 'I'm sure you heard some fantastic tales. These are the facts: I can make you a shield spell, but you can only protect another person, not yourself. If your chosen one was fated to fall to the plague, you will instead. You have three daughters? So, which will it be?'

Marisha leaned closer in interest. She had never heard that a successful shield spell meant the protector fell asleep instead of the protected one. The woman looked in horror at the koldunya. 'I don't—'

'And if you do shield her from the plague, how will she survive without her mother? Or perhaps, you wish to shield your husband?'

The woman's eyes were wide and unseeing. Then she pressed her lips together and squared her thin shoulders. 'If I could be sure that just one of them would be safe . . . it can't be all three?'

'No, I'm afraid not,' Baba Zima said firmly. 'One for one. And be warned, most people who ask to be another's plague shield become deep sleepers, should they succeed. Now, if you're still interested, come back tomorrow. But think long and hard about it–such choices are not made lightly.'

If anything, the woman's eyes had only grown wider. She nodded and ran out of the receiving room. The door slammed and the silence grew. Baba Zima sat back down behind her desk and reached for the teacup before dropping her hand. Marisha suddenly felt like she should be very far away, perhaps by the oven, refilling the teapot from the samovar. She met the koldunya's eye.

'Well?' Baba Zima said.

The peacock feathers in the koldunya's red turban bobbed, but Marisha was not inclined to laugh. She walked over to Baba Zima's desk and picked up the teapot. She hesitated at the door and looked back over at the koldunya. Part of her wanted to say she would be right back with the water, but she screwed up her courage and asked, 'Is it true?'

Baba Zima raised her eyebrows and sat back. 'You'll have to be more specific.'

'All of it.' Before Baba Zima could tell her to be more specific again. 'How would a shield spell even work?'

There was an edge of triumph to Baba Zima's grin. She could feel that she had been waiting for her to ask about the mechanics of koldunry. 'You're getting ahead of yourself. You don't even know why kolduni commune with the spirits. I'll try to explain.' Baba Zima placed her elbows on the table and touched her fingertips together. 'Many of the forces that shape our life–our fate, love, luck–come from the other world and are influenced by spirits. People, being idiots, offend spirits all the time, and so kolduni use their knowledge of spirit forces to help those afflicted.

'The difficulty comes from communication: telling the evil eye to leave that poor child alone is not possible on the damp earth. No matter how hard you scream or stamp your foot, the spirits don't understand. But, the rituals and incantations help convey our intent, though they're not always reliable. Whispering words into water and using herbs can bind their effects as well as relieve the supplicants' physical symptoms. A koldunya could appeal to the spirits directly by travelling to the other world in spirit by, say, dream-walking, but it takes a great deal of practice and is as dangerous as bathing in boiling water. And so, it's easier to ask spirits to help supplicants with our rituals and incantations. The result is less flashy, but no less effective.'

Marisha frowned. 'I see.' She thought she almost understood when Baba Zima spoke, but now that the koldunya had fallen silent, Marisha's comprehension slipped away. Baba Zima's gaze slipped from Marisha's face.

'No, you don't,' Baba Zima said. 'But it's all right. I did not expect you to.'

Marisha's face heated. 'Some would say there's nothing wrong with a baby who cries all night.'

'And what else would those people say?' Baba Zima's voice was soft and dangerous.

Marisha looked at the wall and shrugged. She should have stayed silent. Surely Baba Zima would not tolerate talk of reasonable philosophy. Marisha spared a glance upward at the koldunya. She was looking straight at her, a knowing smirk on her lips. Baba Zima wanted her opinion? Fine.

'Some would say there is such a thing as possibility. And coincidence.'

'Ha! Matrionka Serafima, save me from the deliberately stone-headed. I knew you were more than simply ignorant.' But Baba Zima's eyes sparkled with amusement. She looked at Marisha like she was an unruly plant that needed to be pruned into a correct shape. 'Believe what you want. I don't care.'

'You don't?' Marisha frowned.

Baba Zima grinned. 'It won't change the fact that coincidence is what those silly philosophers use to describe patterns they can't explain. And believing in coincidence won't stop that woman from returning tomorrow and begging for a shield spell to save her favourite daughter. And you can be certain that if her daughter was fated for the plague, in a few months from now, or in the next cycle–whenever her daughter would have been claimed–that woman will become a deep sleeper.'

Marisha resonated with the certainty that rang in Baba Zima's voice, the same certainty that the koldun had, ten years ago, when he had pronounced that her father had fallen to the plague and would stay asleep. His cold eyes had condemned him, for surely, they implied, *surely*, he must have done something to deserve this fate. And reasonable philosophy had been the buoy that had saved her from drowning in the taint that the koldun had silently implied. Reasonable philosophy said that having two deep sleepers in one family was just a trick of possibility. It was not fate. And yet, it was so hard to not be afraid, no matter how many tracts of philosophy she studied. Marisha's anger at all the koldunic fearmongers in Chernozemlya gathered and swirled in a hot ball in her chest, but it emerged in a wisp, not a roar.

'You're wrong,' Marisha mumbled.

Baba Zima's mirth vanished. She looked much older than her years. 'I am not,' she said. 'This isn't the first time I've had people come to me for shield spells. Becoming a deep sleeper is rare, yet when they inevitable do after a shield spell, their loved ones find me after the plague, begging to reverse it.'

What if Baba Zima actually *could* cast a shield spell that actually *did* what it was supposed to do? Marisha imagined herself, ten years old and discovering her father had bought a shield spell, begging Baba Zima to take it back. Her hands clenched into fists and she centred herself as though the house's floors were rocking. She cried out, 'Then why sell them at all?'

'You would judge them? Who are you to do so? People want to feel that they have control over their fate. They can't help it.

But it has a way of catching up with them.'

Marisha reeled, her mind still catching up with the koldunya's words. Baba Zima smiled broadly at her like a toad contemplating a juicy fly. 'Philosophers say they don't believe in fate, don't they? But I know you believe in more than silly philosophy. You know how?' Baba Zima took Marisha's silence as assent. She leaned forward. 'Because if not, you wouldn't be here. Ha! Didn't need the spirits to tell me that one. You're just as scared as the rest of them.' She made a shooing motion with her hand. 'Now go. I'll waste away without more hot water.'

Marisha sprang forward to grab the teapot. Her fingers had trouble gripping the handle. She fled the receiving room, Baba Zima's laughter reverberating off the walls.

The koldunya was right, curse her. Marisha was afraid. She thought of those hours sitting in cafés, listening to mathematical philosophers expound on the theory of possibility that made personal fate a fallacy. But it wasn't enough. Her aunt thought it inevitable that she would follow her parents' fate, and these thoughts crept into Marisha's mind as well.

Her aunt and cousin had had a horrible habit of speaking about her as though she were not in the room. Not long after she had arrived, her cousin Katya had blamed her for her dog running away even though she hadn't allowed the dog to go near Marisha at all.

'Why is she here? Can't you send her away?'

'She is to be pitied,' Aunt Lyubov had responded. But her voice held more satisfaction than empathy. 'Her life is full of misfortune. It's my sister's fault, she should never have married that . . . merchant. Look where she ended up, in a sanitorium bed! And now her bad fortune has attached itself to Marisha, poor girl. Her parents plague-stricken, her brother a reprobate . . .' She shook her head.

'I guess she won't be here long, not when the plague year—'

'Hush! You'll call evil eye!' Then Aunt Lyubov's voice became even again, 'She is an unfortunate girl, and you will be kind to her.' But Aunt Lyubov's voice had a duplicitous tone. She was one of those superstitious people who would call a newborn baby ugly as a toad instead of beautiful to avoid the appearance of boastful or jealous behaviour and calling the evil eye's attention. But it was all fake. Her offer of sanctuary was fake, and only done to avoid the spirits' retribution for turning away a relative. Even though Marisha had grown heated with anger at how they spoke about her, and shame that she had nowhere else to turn, a tendril of fear had curled around her heart at the thought of her parents' fate falling on her.

If only Papa had not fallen asleep to the plague. Marisha wondered if, deep down, her father had been afraid as well. Once her mother had fallen asleep to the plague, had he also been kept awake at night by the superstition that his wife's deep sleeper tarnish had spread to him?

Her mind turned inevitably to the conversation with Papa which must have informed her impressions of koldunry, a memory she handled so frequently it was a well-worn stone. She had been eight or nine years old. Papa had taken her along to Severny without Dima, and it was a rare treat to have her father's complete attention. Marisha played with a loop of yarn while Papa talked to some potential investors for the copper mine. One of the men had a ring that shined faintly even though there was no light shining directly on it. Marisha was so fascinated that she forgot to pretend to not be interested in the conversation.

Later, as they walked to a teahouse for a cup of hot chocolate, Marisha asked, 'Who was the man with the shining ring?'

'A koldun,' Papa's mouth tightened with distaste. 'So he says.'

'What did he mean when he said there were other ways to find precious metals than by prospecting?'

'He meant that he knew some shortcut through koldunry.' Papa shook his head. 'There's no such thing.'

'No such thing as koldunry?' That in itself was not surprising, Papa said often enough that kolduni were liars.

'No such thing as shortcuts, Maryonushka. People offering an easier way forward with one hand hide a hefty price to pay with the other.' The twinkle in Papa's eye disappeared and he stopped walking, right in the middle of the street. He said, 'Never make a bargain when the cost is hidden, Marisha. And especially, never bargain with kolduni.'

'Why?' Marisha couldn't help letting the word slip from her mouth.

Papa smiled a little, even though he was so serious. He always said Marisha asked so many questions that he was surprised there were any left in Chernozemlya for others to ask. 'Why never bargain with kolduni? Because, if you're lucky, and you've made a bargain with a scammer, then all you lose is money and pride at being swindled. However, if you're very unlucky and you've happened upon the rare koldun who is genuine, you may lose so much more.'

His left hand went to the sleeve on his right wrist, which Marisha knew hid the whorled scar. The back of Marisha's neck tingled. Papa always answered her and Dima's questions about the scar's origins with fantastical stories of beasts with strange teeth or being branded by a gang of criminals. But this time, Papa was telling her something *true*. 'This is important, Marisha. Don't bargain with kolduni. Don't make them binding promises. You never know what you might be agreeing to.'

Marisha remembered nodding and feeling acutely that her reality was a bubble, and with Papa's request, the weight of the real, grown-up world with all of its mysteries and dangers, pressed in.

Some of Papa's fear must have rubbed off on her. Maybe that's why she was so wary of koldunry, and why she had turned to reasonable philosophy in the first place. Marisha had not realised how much the prospect that Baba Zima could be a genuine koldunya scared her, not until now. And if Papa had had an encounter with a genuine koldun that ended badly, how did that bode for her in this house? She would have to be careful, very careful, with what she agreed to do around Olena and Baba Zima. Assisting was all well and good, but any more than that and Marisha should leave. It wasn't worth the risk. Papa had made her promise she wouldn't take the risk. And she wondered for the millionth time what it was he'd bargained for with a koldun.

Marisha wiped her eyes. It wouldn't do to let Baba Zima think she had rattled her. She reached into the oven with the tongs and plunked the red-hot coals into the samovar's chimney one by one. She pictured the little girl who lost the full pail of milk returning after the plague had passed, wailing and wondering what had happened to her mother. Marisha could have been that girl. She dropped a coal onto the samovar's chimney and it rolled onto the floor. The samovar had brimmed over. She retrieved it, cursing loudly.

Could one of her parents have bought a shield spell? A true shield spell, one that actually worked. Mama falling asleep to the plague because she tried to protect her family would certainly be enough to cause Papa's stricture against bargaining with kolduni. But then how did his ill-fated bargain with a koldun factor in? Once the coal was safely back in the oven and all escaped embers stamped out, she hung up the tongs and sighed. Could she even know if either of them had bought a true shield spell if it had already been cast?

And besides, if she survived the plague for the third time in her life, Baba Zima would say that it was because the house had protected her, not the lingering effects of a shield spell. *If you want to find out, why don't you leave?*

Maybe she would simply fall to the plague despite the house's supposed protection. Or, maybe her fate would have a much more twisted way of catching up with her for trying to evade it.

Baba Zima's voice echoed in her mind: *You're just as scared as the rest of them.*

SEVEN

arisha gritted her teeth as Olena quizzed her in the oven room on the healing uses of herbs and plants. She had done her best to learn these past two weeks, and she liked the tabulation of the plants and the rules of their uses that went with it, but it was difficult to find time between all her chores. At least Olena had not deliberately sabotaged her again. Marisha was not sure why, but with all the chores and the studying Olena had assigned, deliberate sabotage was hardly necessary.

'Wrong, wrong, wrong!' Olena chanted. 'Didn't you study at all yesterday?'

Marisha had in fact had no time to study yesterday because Baba Zima had ordered her to file and buff the eight sharp nails that tipped the house's feet. It should not have taken all day, but Marisha had begun the task with some trepidation. Each of the three front toes spanned the length of her body (the back toe was only the length of her arm), and the house did not seem to particularly want its nails buffed, given that it rustled and shuffled away when Marisha approached with the file. She was very aware that the house was capable of squashing her by folding its legs and sitting, and so it took Marisha a lot of time to work up the courage to touch the enormous talons. As she stretched her hand forward the ridiculousness of the situation brought a smile to her lips—imagine, trying not to spook a house with abrupt gestures. And when she touched the scaly skin of the house's feet, she was surprised to find it warm. Again she marvelled that the house actually felt *alive*.

Marisha's marvelling ended rather abruptly when she absentmindedly filed at the foot's skin instead of the nail and the house stood straight, knocking Marisha back into a snowdrift. The house ran a few hundred feet away and sat down, acting very much like an enormous, irritated orange hen. It took Marisha many minutes of coaxing before it would stand up again and let her tend to its feet. She was sure she had seen Baba Zima laughing at a window.

Olena opened a drawstring bag by laying it on the table and parting it open with her thumb and forefinger. Despite Marisha's animosity, she could not help but admire how Olena did everything differently: the tasks Marisha could only conceive of being done with two hands, Olena did with one.

'What's this?'

Marisha studied the powder's colour and sniffed it. 'Vervain?'

Olena nodded slowly. 'And what are its uses?'

'In an infusion it can calm the nerves, improve focus and intensify certain amorous desires.' Marisha got the next few right as well and felt good about it. She shot Olena a triumphant look. 'Told you I learn fast!'

'Don't get cocky. You've mastered maybe twenty herbs? There are hundreds to know. How about this one?'

'Um . . .' Marisha caught herself staring at Olena's face. She thought she was getting used to the apprentice's birthmark, but her gaze often strayed to it as though magnetically attracted.

The crimson and cream halves of her face were so strikingly different, and the pebbled scaly patches of purple on her nose and cheek both captivated her gaze and repelled it.

Marisha quickly lowered her scrutiny to the bottle. She racked her brain. She knew the straw-like stems and the rotting sweet smell. 'Skullcap?'

'Wrong. Chickweed. Kchort, this is hopeless. You're an utter waste of time.'

'I made one mistake out of eight and I'm an utter waste of time? I've only been here two weeks! And I thought kolduni were supposed to lift curses, not memorise the contents of kitchen cupboards.'

Olena snorted in derision. 'What you know about kolduni couldn't even fill half a quail egg. A koldunya must know both the physical and spiritual arts. Plants and water–you know them as kitchen cupboard contents–draw power from the damp earth and can be used to relieve bodily symptoms caused by harmful spirit forces. Yes, the physical arts are a lot less subtle and intuitive than spiritual work, like lifting the evil, hence all the memorisation. Though at this rate, we'll be lucky if you can learn to make a tincture to calm a toddler by the time the plague strikes.'

'I'm doing better than you give me credit for.' Marisha hated the whiny note in her own voice.

'If you're so good, tell me, what's this?'

Olena rummaged around her drawer and handed Marisha a bottle. Marisha opened it and tipped a drop onto her handkerchief like Olena had taught her. The smell was caustic, plummy, and infuriatingly unfamiliar. Of course, Olena would give her something she had maybe only seen once. She studied the bottle to buy time when she noticed the inscription. It could not be that easy.

'Bearweed.'

Olena's eyes went wide. 'How did you know that?'

Marisha bit back a smirk. 'Told you I studied hard.'

'But,' Olena pressed her lips together, 'really, how did you know? Have you been rummaging through my stores? I told you not to do that. This is very rare.'

'You mean you didn't assign it to me?'

Olena stared Marisha down. 'Did you rummage through my stores?'

'Of course not,' Marisha said, enunciating very clearly, '*I* wouldn't stoop to rummage through someone else's belongings.'

Was that a flicker in Olena's eyelid?

'How did you know?' Olena persisted.

Marisha pointed to the inscription on the bottle.

Olena's eyebrows shot up. 'You can read Old Slavonic?'

'Of course. I had a classical education. As I told you.'

Olena shook her head and dragged Marisha to the bookshelf. 'So, these. You can read these?'

'Yes, I can. Can't you?'

Olena looked away. 'I can, but it's slow. Unlike you, I didn't have a *classical education*. I usually prefer taking a more practical approach to problems, but these histories might contain records of the first instances of the plague, and accounts and stories about it. I just haven't got through much of them.'

'Accounts and stories—and those would be useful to you?'

'They would be if they have clues about the plague's cause.'

Marisha frowned. 'And knowing what caused it can help you cure it? How?'

Olena glanced from the bookshelf to Marisha. Perhaps she could tell that Marisha was genuinely interested, because she turned towards her. 'Hmm. As you should well know by now, there are differences in the degree of misfortune a person can experience. Curses are just one way that spirit forces manifest in our lives as misfortune. Ill thought can call the evil eye. Oh, and of course, misfortune can be caused by offending a spirit directly, by say, forgetting to bring the domovoi salt and bread on the first day of winter.'

'Of course,' Marisha echoed, only half-pretending to take what Olena said about house spirits seriously.

'Now, unless you've been wilfully blind and deaf for the past month, I'm sure you've understood by now that it is much easier to lift the evil eye, which is cast unintentionally, than a curse.'

Marisha crossed her arms. 'Yes, but why?'

'When you cast the evil eye upon someone through ill thought it is like throwing a stone in their path. They might trip over it and hurt themselves, but it's fairly easy for a koldunya to remove that stone and help them back up. When you cast a curse upon someone with intent it is like throwing a stone directly at them. The hurt is greater. Thus, the physical remedies,' Olena gestured at the table near the cabinet in the back that was strewn with several mortars, 'must be stronger, as must the koldunya's connection to the spirit world for her incantations to take any effect. Now,' Olena leaned forward, 'knowing what to ask of the spirits, that's the real trick. And knowing what the cause of the misfortune is–that's the signpost on the way to the question.'

'And the sleeping plague,' Marisha said. 'No one has been able to figure out what causes it? In all these years.'

Olena shook her head. 'The victims who wake, they have no trace of the evil eye on their spirits or bodies. It is the people who used to know them who complain they are different. And those who stay sleeping, well, it's like they're frozen. No change to their body. Just sleep. That is, until their eventual death.' Olena said the last with a shrug. Marisha did her best not to think about her parents. 'At least, that's what the accounts say.'

'So, this research,' Marisha said quickly, 'Would help you, in theory, learn about the plague's origins, which could help you find a cure.'

'Exactly.'

Marisha smiled. 'So perhaps I may be of use after all?'

Olena nodded her head slowly. 'Maybe so.'

THE NEXT DAY, Marisha was supposed to begin helping Olena with her research, but Baba Zima made crumbs of those plans. 'I have an announcement,' Baba Zima said after taking a healthy draught of tea. 'We're leaving for Gulervo tonight to pick up Valdim, my son. He will probably stay until after the krug.'

Olena slumped noticeably in her chair.

'Will he also be presenting at the krug?' Dunya asked.

'No,' Baba Zima said with a short laugh. 'Valdim's no koldun, he's obsessed with his instruments. Violins and balalaikas. I don't know how it happened, but there it is.' Baba Zima had a son? Marisha was less interested in Valdim's obsessions than she was in his parentage. Had Baba Zima been married? And if so, where was her husband? Perhaps stashed in one of the many closets that only opened to the keys dangling on Baba Zima's belt.

Instead of asking the more interesting, but impolite, questions about Valdim's parentage, Marisha asked. 'What's the krug?'

'A meeting of kolduni, held every year. It is a chance for us to gather to celebrate the Marazovla, the sacred turning of winter into spring, as well as share news and show off our advances to each other. And with the plague arriving this summer, well, many more will attend than usual. Anatoli will certainly be at the krug,' Baba Zima said to Olena, 'So you had better have something to say about the cure by then.'

'I will,' Olena said. She rubbed a red blotch on her nose, darkening its scaly edges to purple.

Baba Zima added, 'And you'll play nice with Valdim?'

'I'm sure we'll stay out of each other's way.'

'You had better. Two grown adults of your age–Baba Serafima would never have tolerated such squabbling in her household.' She shook her head and continued to speak, her voice becoming crisper, 'It's our last day in Aksorka. Olena, I had promised I would go visit a man about his sick cows.' She shrugged. 'He probably did not place the iron bar across the barn's threshold correctly–but still, he was very anxious, apparently his son is distraught, and I said I would visit. But I have no time, would you mind going?' Baba Zima was clearly giving an order rather than a request.

Olena stiffened. She said, 'Of course not.' But she could not hide the disappointment from her voice. So, Marisha supposed, they would not be working on research today. Olena's voice became more business-like. 'His cows are sick? You couldn't just give him an incantation?'

'If it is a threshold issue, it's best to visit. I have already agreed to it. Besides, it's good for you to go outside.'

Olena settled back, resignation written all over her expression. Marisha almost felt sorry for her. Olena avoided dealing with supplicants, and being forced to tend to sick cows when she could be working on the plague cure must be very disappointing. Marisha tried to remember which supplicant Baba Zima referred to. Yesterday, after Olena quizzed her on her plant knowledge, Marisha had assisted Baba Zima with the supplicants again. Baba Zima had only agreed to one request for a visit, from a man with sad eyes who wrung a cap between his fingers. Although, hadn't he said that his wife had died? Marisha began to open her mouth but figured that, unless she was certain, it was much safer to not say anything at all.

That evening, Marisha passed one of the storerooms on the way up to the attic. The door was open and Marisha could spy Anka-ny high up on a ladder, clearing one of the top shelves. It was unusual to see her working so late. Marisha had quickly learned that Anka-ny was the model assistant: quick with her chores and with an incredible memory for incantations and ingredients. Anka-ny had a natural talent, efficiency and focus that Marisha would often dwell on in glum comparison with herself. Marisha asked, 'Anka-ny, what are you doing? It's late.'

'Hi, Marisha,' Anka-ny turned from her task. 'It's fine. I should have done this earlier, but I took a while responding to my sisters' letters.'

'Is your family well?'

'Well enough. Someone asked my sister if I knew how to calm an angry domovoi. Apparently, she came home and the pantry contents were all inverted.'

Marisha had learned that, besides wishing to find a way to alleviate her aunt's symptoms of the plague, Anka-ny wanted to open up her own apothecary one day in her village. Marisha grinned, letting herself feel pride for this quiet, determined girl, 'Not yet a full year of being Baba Zima's assistant and already everyone is coming to you for advice.'

Anka-ny smiled bashfully. 'Yes, well, I couldn't tell her much without knowing more details. But still.' She looked pleased.

Marisha asked, 'Do you need help with cleaning?'

'No, I'll be done in less than an hour. You should go to bed.' She paused her rummaging. 'Actually–would you mind changing my water and fetching some more rags? I hoped the Hands might come by, but no luck.'

Marisha was only too glad to help. After all, Anka-ny had helped her with the laundry on that first awful day and Marisha would never forget what a difference that small kindness had made to her. She was on her way back from lugging the bucket of water up the stairs when she heard Olena and Baba Zima in the receiving room. Marisha could clearly see them squaring off in front of the oven.

'How did it go today?' Baba Zima asked.

'Fine,' Olena said, her voice short.

'Oh? And how did you end up curing the man's cows? Was it the iron bar as I suspected?'

'Actually,' Olena said, 'When I got there, the man had no idea why I was asking about the cows, when he had come to you about his wife's death.' Ah, so Marisha had been right!

'What? Oh . . . dear me, I must have got them mixed up.'

'Mmm.'

Olena seemed calm, but Marisha thought that she could detect some tension in her shoulders.

Baba Zima prompted, 'So, what seemed to be the issue?'

'He told me his wife's shade haunted their child's bedroom. When they opened the door, it began whispering, throwing things around the room. The family was terrified. I had brought all the wrong ingredients with me, my incantations were useless.' Olena's voice gained an angry edge towards the end of her telling. And no wonder. Marisha did not envy her that situation.

'And,' Baba Zima said softly. 'What did you do?'

There was a pause, and Olena's voice returned to its cool cadence. 'I found a packet of letters in the drawer. They were concentrating the woman's ire. I burned them and used water to cleanse the room, and the shade left.'

Marisha could feel Baba Zima's proud smile. 'Ha–throw you into the fire unprepared and you do not falter. My buttered blin, you're a credit to the house's bolshina. A worthy successor.'

Olena's shoulders relaxed and her lips curved up at the praise. But still, Marisha wondered whether Olena resented Baba Zima for treating her like that. Marisha knew that she would.

Baba Zima must have known that she had given Olena the wrong instructions. Marisha's skin crawled with revulsion. Why was Baba Zima doing this? For her own amusement? That sadistic streak conflicted with how Baba Zima looked at Olena with such glowing pride.

And unless there was another interruption, Marisha would be helping Olena tomorrow. Nothing bad had happened since she had come upon the contents of her reticule strewn all over her bed, no tricks whatsoever, but after today . . . Marisha could only hope that Olena did not have the same taste for tormenting her helpers as Baba Zima did. Luckily, Marisha had the feeling that, though Olena was extremely easy to ruffle, she did not have Baba Zima's inclination for power-playing. Marisha felt that Baba Zima's intentions were like the house: complicated and full of twists, whereas Olena's mind was one long narrow hall of single-minded focus.

And so, after almost three weeks of waking up and knowing what to expect (chores, mind-numbing drudgery, more chores), Marisha woke up with cautious excitement. Olena had asked her to come to her workroom. The house had begun to journey again, leaving Aksorka and its supplicants behind. Marisha was thrilled by the prospect of getting a break from laundry, but also, after all Olena's lessons on physical koldunry and seeing Baba Zima interface with supplicants, Marisha was curious to see Olena apply both sides of the koldunic coin, spiritual and physical, to the impossible task of curing the plague. As she walked downstairs to breakfast, Marisha heard Dunya tell Anka-ny that she only expected Marisha to last one day in Olena's workroom. Marisha knew the comment was more about Olena being difficult than her own abilities, but it still stung.

Baba Zima insisted that Marisha finish helping Dunya and Anka-ny with the inventory of one of the still-rooms, and after Baba Zima's anger the previous day, Marisha did not protest. So, it was only after mid-morning tea that Marisha was free to join Olena in her workroom on the first floor. Marisha knocked on the door and pushed it open.

'Ah, good. You finally decided to show up.' Olena sat at the table next to a huge pile of books. Her back was straight, her black hair pulled into a tight bun that hurt Marisha's scalp just looking at it. How did Olena pull her hair back so tightly with only one hand?

'Don't just stand there, sit.'

Marisha did and Olena looked at her as though her inability to even sit down right away exhausted her. Marisha returned her gaze but kept her face blank. She folded her hands in her lap.

As the silence wore on for seconds, Marisha looked around the room. She had been there before to pick up remedies from Olena for Baba Zima's supplicants, but she hadn't had a chance to really look around. The desk at which she sat facing Olena had been pulled out from the wall to make room for another person. Against the wall to the left of the door was a large, gimbaled workbench which took up almost the entire length of the room.

A small iron stove was crammed into the corner. Nailed to the wall above the workbench was three layers of shelves, each containing a hodgepodge of glassware, jars of dry ingredients, and bottles of muddy-looking concoctions. The walls were empty of decorations, save for a large wire frame where bundles of drying herbs were hung. Next to the desk was another door, maybe to a pantry. The sweet and grassy scent of the drying herbs battled with a caustic, earthy aroma that Marisha assumed came from Olena's concoctions. Even though the room was wholly Olena's, there seemed to be no thought to embellishments. Rather all the space was taken up for practical purposes and was organised in a way that could only make sense to the apprentice koldunya's mind.

Olena drummed her fingers on the table. 'The book is over there, do you think you can handle the entire thing in Old Slavonic?'

'I can, I've even taught others to read it.' She pointed to the other book by Olena's elbow. 'What's that one?'

'Pan Feodor Ivanovitch's treatise on the plague. He was the house's master for a short time and koldun to the Grand Prince two hundred years ago.'

'So, what exactly is our strategy here?'

Olena's birthmark flushed purple. 'Our strategy? You don't take part in the strategising. You do what I say.'

Marisha sighed. This would be very tiresome. 'Olena. I'm on your side.'

'Are you now.' Olena opened Pan Feodor Ivanovitch's treatise.

'I want to help you find a cure.'

Olena looked up from her book. 'Really.'

Marisha held her gaze.

Olena said, 'Let me guess, you'd rather it not happen to you? You're scared of falling asleep?'

'Of course I am,' Marisha said in a matter-of-fact tone. She did not add, *and I need to help you if I want to stay employed.* This quest of Olena's may be a dead end, but Marisha was damn sure going to get paid for it.

'And you have a deep sleeper in your family,' Olena said. 'Someone close to you, a parent, or maybe a sibling.'

'What? How–how did you know?' Marisha acted shocked even though on the inside, she seethed. She knew Olena had been the one to rifle through her reticule!

'Please. You're unmarried, alone, and you agreed to jump aboard a house on chicken legs without even returning home to fetch your things. So, there's nothing and no one you cared about leaving behind. Besides, you were obviously hiding something you are ashamed of. Hence, a deep sleeper.'

Marisha started to push back from the table but remembered that Olena may still be trying to provoke her dismissal. Her hand smoothed out flat against her skirt. 'And you? Why do you want to cure the plague? For rewards and glory?'

'Yes. Something like that.'

Really? Marisha thought to herself. Was that really all that motivated Olena? Marisha thought of her own parents, asleep in a bed in a faraway, nameless sanitorium. Olena being unwilling to admit a personal connection to a deep sleeper was a way to put herself above the problem. It made her desires to cure the plague seem clinical and cold. 'Good for you,' Marisha's voice dripped with sarcasm, 'I hope you get it all.'

Olena did not answer but pushed the Old Slavonic book towards her. Marisha grabbed it with both hands. It was a heavy tome, and dusty too. It smelled like a mildewy attic and something distinctly animal, probably from the sheepskin it was written on. She opened the book and rubbed her forehead at the spidery script that faded in the margins.

The two women quickly pretended to grow absorbed in their books. Marisha had a piece of paper at her right elbow for noting any interesting mentions of the plague, and after what seemed like ages, it was still blank. Her neck hurt. Marisha sat back in her chair and groaned.

'Stop moaning, will you? You sound like a cow in labour,' Olena said.

'It would be the quietest birth ever,' Marisha snapped back.

'Well, just be quiet, will you? I can't concentrate.'

'I'm surprised you can hear your thoughts over your foot tapping.'

Olena opened her mouth to say something but must have realised her foot was indeed tapping. She stopped and shot Marisha a dirty look. They turned back to their books.

A few minutes later, Marisha chuckled. Olena said, 'What now? If you can't stay quiet I'll have to tell Baba Zima you're more pain than you're worth.'

'He's just writing about goats. Seven pages, and not even anything interesting about goats, just listing all the goats in Kul and their ailments. And the squabbles between neighbours. Over goats.'

'Quit your whining. And don't skip, you might miss something important.'

'Like one of the goats catching the plague?'

'Exactly,' Olena said in seriousness.

'If only.'

Olena snorted.

'Oh,' Marisha said in a sing-song voice, 'to miss out on the sweet, sweet sound of a snoring goat.' Olena shot her a look. 'Sorry.' Marisha bent her head back over the book.

But Olena said, 'At least it would be more interesting than reading about hoof rot or whatever other ailments goats are susceptible to.'

Marisha leaned forward. Anything to delay returning to her task. 'Don't be too sure. One Vasily of Kul woke the whole village because his goat climbed a tree and refused to come down. Ha! Listen to this. The blacksmith tried to rescue it and got bitten, and they ended up having to chop down the tree.'

'My, how fascinating. I'm almost jealous you can read the Old Slavonic so well.' The right corner of Olena's mouth curved up. Olena caught Marisha's glance and sat up straighter. 'I think it's time we had a tea break.'

Marisha stood up and walked to the doorway. She paused when Olena did not follow her. 'Aren't you coming?' Marisha asked.

'Oh. No. I'll have the Hands bring me tea up here.'

'Is that what you always do?'

'Why? Do you all miss me so much? You have ten minutes.'

Olena buried her nose back in the book immediately. Marisha shrugged but her footsteps were light as she ran down the stairs. Olena had smiled. Maybe there was hope after all.

EIGHT

he stack on the table soared up to her chin. Olena did not love reading, not the way she loved experimenting with tinctures. She loved the green smell that would waft from her mortar, the ideas that would flow in the space created by simple movement. But she had experimented enough already, to no avail. Now, she needed the books. And thank goodness Marisha had shown some proficiency at something besides wasting Olena's time. The tightness in Olena's chest upon seeing the huge stack had nothing to do with the enormity of the task of reading them. *Please, please let them be enough.*

They had made a quick stop in Gulervo to pick up Valdim but now the house was skiing again–and would be for quite some days. Olena was grateful for it. Now she would have the time to focus on her research. Besides, since Baba Zima had pushed her to make that house visit in Aksorka, she hoped that her mistress wouldn't bother her so much anymore with tests disguised as requests. It was hard to be certain. Baba Zima was unpredictable in her whims. Sometimes Olena was sent on a house call and got sick cows, as promised, while other times–Olena smiled grimly–she got a vengeful spirit instead. She ought to be used to it by now. But just because she was used to it, just because Olena understood *why*, didn't mean that she had to like it. Her mind leapt to a memorable moment only a few weeks into her apprenticeship when Baba Zima had sat her down in front of a line of jars and told her to separate out the poisons without any further information–except that she better act fast because some of the poisons were breathable and the jars weren't well sealed. Olena had been terrified, but she had not been surprised. Baba Zima had stated her intentions clearly in the first conversation they had.

Stomp, stomp, stomp.

Olena pushed back from her chair, her thoughts interrupted. The sound of stomping was coming from directly above her, on the ceiling of her work room. She went up the stairs and found the door to the room directly above hers flung open. Inside, Valdim walked from one side to the other, opening a chest and taking out instruments, laying them down on a table.

Something in the way he focused on his task reminded her of the awkward, gangly boy he had been when they first met. Baba Zima had neglected to tell Olena about her son, and when they met by accident in the hall the day after Baba Zima brought Olena in, both were unpleasantly surprised by the presence of the other.

'Who are you?' she had asked. It had not crossed her mind that there would be other children in this house, not when Baba Zima had said that she would be her only apprentice. Olena asked, 'Do you serve Baba Zima?'

'No,' he said, clearly offended. 'She's my mother.'

'Oh.' Baba Zima had a child? She didn't like that. Would he make her life difficult?

'Who are you?' he asked.

'I'm the new apprentice.'

A frown appeared between his eyes. 'An apprentice? My mother doesn't take apprentices.' He looked at her more carefully. Olena hated the scrutiny, but she did not shrink away. She was going to be a powerful koldunya one day, and this house would be hers. His demeanour retracted into politeness. 'Come on,' he said. 'It's almost time for breakfast.'

Even more unpleasant than finding out that Baba Zima had a child was noting how the house *changed* around him. The light seemed to shine brighter where he walked. He led her down the stairs to the oven room for breakfast, and when he touched the banister, it widened and turned into a slide for him. 'Come on,' he had shouted, jumping onto the slide. But by Olena's touch, the wood shrunk back to normal, and she was forced to follow on foot. She remembered feeling shame and confusion. Baba Zima had said that if Olena stayed, if she worked hard and learned, she would inherit this house. But it responded in a much friendlier manner to this boy than it did to her. She had taken deep breaths to calm down. Then she remembered thinking with forced conviction: the house didn't know her yet. It would. And it would love her just as much as it loved this boy.

And now, their roles were reversed: she the permanent fixture, he the interloper. The house had long since warmed to Olena. But even though Valdim had been away for many months, the wrought-iron roses in the hallways that held candles still bloomed when he returned.

'I thought you were only here for a short visit,' she said.

Valdim looked up. He hadn't noticed her. He straightened. 'Olena. Good to see you again.'

Olena wondered again how Baba Zima could have a son that looked and acted so different from her. Valdim had none of Baba Zima's physical presence: he was only a little taller than

Olena, and while Baba Zima sometimes seemed as solid as an oak trunk, Valdim had that sensitive, malnourished artist look that silly girls like Dunya found appealing. He had none of Baba Zima in his face: his face was not long, nor his eyes deep-set. His hair was a frothy brown mess while Baba Zima's was black and pin straight. But he did have Baba Zima's piercing gaze, and the way of looking at someone and fixing them in place. And now he was looking at her, assessing her as she was him.

'Why are you here?'

Valdim looked taken aback. 'I've come for a visit, I know it's been a while—'

'No, I mean, why are you *here*?' She knocked against the wall. 'This room is directly above mine. I can hear every step you take. It's distracting.'

'Oh. My mother said I could take any of the rooms in this wing. Golgolin flew into this one, so I took that as good enough a sign as any.'

Now Olena noticed the guinea pig-fowl roosting on top of one of the chairs, sound asleep. The little traitor. Olena's mouth curved up at the sight of the way the furry creature tucked his head into his wing. But her smiled disappeared as she looked back at Valdim.

It had been almost a year since his last visit. He would come to the house whenever it was in Severny once or twice a year, and then he would sometimes stay for short jaunts, but never for long. He couldn't leave his violins and the society in Severny which required his presence for cultivating patronages and damp earth knew what else. But if he was moving his workshop here, then it was clear that he would stay for a while.

Olena said, 'Is there any way I can persuade you to change rooms?'

Valdim looked around, 'I just unpacked.'

'Barely.' She drummed her fingers on the doorframe. She stopped when she noticed his repressed wince. She had drummed her fingers thoughtlessly, not to annoy him, but she knew that he would take it as a direct offence, as with everything she did. She dropped her hand to her side. 'Sorry,' she said.

He set his book down with exaggerated calm. 'The irony isn't lost on me that for once you are annoyed by my ruckus instead of the other way around.'

Olena rolled her eyes. 'Then you have sympathy for my plight.' She wanted to start drumming her fingers again but decided against deliberate provocation. He had only just arrived and for once, *she* was asking *him* a favour. 'But to be fair, it isn't hard to offend your . . . delicate ears.'

Valdim raised his eyebrows and smirked. 'While you're a fortress of tranquillity. Can't you put a charm on the ceiling to stop the sound from going through? My mother did that for my rooms in Severny.'

'Yes, well, it would be easy enough in an ordinary house. But this one does what it wants.'

Valdim smiled cheekily at her. 'Are you saying that the house *wanted* you to hear my footsteps?'

Olena's face heated slightly. She said, 'Maybe. I'm easily aggravated. And the house likes to test my patience at times.'

'Hmm. And so, you'd rather ask me to move rooms than figure out how to persuade the house to block the sound of my footsteps? I'd have expected more from the future mistress of the house's bolshina.'

'Forget it,' Olena turned to leave.

'Wait, Olena.' He had laughter in his voice. 'You're right, you are easy to aggravate.'

'It's not like that's news to you.'

'Look, if you want me to change rooms, I'll change rooms.' He crossed his arms. 'Why don't you tell me which one will would suit you best. So I know you won't come complaining again.'

Olena blew out a long breath of air. 'Fine.' She looked around. 'Baba Zima said any room in this wing?'

'Yes.'

She walked down the hall until it ended to be as far away as possible from her workroom below. The room was further from the stairs, and the ceiling slanted in one corner. But Valdim didn't seem to mind: at least the window was bigger. Olena gestured inside. 'Well?'

Valdim poked his head in. 'It looks well enough. What do you think, Golgolin?' The guinea pig-fowl sat on his shoulder. 'Has Olena picked a good replacement?'

Golgolin flew away. Valdim raised his eyebrow at Olena. 'He seems to disagree with your choice.'

'He's a guinea pig-fowl. He flies away.' Olena was irritated. Valdim wasn't here that often, it was unfair that he should have such a strong connection with Golgolin when it was built on so little. Golgolin must be excited by Valdim's novel presence, that's all.

'Luckily,' Valdim said. 'It's your approval I'm interested in at the moment, not his. I wouldn't want to get on your blacklist, not when I'm here for so long.' He looked at her with the trace of a grin. 'Golgolin is much more forgiving of my faults.'

Olena sniffed. 'If you say so. But, I'd check the corners every day if I were you. And maybe don't leave some of your more precious objects lying around. He can throw some right hissy fits if he wants.' Olena's lips curved up at Valdim's horrified expression. No doubt he was imagining Golgolin making a mess of one of his precious violins.

He said, 'I wouldn't want to incur Golgolin's fury. Maybe you're right, maybe I should stay put.'

He was teasing her again. She took a deep breath, gathering back her dignity, 'I would greatly appreciate it if you would move.'

Valdim flashed her one last smile and said, 'Fine. Now, I'll stomp around a little bit and you tell me if you hear anything. I don't want to have to move again.'

Olena went back downstairs and sat in her workroom and waited. It was silent. After a few minutes of sitting and then organising her work bench she went back upstairs. Valdim's new workroom was empty. She frowned and went to the old one, the one right above hers. He wasn't there, but all of his stuff still was. A violin was on the table, gleaming.

She stopped, remembering the first violin that Valdim had received twelve years ago, shortly before she had arrived at the house. He had spent many hours practising. Olena loved the sound of it and wanted to strum it so badly, but she had been too shy to ask. So, she had taken it in secret. She tried cradling the violin's neck in the crook of her left elbow, but almost dropped it. Holding it with her hand worked better. She brushed the strings with her little arm and delighted in how the twangs layered upon each other, one by one. Then Valdim walked in.

His eyes grew wide and he yelled, 'Don't touch it!' running at her and tugging the violin. Olena held on to it instinctively, until *crack*. His mouth gaped open in horror. They had both been punished. But Baba Zima's look of disappointment had hurt even more. It made Olena feel like she had fulfilled some small expectation of Baba Zima's. She hated Valdim for the part he played in making Baba Zima think less of her. Valdim was sent away soon afterwards.

A lump rose in Olena's throat as she relived the memory. Yes, time may have passed, and maybe Valdim was being slightly more agreeable now, but he would always be that boy who had made her feel a little bit more like the girl who always broke everything.

She heard footsteps. Valdim walked into the room. Olena took a deep breath. 'I thought you were moving rooms. Did you even bother to stomp around?'

'Ah, so you didn't hear anything. Wasn't that rather the point?' He looked between her and the violin.

She suppressed the urge to grab her little arm at the elbow. 'Don't worry,' she said. 'I didn't touch it.'

'I wasn't worried,' he frowned. 'You can hold it if you like.' He picked it up carefully by the neck. 'I promise I won't tug on the other end this time.' He said the last with a small smile. But Olena did not appreciate the joke.

'That's all right,' Olena said. 'I should get back to work. Thank you for switching rooms.' She added the last as an afterthought.

'You're welcome,' he said. He still held out the violin but when she did not make any move towards it, he set it back down carefully. He drew back. A frown of indecisiveness crossed his face. 'I should tell you,' he said, 'I met Anatoli before I left. He has been in Severny quite often, and we find ourselves at similar functions. When I told him I would be leaving to visit my mother, he asked me to pass on his regards to you.' Valdim looked at her. 'So, I'm passing the regards along.'

Valdim's brow wrinkled further. She knew that Valdim had internalised his mother's prejudices against Anatoli. But the few times that she had spoken with him, she had found him quite pleasant. She liked the way he spoke to her, like she was an equal in intellect. And his gaze was direct, never darting to her cheek or arm. For that alone she would have regarded him highly. But he also asked for her opinion and listened when she answered. And that was almost equally as valuable.

'Thank you, I suppose.' She shrugged but would not condescend to defend herself. Let Valdim think what he wanted. Valdim caught her gaze. Olena's brow crinkled, matching his expression. She was no fool. Anatoli was older and a much more experienced koldun than her, more powerful. Valdim had no cause to suspect her of anything, especially since she had done nothing wrong.

Olena said, 'Don't look at me like that. He knew you were coming here and wanted to send his regards. Sometimes it's as simple as that.'

He raised his eyebrows in a way that told her that he believed nothing of it. 'So, what are you doing that requires so much concentration that a few footsteps interrupted you?'

'I'm looking for a plague cure.' She tried to be nonchalant, but the words stuck in her throat a little.

He raised his eyebrows. 'Why? Did my mother ask you to?'

Olena shook her head. 'No. I decided to.'

'Really? Haven't kolduni been working on it years? You must have quite the big idea if you think you can do better.'

Well, if Valdim had one thing in common with his mother it was his ability to make her doubt herself. 'Oh, I have many ideas. Whether they'll work . . . we'll see.'

He looked at her closely, as though trying to unravel her. 'But it's important to you that you succeed. Why? You don't need to prove anything. My mother has practically yelled to the spirits that you will succeed her in the bolshina.' Valdim paused, bitterness splayed on his face. So, he still hadn't forgiven her for being his mother's successor. Even though he had made it clear that he wanted no part in koldunry.

'Has it even occurred to you that I'm simply doing this to help people?'

His flashed a grin at her. 'No, it hadn't.'

'That says more about you than it does me.'

'Is that so?' He was laughing at her again.

'Not all of us can be satisfied by being simply adequate.' That shut him up. Olena took advantage of the silence to press her point. 'How many people are you helping with that?' She jutted her chin towards the violin.

He said, 'I hope that the person who gets that violin will have almost as much joy as I've had in creating it.' He shrugged. 'Though I'll be the first to admit if you succeed at your task, it will have a lot more impact than mine will.' He met her gaze. 'But at least I'm honest with my reasons.'

She guffawed. 'Think yourself superior, I don't care. Whatever my reasons are, my work is important, so stop interrupting it.'

'Very well.' He looked away and shook his head. 'You know, strangely enough, I was looking forward to seeing you again.' He waited as though to hear that she too had been looking forward to seeing him. But she just glared. He flashed her a tight smile. 'I have to move my things.'

The more she thought about their interaction, the more irritated she became. She hated how easily Valdim made her feel off-kilter. She knew how to act with Baba Zima, her mistress, and she certainly knew how she related to the assistants, but Valdim–they were always on somewhat equal, if uneven, footing. Perhaps it was because the house was more hers than his now. In fact, it had been so ever since Baba Zima brought Olena in, and then sent Valdim away. She knew that part of him resented her for her position, how could he not? She worked with his mother, was her named successor, lived in the house that he had spent his childhood in. And yet, he belonged to it in a way that she did not, because he was Baba Zima's child. But he had never wanted to be a koldun, so it was not fair that he should begrudge her.

Hopefully, they would stay out of each other's way, each of them absorbed in their tasks. As she turned back to her books, she did her best to keep him out of her mind. But she thought she could still hear his footsteps, however faintly, and the plaintive note of a violin.

NINE

s a few days turned into weeks, Marisha's optimism quickly dwindled. She learned many more uninteresting tidbits about goats and soon moved on to interminably boring wars. The plague was mentioned alongside lists of numbers of sleeping victims and the words that began with 'd' like 'devastation' and 'disaster' and 'decimated'. Often she found herself reading and rereading the same sentences.

Luckily, she got to take a break from reading every two to five days when the house stopped in towns and villages to receive supplicants. While Marisha found assisting Baba Zima during those days fascinating despite herself, it was exhausting to run to Olena's workroom and back to the receiving room all day. The only break in the pattern had happened ten days ago when a snowstorm hit the house, perhaps a month after she had begun reading the books. The house had hunkered in place while the wind whistled and rattled the windows. The next day, the house shook off almost all the snow on the roof but was unable to knock over the snow that piled up on the wraparound balconies that spanned almost the entire third floor. While Olena and Baba Zima were shovelling balconies that were not so easily accessible (or so Baba Zima said), the three assistants were told to clear the snow off the wraparound one. Marisha welcomed the exercise and the fresh air. With the house standing still and its legs and feet tucked so that the bottom of the house rested on the snow, Marisha could almost forget that the house was much livelier than a house ought to be.

Dunya sent a snowball flying from the opposite end of the balcony. It only took two snowballs for Anka-ny to be goaded into retaliation. Marisha, who at first was content to just watch, scooped up a handful of snow and joined in after a rogue snowball from Anka-ny hit her square in the chest. The girls yelled and ducked and slid and so many snowballs flew that Marisha wouldn't have been surprised if the Hands were partaking.

Suddenly, the balcony tipped as the house got to its feet and Marisha slid away from the relative safety of the house's side and crashed into the railing. Dunya squealed and laughed as the house shook from side to side, flinging more snow out of the gutters. Marisha looped both her arms around the balustrade, overcome with the vertigo and feeling that the house would think nothing of throwing her off into the snow below. But Dunya seemed unbothered and even exhilarated. She patted the banister when the house stopped stomping its feet and settled back down on the ground. Marisha was much slower to unwrap her arms from around the railing before picking up her shovel again to finish the task.

That had been over a week ago. Now, Marisha was back to puzzling through the Old Slavonic and wishing a snowstorm would hit the house, if only to alleviate the boredom of the task. Olena looked through Marisha's notes with the Old Slavonic book open next to her, cross-referencing between them. 'What's this?' she said.

'What's what?' Marisha looked up from her current volume.

'This,' Olena pointed with her finger and began reading. 'The lord of Kul moved against Onin with the force of five hundred men, his ranks thinned by the sleeping plague.'

'Yes, I wrote that down.'

'But what about here?' Olena's voice rose with excitement, 'The same year, Nightingale the Robber, a *plague* upon Kul—' Olena's voice rose even higher at the word 'plague', '—terrorised people with a fearsome cry that felled whoever heard it.' Olena looked at Marisha and repeated 'plague' again, pointing her finger at the word in the book.

'So what?' Marisha said.

'So, I told you to note down every instance of the plague being mentioned.'

'The *sleeping* plague, not monsters!'

'I was very clear with you. I want you to track any mention of the plague in these histories *and* any associated myths and stories.'

'But this has nothing to do with the sleeping plague! Did you read the next sentence?' Marisha walked over and leaned over the book. 'See, the bogotir Grisha slayed the monster and desecrated its body for good measure. It's not relevant!'

'*You* record mentions of the plague. *I* decide whether or not its relevant.'

Marisha silently fumed then burst out, 'If you want me to write down every little thing that *may* be important, I might as well copy the whole book. Why am I even doing this?'

'I told you. You're reading so we can track patterns associated with the plague: the number of victims, the cycle of the years, the symptoms. This will help me understand whether the root spiritual cause has remained consistent through the years. And the myths and stories may help me understand what caused it.'

'Because once you know what caused it, you'll *certainly* be able to lift it.'

Olena ignored Marisha's sarcasm and picked up a page of notes, scanning the text. 'It would make it easier. Physical remedies like tinctures wouldn't be enough without binding them using an incantation that pinpoints the spiritual source.'

'But not certain,' Marisha shot back.

Olena looked up from the notes. 'I will not pretend certainty. Sometimes the curse caster is stronger than the koldunya seeking to lift it. And some cures are beyond our power to ask of the spirits.' She traced the edges of her birthmark on her cheek and jaw with her index finger.

'Oh.' Marisha did not know what to say to Olena's uncharacteristic humility. Her gaze darted to Olena's birthmark. 'Did–did your parents think . . . ?' Marisha's voice trailed off.

Olena sniffed. 'Did my parents think what?' She dropped her hand from her cheek and finished the question. 'That I was cursed?'

Marisha knew she was skating on cobwebs. 'I thought, maybe because you're Buryat that they may have thought differently.'

'I never told you I was Buryat.'

'I just assumed.' Marisha paused. She scanned the left side of Olena's face again for evidence: the high cheekbone and the long, narrow, slightly downturned eye. 'But I can understand if you don't want to talk about it. Pardon my curiosity.'

'Ha. Well at least you admit you're curious.' Olena looked out the window and crossed her arms, grabbing her left elbow with her right hand. She had made the same gesture when Baba Zima had told her she interfaced badly with the supplicants. Olena had replied then that she couldn't help what she looked like.

Now she looked soft and still, like a birch tree whose bark had peeled thin after a long winter. 'I come from a village in a cold, silent forest, far, far away from here. So far it took the house over a year to ski back to Severny. I bet that when you think of the Buryat you picture the nomad Zabalaisky that follow the reindeer herds. But my village was like any other one in Chernozemlya.' Olena paused, her gaze flicked down. 'I was only allowed to live because my grandfather decided so. It was not a kindness: he forced my mother to keep me because he thought I was her punishment. She loved me those moments she forgot about it.'

Marisha did not know what to say. She thought again of the woman in her village who drowned her malformed baby. Olena had been allowed to live, but the idea that she had been told she was her mother's punishment made Marisha feel sick with an inexpressable rage and sympathy. 'That must have been . . . very hard for you.'

Olena let out a slight snort but did not answer. Marisha wished she could express herself in a less clumsy way, but she could not think of any solace that Olena would accept. Instead, she asked, 'What had she done? Your mother.'

'I don't mind talking about my own shortcomings, but I don't want to talk about hers.' She turned to Marisha. 'And it doesn't matter. She brought me to the shaman–a kind of koldunya–once. But it didn't help. In the end, I was my own curse.' She raised her hand to touch her face but stopped mid-gesture and smoothed her dress.

Marisha wanted to shove her foot in the doorway that Olena had opened on her life, but before she could find the words, Olena moved on. 'The sleeping plague is different than that, it's not born from the actions of one person. And yet the kolduni have no feeling for what caused it. There have been many theories, but nothing fruitful.'

'And no one has tried looking at these books before?'

'Not with a koldunic eye. Baba Zima had to personally ask for them, I doubt they've been out of the Grand Prince's archives these past two hundred years. This will work, you'll see. Knowing that the plague cycle has been stable across centuries has already helped me refine my ideas for a cure.'

'And then what? How are you planning on testing out your cures?' Marisha asked. 'Have you written to the sanitoriums to ask permission to test them? I doubt even Baba Zima's clout would get you so far.'

Olena's expression became wooden. 'I'm working on it. Don't you worry about that, keep looking for mentions of the plague, and stop selecting which ones you think are important.'

Olena made Marisha comb through the surrounding pages for any more allusions to Kul's brushes with the plague and Nightingale the Robber, and by the time lunch came around, Marisha's head was swimming. So, it was with less gusto than usual that Marisha surveyed the options of palm-sized savoury pies that the Hands laid out on the table. Her appetite returned along with some of her good mood as she ate the warm potato and sour cabbage filling.

Baba Zima was going on and on about reasonable philosophers that morning and it was making Marisha angry to listen to. She said, 'Baba Elizaveta said those ridiculous philosophy stone-brains have written another manifesto about an alchemical discovery. Ha! Alchemy. They don't know what real magic is.'

'Why don't you show them?' Marisha asked. Her question was voiced so softly she did not realise anyone else had heard until the table fell silent.

'Why don't I *show* them?' Baba Zima repeated, her voice low.

'Yes,' Marisha said hesitantly, 'If they knew about this house, their doubts would—'

'Disappear? Evaporate into the ether? Ha! You think that's the way the world works?'

Marisha felt her face turn red. 'They might.'

'No. I will not let *my* house be a thing to be poked and prodded. Turning the mind of one sceptic is tedious enough. Tell me, would you have been satisfied with a gazette article about this house? Or even a demonstration?'

Marisha wanted to say yes, but the word was stuck in her throat. She remembered her own incredulous reaction to seeing the house unfolding its chicken legs for the first time. She had assumed it was a trick of hydraulics. What would she think about it now, had she not been let into Baba Zima's coterie? Certainly not that the house's ability to ski was a feat of koldunry rooted in the other world. Surprisingly, the thought elicited no reactionary inner scoff. How disconcerting. Under the table, Marisha's fingers wrapped around the edge of her chair's seat. She felt unmoored from herself. After all, her unwavering belief in reasonable philosophy had been part of who she was for a long time.

One of the Hands dabbed Baba Zima's lips with a napkin. She said, 'Enough. Instead of pointless questions about my nonexistent concerns over these philosophers, tell me of your progress with the cure.'

Marisha's cheeks were still burning. She rolled back her shoulders and said, 'Well, we're making a good deal of progress in identifying patterns in the victims' characteristics and charting the plague's virulence through the ages. It seems that the ten-year cycle has gone unchanged–at least, it was the same five hundred years ago.' She stole a glance at Olena. The apprentice looked determinedly ahead, her hand flat on the table next to her saucer.

'I see,' Baba Zima said. 'So you have nothing. I know I told you that you did not need to prepare anything for the krug this year, but that does not mean you can skate by on empty snowshoes.'

'It's not nothing.' Olena said, 'The patterns are helping me narrow down my remedies, and we're recording accounts of the plague's mythic origins which may help pinpoint its spiritual source. And there are still several Old Slavonic histories to go through.'

Baba Zima snorted. 'At this pace, you'll still be studying the plague's history by the time the Grand Prince is dead of old age and the reward will be of use to no one.

'I will get there,' Olena said, 'I'll find something. I promise.'

Baba Zima raised her eyebrows. 'Don't devalue your word to me. A koldunya's words are her power. Your promises are about as satisfying as a dry white cake. If you keep this up, the next time you whisper into water, the surface might not even ruffle.' Baba Zima snorted and shook her head. One of the Hands at Baba Zima's shoulder zipped over the side table and brought a slice of cake on a small dessert plate and set it down by Olena's elbow. Olena looked at the Hand and moved her elbow a minute inch away from the cake. Baba Zima smiled a small self-satisfied smile. 'Instead of trying to tide me over with pretty promises that have no substance, convince me. You know how to convince me, don't you?'

Olena's eyes widened.

Baba Zima's smile became gentle, a contradiction to the harshness of her admonition to Olena. 'Results, my buttered blin. You're not the first to promise to cure the plague.'

Olena stood up. She said, 'I'll have something.' And she left the table without another word.

Marisha gobbled the rest of her kartofel pie and found Olena pacing around her work room. Marisha said, 'Baba Zima is really getting cranky about our progress.'

Olena did not stop pacing. 'I need to move forward. I need to test these remedies.' She stopped walking and ran a finger along her cheek and jaw, tracing the outline of her crimson birthmark. Marisha wondered if the skin texture felt different or if she had memorised its edges.

After the silence went on for a few more seconds, Marisha sat down at the table in front of her book and tried to to focus on the spiky Old Slavonic script and ignore the caged animal tension that rolled off Olena as she paced back and forth. The tapping of Marisha's pencil on her empty page of notes matched the thump of Olena's footsteps.

'Are you committed to this project?' Olena said. She had stopped pacing and stood in front of Marisha.

'Of course I am,' Marisha answered, startled.

'Prove it,' Olena said. She had tight-lipped smile and her eyes sparkled with nervous excitement. 'Swear an oath that you will support me in this endeavour to whatever end we may meet.'

Marisha hesitated. Her father had cautioned her not to swear oaths or enter bargains lightly. It was one of the few things he had been firm about. 'I can't swear to follow you blindly.'

'So you don't trust me. Ha.'

Marisha stamped her foot and stood up, crossing her arms. 'Olena, I will work *with* you, not *for* you. I can even be your friend if you let me. But if you require blind obedience from me to continue working, well, I'll have to tell Baba Zima these conditions are no longer suitable.'

'She will ask you to leave.'

Marisha shrugged. 'I'd rather leave and keep my soul intact.'

'You think I'd ask you to sell your soul?'

'All I know is that you're smart and bitter and about to do something very reckless.'

Olena's nostrils flared but she did not counter the statement. 'If this is really how you feel, you can tell Baba Zima you're no longer willing to work.'

Marisha hoped Olena would take it back, but she just silently sat down and returned to her notes. Marisha had no choice but to turn and leave. She stood in front of the door after it closed. Had she made a mistake? She could have simply agreed to swear the oath. But she knew deep down she shouldn't. She could hear the echo of her father's voice in her mind, his eyes misting over with some painful memory, his right hand rubbing his left wrist, telling her that swearing an oath or entering an open bargain was like selling a piece of one's soul. Baba Zima would order her to leave, and she would lose so much: safety from her aunt's reach, maybe even the opportunity to wake her parents. *Come on*, she told herself, *it's impossible*. Olena would never manage to find the cure. But would Marisha regret missing this chance to try? Her footsteps were heavy as she walked down the stairs to find Baba Zima.

The older woman stood next to the table in the oven room, arms folded, supervising the Hands kneading dough in a bowl. Marisha's gaze fixed on them instead of Baba Zima, on how they grasped the dough and shaped it into balls, placing them delicately on a tray next to the bowl.

'What do you want?' Baba Zima asked.

'Olena asked me to come see you because she has created conditions in which I do not feel comfortable working.'

Baba Zima placed a hand on her hip. 'What in the damp dark

earth is that supposed to mean? Do you need more tea breaks?'

'No.'

'What is it? Speak plainly.'

'She has asked me to do something I do not feel comfortable doing.'

'Ah,' Baba Zima said. 'And?'

'And, I don't feel comfortable doing it.'

Baba Zima exhaled loudly and raised her gaze to the ceiling. 'Dear Matrionka Serafima, I bet you never had to deal with such wilting help.' Marisha rolled her eyes. Baba Zima lowered her gaze. 'Did you think this would be easy?'

'It's not that—'

'Did you think that being a koldunya is just waving your hands over water and saying a few words?'

'I don't—'

'The point is you have to take risks to be great. Olena sees that.'

'I don't mind taking risks I just don't want to be bound to—' Marisha shut her mouth.

'Hmm.' Baba Zima made some hand motions and the Hands flew away. 'I take it that you do not want to leave.'

'No,' Marisha said honestly. She wanted to stay, and she wanted it with a certainty that surprised her.

'If you do not find a way to work with Olena, you will have to leave. And I need both Anka-ny and Dunya where they are, so I will have to hire a new assistant for her and she will drive that one away too and it will all be such a bother. I thought you were tougher than that. Disappointing.'

'If it's so much of a bother,' Marisha's voice caught in her throat, 'don't ask me to leave.'

'But I have no choice. I can't force Olena to work with you

after this, she won't trust you. Don't look so surprised. I've had that girl with me for many years, I know how she works. She'll get suspicious and think I'm putting you up to something.'

'And?' Marisha asked. 'Are you?'

'Of course not,' Baba Zima said without batting an eyelid.

'Why do you care whether or not Olena trusts me?'

'She won't work as well if she doesn't trust you, and then what's the point of having you help her find a cure for the plague?' The corners of her mouth turned up a little. 'Now. If you want to stay and save us both the hassle you must find a way to satisfy Olena. If she's setting disagreeable conditions for you, change the conditions.'

Marisha bit her lip. 'How?'

Baba Zima shrugged. 'Figure out how to give her what she wants while changing the conditions so they are less unacceptable to you.'

An hour later, Marisha stood in front of Olena's door. She wiped the palms of her hands on her skirt. She knocked and entered.

'You're back,' Olena said. She stopped pacing. 'What is it? Come to say you've changed your mind?'

'I will not swear you an oath, Olena. But—' Marisha took a deep breath. 'I will help you with whatever reckless thing you want to do next, so long as it lies within reason.'

'Really? And what would you consider unreasonable?'

'I won't kill anyone.'

Olena scoffed. 'Murder? That's the best you can come up with?'

'It's just an example!' Marisha gritted her teeth.

'A koldunya must be more creative than that.' Marisha hated the small Baba Zima-ish smirk at the apprentice's lips.

Olena said, 'So you will help me out of your own free will. But you should know, swearing an oath to do as I say would tie your actions to my intent. If you do not swear, you will be responsible for what you do.'

'I will not be blind in this. I will not.'

Olena rubbed a finger back and forth on one of the purple pebbled patches on her cheek. 'All right. You may continue to work for me.'

'With you, Olena.'

'Isn't that what I said?'

Marisha shook her head.

'Either way,' Olena said. 'I will need someone to do the heavy lifting.' She paused and scanned Marisha's face. 'I may ask you to do something tonight, and if you refuse, I will expect you to leave this house tomorrow. But if you do as I ask without swearing an oath to help me, the consequences are on you.'

Marisha nodded and swallowed around the lump in her throat.

'Fine. Meet me here at midnight. Wear something dark. And we'll see how far your word is worth.'

TEN

arisha crept downstairs. What would Olena have her do? Her mind raced, but other than imaginings of dark pits and searing cold, Marisha could not come up with any ideas. Maybe Olena was right, maybe she did lack some sort of creative quality.

The staircases and floorboards were uncharacteristically creaky. Marisha told herself it was just because it was night and the house was quiet, but that didn't stop her from thinking that the house somehow knew Marisha did not want to draw attention. When she reached the bottom of the stairs, the floorboard grated so loudly that she froze, waiting for the sounds of doors being flung open as the awakened inhabitants came to investigate the source of all that noise. After a few seconds of intense listening, she relaxed. It seemed like the house's antics wouldn't get her into trouble this time.

Marisha stood before the door of the oven room, uncertain of whether or not to enter. It was the quickest way to the back staircase to Olena's workroom. Marisha turned the doorknob and pushed, expecting the door to creak loudly as it swung. But the door opened silently and Marisha peeked her head around the corner. Just as she hoped: complete silence and no movement. Perhaps the house had lost interest in her. Marisha opened the door wider and slid in. She was pleased she had almost passed the first hurdle of sneaking to Olena's workroom undetected. Then her gaze alighted on the oven coals' glow reflected on the clock's face. Eleven fifteen. No, no, no! She was early. What was she going to do for forty-five minutes?

She stared at the oven coals and debated whether it was worth staying or going to Olena's workroom immediately. The longer she prowled around the house, the more likely it was she'd make a noise that woke Baba Zima, or even the Hands. What did they do at night? Did they slowly revolve around the koldunya's room and guard her bed, or perch on a gilded pillow while she slept? Surely Olena would have told her if they patrolled the halls. Marisha grabbed the poker that leaned against the tiled mantel and prodded the coals. When she realised what she did she hastily put the poker back. She couldn't believe she was so on edge that she forgot only Baba Zima was allowed to stoke the oven.

She heard a rattling in the kitchen. Her head snapped up. There were footsteps, low muttering, now a big clatter. Marisha froze, her gaze fixed on the door that connected the kitchen to the oven room. *Please let it be Olena.* The door opened. For a split second, Marisha was torn between relief and confusion as she realised that the person traipsing through the door was decidedly not Baba Zima, but neither were they Olena because they had the stocky shape of a man.

Marisha grabbed the poker and brandished it. 'Who are you?'

'Shh. It's me, Valdim.' The man held out his hands in a gesture of peace.

Inwardly cursing the terrible timing, Marisha lowered the poker. 'Ah. Of course.' She and Valdim hadn't talked very much at all since he had first arrived. She only really saw him at mealtimes.

Valdim smiled sardonically. 'You know, you really shouldn't be touching that.' He gestured at the poker with his chin.

She hastily returned the poker to its hanging spot next to the oven. She worried for a moment that he might threaten to say something to his mother, but at his smile her fear dissolved.

'What are you doing down here?' Valdim asked. 'It's late.'

Marisha crossed her arms. 'I could ask you the same thing.'

'I was awake,' Valdim said, his gaze darting to the side. 'I couldn't sleep.' So he had decided to raid the kitchen? Maybe he was hungry. But instead of elaborating, he looked at her, clearly waiting for her to say why she was out of bed.

'I could not sleep as well,' Marisha said truthfully.

'Happens a lot in this house.' He grinned and asked her how she was liking learning about koldunry. Marisha launched into a babbling explanation while her gaze darted to the clock and she wondered if she could excuse herself without appearing rude. She soon noticed that Valdim seemed to be listening to her with half an ear as well. He looked at her, but he was frowning and he kept wincing every few seconds.

Marisha interrupted her own stream of speech, 'I'm sorry, is everything all right? You look a little . . .' Marisha did not continue explaining, but Valdim seemed to understand because his frown dissolved.

'I'm sorry,' he said, 'It's just I can hear this—' he winced again, '—this drip of water. And it's driving me up the wall. Can't you hear it too?' He looked away from Marisha and his gaze darted around the oven room. He strode over to the table where one of the samovars stood and lifted the chimney off. Marisha walked over to join Valdim at the samovar, and she spied the kitchen through the door that Valdim had left open. It was quite a mess, with bowls and cups on the counter.

Marisha said, 'And you could hear it from your room?'

Valdim put his hands flat on the table, leaning onto it and sighed. 'There's always the odd drip in this house, what with all of the barrels of hale water and snow melting and Olena's distilling and my mother's never-ending streams of tea. My mother did something so that I don't hear anything in my rooms. But either the drip is so loud, or it comes from everywhere—'

He winced and pushed away from the table and began rummaging around one of the corners. His search had a franticness that Marisha found distressing to watch.

She focused and thought she could maybe hear some water dripping, but it was hard to know if she'd imagined it. She said, 'I don't think any laundry is happening at the moment. Did you check the pantry?'

Valdim shook his head distractedly and he followed Marisha through the kitchen into one of the pickling pantries. It took a bit of looking, but Marisha remembered that Dunya had brought in some tubs of snow for easy water access the next day and had put them next to a barrel of salted cabbage. And indeed, a bucket had been put on a shelf and was dripping onto the tub below.

Marisha moved the bucket onto the floor put it into a larger one to stop it from leaking everywhere. Valdim's chin lifted, body still with tension, and then after a few seconds he relaxed and an expression of relief spread across his face.

'Thank you,' he said. 'That's so much better, you can't imagine.'

'You're welcome.' She lapsed into silence, pleased with Valdim's gratitude. Truth be told, she had never really noticed how noisy the house really was. But she couldn't hear anything now. Then her stomach growled.

Valdim said, 'Ah, you're hungry. Let's have some tea.'

'That's all right—' Marisha started saying, but Valdim had already grabbed a loaf of bread and a jar of brined mushroom off the shelf. Her stomach growled again.

Back in the oven room, Marisha relaxed when she saw the clock. She still had a half hour before meeting Olena. Though she itched to leave, she sat down at the table and folded her hands in her lap. It would be more suspicious to scurry off now that she had agreed to drink a cup of tea. She filled a teacup with hot water from the samovar and passed it to him. As she filled her own teacup, she couldn't help glancing at Valdim. Marisha thought of how Baba Zima had replaced all their plates and bowls with wooden versions. She asked, 'So it's just dripping water? And cutlery on plates?'

Valdim shook his head. 'Unfortunately, no.' He paused, as though considering a long list. 'Mostly loud noises, wrong notes. It feels like . . . you know that feeling that you get from biting into ice? It feels like that.'

Marisha shivered. 'I hate that.'

'The last concert I tried to sit through, the cello was horribly flat. It made me go yellow all over.' His whole body shuddered. 'I had to leave.'

Marisha frowned. 'But you make violins, don't you?'

'Yes,' He chuckled. 'I know it must seem masochistic to you. But as much as off notes are painful, the right ones . . .' he gained a faraway look as though there were no words.

'So, you never wanted to be a koldun. Huh. I was under the impression that Baba Zima had taken Olena on to replace you.'

Valdim smiled slightly, 'To replace me?'

'I mean, as her apprentice.' Marisha's cheeks flushed. She looked at him over the rim of her teacup.

Valdim blew on his tea. 'No. I never had the inclination nor talent to be a koldun. I wanted to be a musician. A composer. My mother sent me away to a tutor with an excellent reputation shortly after Olena came along.' A slight indentation between his brows appeared.

'How long ago? I think Olena said that she has been here twelve years.'

'Twelve years. That's right. I've lived away since.' He shrugged ruefully. 'I didn't last long with that first tutor. He had three students besides me and the cacophony was endless–enough to drive a domovoi out of the house entirely. So, after a few minor incidents, the tutor sent me to a luthier to . . . work off the damages. I wanted to be a musician more than anything, and Mother did send me to other tutors, but after some time I ended up returning to the luthier. It was easier.'

'So, you had to stop studying music? How disappointing. And Baba Zima couldn't do anything to help?' Marisha asked. She glanced at the clock. Eleven forty-five.

Valdim's frown deepened. He looked into his teacup. 'She did what she could.' He did not elaborate. He said, 'I still play. Though the pleasure of crafting an instrument for a person, to make it beautiful and perfect just for them, is almost as good.' He smiled, but it was a sad smile, and sipped from the cup. 'When did you know the koldunic arts were your passion?'

'I don't know what my passion is. I don't know if I even have one.'

'Sure you do. Everyone has one.'

'I must be deficient.' She had not meant to be short. It was obvious Valdim was being courteous by making small talk, but she could not be late to meet Olena. She breathed in deeply. Maybe she should say she was ready for bed. Would he think it strange that she went down the hall to the back stairs?

'It could be a good thing,' Valdim said, 'that you're not overly passionate about koldunry.' He swirled what was left of his tea. 'My mother can make people crazy. Look at what she has done to Olena.'

Marisha's gut knotted, her worry about the time forgotten. 'What do you mean?'

'You must have noticed . . . my mother likes to toy with people. And with Olena, well,' he shook his head, 'she's constantly setting impossible little tests for her. Best try and stay out of it as much as you can–it's what I do.'

Marisha tried not to show how much Valdim's words rattled her. What was she doing now except succumbing to a test of Olena's own? But she had no choice. If she wanted to stay, she had to see what Olena wanted her to do. She could refuse now or later, either way it would mean leaving the house. And she was not ready to do that yet.

She got to her feet and he mirrored her. 'I should probably get to bed,' she said. He reached for the bread and teacups but she swept them up into her arms first. 'Oh no, let me. It's on the way.'

'I can help,' he said, putting the samovar back on the ledge and gesturing to take the jar of mushrooms.

'Don't be silly,' Marisha said. 'I can carry this myself.'

To Marisha's relief, he relented and with a wave goodnight, he headed out the door. She listened to the fading squeaks of the staircase and her arms hugging the bread, mushrooms, and teacups to her chest relaxed. She glanced at the clock. Ten minutes to midnight.

She walked quickly to the pantry and stuffed the bread and jar on a shelf. She had liked Valdim, despite his eccentricities, though she wondered again how he could have a koldunya for a mother and still suffer from such sensitivity to sounds. She also wondered at that frown that appeared between his eyes whenever she had mentioned Olena. It was obvious they did not get along, she noticed that much herself these past few weeks.

She tried not to think of the other things he had said, of Baba Zima setting hard and impossible tasks for Olena. She closed the door to the oven room. Five minutes to midnight. Too late to turn back now. And with a tingling through her fingers that Marisha could not deny was mounting excitement, she hurried down the hall to meet Olena.

ELEVEN

he candlelight threw trembling shadows on the stairwell walls. Marisha followed Olena down to a door that she had not previously noticed as it had neither a handle nor a keyhole. Olena took something out of her pocket that glinted silver.

'A feather from Golgolin,' Olena said. 'Haven't you ever wondered how he delivers letters so quickly?'

'I have many times, and I thought maybe the guinea-pig body is particularly aerodynamic.' Marisha thought the philosophical word might annoy Olena, but she caught the shadow of a smile on her face.

Olena said, 'A reasonable guess, but no. Golgolin can travel between places.'

'Isn't that what travelling is?'

'No. I mean, he can travel from place to place by going *between*. It's a very remarkable skill. And with Golgolin's help, we can do the same.' Marisha stared at the silvery scrap between Olena's fingers and leaned in closer. Olena withdrew her hand and the feather as though Marisha had tried to snatch it.

'It's very rare,' Olena said as way of explanation to Marisha's raised eyebrows. 'He only moults once every seven years, and Baba Zima likes to keep all the feathers to herself. But I persuaded Golgolin to hide a few for me last time he moulted.' She said the last with an affectionate smile. She could not hide her love for the half-guinea-pig-half-duck even if she tried.

'Give me your hand,' Olena said.

Marisha hesitated. 'It's not dangerous. Right?'

'What, the feather? No, I've used one before.' Olena put the feather back in her pocket and raised her arm so that her sleeve fell, exposing her wrist and forearm. 'See, not even a mark.'

Marisha drew back. 'What do you mean by that?'

'Nothing!' Marisha pulled her hand to her chest and Olena sighed. 'When you touch certain very powerful magical objects, *not* Golgolin's feather, you enter into a covenant with them and they can leave marks–a raised scar, usually in the shape of a sigil. But this is not one of those times. Just give me your hand.' Marisha's mind jumped to the raised whorled scar that her father had on his left wrist. He said it was from the bite of a beast in the icy North, but even when she had been a young child, she knew that was not true. Was this the kind of thing Olena meant?

Before Marisha could ask, Olena had pulled Marisha's arm and pinned her hand against the wall with her stump. She took a vial out of her pocket, which she uncorked with her teeth and set on the floor. She then jabbed Marisha's hand with a needle. Marisha whimpered.

'Quiet,' Olena hissed, and pulled Marisha's hand down until they both crouched over the tiny bottle. Olena let a drop of blood fall into the water where it diluted from crimson to a weak tint of red. Olena picked the feather up again and dipped it into the bottle. The feather absorbed the water, growing red with Marisha's blood. Then the red colour drew from the vane into the quill until the feather returned to its silvery green sheen.

'You could have warned me,' Marisha said. She sucked the

puncture mark near her ring-finger knuckle. 'What was it for?'

'You'll see,' Olena said.

She stroked the door with the feather and it melted into the wood, forming a silver handle. Olena twisted it down and pulled the door wide open. She stopped Marisha from stepping forward with her shoulder. 'Careful when crossing. You would not want to fall through the threshold.'

Marisha nodded though she did not understand what Olena meant. Olena jumped through the doorway, as one would when avoiding a puddle. It was dark on the other side and Olena set a lantern that was hanging from her belt onto the ground and struck a match in her clever one-handed way. The light illuminated Olena but failed to reach Marisha. A narrow chasm gaped between Olena's feet and Marisha's where the door hinged. Marisha did not know how she knew it was a chasm, but she could almost feel it yawning endlessly, a bottomless well that existed only at that point in space. The back of her neck prickled. Olena shook the lantern on the other side. Marisha gritted her teeth and forced herself to step closer, right to the edge of the threshold. A strange chill seemed to emanate from it. She paused, wanting to dip her toe in. Then she lunged back and jumped and landed ahead of Olena.

'My, my, what athleticism. You needn't have been so worried. The threshold is very thin here.'

'It can be wider?'

'Yes. The further the distance you seek to cross, the wider the threshold.'

Marisha thought about the emptiness emanating from the threshold and shivered. 'What happens if you fall in?'

'You'll fall to the other world.' Olena waved her hand through the open doorframe. 'But, getting to the other world is not as simple as jumping into the threshold. You need to know where you're going, or you may fall forever. Visiting it in dreams is safer.'

'You can do that?' Visiting the other world, interacting with spirits–Marisha shivered.

'I can't, but other kolduni can. It takes a lot of concentration and practice to make travel to the other world possible. Years and years of practice.'

Olena jumped back over to the doorway in the chicken-legged house and wedged a bundle of dried herbs between the door and its frame. She leapt back to Marisha and the door swung but stopped from slamming shut by the bundle of herbs. 'It will keep the door from disappearing,' Olena said, anticipating Marisha's question. 'I'd rather not waste any of Golgolin's feathers if we don't have to, and I doubt anyone from the house will want to follow.'

'Why do you think that? Where are we?'

Olena shrugged. 'Nowhere truly interesting. To Baba Zima, that is. To you . . .' Olena flashed an enigmatic smile. She started walking down the hall, and Marisha scrambled to keep up.

Something felt off about this place. It was more than the absolute silence. The hallway felt unused. Neglected. And not only that, but Marisha had the feeling she had been in a place like this before. She felt like an intruder twice over.

'We're here,' Olena said softly and opened the next door. It swung open without a squeak, as though it dared not offend the heavy silence of the place. The new room was large, as wide as the mess hall in the preparatory. Olena raised the lantern.

The room was filled with rows of beds. Marisha's chest tightened at the sight, but she stepped forward when Olena did. The beds were filled with women, men, children. She paused to examine a young man with dark blond hair scattered about his forehead like old straw. He had faint stubble on his chin and his lips were slightly parted. His hand rested above the sheet. And the fingers on the hand twitched.

Deep sleepers–plague victims. Marisha froze. Her parents. She had been in a sanatorium like this before. She tugged on Olena's sleeve, her heart beating loudly in her ears.

'What?' Olena hissed.

'My parents are here,' Marisha said. It wasn't a question.

'Your parents? *Both* your parents are asleep?'

Olena's eyes were wide. At least she had the decency to pretend it was new information and not something she'd already surmised from Dima's letter.

'Yes.'

'Well. That is . . . most unfortunate for you.'

Marisha's voice rose above a whisper. 'I offered to help you, but I will *not* allow you to test your hare-potted cures on my parents.'

Olena shook her head. 'Calm down, I don't want your parents.'

'Then why did you use my blood?'

'I knew you had a deep sleeper in your family, and I figured you have enough money to keep him–them–in a private sanitorium. You need a link to your destination when you travel between, and the desire to kidnap a sleeper is a weak link. A blood link to a sleeper, to your parents, is a strong one.'

'You could have used your own blood. Surely you must have a deep sleeper in your family.'

Olena shook her head. Marisha was surprised. If she did not have a deep sleeper in her family, why did she want to cure the plague so badly? Just for glory and a chance to prove herself to Baba Zima? Surely there was a simpler task to achieve that.

'You could have broken into the public sanitoriums.'

'A private sanitorium is better. There's fewer people going through. When's the last time you visited your parents?'

The question was like a punch to the gut. Marisha decreased the number of years out of shame. 'Two years ago. But it wasn't here, they had a small room of their own.'

'Exactly.' Olena gestured expansively to the ballroom-sized hall filled with beds. 'These are the ones no one visits. They had enough money to secure a more comfortable place, but do not need to be kept in comfortable appearance. The ones that won't be missed.'

'So, you want to kidnap one of them?' Marisha looked at the rows and rows of sleeping bodies. Her skin crawled with disgust. 'Can't you pay a family for the privilege of examining their sleeping relative?'

'No, the Grand Prince made it illegal. Probably to discourage quack kolduni and philosophers from harmful experimentation.'

'But that's what you want to do.'

Olena grinned. 'Yes. But luckily for our victim, I know what I'm doing.'

'That's exactly what a quack would say.'

Olena's grin only grew wider. 'You said you would help me. Here's your chance. Pick one and be quick about it.'

'I can't do that!'

'Come on, we must hurry in case one of the night babushkas finds us.'

Marisha backed away and bumped against one of the beds, the one holding the man with the dark blond hair. A girl with long brown braids lay on the next bed over, and a man with the papery skin of a grandfather was in the next one. She could not pick someone to kidnap. These were *people*, this girl was someone's daughter, that one a father or brother. Marisha's chest contracted. She leaned on the bed for support and her hand brushed unexpectedly warm skin. The man's twitching hand lying on the coverlet.

'This one,' The words slipped from her mouth.

'Very well.' Olena said and grabbed hold of one of the brass bedposts. She tugged on the bed and Marisha watched as it slid easily on wheels. 'Help me,' Olena hissed, and Marisha set herself to the task. She felt slow. Her body moved as though through water, pushing the bed of its own accord. Perhaps she had decided that since she had picked the victim, there was no turning back.

Marisha shifted other beds out of the way and the two drove the one holding the victim Marisha had picked towards the door. Olena pulled and Marisha pushed. The bed's wheels made clunking and squeaking noises. The noise would have been enough to wake a heavy sleeper, but no one stirred. The bed made a loud thunk as they pushed it through the door and into the hallway.

'We need to arrange the beds so no one notices,' Olena said, and they hurried to straighten them out. They were finishing when Marisha heard something other than the scraping of bed wheels.

'Quick,' she whispered. 'Someone's coming.'

Olena swore. They pulled and pushed the bed down the hallway. Olena ran ahead to swing the door open. Marisha pulled the bed to a halt before the threshold. She had a wild urge to let go of the bed and run to the room where her parents were asleep, but with that thought came revulsion at the prospect of the still air, the dried yellow roses at their bedside, the heavy brocade drapes forever drawn at their window. For a moment, she was glad they had been out of the way, asleep in their private room.

The bed rattled. Olena had already jumped to the other side

of the threshold. She returned with a length of rope slung over her shoulder, the end trailing back through the doorway to the chicken-legged house.

'Tie this around our guest's waist,' Olena said while bracing the sleeping man in a seated position. Marisha was not an expert in knot tying and she looped the rope several times around itself to make it more secure.

'No, no,' Olena said before Marisha finished. They switched places. Olena undid Marisha's work by anchoring the leading end with her stump and picking it open with her one hand. She made a different set of loops around the man's waist. 'What's the point of having two hands if you can't even tie a good knot.' Marisha's cheeks flushed.

'We may have to abandon the bed,' Olena said, 'But the less evidence we leave, the better. On the count of three, we'll jump the bed over.' The two stood at the threshold. It sliced open in front of them, about a foot wide. They each held on to a bedpost, the man's sleeping head between them. Olena's stump was braced against the door's hinges. 'One, two, three,' Olena said, and they jumped. The bed was heavy, but they made it. Now the bed straddled the threshold.

'Let's get him out, at least,' Marisha said, and the two tugged him out of the bed. He fell into a heap on the floor. Marisha winced, but at least he was safely through the threshold. They both looked back at the bed.

'I'll climb back and push it through,' Olena said. On the count of three she pushed and Marisha pulled. At first it seemed like it would work, but the bed began tipping on Olena's side. It seemed too long to fit into the threshold, but it tipped more and more, tugging on Marisha's grip. Olena cried out for Marisha to let go and the bed tumbled away. Marisha could feel it fall very fast, as though it wanted to reach the bottom. Olena jumped and landed beside her but leaned back, out of balance. Marisha grabbed her arm and pulled her forward a few steps away from the chasm.

'Thanks,' Olena said, and looked down into the threshold. 'It can't be helped. Hopefully the spirits won't mind.' Marisha imagined puzzled spirits inspecting the crashed sanitorium bed and looking up to the dark earth, wondering who had thrown it down and why. She grinned.

The two women caught their breath and looked at their prize. Marisha tried to arrange his limbs in a more comfortable position.

A few minutes later they struggled up the stairs. 'Couldn't you have picked a child?' Olena huffed, one of his legs draped over her arm and the other one balanced on her shoulder.

'Couldn't you have asked the Hands to carry him for us?' Marisha said from the other end, her arms hooked under his armpits. The man was behaving like a sack of buckwheat and Marisha silently wished she had indeed picked a child.

'No. Not when Baba Zima might be able to get them to confess.'

'If I had known you were so paranoid—'

'Shouldn't you have figured that out by now?'

The two bickered as they carried their sleeping victim up a few steps, rested, and started again. Luckily, they only needed to go up one flight. Olena let the man's legs go and opened the door to her work room. Marisha tugged the man in, no longer worrying so much about his comfort.

Olena opened a door in the back that Marisha thought was a closet but in fact led to another, smaller, room. It was cramped with linens piled to one side but besides the smell of lye and mildew, it seemed quite comfortable. Except for the lack of a window.

'You want to keep him here?' Marisha asked.

Olena shrugged. 'It's fine. It's not like he'll notice much. Let's arrange some of these blankets into a bed.'

'Shouldn't he at least have a mattress?'

'He's asleep, he can't notice anything.'

Marisha put her hands on her hips. 'He's asleep, not dead. Just because he's sick doesn't mean he can't feel anything.' Marisha thought his brow was more scrunched than in the sanitorium. At least his hand was still. 'He's dreaming,' Marisha said.

'Hmph. I'll tell the Hands to fetch a spare mattress.'

Olena left the room. Marisha slumped down next to the man, arms and back aching from heaving him up the stairs. She reached for the lantern and drew it closer. He looked younger than she had thought, maybe a few years past twenty. His dark blond hair fell far past his ears and eyebrows and Marisha wondered if anyone at the sanitorium bothered to cut it. There was something extremely intimate about watching him sleep. He did not breathe loudly, but she could see his chest rise and fall a little, and when she drew her ear close to his mouth, she could feel his breath. He had a thin scar on his chin shaped like a horseshoe. Marisha thought again about what Olena said about magical objects leaving a mark, but this looked like the result of a fall or a knife. She brushed the hair off his forehead. His skin felt cool to her now. She remembered how hot his hand had been before, in the sanitorium. She wondered if he could feel her touch in his sleep.

'My, you're quite taken. How sweet,' Olena said from the doorway.

'Not at all,' Marisha said, rising slowly as though she were not embarrassed. 'I was just looking for any identifying features.

Anything that could tell us who he is.'

'I don't think you'd find his name written on his face. No matter how hard you looked.'

Marisha tried to hide her blush by bowing her head back towards the young man. She noticed something around his wrist and pushed his sleeve up. She held the lantern closer to the black letters on the leather bracelet. 'Kiril Vladimirovitch Begundov,' she read out loud. 'His name. It's Kiril.'

'I guess that's better than "that body in my closet". We'll need a code though. Not Kiril.' Olena looked around the room. 'How about linen?'

'Linen?'

'Yes, soiled linen. Because he's our dirty little secret.'

'Olena, is that a joke?' Marisha said, surprised.

'Sure, it's a joke. I'm hilarious. But really, if I ask you to tend to the linen, you'll know what it means.'

'"Linen needs folding" means go to the secret back room where we're keeping our kidnappee.'

'Ha! Oh, I'm glad, this will help us immensely.'

'Olena, don't you feel bad that we've done something wrong?'

'Why should I? He wasn't doing anything over there, just taking up a bed in a sanitorium. Now he's being useful. And if–when–we're successful, he'll be the first plague victim to wake. Won't he be grateful?'

'I guess. But . . . I hope no one will come looking for him. They'd be so sad to find him gone.'

'Don't worry, he has no pining wife.'

'How do you know?'

Olena looked at her like she was an idiot. 'No ring.'

Marisha was an idiot. 'Of course.'

'My, you really are quite taken with him. Just don't do anything . . . untoward.'

'Olena! As if I would.'

Olena shrugged.

Marisha tried to explain. 'I just wouldn't want anyone to think he disappeared. That he was lost.'

'Don't worry. No one will miss him. If he had a lover, she'd be long gone. No one wants to remember the deep sleepers.'

Marisha felt a prickle of guilt. She really ought to go visit her parents. A bubble of laughter escaped her lips at the thought that she had actually just been there.

'I think we had best go to sleep,' Olena said. 'We must be up bright and early tomorrow to get to work.'

Marisha groaned. 'Bright and early?'

'Absolutely. We have a lot to do, all the tinctures to test! I am so excited I might barely sleep.'

Marisha felt the exact opposite way. It was only when she drifted off that she realised Olena had talked about 'their' tasks tomorrow instead of 'her' tasks. Marisha smiled into her pillow. As bone tired as she was, it had been worth it. She had passed Olena's test. And all it had taken was a little blood and a big choice.

Marisha pushed away the guilty thoughts of standing over Kiril and saying, 'This one.' Instead, she relived the moment before entering the sanitorium, when the door handle absorbed Golgolin's feather dipped in her blood. Olena tugged the door open and somehow, the gaping darkness of the threshold had felt more real to Marisha than so many other impossibilities that she had lived through these past weeks. And when she had jumped over the narrow chasm, she had felt a force emanate from it, like a gaze that was impossible to ignore. It was almost as though part of her brain had finally processed that she was living in a house that was more or less, well, *alive*, while the other half of her brain was able to look elsewhere. But faced with the threshold, she was unable to look anywhere else. Marisha had an uncanny feeling that by crossing the threshold to the sanitorium, she had made herself known to it, and once known, she could not be forgotten. But she felt strangely unafraid of it. Afterall, she hadn't fallen through the threshold.

Marisha was more surprised by her euphoric sense of triumph than her lack of fear. Willing or not, Marisha had participated in opening the door to the sanitorium with her blood. She had helped Olena with koldunry. And she realised that for all the horror that they had kidnapped a person, she was excited about helping Olena tomorrow. Koldunry was a tool, it could do things for her, like open a door onto a building a month's journey away. Now that she had felt the chill of the chasm, the thrill of jumping over the threshold, she wanted more. She wanted to learn about koldunry so that she could use it herself.

And yet, the nagging sense of disquiet remained. Who was Kiril? And how could she have acted the accomplice to such an awful transgression? She tried to internalise Olena's rationalisation for their kidnapping but her thoughts drifted to the sanitorium bed crashing into the spirit world. She pictured spirits looking up at the dark earth, angry at the disturbance. Their eyes burned when they found her, an accusatory finger raised. She burrowed deeper into her blankets. The house protected her. The threshold was closed. She had nothing to worry about.

But even the philosophers who discounted fate believed in the forces of cause and consequence. Her hand twitched at the memory of the warmth from Kiril's skin when she had picked him.

TWELVE

arisha's clothes felt heavier than usual. She wore a dress of woven cloth in a deep wine red. The material was heavier than linen, lighter and softer than wool and covered in beautiful embroidery. Looking at the cuff of her sleeve made her eyes swim: the patterns of fawn grey and indigo swirled and crossed each other. But the dominant embroidered colour was that hateful shade of sickbed yellow, thin and runny like an old bruise or a forgotten rose that wilted in a vase for days. The sickly yellow swirled against the beautiful red in swathes of tiny perfect stitches, rising from the bottom of her skirt in splotches that could have been leaves or waves. She picked at it, but the strong thread did not break.

Black belts of knotted and braided leather gathered the dress at her waist and wrists. The dress reminded her of the ones the village girls wore for the summer solstice festival, but with finer embroidery and wilder colours. Too wild for her, she would draw eyes. But she loved the deep burgundy underneath the yellow. The richness of the colour made her feel the way she did when she tried on her mother's opals as a little girl.

She swung her head. Heavy. Her hair was much longer now and parted in six braids that reached her waist, each twined through with ribbons of burgundy and sickbed yellow. She touched her forehead. She wore something cold and smooth, a metal circlet of some kind. She tried to take it off to examine it, but it was twined into her hair.

A balalaika's twang grated and distracted her from her appearance. She stood in a clearing, a field or a village square. No, not outside. She could see it now, a wide hall. The back of her neck prickled. Something was familiar about this place. And all around, people danced.

The dancers wore similarly outrageous clothes: wools and silks, all beautifully dyed and embroidered. The swirling figures made her head spin. They formed lines or danced in small circles, shifting and twisting their waists, feet following in tiny, quick steps.

Even more unsettling than the quick-stepping figures and tingling balalaika music were the dancers' covered faces: curved copper masks, gauzy veils, colourful woven ribbons, masks of feathers that extended from noses like cat whiskers. Though Marisha could not see their eyes, the way they turned their bodies towards her as though in a lingering glare at her naked face made her feel like she wore no clothes at all.

But now they pressed into her.

Marisha dodged a few of the dancers, but openings were few. She could barely move forward. Someone stepped on her skirt, nearly sending her falling to the floor. The dancers whirled right in front of her nose, cutting her off. The heat was terrible. Some of them turned their heads towards her, their masks exaggerated their brows and mouths into downturned stares and twisted cruel smiles. She revolved on the spot, searching for an opening, her breath and heartbeat roaring.

A man in a cobalt blue kaftan edged in yolk yellow held out a hand. He wore a mask of blue, yellow and white feathers that hid his eyes and forehead. Marisha had not seen the circle of dancers part for him. She took the hand without thinking.

They danced around a circle, increasing their speed with the balalaika's rhythm. Marisha had to pay attention to her feet, she was so out of practice, but at the same time her mind was occupied with the thought that she held the hand of a man. Of course she had only ever danced with girls, she was neither loose enough to dance with a man in public nor daring enough to do so in private. She tried not to think about how warm and firm his grip felt, but all the sensation in her body seemed drawn to that seam where their skin touched.

'Where are we?' she asked, 'Who are all these people?'

'The zal sumerek. You weren't dancing before, but you must,' he said. 'Otherwise, they notice you.'

'Why?'

The man shook his head. 'Your face. It's uncovered.' His mask's feathers fluttered.

'I shouldn't be here,' Marisha said. 'I don't know how I got here.'

'None of us should be here.'

'But what is this place?' Marisha noticed something, a dais at the far side. 'What is that?' she asked.

The man did not answer but skilfully directed them out of their circle and into another one closer to the dais so she could see it: several figures stood watching the dancers. If she had thought her outfit fine, it was nothing compared to these. Two thrones stood near the edge of the dais. A lady sat in the left one, while the right one was empty. She wore a midnight blue gown, so dark it was almost black, and picked over with silver threads. Everything about her shimmered, her diamond headdress, her embroidered sleeves, the feather swinging from her high-waisted black pendant belt. A dark veil hung from her headdress, obscuring her eyes and nose.

Marisha could not look away from her. Other figures crowded around the woman in the midnight blue, vying for her attention. One lady in an ombre dress that smoothly changed from blush pink at her neck to deep violet at her ankles curtsied and gestured expansively at the hall. At the seated woman's shoulder, a man wearing a black-and-orange striped kaftan with a matching spiky collar bent down to whisper in her ear. One of the orange spikes grazed the woman's shoulder as he leaned forward. His face was surprisingly uncovered, but perhaps the woman liked his fashion-defying boldness. The woman on the throne swept the dancers with her unseen gaze. Marisha's skin crawled. She told herself she only imagined the woman's gaze riveting on her. The woman's lips curved into a smile.

Her head tilted slightly to the right, to the empty throne. An unknown fear coursed through Marisha's body, greater than the one roused by the woman's gaze. Even her dance partner's skill was not enough to keep her moving.

A small child tugged at her dress. Others pressed in.

'You will come back?' he asked.

'I don't know. I don't even know where this is.'

'Don't you recognise it?'

Marisha realised with sickening certainty that the dimensions of the hall were the same as the dimensions of the bedroom in the sanitorium.

'No.' She shook her head to clear dizzying nausea. 'No. This can't be.'

Someone wrenched at her arm again. Two of them this time. Others clamped on her partner's shoulder. She tried to hold on to him as the balalaika music soared and hands plucked at her sleeve, her hem, pulled her hair.

'I'm sorry,' he said before he was tugged backwards, her fingers slipping out of his grip.

Someone wrenched at Marisha's braids and she shook off the attack, but when she looked back, she screamed. Her partner had disappeared and, in his place, stood a man dressed entirely in black with a mask covering his entire face. Her gaze immediately drew to the beak he had instead of a mouth. It was slightly hooked and longer than her forearm. Light glinted off its wicked sharp tip. The rest of the mask covering his face looked scaly, like a snake's skin, with small scraggly feathers growing in. He took a step forward and raised his arms from his sides. He had talons where hands should have been.

The beaked man grabbed her throat with a talon, pinning her in place. His eyes were deep, colourless pools. Marisha couldn't breathe. She beat her fists uselessly against the arm that pinned her. He bent his neck impossibly far so the beak pointed straight up into the air.

And in a moment, he would bring it crashing down through her chest.

MARISHA AWOKE AND PRESSED A fist on her breastbone and drew in deep, ragged breaths. She was in the attic of Baba Zima's chicken-legged house. The air was delightfully cool and nothing more than air and blankets touched her limbs. Her heart raced as she brushed her hands over her body, smoothing away the terrible feeling of the crowd pressing her everywhere. She breathed deeply a few times with more calm, savouring the feeling of her lungs inflating, willing her heart to slow down. Everything was fine. But she trembled so badly she could not sleep for a while.

And though the next morning she forgot the dream's details, the feeling of terror remained.

THIRTEEN

id the plates have an unlucky accident as well?' Dunya remarked at breakfast.

Even through Marisha's fog of sleeplessness she agreed it was strange to eat on wooden plates. The crockery had slowly disappeared since Valdim's arrival. It had been several weeks and teacups were the only remaining porcelain. Even the spoon Marisha used to stir in the sour cherry jam was wooden.

Valdim said, 'Sorry, Dunya. I couldn't take the sound anymore. I hope you don't mind too much.'

Though she raised her eyebrows, Dunya did not comment. She asked instead if he had heard from Severny whether Princess Olga's marriage prospects had improved and Marisha let her mind wander as Valdim talked. Her tongue felt thick as she forced herself to swallow the gluey kasha. She had been having nightmares almost every night for the past week, and the sleeplessness was taking its toll on Marisha's body.

Baba Zima spoke now. 'Last week, a man came to me and said a leshi had been stealing all the mushrooms in his regular hunting spots. Now, say someone came to you with that story, what would you do?' Baba Zima's head swivelled and she selected her victim. 'Marisha.'

Panic and surprise cut through Marisha's fog. She had just put a spoonful of kasha and sugared lingonberries in her mouth.

'Umm,' Marisha chewed her kasha as a bid for time. 'I would start maybe with that incantation you had given to that woman, the one who said that she had wandered in the forest for two days, though she was only gone for an hour. Ask for protection from the woods and over the mountain and—'

'Quit your babbling, you sound like Dunya.'

Dunya lowered her head and looked at her bread, the smile gone from her face. It made Marisha angry. Anka-ny squeezed Dunya's hand under the table. Marisha said, as slowly as possible. 'Excuse my unseemly babbling. I do not know what you wish for me to divine from that story.'

'That is because you do not *think*, and before you think, you need to *listen*. But how can we get anything through that thick, stone skull of yours? Let's try again. A man comes to you and tells you that a leshi has been going to all his mushroom spots and stealing them. What do you say to that?'

Marisha looked out into the distance. A leshi, stealing mushrooms? A few weeks ago, she would have never considered it, but now . . . she imagined a small man with flinty eyes and mossy beard, tramping through the forest, mushrooms sprouting in his footsteps. If she thought about it logically–and part of her mind couldn't believe that she thinking about this problem from the starting point that leshi were real–why would a leshi steal mushrooms? According to the superstitious stories of her aunt, leshi were protectors of the forest. They led people astray, but would they wipe out a mushroom patch? Unlikely. People on the other hand . . . She thought for a moment of following Dima through the brown tree trunks to a new patch of mushrooms where a profusion of yellowish stalks sprouted through the layer of brown pine needles, his step quick and his expression impish with delight. He'd grab her hand before letting her run over to inspect the patch, first making her promise not to tell. She shoved the thought of her brother away with a guilty twang. Marisha said under her breath, 'I'd think he was kidding himself.'

The dull clunking of wooden spoons against wooden plates stopped. Baba Zima said, 'Elaborate.'

Marisha said, 'Um. It's just . . . a *leshi*? Isn't it more likely that one of his neighbours found his mushroom spots?'

Baba Zima chuckled to herself. 'Marisha the sceptic. Sometimes your thick, stone skull comes in handy.' Marisha was annoyed. Baba Zima had misinterpreted her answer: it wasn't that she was sceptical of the leshi's existence, it was more that she was sceptical of its behaviour. Baba Zima's beady gaze swung from Marisha to Olena. A malicious smile caught the corner of the koldunya's lips and she said, 'Heh, Olena, your assistant has some use after all! She knows how to question stories. But–you may not want her to question you too hard, do you Olena? Wouldn't want her to question whether your cure will bear fruits.'

Baba Zima laughed to herself, and she did not seem to mind that no one else did. Then she fixed her gaze back on Olena. 'Of course, *I* fully believe in you.' She smiled, and that icy smile made her warm words feel like the exact opposite of encouragement.

'Thank you, Matrionka,' Olena said stiffly.

'Anything for you, my buttered blin.'

Then Olena looked down at her plate in silence. Valdim left the table, a disgusted look on his face. Marisha also excused herself as quickly as possible and escaped to Olena's workroom and Kiril's hideaway.

The morning after they had kidnapped Kiril, Olena had handed her a key to her workroom and the linen closet. She had also taught her the words to lift the wards so she could enter the rooms safely by herself. Marisha was grateful to receive the token of trust, though she noticed several shelves barer than they previously had been.

When Marisha entered the backroom and closed the door. Kiril was laid out on a thin mattress on top of a table. She placed his arm on top of the coverlet to check his pulse. It was faint and slow, but it was there. Her hand was too small to close around his wrist. She slid her thumb up and pressed the centre of his palm and the fleshy muscle at the base of his thumb. His fingers curled in a little. She smoothed them out and let them curl back in over her hand. Almost like he held it.

She sat down on the shelves next to the bed. A feeling of peace overcame her, making her realise how anxious she had felt throughout breakfast. Marisha thought of Baba Zima's little smile when she voiced doubts about Olena's abilities in Marisha's name. She felt a wave of anger against the koldunya. Why did Baba Zima nettle Olena so? Olena was frustrated enough that her first attempts at a tincture had not immediately woken Kiril up. And now, because of Baba Zima, Olena would take her frustration out on Marisha. She shook her head. Really, it was absurd how easily Olena allowed herself to be baited by Baba Zima. She sighed deeply and braced herself for the upcoming onslaught.

She just wished she did not feel so tired. She looked down at Kiril. He had been asleep for nine years. She shivered at the thought. Had he been afraid while waiting for the plague year to pass him by? It all felt so hopeless, so futile–being anxious about the plague, worrying about something that could not be changed. Kiril could have lay awake at night from fear, he could have run, he could have got on with his life, but nothing would have changed. He would not have escaped the plague. Hopefully his dreams were more pleasant than her nightmares.

Marisha stood up to dispel the feeling that something was closing in on her, like the rusty jaws of a bear trap. She was awake. She could escape her dreams. Unlike Kiril.

An hour later, Marisha helped Olena apply a fresh tincture of roses, lavender, and marjoram to Kiril's eyelids, wrists, and ankles. Marisha was silent while Olena recited an incantation. Nothing happened. Olena poked his foot with the sharp corner of her notebook but garnered no reaction. She poked it again, harder.

'Don't do that,' Marisha said.

'Do what?'

'Prod him like that. He's a person, not a slab of meat.'

Olena did not even bother to look at her. 'I'll be sure to keep that in mind.' She scribbled in her book. Then she pushed up Kiril's sleeve up over his elbow. 'Pass me the flask. That one, with the wide neck, and the knife.'

Marisha's hands stilled. 'What? Why?'

Olena sighed in frustration and got up. She grabbed the flask from Marisha's limp hand, set it down on the table next to Kiril, and picked the knife up off the table and turned to the hearth. She ran the blade through the flames and muttered an incantation. Marisha watched dumbly as Olena at back down next to Kiril, knife in hand and leaned over his arm.

'Olena, stop!' Marisha rushed over to Olena's side, and reached for the knife, but Olena turned and jerked her arm away before Marisha could grab it.

Olena looked at her, eyes glittering, 'You really should not yell at me when I am holding a knife. I only need a little venous blood. I'll just nick the skin. Now hold the flask.'

'No.'

'No? Fine.' And before Marisha could react, Olena leaned over Kiril and pressed her knife to his elbow. Red welled up. Kiril's face, which had been serene and blank before, twisted into a frown.

'He felt that,' Marisha said, balling her hand into fists to keep them from lunging at Olena. 'You hurt him.'

Olena had set the knife down and now held the flask to the cut. Blood dribbled inside. 'He's dreaming. He's been reacting to the dreams more since we started. It's progress.'

Olena walked to her work bench, carrying the flask of blood and turned her back to Marisha. Marisha rushed to Kiril and pressed a wad of cotton to his elbow. The cut that Olena made was larger than Marisha had expected. The blood had dripped down his arm in warm rivulets. Marisha's fingers trembled. '*Never* do that again.'

'I won't need to,' Olena said from somewhere behind her. 'This is more than enough for as many exploratory analyses as I'd like. Though if I needed fresh blood—'

'No! It's not right!'

There was a pause and then Olena said. 'What isn't right is that you're supposed to be my assistant and you're obstructing my progress. I needed some blood to try and detect any lingering components of the plague, and also to strengthen the marjoram tincture. If it works, Kiril will wake up.'

'And he'll awaken to find that he's been poked, prodded, and bled dry. That's not a way to treat someone.'

'You're thinking too small. I'm trying to find a cure that will help alleviate the misery of thousands and thousands of people. Isn't that worth a miniscule cut and some donated fluids?

'You're downplaying what you're doing, Olena. Helping people does not cancel out hurting others. We don't know what Kiril might be thinking or feeling, we don't know if he would have agreed to be your test subject. I certainly wouldn't have.'

'Well then, we should be glad that Kiril's the one we're working with. Not you.'

'But it could have been me! I could have been the one asleep on that table.' Marisha's fist went to her sternum and pressed down to dispel that awful feeling of compression. It could have been her. She would have been the one asleep and nothing more than a test subject to Olena.

Olena tipped her head back and gave a slow nod. 'Ah, now it makes sense. Yes, it could have been you.' Olena sniffed, 'Though at this point one of your parents would have been more likely.'

'Stay away from my parents!'

'Oh, I have no desire to go anywhere near your parents. Though, aren't you happy that you came with me to pick Kiril so that you could spare your mother or father the torture of being my victim? Oh, the horror of being stuck with a pin by the terrible Olena, how could the terrors of unending nightmares ever compare?'

'Shut up!'

'No, you shut up. Baba Zima called you a great questioner at breakfast, but you're nothing of the sort. You're just a selfish brat who can't see the good that we could be doing for so many people, including your parents!' There was a crack and Olena set the flask of blood down with a cry. Miraculously, the blood had not spilled, but the neck of the flask had broken off into jagged spikes and cracks propagated through the body of the glass. 'Now look what you made me do!' Olena immediately grabbed a new flask from the shelf and set it down. She steadied the empty flask with her stump and poured the blood in. The red liquid smeared across the sides and into the cracks. Olena set the cracked flask down and took a deep breath. 'You of all people should want to work as hard as possible and do whatever's necessary to find the cure. If you don't care enough to make sacrifices for it, then what are you here for? Just leave.'

Marisha shook her head. 'I'm not going anywhere. Who knows what you'd do to Kiril if you were alone. You keep saying that the cure will help thousands of people, but you don't care about them. You don't care about Kiril's wellbeing. You just want to find the cure to *finally* earn Baba Zima's respect. And you keep on talking about the cure like it's a given, but Kiril is still asleep and it doesn't look like that's changing any time soon.' Marisha glanced over at Kiril. His brow was still furrowed slightly. 'At the end of the day, he's just a poor soul at your insufficient mercy.'

'Just like you would have been,' Olena said softly. 'And that's the only reason why you're making a fuss.'

'That's not true,' Marisha shook her head.

'Ha! Lie to yourself all you want, doesn't matter to me. If Baba Zima wishes to test me with the most idiotic assistant who walked these halls, fine. Stay. But stay out of my way.' Olena turned away from Marisha and pretended to focus on her flask of blood.

Marisha breathed heavily as though she had just sprinted. What had happened? Had she overreacted? She looked back down at Kiril, and her anger returned at the sight of the dark patch of blood on the surface of Kiril's bandage. No, it was not right, Olena should not have hurt Kiril. Kiril was defenceless, prone on the table, no movement except for some occasional twitches and moans. He had been asleep since the last plague, at least nine years. And he would sleep for the rest of his life.

It could have been her. And if Olena did not find a cure to the plague, it would be her. Going to the sanitorium, kidnapping

Kiril, being surrounded by so many plague victims–somehow it had triggered her nightmares. Marisha remembered the feeling of a dark chill emanating from the threshold when jumping to and from the sanitorium, like some force had seen her. Marisha was safe, as long as she was in the house. But how long would that be if Olena barely tolerated her? And if she had drawn the plague's attention, if her nightmares were truly terrible portents, then how long until she was claimed by her fate and was nothing more but a sleeping body on a table somewhere? For the rest of her life?

Marisha silently drew a cup from the bucket of clean snow melt in the corner and returned to Kiril's side to wash the dried blood on his forearm. Marisha was safe, as long as she was in the house. But would that be enough to dodge her fate? Some of her old anger struggled and flared in her chest. Koldunry had brought her into this mess? Fine, it could also take her out of it. She would figure out how to banish her nightmares and avoid the plague, and she would figure it out on her own.

FOURTEEN

lena could not leave her workroom fast enough. Who was Marisha to tell her how to run her experiments? The girl had no feeling for koldunry, and worse, even though she had arguably bigger stakes in the plague cure than Olena did, she took no initiative in the research. If someone that Olena loved, if Fedya–she closed her eyes–if Fedya were asleep from the plague, and she had had the good fortune to be brought into Baba Zima's household to work on this project, Olena would have spent day and night pursuing any idea to fix him. *But you can't fix him, can you? That's the point.*

Olena pushed the thought of her brother away with twelve years of practice and focused instead on boiling her anger at Marisha's accusation that she did not respect Kiril. And after staring at him indecently, no less! How dare she, when she did not even know real disrespect. Olena clutched her little arm at the stump, feeling the echo of a stone's sharp impact to her shoulder, and remembered looking up from her mushroom basket to the cruel laughing faces of gangly teenagers. They shouted ugly things about what her mother must have done to conceive her, about what other deformities she might have hidden under her skirts. She hated them, and hated the fear that burned through her as she ran, slipping on the still, frozen earth.

She shook her head as if it would shake out the memory. Olena willed herself to breathe and focused on feeling the wall's plaster beneath her hand. Cool and bumpy. The air rushing through her nose had a stale aroma of baking bread and dried laurel. She thought she could hear a murmur. A shrill laugh. Definitely Dunya.

Golgolin flapped near her shoulder, startling her. She had not heard him at all, but perhaps he had come from somewhere much further away than the corridor behind her. His clumsy grace as he settled on her shoulder made Olena chuckle. She reached over with her little arm and hugged the creature, pressing his furry body close to her collarbone. His little claws gripped her skin through her shirt, and he snuffled her neck. The tightness in her chest loosened. Olena stood there for a long moment, stroking Golgolin's feathers and fur, and thinking what to do next.

Olena had dismissed Kiril's grimace as dream-induced, but what if had actually felt her knife nick his skin? Maybe her tincture had more of an effect than she thought. Maybe she should consult Pan Boris's journal again about rituals and incantations to complement tinctures for drawing the soul back in the body. Golgolin began to fidget and Olena loosened her grip. He flapped away from her and to the door that led back to a storage room. It opened a crack and Golgolin disappeared through it. Tempting as it was to open the door to see if Golgolin had actually gone to the storage room or somewhere else altogether, Olena turned around and headed down to the library.

The next day, Olena sat at her desk and tried paging through her notes, but she kept looking at the closet with the cracked door. She imagined she could see Kiril on his mattress, his chest rising and falling slowly. She tapped her pencil against the pages. She didn't need to look down at them to see that her list of untried remedies was extremely short. In fact, once she crossed off her last failure, there was only one item on the list left. Tincture of paporotnika; a plant with limited applications, and she had already set it soaking into alcohol. She set the pencil onto the page. Nothing. When she removed her hand, she realised that she had pressed her pencil so hard into the page that she had torn a hole through the paper.

She shoved herself away from the table. Panic pressed in at the edges of her throat. It was her own fault for being so arrogant to think she could tackle this challenge. There was a reason the cure to the plague remained undiscovered! But she was apprentice to Baba Zima, the greatest koldunya in all of Chernozemlya; that ought to mean something. Except that power and success was not a transitive property. And in that moment, Olena thought something irrational that she had not thought in years: Baba Zima would wake up one day and realise she had made a terrible mistake in choosing Olena as the next holder of the house's bolshina.

Enough! Olena walked to the cabinet against the back wall of the room and pulled the doors open. The shelves were crammed with various glass bottles all neatly labelled and filled with liquid and various plant matter. She pushed through her most used tinctures with her little arm and scooped forward the fuller and dustier ones, looking for some additions to increase the potency of her mixture. The act of lining up the bottles on the table brought a measure of calm and order to her mind. She did not have nothing. She had tested her cures, and they were not without effect. Why, it was only a few days ago that Kiril's hand had moved! Not only that, but since she had tried a mixture inspired by Pan Boris Helgavitch's work, Kiril's fingernails had grown so noticeably that Marisha had trimmed them. That was not nothing. But it felt like whatever Olena tried to do to tug wakefulness back into Kiril's body, he resisted.

Olena took out her list of stories around the plague, gleaned from both Marisha's reading of the Old Slavonic books and Olena's own research. When Olena had first started her research, her plan was to find the spiritual nature of the plague's source and use it to strengthen her tinctures with an incantation. But the plague's origins were murkier than she had imagined.

Her gaze paused on an item penned near the bottom of her list. The waters of life and death, which were said to heal any ill. Ha! That was the mythical substance for which fanatics of the Morskoi Prince cult gave up their worldly possessions to wander the forest, searching the pools of water that gathered between the tree roots for any hint of magical properties. Still . . . The waters of life and death would probably be powerful enough to cure the plague on their own without any additional tinctures or incantation. The only trouble was finding them. But it was best to not think too hard about it–these were the substance of myths and she needed an earthly solution.

She tapped her pencil to the page and found that she was tapping the spot next to one of Marisha's notes about Grisha, the slayer of Nightingale the Robber: 'It is said that Grisha visited the grandfather of the forest and received a sigil on his right arm to shield him from the monster's cry.'

Olena frowned. It was difficult to explain why she was so drawn to this story, except that she felt it had something to do with the sleeping plague, even though, as Marisha had so bluntly pointed out, the story and the sickness seemingly had nothing to do with each other. But Baba Zima had taught Olena to trust her intuition: her intuition fed her koldunic ability to *know*. She meditated on the problem while working on the tincture, sinking into that narrowing of focus where she did her best work. She pictured the bogotir Grisha running to confront the monster. People fell senseless around him from the monster's cry, but not him, no, because he was shielded. Olena's hand stilled. The shield spell. The shield spell protected one from the plague by deflecting it onto another person–but could it also be the key to separate the plague from the body?

Olena sat completely still, suspended in the clarity of the beautiful thought. The door burst open and one of Baba Zima's Hands came through, shattering the moment. The Hand was not carrying Olena's usual bread, butter and honey, which meant that Baba Zima had wanted her hungry enough to come to lunch. And indeed, the Hand crooked its finger, beckoning. Olena huffed and paused long enough to write 'shield spell' in large block letters on her list of possibilities and followed the Hand downstairs.

Valdim flicked his gaze at her when she arrived. He raised his eyebrows and returned his gaze to his plate, or Dunya or wherever he had been looking before.

'What?' Olena snapped.

'You're in an even lovelier mood than usual,' he said, looking back at her with a hint of a grin.

There was nothing she could say to that at the table, so she simply scraped the legs of her chair against the floor as she pulled it out and enjoyed seeing him wince.

Baba Zima blew the air out of her cheeks. 'Now is this really necessary?'

Neither of them answered.

All six of them were seated at the table, which had become a rare occurrence. Baba Zima at the head of the table, Olena at the foot, Dunya and Anka-ny on the left side and Marisha and Valdim on the right. Baba Zima insisted on everyone's presence for dinner, but lunch was a more casual affair and Olena preferred to skip it and continue working, despite Marisha's protests. Today, when the Hands flew to the table carrying a plate piled high with pies the size of her palm, steam escaping the crust in a delicious buttery scent, Olena felt mollified at being corralled to the lunch table. Having epiphanies was hunger-inducing. Olena smiled and stabbed the mushroom and tarragon pie with a fork.

'I have received letters from supplicants in Vorevka, our last stop before the krug. We will need to prepare before we arrive in two days.' Baba Zima said.

'What do they need?' Dunya asked. Whenever supplicants wrote letters in anticipation of Baba Zima's visit, it was usually for incantations that required extra payment, extra care and extra thought.

Baba Zima said, 'Three curses, all against former lovers, two shield spells and–ha! One woman wrote saying that no one in the village will sell her fish anymore, because they say that when they do, their nets stay empty. Anka-ny, what would you recommend?' Olena blocked out Baba Zima's quizzing of the assistants, though she was irritated that Marisha stumbled over her explanation of why the supplicants who requested curses needed to stick pins into the dove hearts themselves. She ought to be studying harder.

Olena's ears perked when Baba Zima turned to the plague shield spell. Baba Zima said it was simpler in execution than the curses, at least for the supplicant. The preparation, however, was difficult, as it required a long incantation invoking the spirits that was whispered into the water, and the water itself had to be buried in the ground over winter.

Olena felt as though she was vibrating with secret energy. Could Baba Zima sense her discovery? She felt a warm connection to her mistress. Perhaps Baba Zima had an inkling that the shield spell might be useful and had been trying to guide her towards the possibility.

'You don't always see that,' Baba Zima said in response to Anka-ny's question of why the water had to be buried. 'But closer to the spirit world, the water can absorb the protective properties of the earth. It was actually one of my Matrionka's innovations.' Baba Zima's countenance took on the misty look she always did when she spoke of her former mistress.

Olena had let Baba Zima's words flow past her, but then her mind snapped onto their meaning and she reeled them back. 'Baba Serafima improved the shield spell?' Olena's feeling of warmth brimming over a cup shattered. If Olena had known that Baba Serafima had worked on the shield spell, would it have taken her so long to think it could be important for the cure?

'Yes,' Baba Zima replied. 'She perfected it.'

'Why didn't you tell me this before?'

Baba Zima looked nonplussed. 'My dear Matrionka did so many things, I couldn't possibly relay them all.'

But the fact that Baba Serafima had worked on the shield spell was relevant to Olena's work. How could Baba Zima not tell her? Olena looked at Baba Zima for a moment, looked at the politely puzzled expression on her mistress's face. Olena excused herself and headed to the library.

Seven shelves spanned the length of the library wall which held the curated notes of past kolduni who were mistresses and masters of the house. As she did whenever she consulted the library, Olena first dusted the shelves and spines before lifting the books of interest from the shelf. Baba Serafima's section had been relatively thin, but that could be explained by her predilection for writing in clear terse sentences compared to the flowery language of Baba Ekaterina, whose entries comprised almost a quarter of one shelf. Olena sifted through the pages of Baba Serafima's notes and skimmed them quickly. Not one mention of the shield spell. In fact, it seemed to Olena that Baba Serafima's incantation book was missing. 'You're not hiding anything, are you?' Olena asked. The shelves did not even quiver in response.

When Olena had first arrived in the house many years ago, she had been a painfully slow reader. Baba Zima told her that she would do well to tend to the library: dust the floor-to-ceiling shelves and the edges of the books' pages. Olena assumed it was so she would become more comfortable with books after the scarcity of reading material in her youth. Soon, she was spending many evenings in the library, hungrily reading accounts of the otherworldly spirit forces. She began finding books left out for her on the table which naturally followed the last in her course of study. Some of them she was sure were left by Baba Zima, but others contained answers to questions she did not realise she had until she opened the covers. She continued to pay attention to the library's upkeep, and she continued to be rewarded for her attentions. But it seemed that her current problem was not one that the library could help her with. She frowned and returned the short stack of slim volumes to the shelf.

Olena walked downstairs to the receiving room where, as she expected, Baba Zima was drinking tea and reading letters. One of the red Hands held a page up to her eyes, while the other stacked the papers neatly. Marisha stood before the koldunya, listening to the list of items Baba Zima wanted her to check in the inventory. So, Baba Zima had asked for Marisha to assist her, yet again. As long as Marisha tended to Kiril, which she did most assiduously and with disgusting levels of solicitude, Baba Zima could monopolise Marisha's time as much as she wanted. But was using Olena's assistant a way to make a point? Did Baba Zima surmise that besides reading the Old Slavonic books (and secretly tending to Kiril), Olena had little use for Marisha at the moment? Olena frowned at Marisha as she left. Really, her assistant looked like an awful slob. Her brown hair was lacklustre with pieces of it escaping her bun, she was as pale as winter milk, and she slouched most horribly when she walked.

'It seems to me like you might be overworking your assistant,' Baba Zima said.

Olena stepped in closer. 'Me, overworking someone?'

'It's the only excuse for her slovenly appearance.'

'On that we agree.' Olena sat down in the chair facing her mistress. Olena forestalled the inevitable tirade on the importance of appearances in making a good first impression by saying, 'Matrionka, I noticed something odd today.'

'Oh?' Baba Zima signalled to the Hands with an almost imperceptible movement of her pinky to lift the cup of tea to her lips.

'I was looking in the library for something that Baba Serafima had written on her idea for the shield spell, but I couldn't find anything.'

Baba Zima waved a hand into the air. 'Not surprising. Baba Serafima's mind was such that she rarely needed to take notes. A boon for her, but a terrible loss for those that she left.'

Olena hesitated. She worried her mistress might take her next question the wrong way.

Baba Zima chuckled and said, 'You look like you've got a mouth full of fishbones. I know what you wish to ask. No, I have no way of contacting my former mistress.'

'But surely you must know something. She truly left you no way of contacting her, even in emergencies?'

'Baba Serafima was in quite a hurry when she left.' Baba Zima's expression was all careful nonchalance and she signalled the Hands for another sip of tea. 'Of course, I understand that she had something she needed to do, something important.'

Olena understood that Baba Zima had still not quite forgiven her mistress for leaving so suddenly, with no warning. 'And, you're sure she's not dead?'

'One cannot be sure of anything. But I believe she's alive.' And she said quietly, almost to herself, 'She would not leave without saying goodbye.'

They sat in silence for a moment. Olena's throat constricted at the thought that Baba Zima might follow in her mistress's steps and leave without a warning, but she hoped that she had the felt the pain of it enough that she would not inflict such a thing upon her own apprentice.

Olena slumped even further into her chair. 'So, there's nothing,' she said. She could hear her own voice turn tinny.

'No,' Baba Zima said. 'Nothing.'

Olena sat silent for a moment, lost in thought. 'Nothing? Really, no other writings? In this whole house?'

Baba Zima shrugged, 'You can look around if you like. But I can assure you the search would be fruitless. There's nothing in this house that does not come to my attention.'

'But perhaps your attention is not always well-placed.' Olena had said it more to herself before she realised that her words could be taken as a criticism. Luckily Baba Zima let out a booming laugh in response.

'There is little I don't notice. However, I do not choose to pay too much attention to everything.' Baba Zima's gaze became a bit too knowing and Olena decided not to engage with it.

'I might still look,' Olena said.

'Be my guest,' Baba Zima said with an expansive gesture that the Hand at her shoulder mimicked. 'Even though it seems like a wild waste of time to me. Tell me, how are your preparations for the demonstration going?

'Huh?' Olena was still thinking about Baba Serafima.

'The demonstration,' Baba Zima repeated, somewhat impatiently, 'At the krug. It's in only a week.'

'I—' a different kind of panic began pooling into her throat '—I thought that you would be representing our household.'

'Yes, I'm certainly preparing something, but that does not mean you're out of the frying pan, my buttered blin.'

'But–I thought I should focus on the plague cure.'

Baba Zima tsked. 'You have focused on the plague cure enough, you ought to give thought to focusing on our house's reputation. It will one day be your reputation. It is up to you to uphold it.'

'Yes, mistress.' Olena tried her best to stop the edge of anger from creeping into her voice, but she failed. She was sure that Baba Zima had told her that she did not need to give a demonstration at the krug. At the time she had been grateful that Baba Zima valued the importance of her work on the plague cure.

Olena did not know why she was caught off-guard by Baba Zima's changing tune and misleadings, she did it often enough. Olena remembered the familiar dread, the cold slip of wondering whether she had heard correctly, followed by the inner roar of her thoughts as they scrambled to find a solution. Just as she had a few weeks ago when Baba Zima had sent her to that house to administer to sick cows, when the supplicant's plea was actually to dispel his dead wife's shade. Olena had to acknowledge that the many instances of Baba Zima's forgetfulness, whether feigned or real, had made Olena more resilient, but she hated feeling that Baba Zima laid out these broken stairs for her.

And to forestall Baba Zima from scolding her again, Olena asked, 'What are you preparing, Matrionka?'

'I was thinking of walking through fire. Now don't you roll your eyes at me, that would be quite the feat, don't you think?'

Olena raised an eyebrow. She said begrudgingly, 'I suppose so.'

Baba Zima seemed almost more animated about the idea of giving an excellent demonstration at the krug than about finding the cure to the plague. Was her rivalry with Anatoli so much more important to her than helping others? No, Olena reminded herself, Baba Zima dedicated more than half of her time to seeing supplicants, which was much more than Olena could say about herself. Olena was grateful for this; she hated seeing supplicants herself because they always stared at her, their gazes darting from the floor to her and back. When she was the mistress of the house, she would delegate the supplicants to apprentices and assistants so that she could do the more interesting tasks.

'Just imagine!' The Hands grabbed Olena's shoulders in Baba Zima's excitement. 'To be able to rescue someone from a burning building and come out unscathed.' Olena felt ashamed of herself. Of course, her mistress was interested in more than just theatrics.

Olena said, 'But is it not simply a matter of coating your entire body with our poultice?'

'Think, girl! Then your body would not burn, yes, but what actually kills you in a fire?' Baba Zima waited while Olena thought about it. 'The smoke,' Olena said.

'Exactly,' Baba Zima replied. 'I must find a way to repel the smoke as well, at least from around the face.' Baba Zima cocked her head in thought. 'If coming up with your own idea for the demonstration is such an onerous task, you can always help me with mine.'

Did Olena have any ideas left? An image of a life-sized doll sitting in a pile with broken legs came into her mind. Blood dripped out of his ear. She imagined waving her hand over it and the legs straightening so that the boy could walk again. *Well, that's unlikely.*

'Yes,' Olena said, 'I can help you.'

As Olena brainstormed ideas with her mistress, she was easily caught up in the enthusiasm of the idea. Still, the demonstration for the krug, as interesting as it was, was nothing more than a distraction. The idea of the shield spell filled her with a wild hope. Olena needed a spiritual anchor for her tinctures and her strategy up until now was to find the spiritual nature of the plague's source to do so, but maybe the shield spell would be even better. It was something that she already knew worked against the plague in limited circumstances. And if Baba Serafima had perfected it, then that meant that she had understood it. And if she had left some explanation of it, then Olena would find it.

Baba Zima said, 'I think we have enough to start with here. My buttered blin, I am always amazed by your quickness of thought. With your help, the demonstration will be a resounding success.'

Baba Zima smiled at her and Olena smiled back, but her expression dropped as soon as Olena looked back to her notes. She tried to quell her rising resentment, after all, her mistress had said she could look around the house for something that Baba Serafima had left behind. But in the back of Olena's mind was the truth that Baba Zima had not told her that Baba Serafima had worked on the shield spell. She did not lie to Olena, but keeping information from her was just as bad. Why hadn't Baba Zima told her? Why did Baba Zima always seem to help her with one hand, but obstruct her with the other? There was something that Baba Zima was hiding about Baba Serafima, it was more than simply grief. More secrets. Olena was determined to find out what she could.

FIFTEEN

Marisha tried to wrap her tired brain around a plan, but any useful thoughts floated like feathers at the edges of her mind, blown out of reach.

It had been ten days since she had helped Olena kidnap Kiril, but her dreams had not disappeared. Though she could not remember their contents, she remembered the feeling of terror that they inspired; and it was that terror that caused her to lay awake at night, her body electric and tense. Sometimes she stole a few hours of restful sleep in the small morning hours, but more often than not, she woke in a knot of cold sweat, blankets and suffocating certainty that she would never have a good night's rest again. Marisha pushed that thought away during waking hours. She reasoned with herself that her terror was unfounded, that the dreams would go away on their own. Sometimes she almost believed it.

Could she ask Olena for help with banishing her nightmares? The idea of mashing linseed with her thumbs instead of a pestle was more appealing. While relations between her and Olena had returned to stiff cordiality since their fight two days ago, Marisha no longer felt the camaraderie she had when Olena had first asked her to read the old Slavonic histories for her. Pride struggled with practicality. And pride won.

She just wished she didn't feel so dull and sick all the time. It was likely due to her chronic exhaustion that she was not particularly careful when asking Baba Zima about a sleeping spell.

'A sleeping spell?' Baba Zima said. 'Why would you ever want that?'

'I, um, have been waking up a lot at night. Dunya snores,' she added quickly, then silently cursed herself for the addition. Wouldn't Baba Zima know if Dunya snored?

'Well, you can't be tired enough if a bit of snoring keeps you falling asleep. Baba Serafima worked me so hard that a bear could have roared in my ears without my waking.'

'I'm a light sleeper.'

Baba Zima sniffed. 'I have neither the time nor inclination to make a spell for you. I can give you more chores to do. The basements can always use a scrubbing.'

'Um, Olena has my day pretty much full. Can't you simply teach me how to make it myself?'

'My dear. That is far beyond you. Don't you remember I have no obligation to teach you until you have completed your first year with me? And didn't you say when I hired you that you have no interest in learning the koldunic arts?'

'I never said that!'

'Are you saying my memory is faulty?'

'I just think you may have misunderstood me.'

'Ha! Misunderstanding. Misspeaking or not, a year has not passed. And unless you are taught, I expressly forbid you to try to perform spells. The results could be disastrous.'

Marisha gritted her teeth. Baba Zima continued to sip her tea, unconcerned.

Marisha turned away to leave, but just as she put her hand on the door handle, Baba Zima said, 'Of course, I might be convinced to overcome my . . . disinclination.'

'What?' Marisha turned around.

'Tell me something interesting about Olena's activities, something that I may not know. And I can help you overcome, ah, Dunya's unpleasant *snoring*.' Marisha's face grew warm.

'I can't imagine you don't know everything that goes on in this house,' she said.

'Ha! Well, as the holder of the house's bolshina, I do know most things. But there are ways to turn my eye, and Olena . . . well, I certainly would hope there was nothing she think needs to be kept hidden. But you're saying there's nothing she's done that you think I should know about?'

Marisha looked down. Could Baba Zima know about Kiril? Maybe she did already, but maybe she did not want to be caught spying on Olena, maybe she wanted Marisha to tell her so that she could place the blame for the information squarely on her. Marisha would be turned out.

'I can't think of anything,' Marisha said.

'If you do, you know where I'll be.' Baba Zima signalled the Hands to pour her some more tea.

Marisha left the room and stood at the window in the hall. The house's movement was smooth. It snowed again, large wet clumps that erased them from the landscape. She considered the possibility of Baba Zima's offer. She did not like the way that Baba Zima was trying to manipulate her. Despite their quarrel, Olena had not tried to turn Marisha out, though she certainly would if she told Baba Zima about Kiril. But would it matter if Marisha was turned out? Would she still have nightmares outside this house? *What about the plague cure*, she thought to herself. Olena was too arrogant, her motivations so misplaced, she'd never find it. *Or are you dismissing the possibility to protect your-*

self from hope?

Marisha could not think clearly about the plague cure. There was no need to get unnecessarily turned out of the house's security and salary. Besides, she needed to shield Kiril from Olena.

She would figure out how to banish her nightmares on her own.

That afternoon, Marisha took her stack of Old Slavonic history books to the library. On the way there, she had passed Dunya and Anka-ny sitting together in an alcove behind one of the staircases, where the windows formed a perfect nook. Dunya had laughed her sparkling laugh, making Marisha pause as she passed. The light streaming from the window illuminated Dunya's mess of blonde curls and Anka-ny's single black braid as they bent their heads over something that Anka-ny held. Marisha was struck by a pang of longing. She wished she could laugh. She wished she didn't feel so alone.

Marisha sped up past the pair and entered the library. She sat at the small table next to the window, books stacked precariously in the corner, one of the histories open at her right elbow and Ansiev's account of Southern Chernozemlya myths on the left. On top of the Ansiev book, was a smaller, slimmer volume, written by Baba Valeriya. Marisha paged through it, skimming the text for incantations to banish nightmares. Besides something about a tincture of lavender to invoke peaceful sleep and an incantation to protect children from soul-sucking ghouls, Marisha was not finding much. Marisha had told Olena that she wanted to go to the library to research Nightingale the Robber, and indeed, the Ansiev book was open to a story about the bogotir Grisha of Kul, the monster's slayer. Olena had raised her eyebrow at Marisha's request, as Marisha had not shown enthusiasm for her theory, but she did not stop her. Marisha sensed that Olena felt relieved that she was leaving for the library.

However, Marisha had another reason besides illicit incantation research for wanting to be in the library. Since her nightmares kept her from sleeping, she found reading to be a much more arduous task than it had been before. Her eyes glazed over the words, and they seemed to immediately flee her mind, taking all meaning and sense with them. Worse, she had fallen asleep at the table. Olena had shaken her awake and told her that her laziness was intolerable. Marisha could not let it happen again. In the library, she felt a lot less conspicuous about standing up and walking whenever she felt herself nodding off. But she must have been even more exhausted than she realised, because one moment she was reading, and the next someone was tapping her shoulder.

Marisha's eyes shot open and she almost fell out of the chair onto the library floor. Valdim stood over, his gaze concerned. 'You were having a bad dream.'

Marisha nodded, trying to calm her racing heart. She did not remember her dream, but thought she felt the echo of something sad, of music. She took several deep breaths and tried to focus on what Valdim said. Valdim, who made musical instruments, but did not play them; not the mournful tune that belonged in her dream and made her body crest with yearning for something she had lost. For someone.

'Why do you think music makes us feel things?'

Valdim paused to consider her question. 'Because music, I think, is the language of the soul. It speaks, but not with words our mind can understand.'

'I guess that's why I feel sad, but I don't know why.'

Valdim smiled as though he knew exactly what she meant. Marisha leaned back against the windowsill, hoping she could try to recapture her dream with stillness. But she was left only with the feeling of something soft but bristly brushing her cheek, like feathers.

She noticed a violin on the corner of the table, as though set down hastily. 'You've been playing?'

'Yes.'

'Could you play something now? Something happy.'

Marisha expected him to be flattered by the request but instead he shifted as though mulling something over and looked outside. 'I would but–I'm sorry, I can't play if there are other people listening, even the thought of it—' He shivered.

'Oh.' His answer made her feel small, bereft. She wished she could have something to lose herself into. The way Valdim had music. Or the way Olena's gaze turned inwards when pounding herbs.

He smiled. 'Maybe one day.'

She smiled back, even though she knew it was an empty promise.

'No wonder you had a nightmare.' Valdim said, reaching for the strewn books. Marisha's heart raced, but he picked up Ansiev's tales. He read the chapter title out loud, 'How the Bogotir Grisha Slayed the Monster of Kul.'

'Yes,' Marisha said quickly, wishing to distract him from seeing the slim volume of incantations open on top of the Old Slavonic history. 'Olena is having me research Nightingale the Robber. Ever heard about him?'

'No,' Valdim said, his head bent over the book, eyes scanning the text, 'Why does she want you to research this?'

Marisha shrugged, 'She thinks it has something to do with the plague. The monster was described as a "plague on Kul" in one of the histories, and people fall senseless when they hear his cry.'

'Ah,' Valdim said, looking up from the book to Marisha. 'A bit of a stretch in my opinion. But then again, I'm not a koldun.' He returned to scanning the recent edition of Ansiev's tales, 'I see that Ivan the Fool makes another bad decision. And all to learn the language of birds.' He raised his eyebrows, 'I don't think I've ever wanted something so badly I'd trade my face for it.'

'He didn't know the demon would take his eyes, ears, and mouth in exchange. The demon tricked him. Though, at least he got to understand the language of birds.'

'It doesn't sound like he enjoyed it. Considering all the killing and kidnapping he did.'

'That's how it goes in stories,' Marisha said, 'There's always a price, always a trick, when it comes to magic.'

Valdim frowned slightly, scanning the text. 'Yes. And even though people know it, they still promise to pay. Then they're unsatisfied with the results.'

That reminded Marisha of what Baba Zima had said about supplicants begging for plague shield spells for their loved ones and the loved ones returning, heartbroken when the spells worked.

Valdim smiled and, as though he meant to lighten the conversation, he said, 'Luckily, mother is usually happy with charging a few rubles for her efforts. Then the supplicants go on their merry way.'

'That's not all she charges,' Marisha thought of Baba Zima's offer of help in exchange for information.

'Really?' Valdim looked at her.

Marisha shrugged. She had said too much. Her shoulders hunched over. What was the matter with her?

Valdim frowned and said, 'I hope she's not overworking you.

You've seemed a bit . . . diminished lately. And then I find you sleeping here in the middle of the day. Is everything all right?'

No, she wanted to say. No, everything was not all right. But she wouldn't say it. 'It's nothing. I've had insomnia all my life,' she lied, 'It's flared up.'

'Ah,' Valdim said, frowning. 'Have you asked Olena for help? I'm sure she wouldn't want you suffering, if only because it would reduce your energy for work.'

'Yes,' Marisha said, lying once more, 'I asked her. She said tincture of lavender would help. She wanted me to look up the ingredients first though.' Marisha smiled weakly, 'Everything is a learning opportunity.' She clamped her mouth shut before she could let another lie escape. Her tongue was running without any control, and she usually felt so measured with her words. It was all because she had been robbed of her sleep. She recalled the terror of her nightmare and how futile she felt against it in her exhaustion, and she wished she could just be honest with Valdim. But she also knew that information was currency, and since she was afraid of appearing weak before Olena, she couldn't appear weak before anyone else in the house lest they tell her. But at least he had cared enough to ask, which was much more than others had done. 'Thank you,' Marisha said, 'For your concern.'

'No problem,' he said. 'Don't worry too much about it. I'm sure Olena is not making your life easy, especially with the krug next week. But you would not be here if she did not want you to be.' Marisha thought of her upcoming three-month review and thought she may not be with the household for long. Valdim filled the silence. 'I know Olena wants to show up Anatoli at the krug. Does she know what he's planning?'

'No. I don't think so. How would she know?'

He shrugged. 'I run into him sometimes in Severny. Before I

left, he said something to me that made me think they were in contact.'

Marisha studied his expression, so carefully mild. His arms were tense. This was important to him, but he did not want to let her know how important. He did seem like the kind of person who always had his guard up, but she had long concluded it had to do with controlling his reactions to the particular sounds that bothered him so much. Now, she was not so sure. She was glad more than ever that she had not told him all her troubles.

He said, 'Will you let me know if she does correspond with him?'

Marisha crossed her arms. 'Why?' Was he just like his mother and intent on spying on others in a flight of manipulation?

'There's something about him that . . . no other way to put it, makes my skin itch. I'm worried about his intentions.'

'I didn't realise you cared so much about her.'

Valdim started. 'I don't–I mean, it's complicated of course. I just don't want her to be taken advantage of.'

Marisha frowned. Something was not quite right. Then it clicked. 'Worried about your mother?'

He seemed surprised by her insight. Or he feigned it well. 'No. Should I be?'

'She's very outspoken about her dislike of Anatoli. Maybe she rubbed off on you a bit.'

A frown darkened Valdim's expression. 'You've never met him. You don't know.'

Did Valdim have a history with Anatoli too? At least, unlike his mother, his desire to know about Olena's affairs seemed to be out of concern, instead of nosiness. She shrugged. 'Fine. I'll keep an eye out.'

His frown relaxed. 'Thank you. I'll let you get back to Nightingale the Robber.' He walked away from the table but hesitated by the door. He said, 'You know, agreeing on a trade is not the only way to get what you want. Sometimes the demon is the one who gets tricked into looking the fool.'

Marisha lay a hand on the book of stories. 'I don't want to make a fool out of anyone.'

'No, that would be unwise. Still, I would not make a trade with my mother, not unless you had no other choice.'

Marisha thought of the bargain she had already entered into with Olena. Helping her kidnap Kiril in exchange for her place in Baba Zima's household had resulted in the spirits punishing her with nightmares. She shook her head, 'No, I would rather not as well.'

'Luckily,' Valdim said, 'As an assistant, you do have advantages that ordinary supplicants do not.'

Marisha shrugged. 'Not always. I wouldn't mind paying rubles if I thought they would be accepted.' Marisha sighed, but then a tendril of an idea wormed its way through her mind. 'That is . . .'

Valdim said, 'Just be careful.'

Marisha smiled. 'I will.' Her eyes were trained on the door as it closed, but she did not see it. She had finally caught the feather of an idea as it floated by. She sat there for a long while, immobile, her hand resting on top of the story of Nightingale the Robber. Suddenly she got up from her seat and the left the library, leaving the books open on the table. She felt infused with a wild crackling energy.

The first thing that she did was walk straight to Baba Zima's receiving room. Without quibbling about it, she took a small bottle of lavender tincture from one of the drawers. If someone noticed it was missing, she could say that she had dropped the bottle, and Baba Zima would probably enjoy reprimanding Marisha for her clumsiness and docking it from her salary. But that didn't matter. It would help her sleep. They would arrive at the krug in a week, a place full of kolduni. Baba Zima and Olena were not the only ones out there: surely any of them could help her. All she had to do was stay alert enough to not get kicked out of the house before then.

SIXTEEN

'Are you sure about this?' Dunya said. Anka-ny's arm was slathered in a poultice. The fire in the brazier was hot, but not terribly so.

'I already tried it myself,' Olena said, her voice grating with impatience. 'Look.' She passed her arm through the fire and held it there for a moment. Olena felt nothing but a bit of itchiness. It had only been two days of work to increase the poultice's longevity, it would keep the burning at bay for at least five minutes now. 'I need to make sure it works this long on other people.'

'Sh-shouldn't you ask Marisha?' Anka-ny said, still, not sticking her hand in the fire. Ha! Now Olena knew what it took to ruffle the ever-serene Anka-ny.

'Marisha's busy.' Mooning after Kiril. Or hiding from her. Not that Olena minded much.

Olena darted her hand forward to grab Anka-ny's elbow and push it into the fire, and Anka-ny shrieked and jumped back.

'Stop being a baby.' Anka-ny glanced back at her and finally stuck her hand into the fire, and Dunya made a ridiculous squealing noise as she did.

'Well?' Olena asked when the squealing stopped.

'It's . . . fine.' Anka-ny had a surprised look on her face. She flexed her hand in the fire. 'It feels odd.'

Odd? Was that the most awe Anka-ny could muster for such a wonder?

It felt so satisfying to have a problem she knew she could solve. The problem was hard, but the ways to solve it mapped out in front of her like capillaries in a marsh. So many possibilities, crisscrossing, stumbling upon new paths. The feeling was welcome after so much time spent staring at the blank page in frustration over the shield spell. She relished in it, this power of her mind.

Though Anka-ny had been unharmed by the fire, it took some amount of rough cajoling to make Dunya submit to testing the poultice as well. Once Dunya's skin had successfully been unburned, Olena dismissed both assistants and started trying out incantations that would create a temporary barrier around the user's eyes, nose, and mouth. This was the more difficult part of Baba Zima's idea. The barrier must be at least partly physical–perhaps something with an elemental aspect. After all, smoke was small particles of ash suspended in the air, and ash was just earth. Perhaps an incantation to separate earth from air, then? Olena grabbed a bit of muslin cloth and, after quick deliberation, some pennyroyal ointment for clearing the lungs. That was a good start.

It was not until later in the evening that Olena felt she had made enough of a dent into the problem (her incantation successfully caught smoke particles like a net, but only at a low density) to turn back towards trying to dissect the shield spell from Baba Serafima's notes. But with the missing incantation book, she had very sparse material to work with. One of the few lines that Baba Serafima had written about the shield spell read: 'The plague's attention must be deflected onto another object.'

Strange how Baba Serafima wrote about the plague as though it had a consciousness. Maybe the root of the curse was spiritual after all. But how did the shield spell deflect the curse's attention? Unfortunately, the slim volume of Baba Serafima's notes had nothing about the *why* of it all. She had to have written more.

Olena riffled through her papers and picked out a page of Marisha's notes. They were written in a small but rounded hand; so much easier to read that Baba Serafima's spiky, hurried writing. In addition to stories about the monster-slaying bogotir Grisha, Olena had set Marisha onto legends about the waters of life and death. From one of the tracts written by Baba Rushkina, the tenth koldunya to hold the house and whose flowery handwriting was particularly difficult to decipher, Marisha had distilled a two-sentence summary: 'There is a legend that, when the house was still in the other world, it had closed a window on a bird that had bathed in the waters of life and death. As it flew away, a drop of water from its beak and a drop from its claw fell onto the house's floor and two fountains bloomed. Baba Rushkina claims that the house survives on the dark earth because it still has a connection to those mythic fountains.'

Olena could feel Marisha's scepticism drip from her pen. Olena imagined stumbling into a room with two fountains spouting right out of the floor. Could something like that truly exist in the house? The idea of the shield spell, something that she could create herself, appealed to her more than the slim possibility that the waters of life and death could be somewhere in the house.

Olena opened the cover to Baba Serafima's book again and paged through it quickly. But Baba Serafima's hints were too few to be helpful. Yet Baba Serafima must have worked hard to improve the shield spell. She must have written more about it.

Olena thought of something that she knew she should not . . . Baba Zima had not been Baba Serafima's only apprentice. Perhaps Anatoli knew something that Baba Zima did not know—or was unwilling to tell her. But asking Anatoli if he knew anything about the shield spell would be quite a breach of Baba Zima's trust. Besides, sending a letter to Anatoli would be difficult without detection from her mistress. *But at the krug*, a voice in the back of her mind whispered, *you'd be free to seek him out. If you wanted.*

Olena closed the book with a decisive thud. She would not chase after the possibility that Baba Zima's sworn enemy could have the answers she sought. Not when she had not even made a good crack at looking for clues that Baba Serafima may have left behind.

Olena faced the prospect of a search with much excitement. She had spent many hours exploring the house when she was younger. Olena learned of secret passageways that connected the top floor to the bottom one in a few steps, hidden alcoves with wooden icons placed by kolduni long ago, even a roof garden that was only accessible during a full moon. But even though Olena had lived in the house for twelve years, she did not know all its secrets. She would occasionally stumble across an unknown hallway or a new door, usually when she needed to get to the kitchen or receiving room in a hurry. But in this case, stumbling upon the unexpected was not good enough.

Olena decided to make a dowsing rod. The dowsing rod was an ordinary stick that she had used to draw a circle around Baba Serafima's notebook in green pigment. Around and around five times, and the other way seven, around five, and then back seven, and on and on until she could not pull the rod away from the book anymore and had to break the circle with her shoe. Now as she swung the rod, she thought she felt the gentle tug that signalled that it was working, that it was attracted to something of Baba Serafima's. But she wasn't sure.

Golgolin, who had been sitting on her shoulder, took off a with a squawk, his little claws biting into her skin as he lifted off.

'What is it?' Olena said. Golgolin didn't answer, but flapped in front of the door, squawking some more. Olena frowned, not knowing why the door didn't open for him like it usually did. She transferred the dowsing rod to the elbow of her little arm and opened the door, to which Golgolin flapped down the corridor, making a trilling noise.

Dowsing rod forgotten for a moment, Olena followed the guinea pig-fowl down the corridor, up the stairs, taking them two at a time. She had a moment to realise that they were in the corridor directly above her workroom, when a door opened and Valdim popped his head out. His hair and shirt were covered in sawdust.

'What's happening?' He said, looking from Olena down the corridor. Golgolin flapped towards him and settled onto his shoulder. Valdim smiled at the creature and lifted his hand to scratch the fur around his ears.

Olena's chest grew tight. So that's it, Golgolin just wanted to visit Valdim. She transferred the dowsing rod to her hand, and was gratified to feel an actual tug now. She swung the rod around, feeling for where it pulled the most. Golgolin pushed off from Valdim's shoulder and landed in front of a green-painted door on the other side of the corridor, where the dowsing rod led as well. Her heart lightened. Golgolin had been trying to help her after all.

Olena transferred the dowsing rod back to her little arm and pushed the door open. It opened onto a small alcove that she thought had been a storage room for cabbages and root vegetables. But it seemed to be mostly empty.

'What are you doing?' Valdim asked, appearing by her side.

'Nothing,' Olena said. The dowsing rod pulled her to a door at the back of the room. 'Just looking for something. Why don't you go back to your violins?' The door was a small rectangle of wood that she would have to duck through in order to pass. She would never have noticed the door without the dowsing rod. Olena turned the doorknob with mounting excitement and pushed the door open with merely a shove.

Travelling trunks were piled to the ceiling along one wall. Some of them were fancy things covered in red leather, and some were no more than rough-hewn wooden boxes like her own. She took a closer look. They were ancient. These were likely the trunks that belonged to past assistants and apprentices–those who had departed so quickly that they had forgot to take their belongings.

'Wow,' Valdim said. Olena whirled around. Valdim stepped through the doorway behind her. 'This is quite the collection.'

'Why are you following me?' Olena asked. 'Go away.'

But Valdim ignored her and walked over to the nearest stack of trunks. He wiped the wood and read, 'Varvara Polskaya. Goodness, that's over eighty years ago. Do you know whose trunk you want? I can help you look.'

'Luckily,' Olena said, 'I don't need your help. This rod will point me to exactly the right one.' Olena's voice died. The rod was indeed tugging at her arm very forcefully, but it was tugging exactly at to the centre of the biggest pile of trunks yet, against the back wall of the room. The trunks were piled four layers high and six wide. How was she ever going to find anything in that mess?

Valdim appeared next to her. 'Hmm. Not the most accessible. But the Hands should have no trouble with it.'

'No,' Olena answered. She would not ask the Hands to do this for her. They would report back to Baba Zima and she did not want to feel like Baba Zima knew more than she already did. 'I'll fetch Marisha.'

Valdim frowned. 'No need to do that. I'm already here. I'll help you.' Valdim rolled up his sleeves and looked up at the trunks. The lid of the highest one was reachable if he stretched his arms. He had to tug quite hard to get it to move. 'Grab the other end, will you?' She did, but a second too late, and the whole thing came crashing down. Dresses and shoes exploded from the trunk onto the floor.

'Kchort,' Olena said, irritation prickling all over her skin. Now they had made a huge mess, and there were still so many trunks left to move. She glanced over at Valdim who looked like he was doing his best not to laugh. Then Olena laughed in spite of herself. Valdim glanced at her, his eyes crinkled with silent mirth. He began piling the clothes back into the trunk, but they were much harder to get back in than out. Olena's shoulders shook with suppressed laughter as she watched Valdim try to shove the dresses back into the trunk. Oh, this was not starting out well at all. She took a deep breath to get a hold of herself and went back to the tall stack of trunks. Somehow, it didn't seem as bad as it had a moment ago. She tugged on the handle of the one to the left of the empty spot. It budged, but there was no way that she could move it safely to the floor by herself.

Their shared laughter was soon forgotten. Working together to move the rest of them did not go smoothly. There was much yelling and accusatory looks as several more near-misses almost tumbled the trunks. Finally, Olena spied 'Serafima' inscribed on the lid of a trunk. 'That's it,' she said excitedly. Her arms were exhausted. 'This next one. Here.' It was two trunks deep. She reached over and tugged on the handle to bring it to the lip of the pile. It wouldn't budge.

'Here,' Valdim said, 'Let me.' He pushed in next to her, the narrow window in between the trunks squashing them together. Valdim had very pointy elbows. His fingers touched hers as he tried to grasp the handle as well.

'Move over, just a little bit.'

'There's no room for the both of us,' Olena said.

Olena squashed herself to the side, and he was able to grasp the handle more firmly now. 'On the count of three,' Valdim said, 'One, two—' they both heaved and the trunk shot forward. The loss of the trunk's resistance sent Olena careening into Valdim, knocking the breath out of him with a loud, 'Oof.' After much flailing, Olena found herself squashed between the trunk and Valdim. The trunk teetered on the edge of the stack of remaining trunks, its bottom edge digging into her hip while she leaned with all her weight into Valdim. Valdim's right arm pressed against her own as he was still holding the trunk's handle. He reached around with his other arm to brace the trunk more, effectively blocking her in. 'I think I have it,' he said. 'If you'd just get out of the way—'

'How?' Olena said. 'You're blocking me with your arms.'

'I'd think the future mistress of the house could figure it out,' Valdim said through gritted teeth.

Olena moved her hand back to the handle with her little arm bracing the trunk. 'I think I have it now. You can let go.'

Valdim moved away and she felt unsteady for a moment at the loss of his solid body pressed against her back. She hid her moment of wobbliness by tugging the trunk. She had expected it to land with a thud, but Valdim had, without prompting, reached around and grabbed the other end and set it down gently.

They were silent a moment as they both caught their breath. Their gazes met. Valdim's cheeks were flushed and his hair curlier and mussier than ever. She had a sudden urge to brush some sawdust out of his hair.

'Well,' Olena said, still a little breathless. 'Thank you.' She expected him to leave, but instead he crouched down and looked at the inscription. 'Serafima,' he read and looked up at her. '*The* Serafima? The one that my mother won't stop talking about, her old mistress?'

'Do you know of any others?' Olena had caught her breath. She knew she ought to be grateful that Valdim had helped her, but she wanted to open the chest by herself. He got up to his feet and she thought for a moment he might leave, but instead he only walked around the trunk to crouch down next to her, in front of the lid.

'Let's open it, shall we?' Valdim said.

'But—'

It was too late. Valdim threw the lid open. Olena had a moment to feel a bit crestfallen, then elated, then disappointed at the meagre contents of the trunk. The trunk did not contain a mound of papers, in fact, it was almost entirely empty.

'That's it?' Valdim said, peeking his head inside. 'I would have thought her a rock collector, considering how heavy it was.' He took out a small pink sash with one hand and an empty bottle with the other. Olena took the empty bottle from him to examine it. It was made of unusually thick glass. She lifted it up for a closer look and realised that one smaller glass bottle nestled in the first so that they were only connected by the lip. It was a beautiful thing.

She looked back down at the trunk, but it was empty. Olena's lingering elation was replaced by a wave of despair. It looked like a gale had hit the room: the neat stack of trunks was demolished and clothes were still strewn across the floor from the first one that had burst open. A mess and a complete waste of time.

'Well, that's it then.' Olena put the bottle back into the trunk and closed the lid. She took a deep breath. 'I suppose we should clean up. Or I can tell the Hands to. It's not like we found anything interesting.'

She glanced at Valdim, who was looking at her with sympathy. Quite affronting really. He said, 'Whatever you're looking for, I know you'll find it.'

Olena barked out a laugh. 'Why do you say that? You have no idea what I'm looking for.'

Valdim grinned. "Doesn't matter. Remember, with the pineapple—"

"Shut up!" Olena hissed, looking around furtively. She half whispered, half spat, "We swore we would never talk about it. *We shook hands.*"

Valdim held up his hands, "All right, yes, I wasn't going to—I just meant that, you have more tenacity than anyone I know."

Olena searched his face, unsure if he was being serious or not, but considering the way he was looking at her–half admiring, half exasperated, she thought–maybe he truly meant it.

Tenacity. That's slightly nicer than "the most stubborn person in a long line of mules."

Valdim grinned, no doubt also recalling how he had called her that a few years ago. He said, 'I stand by that. But you don't seem to have tipped into self-delusional. Not yet anyways.'

'Thanks.' Olena got up, feeling lighter, even though Valdim's good opinion didn't mean much. Still, it was nice to know he had some regard for her.

They fell into silence for a moment. Golgolin flew into the room but didn't alight on either of their shoulders. He seemed more interested in rummaging around the yellowing gowns, surely searching for a scrap of silk to bring back to his nest. Valdim said, 'This was fun. Reminded me of how we used to explore the house.'

Olena frowned. 'Explore? I remember getting lost with you on *your* alternate routes.'

'Funny, I don't remember that.'

'What about the time we ended up in that room with the flaming skulls? If I recall, you said you knew a shortcut to the pantry.'

'Maybe it was part of the shortcut.'

'And yet I never heard such a scream.'

'You trod on my foot! And the skulls had flames in their eyes.' He shuddered.

Olena shook her head, a small smile on her lips. 'I searched for that room since. I thought you might enjoy one of those skulls as a paperweight.'

He laughed. 'I'm glad you didn't find it.'

Her smile spread wider. 'Who says I didn't?' A warm feeling spread through her at his grin. She looked away, feeling strangely flustered. 'There are many rooms I haven't seen. This house . . . It never stops.'

She glanced back at him. He said, 'I'm glad to have seen a small part of it. I'll be sorry when it will no longer be in my life.' He looked at the mess of trunks. 'But I suppose that's all the more reason to see it when I can.'

Olena bit her lip. Of course, when she became mistress,

Valdim's ties to the house would be severed. She shrugged. 'There's no reason why you couldn't visit.'

'Really. You would invite me back? I didn't think you'd miss me.'

The back of Olena's neck felt warm. She looked at Golgolin, who was busy burrowing into a pile of silk. 'I think he would. I would do anything to keep Golgolin from pining.'

Valdim gave Olena a small smile. 'Very well. I would visit. For Golgolin's sake.'

Olena felt the moment stretch out between them and splinter. 'I suppose I'll ask the Hands to clean up. Or Marisha. She could probably use the exercise.'

Valdim frowned at her slightly. He began to pick up the dresses and push them back in the half-open chest. Olena was itching to leave and see if the dowsing rod would lead elsewhere, but she'd look a complete ass if she left while Valdim cleaned up. So, there was nothing to it but try stuffing one of the dresses along with him.

'I wanted to talk to you about Marisha,' Valdim said. 'I spoke with her a few nights ago. She seemed unwell.'

'How so?'

'She was just . . . very quiet, out of sorts. Tired looking. When I first met her a few weeks ago, she seemed a lot livelier. Haven't you noticed?'

Olena was taken aback. Valdim was trying to interfere with her assistant? 'Marisha's fine. She hasn't said anything to me about feeling unwell.' Well, if Olena was going to be honest with herself, they hadn't exactly been on the best of speaking terms since Marisha's outburst about Kiril a few weeks ago. But she wasn't about to tell Valdim about that. She continued, 'Yes, she's been a bit slow lately, but nothing to be alarmed about. Koldunry isn't for the faint-hearted and Marisha will have to learn that if she wishes to stay.'

Valdim frowned. 'But she's your assistant. You're responsible for her, aren't you?'

Olena stared at Valdim, indignation creeping over her. 'Did she say anything to you during your tête-à-tête? Any complaint?'

Valdim said, after a moment. 'She denied anything was wrong. But it's clear she's lying.'

'Well, there's nothing to be done, is there. She says everything is fine, then everything is fine.'

Valdim shook his head and got up from the trunk. He put his smock back on from when he'd shed it earlier. Olena got to her feet as well and said, 'What?'

'You just reminded me of her for a moment.'

'Of Marisha?' Olena reeled back, now very confused.

Valdim laughed. 'No. Of my mother. The resemblance is uncanny.'

'You say that as though it's a bad thing.'

Valdim only raised his eyebrows at her and said, 'I think I'll return to my work. Good luck with your search.'

Olena felt like she had a knife in her chest, though she did not know why exactly. 'Fine. It'll go a lot faster without the distraction.'

He didn't even look back at her as he left.

Emotions boiled through Olena, indignation, shame, annoyance both with Valdim and with herself. She did not need his condescension. Marisha was fine. Even though she had become distant ever since her outburst about Kiril, Olena would have noticed if something were truly wrong with her. Besides, if Marisha was struggling a little, it wasn't a bad thing. Baba Zima had always allowed Olena to struggle through things herself, which is what had uncovered that tenacity that Valdim had seemed to admire about her only moments ago. Olena wanted to run after Valdim to tell him, but she wouldn't subject herself to the indignity. And so, she took a deep breath and lifted the dowsing rod back up, ready to follow where it led. She left the trunks in disarray.

SEVENTEEN

Unfortunately, the dowsing rod took her to a locked door, which was most unhelpful. This door was not unknown to her. It was on the first floor and out of the way enough that she did not come across it very often, but when she did, she looked at it with curiosity, even once trying to force her way through when she was thirteen or fourteen. It had no handle, only a brass keyhole at the bottom of the door and another keyhole at the top. Baba Zima's keys would be necessary to get through.

Olena wondered what could be behind the door, her frustration mounting. But then the frustration turned inward. Of course, Baba Zima would have keepsakes of her mistress. Olena could ask Baba Zima what they were, but what would be the point? If Olena questioned her matrionka about this, then it would be implying that Baba Zima was hiding something useful from her, and of course she wouldn't. Would she?

Olena stood a long time looking at the door with the two keyholes. She only left when she thought she heard Valdim coming down the stairs. She didn't want him to see her and wonder why she stood in front of that door in particular.

She went back up to her workroom and sat back into her chair and stared at the wall without really seeing it. All the momentum she had felt earlier had fled her. She had not realised how much she had been counting on finding something of Baba Serafima's to guide her. She was so busy staring at the wall that she did not notice Golgolin. His flapping wings brushed her head as he landed on her shoulder.

Olena cried out in surprise and then scooped the creature off her shoulder and hugged him to her chest. She felt better instantly. He let her hug him for five seconds before he squirmed out of her arms and landed onto the table next to her chair. She smiled at his antics. Then her gaze fell upon the door to Kiril's linen closet. She thought about the door with the two keyholes and her smile fell.

'Golgolin,' she whispered, scooping him up again. 'I know there's probably nothing behind that door, the one with the keyholes at the top and bottom, that might interest me. But I can't get through, not without Baba Zima's keys. And I only have two of your feathers left.'

Olena thought of her horded treasure, two silvery feathers she kept hidden in her mother's green veil. Would Baba Zima know to spell the door against Golgolin's feathers? It would be a terrible thing to waste them that way.

'Do you think,' she asked, 'you could open a way there for me? Or if you can't, can you look in there and bring me back something of Baba Serafima's?'

Golgolin wriggled out of her arms and flapped over to Kiril's closet. He made a high-pitched trilling sound. The door opened and he disappeared through it. Olena waited a long while, hoping that Golgolin would do what she asked. Golgolin could travel anywhere by using thresholds to go between, but he could not open a doorway for people, not like Olena could with his feathers and a bit of koldunry. Though asking him to fetch something for her . . . she had never done that before, and she didn't know if he could do it. Still, when she heard the squawk on the other side of the door and opened it, she was disappointed he carried nothing in his beak.

'Oh well,' Olena said, 'Even you cannot disobey Baba Zima. I know that.' Olena peered closer and gasped in surprise. Kiril's bed was gone and the floor was taken up by a mound of paper that reached almost to Olena's shoulders. It was a different room. But Golgolin couldn't do that. She knew she had asked him to open a way through the door for her–but she had not actually expected him to do so! Was this some new power of Golgolin's that she had never seen before? The ceiling was lower than the closet and the floorboards had an old brown varnish. But, more importantly, most of the floor was taken up by the enormous mound of paper. At first, she thought that the paper was simply crumpled and piled, but upon closer inspection she saw that these had been folded into strips and tucked together in such a clever way that the structure held.

'Ah, I see. I know where we are.' Olena said, understanding clicking into place. 'Golgolin, you cheeky thing, this is your secret nest?'

Golgolin was not exhibiting a new and outsized power. Baba Zima had told Olena that Golgolin had claimed a nest somewhere in the house and that only he had access to it. Olena had thought that meant no one else could enter his space, but now she understood that her mistress had meant that only Golgolin could reveal his nest to others. The guinea pig-fowl snuffled at her neck and Olena felt overcome with emotion for the small creature. That he would trust her enough to bring her to this safe place of his. She took a shaky breath. 'What is it that you wanted to show me?'

Golgolin launched himself from her shoulder and perched on the edge of the paper mound before diving into it. Olena lifted herself on her tiptoes to peer over the edge. There was a small hole at the top and though the mound of paper rustled and shook, the structure held together. The strips of paper on the outside were mostly blank.

'They're envelopes,' Olena said, bending her head close to a yellowed strip of paper without touching it. 'But you would never steal any letters, would you, Golgolin? Of course you wouldn't.' Perhaps these were letters that had arrived accidentally. Or letters that had been refused by their recipient. Her hand itched to reach over and pluck one out to read, but instead she waited with her hand folded over her little arm at the elbow. Golgolin emerged from the mound of letters with one in his teeth. He stretched out his neck so that she could take it, as though it were nothing more than an ordinary letter he delivered.

The envelope had been folded in half lengthwise. Olena sat cross-legged on the floor, careful not to disturb the enormous paper nest, and smoothed out the envelope. It had no address on it, which was not that unusual; Golgolin could be easily told who to deliver to. She inserted a finger under the envelope flap and it lifted easily. There was only a single page inside the envelope. Olena pulled it out with a bit of difficulty, anchoring the edge of the envelope to her knee with her little arm and doing her best not to damage the brittle paper.

Despite being folded into Golgolin's nest, it had suffered no lasting damage and she could easily read the spidery ink. Though she had been disappointed to find only a single sheet of paper, she was even more disappointed to see that the writing had not even covered one side of the page. She bent over and read eagerly:

Esteemed Pan Volya,

I have considered your request, but I cannot fulfil it at this time. Your accusation is presumptuous. I have not seen your missing talisman, nor do I know how you think it may have come into my possession. The shield spell is the best defence I have against the plague, but it is not the only one. This house has deep waters, some that you couldn't fathom, some that keep out the unwanted sort, and some that welcome only death–if you come seeking. So, I do not recommend that you do.

Yours,
Baba Serafima

Olena lowered the page. That was it? She reread it. *The shield spell is the best defence I have against the plague, but it is not the only one.* What could Baba Serafima be referring to? It was so frustrating to have such a strong allusion dangled in front of her. She felt like a mouse chasing a piece of cheese on a string. Golgolin perched on the lip of the mound, looking down at her.

'Thank you,' Olena said. 'But is there nothing else that Baba Serafima wrote about the shield spell, or anything else?' Olena reached up to stroke the soft fur between Golgolin's ears. 'Nothing else you can give me?'

Golgolin blinked owlishly at her before plunging back into the mound. He emerged with a second envelope clasped between his teeth and Olena's heart soared with hope and curiosity. Golgolin flapped clumsily over to her and dropped the letter into her lap. Olena unfolded the envelope and read the name written on the centre. Her blood went cold. How could it be? She read the name again and snatched up the envelope, bringing it so close to her face that her nose touched it, as though the name would change at that distance. But of course, it didn't: the letter was still addressed to Feodor Danilovitch Yasenov. How formal of her. Olena didn't remember writing his full name out, patronym and all, as though *Fedya* would not have sufficed–but it was her spiky writing, and it was certainly her letter. It was only then that she noticed that the envelope had not been opened.

Olena had written the letter only a few months after she had moved into Baba Zima's orange house. She remembered her hand skating across the page as it never had before. Her tears came quick and thick, then ran down her chin. It had been a particularly difficult day, and she missed home. She had sealed the envelope, never intending to send it, but the next day the envelope was gone. She both hoped and feared that Golgolin had taken it to Otkazin. She knew he could do it in the blink of an eye. And over the next few weeks and months she had half-waited for a reply. It never came. At least she could tell herself that maybe Fedya had read it, even if he had decided not to answer.

'Thank you, Golgolin,' she managed to say. She picked up Baba Serafima's letter. 'May I keep this? You keep the other one.' It would be more useful to him than to her. She tried to smile.

'MATRIONKA,' OLENA ENTERED the receiving room. She had the empty bottle from Baba Serafima's trunk as well the letter from Serafima to an undisclosed person. 'This is all I could find.'

Baba Zima motioned for her to come closer. 'Let me see.' She scanned the lines. 'Not much to go on, is it.'

Olena shook her head.

'And what else do you have there?'

Olena handed her the peculiar bottle. She said, 'I found them in a room full of travelling trunks.'

Baba Zima smiled slightly, 'The house never does cease to amaze.'

'I was wondering–the bottle, the way it's been crafted with the double glass and the tiny stopper . . . so that the water would not touch the outer walls, I've not seen that design before. Well, the way the letter is phrased . . . about waters that are so deep that they could invoke death . . .' Olena paused meaningfully. It had not taken her long to make the connection to the water of death. It had been on the edge of her mind as an option to cure the plague, what with Baba Rushkina's story about the fountains of the waters of life and death animating the house outside of the other world. Was it so hard to believe, as fantastical as it was?

'Yes?' Baba Zima studied her, 'Out with it, I do not know what you're babbling on about.'

'Is there some water of death hidden somewhere in this house?'

Baba Zima did not laugh at her. She did not even smile. 'Has it truly come to that?' she asked.

'What do you mean?'

'Is your progress so stunted that you must resort to such means?'

Yes, it is. Olena resisted the urge to fold her hand around her little arm's elbow. 'No, I still think that the shield spell might yield some interesting results. But I can't help but be intrigued. Matrionka, if we really did have access to the waters of life and death—'

'There's nothing in this letter about the water of life, just waters so deep they may bring on death.' Baba Zima cocked her head. 'Sounds like someone rattled her off so much that she threatened to drown them. Wouldn't be the first time.'

Olena refused to be cowed into submission by disparagement. 'But the bottle. What else could it be for?'

She was surprised that Baba Zima's mouth broke into a misty smile. She seemed soft somehow, like the angles of her cheekbones had melted. The Hands carried in the large samovar and steam curled from the spout. 'I'll tell you a story. Baba Serafima came from modest means, even more modest than your own. Back then, learning your letters was an even greater luxury than it is now, and Baba Serafima, or Fima as she was known then, would not dream of even seeing the world a mile out of her village. But when her father was asked if he had a child to be put up as a lady's maid, it was Fima, the lively and troublesome child, who he decided to sell.

'Fima was clever. She manoeuvred herself to be sent with her lady to boarding school and she learned everything her lady did. But later, when she became a young woman, she reached past her social bounds and was turned out. Oh, the sordid details are not important, there was a young man involved, as there often is. But Fima did not let herself be beaten. She consulted a koldunya who then gave her an incantation and a small bottle of water to manifest her destiny. She was to recite the incantation and pour a single drop onto the ground. If her destiny did not hasten, she was to repeat the actions the following month. And what did Fima do? She spoke the incantation and upended the entire bottle.' Baba Zima chuckled softly. 'That was Baba Serafima in a nutshell. She said she was tired of waiting for her destiny.'

'She might have died,' Olena said. Baba Zima nodded for she knew just like her apprentice that calling destiny too hastily could inadvertently call death. It was the one fate that could not be escaped. 'Did she know?'

Baba Zima nodded. 'She did, but she did not care. She was bold. And once the water had soaked into the ground, it took only a moment for something to appear on the horizon. She was standing in one of those tussocky landscapes where one could see for miles. The snow was melting and the ground was boggy, but she could see that something grew closer. And what was it but an orange house staggering across the snow on stilt-like legs with knees that bent like elbows. Fima stood in the house's way and she did not budge until the house stopped in front of her. Hands on her hips, she looked the house up and down and said, "Now what do we have here?" It stood on two chicken legs, but it kept lifting one foot from the ground so that the entire house tipped to one side. Baba Serafima always said she could hear the crash of the dishes sliding out of the cabinet.' Baba Zima's shoulders shook with silent laughter. 'She immediately saw what the problem was. A wooden splinter the size of her arm was stuck in the bottom of the house's chicken foot. She pulled it out and the house righted itself. At that, the koldunya, Baba Valeriya, came to the door and when she saw what had happened, she invited Fima in. The rest, you know well.'

Olena looked at the bottle in her hand. 'You think this was the bottle that held the water that Baba Serafima used to call her destiny?'

'It might be. It is the right size and why else would one keep an empty bottle in one's trunk? The point is, Baba Serafima knew she had a destiny and she invited it, even though she may have been inviting her death.'

Olena failed to see how this was relevant. 'And the water?'

Baba Zima shrugged. 'Who knows. But Baba Serafima relied on herself and her own ingenuity and we may all take a lesson from that.'

'But the water of death—'

'A shortcut! Something you could spend your whole life searching for and that would be a waste. Besides, there is none in this house.' Could Baba Zima really know everything about the house? Or maybe she was hiding something still. Olena thought of the locked door with keyholes on the bottom and top. Baba Zima must have divined her line of thought for she said, 'Why would I keep something like this from you? Think of what we could do with such remedies. The waters of life and death can cure all bodily ills. Why, it would certainly put us out of business.' She gave a wry smile. 'Olena, I jest. I would never keep something like that from the world, or you. Forget this folly. The answer will come from you, my buttered blin, from your own ingenuity. Believe in your destiny.'

Olena tried to smile back at her mistress. But it was hard. What was her destiny? She kept her expression a smooth façade though something was crumbling inside. 'Of course, Matrionka. I will.' She would deconstruct the shield spell, and it had better yield something, if not–she could see into the abyss just as though she were looking down a threshold. She thought about meeting Anatoli at the krug. She would not have entertained the idea before. But now . . .

Maybe Baba Zima really knew nothing about Baba Serafima's work on the shield spell, maybe the water of death truly was a folly like she said. But Baba Zima's confident belief in Olena's destiny was no longer enough for her. Perhaps Anatoli could tell her a different story.

EIGHTEEN

They would arrive at the krug in only two days. Olena was distracted and paid little attention to Marisha besides barking orders at her. Marisha barely noticed. Her tincture of lavender didn't work anymore, and she woke up with a racing heart almost every other night. She was so miserable that were they not headed to the krug, she would have told Olena about her nightmares, or even Baba Zima. But she would meet plenty of kolduni there who would be able to help her. It would be easier to talk to a stranger.

The logical part of her mind told her she was ridiculous: she should ask Olena for help, but the idea of admitting to Olena her terror–she couldn't do it. Olena would mock her for refusing to swear her oath before kidnapping Kiril. If Marisha had agreed to it, she could have avoided the nightmares altogether. Olena would not care that Marisha had promised her father never to swear oaths or enter into an open bargain. She thought of his pained gaze and the way he had clutched his left wrist when he had extracted the promise from her, and she wondered yet again what he had sworn that made it so important she not do the same.

The bottom line was that she could not give either Olena or Baba Zima a reason to dismiss her. The krug would last three days. The timing aligned with the Marazovla, the festival that celebrated winter's wane. Marisha had celebrated it as a child by drowning small wooden dolls dressed in wool scraps, and as a teenager by getting stupid drunk with her preparatory friends around a bonfire, but for the kolduni it was a momentous occasion. On the first day, they would arrive and there would be an opening ceremony in the evening. The next day would host a fair with koldunry demonstrations and a banquet. On the third day, the Marazovla festival, the kolduni would perform the blessings of the water ceremony in the morning and the Marazovla celebration in the evening, which entailed staying up all night singing and dancing to help spring be reborn from winter. While the Marazovla celebration was the culmination of the krug, Baba Zima made it clear to Marisha that the blessings of the water was the most important event. The passage from winter to spring would infuse the river water with power, as close to the potency of the waters of life and death that kolduni could get.

The day before the beginning of the krug, the house took off its skis and walked into a dense pine forest. Marisha worried at first that the house would run into all the trees, but it slipped between the trunks as easily as it slipped between houses in towns. The excitement in the household was palpable. Dunya and Ankany were glued to the large window in the oven room and Baba Zima whisked around in her most clashing green-and-pink striped skirt and gold headscarf. Olena stayed silent for the most part, but her eyes sparkled. The atmosphere was infectious, and the idea of finding a way to banish her nightmares kept Marisha in high and hazy spirits. In fact, Valdim was the only one whose silence had an edge of grimness. Marisha could only assume he anticipated the painful ruckus the krug was sure to produce.

As the afternoon light slanted away, the house skittered to

a stop at the edge of a clearing and folded its legs. Everyone, except for Baba Zima who was dignified, and Olena who pretended to be, bundled up and rushed outside. Light snow fell. The huge four-toed footprints of the house tracked back into the trees. The rustling sound of running water cut through the silence. Marisha wondered how water could run in such cold.

It appeared they were early. Two more houses stood nearby, but they seemed small and shabby compared to Baba Zima's handsome, orange shingled house. Several tents were also pitched next to enormous bowls. Mortars, Marisha realised. Baba Zima had said that traditionally, a koldunya travelled in a mortar with a pestle to steer or bang against the sides for encouragement, like whipping a horse. Baba Zima did have a huge mortar which Marisha had used once to grind an enormous batch of willow bark. She supposed one could stand in it, on one foot, but Baba Zima said she preferred travelling by giant teacup, a more elegant mode of transportation. Marisha did not know whether to believe her or not. She had not found an oversized teacup in any of the storage rooms, but many doors opened only to Baba Zima's keys.

Further into the clearing stood a giant tent. It seemed to be made out of a shimmery white fabric, and closer inspection showed rows of thousands of tiny mirrors sewn into the tent with silver thread. Baba Zima said they were for turning the evil eye away from the krug. Marisha thought it must have been awfully expensive to commission and wondered who had paid for it. She then wondered if the mirrors worked.

The day before, Baba Zima had handed them amulets which would allow them to enter the *krug*. The amulet was a locket made out of cheap pewter in the shape of an oval with an eye carved at the centre. It contained a tiny rolled-up scroll upon which Baba Zima had written her permission to attend. Marisha thrilled a little when they approached the tent. She clutched the amulet in her hand but was disappointed when nothing happened as she passed through the tent flap. Yet when she looked back, the trees were as dark as midnight, even though it was only late afternoon. She shivered and told herself it must be a trick of the light.

Their entrance caused quite a stir. The whispers and pointed looks seemed to be an acknowledgment of Baba Zima's high standing, but the lingering stares were for Olena's face. Dunya and Anka-ny's awed expressions matched her own. Valdim looked around, his brow wrinkled. That's when Marisha realised Olena had disappeared.

Baba Zima elbowed past her. Valdim looked where she headed and rolled his eyes. Marisha followed his line of sight to a clean-shaven man of medium height who strolled towards them once he saw Baba Zima. He acknowledged Marisha, Dunya, and Anka-ny with a nod and a smile, and then bowed to Baba Zima who returned the courteous gesture with a curt nod. They kissed each other in a perfunctory way on the cheek.

'Ah, Zima,' he said, 'I'm delighted to see you.'

'Anatoli. Wish I could say the same.' And indeed, she looked like someone had dared to serve her a steeped teabag instead of the best caravan looseleaf.

Anatoli winked at Marisha. 'I'll take it as an achievement, to be so aggravating to the great Baba Zima.'

Baba Zima sniffed. 'Not something to be proud of. Unless you have no other achievements.'

So, this was the famous Anatoli. His open genial face made him look younger than Baba Zima, even though they had to be of a similar age to have apprenticed to the same koldunya. He was quite handsome, Marisha decided, but not classically so. He had dark blond hair, large deep-set eyes, and a thick upper lip with a cupid's bow. His attractiveness had more to do with his easy, familiar manner that made Marisha feel like she was already acquainted with him.

His gaze swept over the rest of the party. 'Valdim. We meet again. It's too bad that you left Baron Ossman's dinner before I could introduce you to Emil Falkof. He has quite an extensive collection of rare items, one that he likes to grow. Could have been lucrative for you.'

Valdim smiled but it looked more like a challenge. 'I can make my own introductions if I wish for it. Next time.'

'If you say so,' Anatoli said. He turned his attention to Marisha, Dunya, and Anka-ny. 'Well look at this. Your brood has grown quite a bit. Do you finally miss the raucousness of the house of our youth?'

Baba Zima focused her stare on Anatoli, 'You wouldn't recognise the house if you set foot in it. Which you won't. Not without asking first.' Baba Zima grinned with relish at Anatoli. It wasn't that it was strange to see Baba Zima take pleasure in causing discomfort in others, but Marisha couldn't recall her ever displaying such personal triumph at doing so.

Anatoli's smile gained a certain fixed quality about it. He said, 'I was disappointed to hear you won't be exhibiting anything, especially so close to the plague year. It's almost a cause for concern.'

Baba Zima smirked. 'Listening to gossip, are we? Some of us like to guard our secrets. Though I suppose, you never worry about people stealing yours, do you?'

'Only around you, Zima.'

'Ha! You are bitter, Anatoli. And tiresome. Only a minute in your company and I feel drained of goodwill. How ever do you do it? No, don't answer. You wouldn't want me to steal your secret.' Baba Zima looked around. 'Where's Olena? I wanted to introduce her to Baba Ekaterina.'

'Ah yes, I want to speak with her: delightful girl, quite a talent you unearthed. What are you looking at me like that for, Zima? Perhaps you need a tighter grip on your underlings.'

Baba Zima laughed. 'Your threats are as sharp as a frog's tooth. Do your worst. But don't expect much, you do not know what it is like to have a loyal apprentice.'

'Hmm. Strange to hear you putting so much stock in loyalty, Zima. I know one who did as you're doing and did not live to regret it.'

For some reason, when he said this Baba Zima took a sharp breath and pursed her lips, as though he had insulted her in the worst way possible. Anatoli turned to Marisha, Dunya, and Anka-ny. 'But why worry when you have so many possible replacements? I did find it hard to believe that you spent so many years alone in that big house with only your son for company. Oh,' he addressed the silent assistants. 'You would have never recognised your mistress when she was younger. She was always trailing around after me, her and Olga—'

'Don't—' Baba Zima seemed to expand, her eyes glittered, her face grew red. 'Be careful Anatoli. Things are different now, as you don't cease to remind me. Know your place now, and don't—' she punctuated her words with a finger jab that stopped short of Anatoli's chest '—test me.'

Anatoli met her stare with a challenge of his own. 'And here I was thinking we could let the past be the past.' He shrugged with feigned insouciance. 'Too bad.' He brushed away his shirt and Marisha noticed that there was a black spot, charred with soot, where Baba Zima had almost touched it. Marisha's gaze shot between the two. What had happened between them to sour relations to this point? Marisha had not imagined she could even see Baba Zima so discomposed.

'Oh, we can let the past be the past, Anatoli, but it won't change anything.' Baba Zima's voice was soft and sweet, and put into Marisha's mind a poisonous snake about to strike. 'Baba Zima leaned in closer to Anatoli, 'I have it all. And you have nothing. When we're done here, I will go back to *my* house, where *I* am mistress. And you? You can sit where you always do. Below me.'

Baba Zima swept away. Marisha followed, her mind rattled. She looked back at Anatoli once. His furrowed brow and bared teeth conveyed such intense dislike that she almost made the forked sign with her right hand to ward off the evil eye. No, not dislike. Hate. Real hate. It was only there for a moment, and it was gone.

NINETEEN

he day of the demonstration fair dawned with a blue sky and a temperature barely cold enough to freeze standing water. Olena was actually looking forward to the fair since this was the first time in seven years when Baba Zima had not requisitioned a booth. Today, Olena would stroll through the various displays to her heart's content without worrying that the assistant she left in charge had broken something or shamed Baba Zima's bolshina. Plus, in the chaos of the demonstration fair, it would be easy to find Anatoli and slip away to converse.

Their uncharacteristic lack of booth was due to Baba Zima's pleasure at the effectiveness of the smoke repelling incantation; she thought it was good enough to drum up interest. There was a culture of kolduni attempting to outdo each other, and the flashiest of them would save their demonstrations for outside the demonstration fair: at the banquet, or in the pavilion tent. Olena had been asked several times in the pavilion what Baba Zima's household's demonstration would be, and she was happy to hint at her mistress's machinations. She did not have to think hard to figure out what her mistress would do. The Marazovla bonfire burned at the centre of the clearing where the demonstration fair would be held and at some point, maybe during the third day when they would burn the man-sized Marazovla doll, a hush would come over the gathered kolduni when they realised a person stood at the bonfire's centre. And then Baba Zima would step out unscathed to raucous applause.

Breakfast was a hurried affair which Marisha did not even deign attend. Olena kept glancing at her empty seat. She knew she ought not to be irritated with her assistant, but why pick now of all times to be sick? Even *she* would be interested by the demonstration fair. Olena meant to go upstairs to see how sick she really was, but Dunya had already left the table with some herbs and water to relieve stomach cramps. Olena lingered by the staircase after Dunya returned, still thinking that she ought to go up, but Baba Zima was already at the door and hollered for the others to hurry. And so, Olena left with only a whisper to Golgolin to check on Marisha and followed Baba Zima, Dunya, Anka-ny, and Valdim through the door.

The noise of muffled chatter grew louder as they approached the clearing. Olena quickened her stride because she was excited, but also to put some distance between herself and the rest of the group. Olena was annoyed that Valdim was accompanying them. She was even more annoyed that as soon as they passed the pavilion, Baba Zima immediately peeled away and called back to Olena, 'Keep an eye on them,' pointing at the assistants and her son.

'But—' sputtered Olena. But Baba Zima had already disappeared into the crowd heading to the clearing.

Olena groaned. They may not have a booth of their own this year, but Olena was still stuck babysitting. Not only that but watching them would make it harder for her to slip away to talk to Anatoli. Kchort!

They showed their amulets to the invisible guardians at the

fair's entrance and were let through. All at once, the din was amplified. The clearing echoed just as much as the pavilion, and on top of that, there were loud bangs and screeches from the demonstrations themselves. Dunya and Anka-ny stopped at the entrance, Dunya's mouth hung open and she clutched at Anka-ny's arm.

The awareness of the large number of kolduni prickled uncomfortably at Olena's skin. She avoided crowds. When the house stopped in towns, Olena rarely ventured into the square with the rest of the assistants and preferred to walk along the outskirts by herself. Even though she knew that no one with half a brain would dare attack Baba Zima's apprentice, when she did venture into villages and people whispered to each other and followed her with their gazes, her mind could not help turning towards her younger days and to her mother, who had hated people staring at Olena even more than she did herself. Her mother's lips would draw together, and she'd jerk Olena's brown shawl tighter around her face and torso. Olena would not protest even though her mother would pull the scratchy wool too tightly over her nose for her to breathe comfortably. She had felt ashamed for causing her mother such embarrassment, even as she had feared those who spat at her feet and made the sign to ward off the evil eye. Sometimes they circled around her to stare at her better, making her feel like a calf among wolves.

But now Olena was safe among kolduni, and though they still stared at her, their revulsion was accompanied with awe and respect. Mostly. Olena resolved not to be bothered by it. Not today. She decided to instead focus her attention on the demonstration fair. The clearing was large enough to fit the receiving room-sized bonfire at the centre without the threat of burning the trees, but not so large that the hundreds of booths could ring around it comfortably. The booths spilled out into the forest. Luckily the trees were thin near the clearing, with yards of room between trunks and only young saplings pushing out beneath the thin layer of snow. Beyond there, the trees quickly grew thick so that a person had to shift sideways to pass between trunks. The clearing was not natural, but there was no sign of what there had been before. Perhaps it had once been pasture for the Zabalaisky reindeer herds. Or perhaps it had been a village, now long gone. Olena was glad to see that the tree branches beyond the booths were thickly hung with mirrors.

'Ooh, how lovely,' Dunya cooed, 'Like a snow fair.'

It was indeed like a snow fair. The day was wintery perfection with a dusting of new snow on the ground and pine boughs. Muddy paths started to form between the booths, but at the edge of the clearing, the snow was unsullied. The sun shone high, causing some of the demonstrators to throw caution to the earth and do away with their canopy altogether. And between the chatter of excited knots of kolduni roving around, and the bangs and low hums from the demonstrations themselves, there were cries of hot tea and warm pies from tea sellers. Olena was reminded of the snow fair that her village used to organise every year, also near the time of the Marazovla. It had been so exciting–ballads would be sung, dances held, blintzes fried. The air smelled of cold and powdered sugar for days beforehand. Olena could not stop that little tug of longing that accompanied the memory. She had wished she had been allowed to go to the fair. She stared at the mirror dangling from the pine needles, but there it was, the thought she tried to stop herself from thinking: *I wish I had not gone.*

'Well, come on,' Olena said.

She intended to circle through the outer ring of booths

quickly once and then spiral in, but after a few steps she noticed she was walking on her own. Dunya and Anka-ny had been distracted by something at the first booth. The first one! If they stopped at every single booth, they would get nowhere.

Valdim stood a bit to the left of her. His face was pale and he looked like he was trying hard not to wince. Of course, the loud bangs and chatter of the excitable kolduni would make him edgy. She caught Valdim's eye, he shrugged and ambled up behind the assistants. Olena rolled her eyes and walked faster to catch up with them.

Dunya and Anka-ny were leaning over a table, close but not touching. Other kolduni passed them with only a small glance. Olena itched to keep going. Had any other kolduni thought about the application of the shield spell for the sleeping plague? And if so, would they dare to demonstrate such a thing at the fair? Olena imagined how her own booth would look with Kiril laid out, bundled in blankets against the freezing cold and sleeping serenely through the hubbub. *See*, she would say, *examine the fingernails, the twitch in his eyelid. He's close to waking!* Dunya and Anka-ny's oohs and aahs broke Olena's reverie. Olena looked. It was nothing more than a clockwork mouse, dancing with a ridiculous parasol.

'All it takes is one dose,' the koldunya–or more likely than not, apprentice–chattered on excitedly, 'and the mouse does your bidding. Of course you need to increase the dosage for larger creatures. Hares fight it still, but we're making adjustments.'

So, it was a live mouse. Olena frowned at the small creature that teetered on two legs, clutching the small parasol with difficulty between its two front paws. The parasol must have belonged to one of the small porcelain dolls that daughters of rich boyars were so fond of. How humiliating. The koldunya continued her demonstration for Dunya and Anka-ny and whistled two notes. The mouse put the parasol down and put its front two paws on the table in an impressive handstand.

Olena stepped closer so that she stood next to Anka-ny and asked, 'And how long does it last?'

The koldunya's eyes widened at seeing Olena, staring at her face and then looking away in the familiar pattern of people who did not wish to offend. Instead, the woman settled on looking past Olena, which was only a slight improvement. 'Quite a while,' she said. 'Up to two hours, depending on the constitution.'

Olena eyed the woman closely. The koldunya was older than Olena, but she had girlishly plump cheeks and wore a coat with fur at the wrists and collar, an outfit that would not be mismatched with a larger version of the mouse's parasol. She looked away from Olena and clasped her hands behind her back as though to keep herself from placing them on the table to shield the mouse. She was hiding something. The table was covered in a plum and cream striped velvet cloth that reached for the floor on all sides. Olena lifted the cloth and the koldunya gave a small cry and tugged it down, but not before Olena had seen the cages stacked under the table and filled with mice. Olena said, 'After which the mouse dies?'

The koldunya's mouth formed a moue of indifference. 'More or less.' Olena sniffed and turned away from the table.

Dunya's excited expression fell. 'The mouse dies? How sad. And the other animals die too?'

The koldunya spread her hands. 'As far as we know. Still, very useful, very promising.'

Valdim said, 'Though death is not a desired side effect.'

Usually, thought Olena.

Valdim hummed a pair of notes and the mouse climbed into

his hand.

'Oh, you've got it!' The koldunya said excitedly. 'See, it's the easiest thing! We'll iron out the other–*undesired*–effects eventually.'

'How did you do that?' Dunya demanded. She imitated Valdim's humming and held out her hand, but the mouse did not approach her.

The koldunya said, 'Not to worry, it's probably winding down.' She bent under the table and reemerged with a new mouse clasped in her hand. It wiggled wildly, but the koldunya held its body firmly so that it could not move its head far enough to bite her knuckle. Olena and the others turned away from the booth as the koldunya fed the mouse from an eyedropper and whispered an incantation into its ears.

They restarted their slow meander through the fair. Olena spotted a flame from another booth nearby. Kchort, she thought, stopping to see a koldunya with her gloved hand in the fire. That was very close to what Baba Zima would demonstrate, she would not be happy about that. Olena lifted her head and looked again for her mistress, but she saw no sign of the purple-and-green ribboned hat Baba Zima had worn this morning. Nor did she see any sign of a certain koldun who had promised to find her if she could contrive to be alone.

She had written a note to Anatoli three days ago, asking him for a brief, discreet meeting at the krug. She had hesitated a long while before sending the letter with Golgolin. She had taken precautions to make the note unreadable save to its intended recipient, but she had braced herself for Baba Zima to burst in and demand an explanation nonetheless. She had passed Anatoli last night in the tent, but Baba Zima had been too close for Olena to partake in anything more than a cool greeting. Once back at the house, she found a note in her pocket saying that he would come to her, but she didn't trust him entirely. And she didn't like feeling that she had ceded control. After all, she was the one with the questions. She kept the bulk of her attention on the booths, but kept looking for Anatoli in the crowd, though he kept frustratingly out of sight.

They drifted through the ring of booths. Olena tried to steer them towards the booths that had the prime spots close to the bonfire. Valdim, on the other hand, tried to steer them to the booths at the edge of the clearing among the trees, surely because they were a bit quieter. Unfortunately, Dunya and Anka-ny drifted together and did not seem to care which way Olena or Valdim tried to steer them. This was vexing as Olena was used to them heeding her orders, but their attention to her desires dissolved quickly when something more pleasing caught their eye. And since Olena had promised that she would keep an eye on them, she had to go chasing after them instead of the other way around.

So, that was how Olena visited a booth where an apprentice advertised an ink that could be stretched so thin the inkwell needn't be refilled for a year, which Anka-ny was happy to purchase and test with her weekly letter-writing devotional to every one of her eight siblings; as well as a booth where roses as large as Olena's head furled and unfurled their petals in a strange hypnotic wave, sending Dunya into a fugue of praise. They also stopped at booths that advertised protection for cattle from thinning milk, needles that prick cloth but not flesh for Anka-ny, and some ridiculous booths that boasted beautifying hair and face creams and charms to attract the object of one's affections. Olena categorically refused to look at these on principle. While love charms were the kasha and honey for many kolduni,

Baba Zima dabbled but they were not her specialty. There was something pathetic in the way that the booths that specialised in love charms and beautifying aids were always staffed and surrounded by female kolduni. At one point, Olena neared a booth to retrieve Dunya and the koldunya looked at Olena with condescending pity, as though she thought that Olena wanted to come over to look at her wares but was not brave enough to do so. At that, Olena grabbed Dunya's arm and pulled her away bodily.

'Oh,' Anka-ny said as they passed a woman who was selling blintzes.

'You're hungry,' Dunya exclaimed.

'No, I'm fine,' Anka-ny said, but her head was still turned towards the blintzes.

'I'll get you some,' Dunya said, patting her pocket. 'Kchort.' She frowned. 'I forgot I had already bought the hair tonic.'

Before Olena could reprimand her for spending her money on fripperies, Valdim swooped in. 'Let me.'

Olena ignored Anka-ny's twittering of, 'Oh, it's not necessary,' and Dunya's, 'Oh, you're so kind, really,' and then Valdim's obligatory male insistence that it was not a problem. She tapped her foot in impatience and watched the tea seller as he moved in a slow circle pushing his urn of water and shouting the virtues of his 'hot tea, hot tea,' only pausing momentarily when a koldun sidled nearby with an empty mug for the tea seller to fill.

'Here you go.' Valdim appeared in front of her and held out a cone. The scent of warm powdered sugar and butter overwhelmed her with its cloying sweetness.

Olena reeled back. 'What?'

'Some blintzes for you.'

'I don't like them,' Olena lied automatically.

'Really?' Valdim frowned. 'But I've seen you eating the ones the Hands make.'

'The ones the Hands make are different,' Olena said, taking a step back. 'And since when do you notice what I eat?'

'I notice when you get to the platter first and there's none left for me.'

He had half a smile, damn him. Olena said, 'And now you have plenty. Enjoy.'

He didn't answer, but just gave a long look and turned away to the tea seller. How presumptuous, to think that she would be grateful just because he bought her a cone of subpar pastries. Next she looked, he stood in front of her with two cups of tea. Olena rolled her eyes at his persistence and was about to lean forward to take one, when he handed the one in his right hand to Dunya. Olena flushed, hoping that he didn't notice. Now she was just as angry as before, and embarrassed, which was worse.

Olena plunged straight to the centre of the clearing. The others, content with stuffing their faces, followed her for once, though Valdim winced in displeasure at the increase in hubbub at the central booths. They had made a full circle, for not too far away was the booth near the entrance with the not-clockwork mouse. Olena could see that the koldunya had not changed up the mouse's parasol twirling act. She surveyed the other options and decided upon the booth with the largest crowd.

'That one? Really?' Valdim had caught up with her. He smelled of powdered sugar.

'Yes,' Olena quickly stepped closer to the booth and snuck to the front of the crowd at the side of the table. The koldun, a man with a booming voice and smug expression, was showing something to the gaggle of apprentices that leaned over the table and blocked her view.

Valdim looked over her shoulder at the display. 'Olena, let's move on. It doesn't look interesting.'

'Why so insistent?' Olena said. 'A little too lively for you?'

'I've seen that man before,' Valdim said, 'He's apprenticed to a koldun who doesn't like your mistress.'

Olena sniffed. 'All the more reason to see what he's up to.' Olena asked, 'What's this?' loudly to get the apprentice's attention. He glanced over at her and his gaze immediately fixed on the left side of her face. He did not try to hide his staring. Then he changed his expression of repugnance to one of delight. He gave a silly kind of half-bow and rushed over to their side of the table holding a jar containing a rather elaborate feather quill.

'It's a simultaneous writing apparatus,' he announced to Olena. The other kolduni who were watching the demonstration either left the table or clustered around Olena and her group.

'Ah, a fancy quill pen, how sweet.'

'Not a pen, a stylus, no ink is used. Observe,' he said with an excess of pomposity. The apprentice leaned over her and took the pen from out of its jar. The tip was not cut like a good quill but looked as though it had been coated in some fine metal powder. And then he took out a large oven tile. Olena thought that it must have been baked but it was still soft as he brushed the surface with a flat rock to smooth it. Then he took out an identical large clay tile and placed them on the table so that they faced the crowd. He brushed his sleeves back dramatically. 'Are you watching closely?' he said and took up the pen. He made an incision in the clay tablet and, it took a moment for Olena to notice, but the exact same incision formed on the one to the left of it.

Dunya's mouth opened in astonishment. 'How is this possible?'

The apprentice said, 'Ingenious, isn't it. Any guesses?'

Another koldun said, 'The clay is mirrored.'

The koldun holding the simultaneous writing apparatus grinned and said, 'No.' He turned to Olena. 'Any guesses, madame apprentice of the illustrious Baba Zima?' Olena held out her hand for the quill pen.

'Ah, I'd rather not,' he said. 'It's exceedingly delicate.'

'And what makes you think that I don't know my way around delicate objects?'

He could not stop himself from glancing at her left sleeve, which was obviously shorter than her right one. She let her shawl come loose so that her little arm was more clearly visible–if he was going to stare, might as well do it properly. She looked straight back at him and held out her hand. The apprentice gave the quill pen to her, though his grin became rather fixed. Olena quashed the angry urge to break the pen in spite. She hated when people thought she couldn't do what they could just because she had only one hand. And it made no sense, you only needed one hand to write!

Instead of stabbing the apprentice with the quill, Olena pricked the tip into the surface of the clay. The small hole formed on its twin. She then hovered the quill pen on the surface and stuck her finger in the clay instead. The apprentice gave a start at that but did not stop her. The clay felt a little smoother than she expected, as though some grittiness had been removed. There was an oiliness there too that she did not expect. She took her thumb away from the tablet and inspected it. She looked at the other tablet and saw that no thumbprint was there.

'Hmm,' she said. 'So, it's not the surface of the clay itself. An incantation for sympathy, no doubt? Activated as soon as the quill comes into contact with the clay. And there's some binding agent in there too.'

The apprentice deflated at her words but perked up. 'True,

true. But you're missing the key! The link to form the pair of strokes, now that's the truly ingenious bit.'

'It's in the pen.'

'Stylus,' the apprentice said. 'And yes. But can you figure out how?' He had regained his grin.

Olena set the tablet down and raised her shoulder. 'I'm sure if I had an hour with the tablet and the pen–I mean, *stylus*–alone in my workroom, I could figure it out.'

'In other words, she has no idea,' Valdim said, leaning over her to get a better look at the marks.

'I have plenty of ideas,' Olena hissed.

Valdim did not answer but took the pen up from where she had set it onto the table, ignoring the apprentice's squeak of protest. He wrote, 'Really?' onto the surface of the clay tablet so that it was written on both.

'Oh, ha, ha,' Olena said, 'If only you were as witty as you were annoying, I might actually be able to stand you.'

'But you still don't know how it works, do you?' he wrote.

'Give me that,' she tugged the pen away from him and he let it go easily. Once the apprentice had recovered from the callous handling of his pen, he became gleeful that Olena could not figure out the secret. He watched her with great big eyes as she made marks with the pen in the clay. Other kolduni sidled to the table and the apprentice pulled out the clay tablets and gave his spiel, though he glanced over at Olena frequently. It seemed that Olena was monopolising his only pen. Now wasn't that a shame? Her vindictiveness turned to frustration as she inspected the pen and the markings they created. Anka-ny and Dunya drifted away to another booth, but Valdim stayed close by to watch her fail. Surely it could not be as simple as a binding between the clay of the tablets and metal dust that coated the pen? Then she felt, more than heard, a crack. She stopped writing.

'What is it?' Valdim asked.

She hadn't thought that anyone had heard.

'Nothing,' she said.

He leaned in closer and looked at her hand wrapped rigidly around the writing implement. 'You broke the pen, didn't you?'

'No,' she whispered. She didn't let go of the pen. 'Go away.'

'Let me see.'

'No,' she whispered a bit louder. She did not want the apprentice to see. Such an apparatus must have cost an immense amount of work to make, what was he doing allowing others to handle it? He would make her pay for it and she surely did not have the money which meant that Baba Zima would have to step in—

Why did Olena always break things? It had been just like this at the snow festival all those years ago. Anger and resentment had boiled through her, and then *crack*, just like the pen. She hadn't even pushed her brother that hard but he had flown into the air as though he had been thrown by a giant's hand right into the trunk of the twisted pine.

'Just put it down,' Valdim whispered, and she finally saw the sense in the idea. Unfortunately, the quill was cracked neatly down the middle and almost fell into two parts.

Valdim leaned over Olena to get a better look. Was he humming? Did he think it somehow made him more inconspicuous? Olena saw the apprentice leave the group at the other side of the table and approach them. Olena grabbed the pen back up and gripped it tightly to keep the pieces of it firmly together.

'Oh,' Valdim yelled, grabbing Olena's little arm, 'What's that?'

A mouse scurried onto the table. It actually stopped in front of Olena and grabbed at the pen and pulled it from Olena's hand.

The apprentice cried out, 'Koschei's bloody needle–what's that? Did you just give my stylus to a mouse?'

'Of course not, it took it right out of my hand!'

The apprentice grabbed for the mouse, but it ran down the tablecloth onto the floor, the pen held with difficulty between its paws. The ostrich feather bobbled up and was all Olena could see of the mouse as it reached the floor and wove between the crowd's assembled feet.

'Where did it come from?' The apprentice shouted. 'Stop that mouse, it stole my exhibit! Oh, Pan Volya will be so angry.' Someone pointed the apprentice to the booth where the koldunya paused her parasol-touting display to look over at the commotion.

Valdim touched Olena's shoulder. 'Let's go.' Olena allowed herself one last glance at the horrified apprentice and almost melted in relief. Then her stomach curled imagining the apprentice's gut-wrenching anticipation about owning up to his master about the incident. She felt awful about it, but not awful enough to own up to her destructive deed, and she scrambled after Valdim, all the while thanking the spirits and the earth for the good fortune of the mouse's intervention. Then she noticed Valdim's eyes twinkling. 'You did that,' she whispered. 'You commanded the mouse! With your idiotic humming.'

'I did no such thing,' Valdim said, but he could barely stop himself from laughing.

Olena let out a guffaw of her own. She glanced back at the booth. The apprentice had clearly tried to jump over the table and had pulled the tablecloth almost all the way off it. He was now scrambling up to his feet and began marching in the direction of the mouse-charming woman.

'How did you get it to grab the pen?' Olena asked. 'I thought it needed a specific tune to activate the order.'

Valdim shrugged. 'I don't find such contrivances all that difficult. Animals listen to me very well.'

'Your talents are wasted on violins,' Olena said.

'So, you think I have talents.' Valdim's eyes were still crinkled in laughter.

Olena rolled her eyes. 'Everyone has talents. Even you.' But she smiled. She felt lighter than she had in days, as though the heavy weight of Kiril in the closet and all her erroneous cures fell off of her. But to feel that way because of something Valdim had done? It was as wrong as sticking the right foot in the wrong shoe.

'Why are you being nice to me?' Olena demanded. 'First the blintzes, now . . .' She waved over at the mess of tables where the apprentice still searched for the mouse that carried off his quill.

Valdim shrugged. 'I thought we could try being nice to each other. It was fun helping you with the trunks the other day. Things could be different.'

'I don't know,' Olena said. Who was this Valdim? She did not know this person who ordered an enchanted mouse to save her from the disgrace of admitting the destruction of another koldun's property. The Valdim she knew frowned when she entered a room. And a moment ago, when she had forgotten that she had barely tolerated him for almost as long as she had known him, she had actually enjoyed his company. Maybe he truly had changed. Or had she simply been working alone for so long that she took any nicety as an offer of friendship? Her mind guiltily turned to Marisha, who she imagined was lying in bed, pale and sleeping almost as deeply as Kiril.

'Why not, I suppose.' Olena said. Why not indeed. And

though she was still not inclined to trust him–a small part of her wanted to.

She craned her neck to look around. ‘Ugh, where are they?’ Olena spotted Dunya and Anka-ny standing in front of a table around which flew glittering insects. ‘It looks like the assistants got pulled in by a swarm of ice bees. Come on.’ Olena started towards the table, exasperated at the assistants, yes, but with a strange buoyancy of spirit that she could not stop probing–confusing, but strangely pleasant. Valdim quickened his stride so he walked next to her and Olena was surprised to find that she did not mind.

TWENTY

arisha felt as haggard as if she had drunk too much blackcurrant vodka the night before. She stumbled out of bed. It was the second day of the krug and the second time she had woken that day. Earlier, Marisha had felt so sick from exhaustion she had pleaded sickness and begged to be excused from the demonstration fair, which earned her a cool look from Baba Zima. Honestly, Marisha could barely bring herself to care that she had incurred the koldunya's frostiness. Daylight streamed through the window with too much ferocity for her current state. She sat upright, her cloak slipped off. She had woken much too late.

Marisha brushed her teeth and got dressed. The house was eerily silent. She walked outside and spied someone moving around the corner of the house. She ran forward, eager to have found another person in her household who had not gone to the demonstration fair. She was almost upon the figure before she realised she did not recognise him. But by this point, he had noticed her and turned around, letting the leaf he scrutinised flutter away.

The man had long silver-and-black whiskers, a fur hat and cold blue eyes. He looked familiar and she wondered if she had seen him in the huge tent the evening before. She was so focused on placing him that she almost did not catch his words of greeting.

'Yes,' Marisha answered belatedly, 'I am an assistant. I started a few months ago. Evdokiya Igorovna.' She did not know why Dunya's name had come out of her mouth, except something about him made her wary. He looked at her the same way that those kolduni who shouted their cures on street corners looked at the gathering crowd. 'You may call me Dunya.'

'Enchanted, Dunya. You may call me Pan Volya. Ah, you're with . . . hmm . . . forgive me, I recognise the house, how could one not?' He smiled at the bright orange shingles, 'And I remember Baba Serafima of course, but my memory . . .'

'Baba Zima is my mistress.'

'Ah yes. Funny, I do remember Serafima having another apprentice.'

'Pan Anatoli.'

'Yes, that's right. A koldun apprenticed to a koldunya, you don't see that every day. Women and men are said to have different spheres of sorcery, you know. Poppycock of course, everyone has their own specific talents, but a koldunya is said to be more skilled at healing and domestic arts whereas male kolduni are supposed to be more skilled at elemental and animal arts. Inwards and outwards so to speak. That's why a greater proportion of dwellings from the other world are in the hands of female kolduni. It's a crude delimitation, but there are always those who are willing to follow the path the damp dark earth laid down before them, and hang the consequences.' Pan Volya paused. 'Do you have any particular koldunic interests?'

'I'm helping Baba Zima's apprentice search for a plague cure.'

'Excellent, another plague scholar.' Pan Volya smiled indulgently. 'I myself am interested in the plague, but with a different focus. I want to understand the edge between sleeping and waking. I know how sleeping works, yes, I know it well. But waking . . . It's terribly fascinating. So many kolduni are interested in curing the plague, but no one seems to care what happens after. And I'm sure you are well aware of what happens when a plague victim wakes up after sleeping for a year and a day.'

Marisha thought of how Anka-ny had described her sister growing more and more silent until she stopped talking altogether. If she was in that state after only being asleep for a year, what would deep sleepers be like if they woke after being asleep for several? Marisha thought of Kiril and her parents. Her breath hitched. She said, 'And what about the deep sleepers–what happens if they wake up?'

'It's my belief that when a person is in the throes of the plague, their spirits change, become diluted somehow. And if one is a deep sleeper, the exposure to the plague would certainly take it further . . . It's hard to speculate, but, at the worst, I think they might wake as empty shells–with a sufficient spark to animate their bodily function but not much more. Or, their spirit might stay somewhat whole, but with such great changes they might not recognise themselves.' The koldun's gaze turned beyond the trees. He frowned and said, 'They might become indifferent to the ones that love them, so restless they leave without a goodbye.' He paused, his expression smoothed and his gaze focused back on Marisha. 'Tragic, isn't it?'

She did not like the way that his smile did not extend to his cold eyes. 'It would be. Not much to do if that were the case.'

Pan Volya's smile twisted. 'No, only let them go–if you can. And if you can't—' He peered at her. He said, 'You have the look of one who does not know enough sleep.'

'You're saying I look tired.' Marisha tried not to let the resentment show but it was hard. She knew she was haggard: her skin sallow, her eyes sunken, her hair limp and dull.

'Yes,' the koldun said simply. 'You know, I'm intrigued by a koldunya's assistant who does not use the arts to aid herself in finding rest.'

'I'm still learning.'

'If you need instruction, I'm willing to help.'

Marisha hesitated. She had intended to ask a koldun at the krug for a sleeping potion, but this seemed almost too convenient. 'Why? You know nothing about me.'

'I am not the kind to turn away from one I could help. And perhaps aid rendered might deserve another happy turn.'

'What do you want?'

'My, you don't sneak around the sleeve do you?' Pan Volya smiled. 'There is something Baba Serafima . . . acquired from me, many years ago. A feather. From a very . . . unique creature.' Marisha's mind leapt to Golgolin. 'I'd be curious to know whether she still has it or whether she left it to her successor.'

'And you can't just ask Baba Serafima?'

'My dear, Serafima disappeared over twenty years ago. No, I cannot just *ask* her. Didn't you know? How did you think the succession happened?'

'I thought . . . Baba Zima said her mistress passed her bolshina to her, that it was time.'

'Certainly, but there was more to it than that, I'd bet my fastest hellhorse on it. Now. Do you wish for my help?'

Marisha was not sure she did, but she felt reckless. 'What kind of feather was it?' If he really referred to one of Golgolin's, she would deny everything. How many kolduni knew the creature existed?

'It's black, almost as long as my forearm but thin enough to slip up a sleeve. It feels and looks as though it were made of steel.'

Marisha breathed a sigh of relief. Definitely not Golgolin. Still, the thought of black feathers unsettled her. 'I've never seen anything like it.'

'Are you answering honestly?'

'Yes.'

Pan Volya looked at her for another moment and pulled up his sleeve. 'If Baba Zima had possessed the feather, she would have this mark on her wrist.'

On the inside of his wrist were two raised interconnected whorls. Marisha barely stifled her gasp.

'I've never seen that before,' Marisha lied.

She had seen the scar before, countless times, on her father's wrist. He always told tales of a beast with strange teeth or an unfortunate encounter with a fishhook to explain its origin, but Marisha had known he was lying, even when she was younger. Except for when he had told her: *Don't bargain with kolduni. You never know what you might be agreeing to.*

And ever since Olena had mentioned that handling certain magical objects could leave a mark, Marisha knew that her father's scar must have been produced by such an object. And now she knew which one. Even though Pan Volya could perhaps shed some light on what her father had done, her instincts told her not to trust him.

He stared at her a long moment and Marisha hoped he could not see what she thought. She said, truthfully, 'Baba Zima has no mark on her wrist like this, I'm sure of it.'

The koldun nodded. Marisha's breathing calmed. She had kept her father's secret. How was it possible that he had possessed the feather that this koldun was looking for? And did he still have it? Marisha wracked her mind, but she had genuinely never seen a feather like that. Why would her father have had it? And how was he linked to this koldun?

'Sir, why do you want this feather so badly? What does it do?'

'I believe it's something that might help contain the plague... It could help find the cure, you want that, do you not?'

Marisha nodded.

'Are you sure you have not seen this mark?'

'I told you, Baba Zima does *not* have that on her wrist. I've seen both, and I would have noticed.'

Pan Volya pursed his lips. 'I suppose you have no reason to lie. Now, what can I do to help you?'

Even though she hungered to know more about what the whorled scar could mean for her father, she sensed it would be dangerous to prod Pan Volya further. So she said, honestly, 'I want to sleep. Without dreaming.'

'I can mix you a potion for dreamless sleep. It is easy enough to do. But dreams are powerful things. Suppressing them is a cheap fix, to truly be rid of them you must confront whatever it is that's tormenting you.'

'I can't. I just want to sleep. I can barely even think...'

'I noticed.'

She bit back a sharp reply and inclined her head in her best image of meekness. He agreed to meet her later and hand over the potion. Marisha was only too glad to get away from the strange koldun.

Finally, she could let in the thoughts she had pushed back as soon as she had seen Pan Volya's wrist. How many times had Marisha traced the pattern of raised skin on her father's wrist when he held her on his lap? How many times had he diverted her questions of what the marks were with fanciful stories about beasts with strangely shaped teeth?

Don't bargain with kolduni. Could Pan Volya be the koldun her father had bargained with? She should have tried harder to get the information out of him. But she could not get away fast enough. There was something eerie and slimy about Pan Volya, but she couldn't pin a finger on it. What's worse, she couldn't shake the feeling that Pan Volya was familiar to her. She definitely did not like the idea that her father had anything to do with him.

If only she could sleep. She longed for the feeling of bright-eyed clarity, the banishment of her headache and nausea, thoughts snapping into place instead of coming together piecemeal like shards. She did not want to trust the man, but she did want to sleep.

It was not too late to ask Olena for help. Surely she could fix a sleeping potion as easily as this strange koldun could. But asking Olena seemed like such an insurmountable task. Worse than taking a chance with whatever Pan Volya gave her. So, she decided to keep her meeting with the koldun and fought against the idea that her pride might prove to be costly, but like a fly attracted to a peach on a hot summer's day, it kept coming back.

TWENTY-ONE

pot anything of interest?'

At that voice, Olena looked around quickly to make sure that she was alone, even though she knew that Dunya had called Valdim and Anka-ny over to point out something at the next booth. She faced Anatoli, putting on an air of self-assuredness, though she was far from at ease. Even though she knew Baba Zima was not nearby, she was still worried that somehow she would find out.

'Some,' Olena said. 'There was a not-clockwork mouse that was most impressive. And a few other things here and there.'

Anatoli stood before her now and gave her a polite bow. 'Nothing you couldn't replicate, I'm sure.'

Olena thought about the broken pen and pretended a small smile of self-satisfaction.

Anatoli said, 'You wrote that you wanted to talk.'

'Yes,' Olena said, 'I have some questions.'

'How coincidental,' Anatoli said, 'I have some questions of my own.'

'Ah,' Olena tried to appear nonchalant though she was still on her guard.

'Shall we go somewhere where there are fewer ears?'

Olena glanced back towards Dunya, Anka-ny, and Valdim.

Surely, she could simply explain she lost them in the crowd. It was the end of the day, twilight was descending onto the clearing, announcing that the fair would soon come to a close. She would say she thought it was easier to meet them back at the house. Baba Zima would believe that–it was the practical thing to do.

But she still hesitated. It was one thing to ask to talk to Anatoli, it was another to sneak off with him somewhere. And asking him information about something because she did not think that Baba Zima knew about it seemed like the worst kind of betrayal. But Olena thought again of Baba Zima's reticence to tell her about Baba Serafima's work on the shield spell. Didn't that also constitute as a betrayal? And more important than all of that was the plague cure. Didn't that goal supersede a decades-long rivalry?

'Let's go,' Olena said, more authoritatively than she felt.

A sound of broken glass followed by a large whooshing noise, like wind blowing a window open, brushed through the crowd. Olena swivelled her head, following the direction of the noise and the murmur that travelled through the gathered kolduni. Their heads turned towards the Marazovla bonfire.

It was larger than it had been in previous years. Before, the bonfire had been confined to the centre of the clearing, still allowing the kolduni to get close to it with ease, whether to warm their hands, or throw in Marazovla dolls of their own to burn for the coming new year. But now, the fire spurted up, so high that Olena was worried the branches of the surrounding pines would smoulder. For a moment, a hush fell over the crowd, and then an inexorable push started towards the fire, as though it had grown a link to each and every one and reeled them in. And with that came the new murmur of concern and curiosity. Olena let herself be carried by the crowd.

'Olena!' Dunya waved at her frantically from the side. Olena wondered for a moment if she should ignore the cry, but excused herself from Anatoli and elbowed her way through to the girl. Dunya continued to wave, while Anka-ny stood next to Valdim, who was slumped over against a tree, his hands clutching his head. What little she could see of his face was grey, and his chest moved up and down with deep breaths.

'What happened?' Olena barked.

'I don't know,' Anka-ny said. 'He was fine and then people started shouting and he became all white and trembling and said he needed a moment. Then the fire started like that.' Anka-ny nodded towards the fire. Olena crouched. 'I'm all right,' Valdim murmured. He took in a deep breath and got to his feet. 'It's fine.' Olena stood up as well. He said, 'You should go see what's happening.' He still seemed pale, but not in any immediate danger.

'Get him back to the house,' Olena said to the two assistants, and she watched them go, half-leading, half-tugging him along. For a moment she thought that she should go with them and make sure that they made it safely back to the house. What if Valdim was in worse condition than she thought?

They'll be fine, Olena told herself forcefully, and she rejoined the mass of kolduni ringing around the bonfire and pushed her way through. When they looked back in annoyance and saw her face, they made room. It certainly paid to have a reputation sometimes. Then there were no more kolduni in front of her and she wished she had a shield of humanity to protect her from the heat of the fire. The flames crackled and the bonfire was so large it seemed brighter than the rising moon in the twilit sky. Olena noticed that the flames' incredible growth extended upwards and not outwards, which gave the kolduni more room to ring around close and watch. *Clever,* Olena thought to herself. *I see she kept some tricks back for herself.*

That was when the figure materialised. Someone shouted and pointed up into the treetops. Olena craned her neck to see her. The Hands carried her in a sort of hammock, which meant that the house was nearby–the Hands' tether to the house did not extend very far. Baba Zima sat back imperiously as though the audience were not there. She had mirror powder scattered on her dress to make her shimmer and had painted her face to make herself look like a Marazovla doll. The doll, which normally ended the evening as kindling, would walk out of the fire, unburnt. Now wasn't that a blunt, unsubtle and powerful message. Olena shook her head. It was entrancing. Even she, who knew how this display would end, could not look away. Then the Hands, staying well away above the fire themselves, lowered the rope so that the hammock settled itself into the fire. The rope must have been coated with the fire-resistant salve for it did not burn either. Already there were cries that she would fall. The more experienced kolduni simply stood back and watched, the jealousy and resignation to the spectacle etched all the deeper on their faces by the flames' shadows.

'Well, well,' Anatoli said from beside her. She had not even noticed that he had regained her side, so focused she was on her mistress. Anatoli gave Olena a conspiratory wink. 'Still as dramatic as always. Good to know some things don't change.'

Olena felt the corners of her lips go up, though she quickly suppressed the smile. She turned her focus back on her mistress. Baba Zima lowered herself from the hammock into the fire. The crowd's twitters became shouts. Baba Zima still hung on. Olena did not think that she could stand in the fire, no matter how much salve she had put on. She supposed that Baba Zima was wearing her boots with iron soles, the ones that were so thick that they could not melt, except by the breath of the firebird. Or at least that's what her matrionka said.

Baba Zima held her arms up and twirled. The crowd's murmurs and fears turned to whistles and claps. She heard the crowd surge with whispers of 'It's Baba Zima' and 'How did she do it?' and 'She can't last for much longer.' Indeed, Baba Zima's skin was shining with sweat and Olena was certain that the fire, though it did not burn her, was hot enough to be causing her excruciating pain. She must get out now. Olena tapped her foot. Should she go after her mistress?

Baba Zima made a movement with her hand and the Hands looked like they would carry her out of the fire. Then the fire roared and a lick of flame reached up so high that it threatened the Hands. Baba Zima reached her own hand up in instinct and the Hand let go of the rope. Olena lurched forward, but Anatoli blocked her way. Baba Zima let out a cry that could still be heard over the roar of the flames. She landed in the mound of burning logs. Olena whipped around Anatoli and rushed forward. The flames reached far over her head and sent out a wall of heat that physically repulsed Olena. She looked inside the fire, blinking her eyes rapidly against the smoke. But Baba Zima was steady on her feet. Her iron shoes held. Olena sighed in relief. Baba Zima stood still for a moment, cocking her head as though listening to something, then took a step toward the edge of the fire. The fire surged again, a wall of flames keeping Baba Zima in. What was happening?

'Are you doing this?' Olena shouted back to Anatoli.

'Me?' He said, looking shocked. 'How could I be doing anything? I'm right here.'

Olena narrowed her eyes at him and scanned the other kolduni. Did they still think that this was part of the demonstration? How could she have worked so hard on an incantation to clear smoke from the lungs without thinking about how to calm a fire?

Baba Zima's eyes were wide and she held out her hands as though to shield herself from something. Olena almost thought she saw the shape of a hand in the fire. Olena yelled out for her mistress and finally made eye contact. Then Baba Zima looked past her and stepped out of the fire. She stood on the edge of the bonfire for a moment. Smoke pouring from her clothing, but they were only singed. The crowd quieted. Stillness hung in the air for a moment then the Hands returned with the hammock and Baba Zima stepped back in and lifted up again. The clapping started quiet but then they were shouting and cheering. Baba Zima smiled and gave a little bow from her hammock. She was all poise again.

Olena wondered if anyone else had noticed the fiery hand that had reached for her mistress and the terror in her gaze. Olena glanced to her side. Anatoli slipped away through the crowd of kolduni. He walked deliberately but slowly, as though to give her enough time to see him and decide. Olena hesitated only a second longer. She followed him, though a voice at the back of her head said that Baba Zima would not approve. But Olena needed answers and Baba Zima was not providing them. And right now, Baba Zima would need time to recover from the exertion of her demonstration. It was now, or never.

TWENTY-TWO

he bright moonlight made Marisha's shadow grow until it was swallowed by the trees on the edge of the clearing. Her hand in her pocket wrapped around the small vial the koldun with the cold eyes had handed to her minutes before. Pan Volya, who had the same whorled scar on his wrist that her father did. Marisha had asked that they meet near the tent covered with tiny mirrors, where other kolduni were nearby. Sleeping potion in hand, she heard giggling and ran into Dunya and Anka-ny who were walking in the opposite direction along the path.

'Oh, hello, where are you off to?' Marisha asked quickly, hoping to forestall any questions of their own. She was glad the Pan Volya's sleeping potion was safely in her pocket.

'Oh,' Dunya and Anka-ny shared a guilty look. Dunya said, 'There's some people gathering at the bonfire.' Marisha spied the crude Marazovla doll made out of wood and yarn dangling from Dunya's hand. She would throw the doll into the fire and whatever sins of the past year and wishes for a better one would go to the spirits in the other world. Marisha thought of how she had gathered around Marazovla bonfires at the preparatory, laughing and drinking lingonberry wine with her friends. Marisha hadn't made any dolls of her own, but she had enjoyed the silly conversations and the atmosphere of merriment. She wondered what sins and wishes Dunya had gathered for herself to cast away. Anka-ny wasn't holding a doll. Did she not want to participate in the practice or was she perhaps waiting for a more private moment?

'Do you want to come?' Dunya asked. And Marisha sensed it was an actual invitation rather than mere politeness.

Marisha was surprised to find that part of her wished she could accept the invitation. 'Thanks, but I'm tired, I'm heading back to the house. Have fun.' She flashed the pair a smile and their giggles faded into the darkness.

Marisha did not want to meet any more people on her way back, so she swung off the path into the trees. The moon was full and high and it was easy to find the stream that led back to the house. She followed the edge of water, when she heard voices.

'I will not do something like that behind her back. I simply will not.'

Marisha raised her head. A woman had stormed out of the trees, and her voice, the way she held herself, reminded her an awful lot of Olena. And the person following—

'So, you always tell her everything you do?' The voice was deep, male. Marisha dared to look up more. It was not Valdim, but she recognised the voice. Marisha let out a small gasp. What was Olena doing with Anatoli?

Marisha longed to take a few steps closer, but she knew if Olena saw her, she would be finished. Her whole body thrummed with nervous energy. She was perfectly positioned behind a small stand of birch trees. Her back cramped from her bent over position and she leaned back against the trees to ease it a little.

Olena said, 'Of course I don't tell her everything, but this would be different.'

'Olena, what is more important here–a twenty-year-old rivalry? Or the chance to cure the plague forever?'

Olena shook her head. 'Why me?' she asked. 'Is it simply because I'm convenient?' She walked away from him with quick steps. Marisha silently congratulated her for not being taken in by his noble-sounding platitudes.

'Olena.' Anatoli's voice was rich with amusement, he caught up with her easily. They both stood still. 'If I wanted someone convenient, I would have asked one of her many simple assistants.'

'They do not have the access I do. You could only ask me.'

'Oh, I'm sure I could have found another way.' Marisha craned her neck to gaze through the gap in the branches. The moon's harsh light accentuated Anatoli's calculating look. Olena must have seen it.

'I'll think about it,' Olena said and started walking back to the clearing with fast steps, towards Marisha's hiding place.

Anatoli caught up with her again and said, 'How much time do you really have to think about it? When the plague has arrived and it's too late?' Marisha held her breath. Now that they were closer, could see Olena's frown of indecision much more clearly.

Olena asked, 'What really happened at the bonfire with Baba Zima's demonstration?'

Marisha had no idea what she was talking about. Baba Zima had returned jubilant from the demonstration, proclaiming its success. She had darted around the house from room to room like a clockwork hummingbird, unable to stay still in the aftermath of her triumph, until she slowed and stopped before the oven. Marisha had noticed that she had stood in front of the oven for a long time without moving, looking but not seeing. She had then flown about the receiving room in a frantic way, opening and closing drawers, saying that she absolutely must have the right broach to wear at the banquet, anything else simply would not do. Marisha had assumed her frenzy was from euphoria, but maybe it was not.

Anatoli said, 'I already told you. I had nothing to do with it. I did not know what Zima was planning. No, when kolduni gather, strange things happen. And on the eve of the Marazovla, the threshold between the earth and the other world is thin. With so many kolduni in one place, the spirits are attracted. They must have felt her power and sought to commune with her.'

Olena did not look at him. She crossed her arms. Anatoli added lightly, 'Besides, I would not ruin my chances to collaborate with you by threatening her.'

Olena sniffed. 'That I do believe. But I don't know that you'd be able to resist. Especially if you thought you could get away with it. I, for one, don't underestimate you.'

'I'm grateful for it. And I hope your regard is high enough to see that I would not jeopardise an opportunity to find a plague cure with petty revenge, as much as I might enjoy it.' He paused and Olena inclined her head towards him but remained silent.

'Oh come now,' Anatoli said, 'Can we let a feud between your mistress and myself be something that is separate from us working together? I'd be happy to mend things, but Zima—' Anatoli shrugged, 'I hope you can see that I don't want to involve you in this petty fight. I tried to come to Zima first, but she wouldn't hear me. And I'm finding that you are much more reasonable. You actually want to bring the cure to people. I find that deeply admirable.'

Olena said, 'She doesn't hold grudges without reason.'

Anatoli said, 'But to hold onto grudges to the detriment of others? Again, I do not wish to discuss my relationship with your mistress with you, that's not what this is about. I know you think I'm only approaching you to get at what I want. But know this: I'm approaching you because I know *you* want what *I* want. And you may see past your mistress's prejudices to work with me, which is the only way we'll be successful. I cannot do this without you, Olena.' He paused. 'Think about it. I'll send you letters telling you about my progress. I hope you will do the same.'

She did not answer. He put his hands in his pockets. 'Zima has been a good mistress to you, I can see that. But there comes a point in every koldun's journey where one must decide—what do I need? What do I want? And what am I willing to do to get it? There is no shame in outgrowing one's teacher, it is a natural part of the process. And if Zima is making you feel like you're being disloyal when you're growing into your power, if she's making you feel stifled, well–maybe you need to decide what kind of mark you wish to make on the world, and who you need to help you get there.' He stepped in close to Olena. 'You have great potential, Olena. I hope you will think on what I said, and consider what is really important here, for your future, and for Chernozemlya's.'

Olena's mouth was set resolutely. *What had he asked her to do?* Marisha willed them to talk about it but they both stayed silent. Finally, Anatoli turned and left.

Olena swayed a little. Marisha didn't move.

'Are you just going to stand there all night?'

Marisha jumped. She fixed her eye on a space between the slim tree trunks. The angry voice came from a figure standing a bit to the side of the clearing, arms folded at his chest, feet spread apart, facing Olena square on.

Olena groaned loudly. 'Valdim. Why are you here?' She stomped towards him, partially blocking Marisha's view of him.

'Are you spying on me?' she added.

'I was taking a walk. And I don't need to spy on you, Olena. Not when you conspire with Anatoli for the whole world to see.'

Olena took in a sharp breath. *Oh, she's going to let him have it.* Marisha almost felt sorry for Valdim. But he did not stand down.

Olena walked right up to him. 'The whole world? What, in this wood? You're the only one here, you ass.'

His mouth became a thin line. 'Olena–how could you? With him?' He made no effort to hide his disgust. 'After everything my mother has done for you? Olena, he's obviously using you to get to her!'

'Shut up! You have no idea what you're talking about.' She drew her head close to his so their foreheads almost touched. 'Don't stick your nose where it doesn't belong. It might get chopped off.'

'Try. See what happens.'

Olena let out a sniff of contempt and began walking away.

Valdim yelled, 'Why are you doing this? Do you really think so little of your mistress to trample all over her like graveyard dirt—'

'Don't you question my feelings!' Olena turned and walked right back up to him. 'She's much more to me than she is to you, you who only visits once a year, who never writes. You're a terrible, ungrateful son. And stop trying to interfere with my business.'

'You think because she doesn't show you my letters, I don't write? You're so self-centred! And you–I know what kind of promises you made when you became her apprentice. Not only are you fickle, you are faithless–and I won't let you do this to her.' He said the last evenly.

'So, what'll you do? Tattle on me?'

'Maybe. That depends on you. Convince me I don't need to tell her what I saw.'

'I have no intention of doing that.'

'You're giving me very little reason to trust you.'

'You think she'll believe you?'

'I think she would. She may love you more than me. But we're still blood.' He could not keep the bitterness out of his voice.

'So, you're blackmailing me.'

'I suppose I am.' His voice was uncertain.

'Ha! And you said you wanted to try being friends.'

'And I did. I do!' Then he said with quiet conviction, 'Olena, he's using you. You have no reason to trust him, he's not a good person.'

'Why do you believe he's so terrible? Do you have any evidence at all?'

He opened his mouth, then closed it. His gaze shifted and he tugged at his coat sleeve.

She asked, 'Do you know something?' He turned away. She pressed him. 'If you know something you have to tell me.'

'I don't owe you anything.'

Valdim turned to the side as though to let her pass by, but Olena squared her body towards him. 'Fine, don't tell me. I bet it's nothing. You have nothing.'

'Then leave.'

'Why the sudden reticence? You were so eager to convince me of his bad character, why stop now?' Something layered her voice besides curiosity. Fear. She must not have been so sure of her plan to work with Anatoli if she believed that Valdim could know something bad about him.

'You'll laugh at me.'

That was unexpected. Now Marisha was more curious than

ever. She was glad for Olena's reasonable tone. 'I won't laugh at you. I promise. Just tell me what it is.'

Valdim did not say anything for a while. Marisha counted one breath. Then two. 'His colours are all wrong.' He said it so softly Marisha barely heard him.

'What? I'm sorry. His . . . colours?'

'Yes, his colours.'

'You'll have to be more specific than that. I don't follow.'

He brushed a hand through his hair. 'When I see people, talk to them, I see colours. It's hard to explain.'

'You see colours.'

'Yes.'

'Is this similar to how you can't stand eating soup because of the spoon's sound?'

Valdim let out a small huff. 'Yes, and no need to sound so sceptical. It causes me actual pain. I don't know why you never did believe me, I really do feel sounds on my skin.'

'Of course I believe you,' Olena said, but her voice had the soothing tone one uses when talking to a small child. He cocked his head. She said, 'Sorry, it just always sounded to me like you were trying to get out of your chores.' He shot her a furious look.

'So,' Olena prompted, 'You see colours.'

'Yes.'

'And? I'm sorry but I'm having trouble understanding what you mean. Do people's skin look different shades?'

'No. It's more like . . . I see colours around a person. They flicker out of them. Like . . . the way the sun does when it's behind a cloud.'

'Ah. I see. What do you see with Baba Zima?'

'Dark purple,' Valdim said, looking past Olena, 'With red at the edges, flickering red, like a burning coal.'

'Sounds pretty,' she conceded. 'And you see these colours with everyone?'

'Yes.'

'Does Baba Zima know?'

'Yes. She thinks the spirits are being extra communicative with me. So, it was even more disappointing when it turned out I had no koldunic inclinations.' He smiled, bitterly. 'She used to ask me to be in the receiving room with her and tell her what colours the supplicants had. She said it was very helpful. At that time, I didn't realise seeing those colours was different.'

'Can you see your own colours?'

'Yes. I'm dark brown, slate blue, and white. All woven together, rippling.'

'Hmm.' Olena paused. Her chin tilted to the side. 'And so, what do you see for Anatoli?'

'His colours are strange. He has this beige layer, it's soft and fluffy, but spikes of orange and black poke out. Sometimes that's all there is.' Valdim shuddered. 'They're just . . . *wrong*.'

The back of Marisha's neck prickled. What did that remind her of? Then Olena talked again, and Marisha concentrated on her voice.

'These are impressions. Your impressions. They don't actually have anything to do with what a person is like.'

Valdim shook his head. 'No, they're more than just impressions. They're the colours of people's souls.'

'Really? What are my colours?' Olena had her good hand on her hip, lips pursed, and looked at Valdim defiantly.

He took a step closer. 'Green,' he said, locking her gaze. 'But not a bright green. A sage green, maybe. And at the edges, gold, almost like dripping beads. It covers you sometimes.'

Olena looked like Valdim had punched her in the stomach,

her mouth hanging open, her eyes wide and unblinking, her body frozen in mid-hunch.

'Complete and utter horse shit,' she spat out, and walked quickly. Olena would surely never own up to it, but if asked, Marisha would have said she ran away.

TWENTY-THREE

arisha hurried back to the house. She could not believe what she had witnessed. What could Anatoli have wanted from Olena? It wasn't Kiril. Surely Anatoli could procure a deep sleeper to experiment on if he really wanted to. But he did want something. The covetousness in Anatoli's voice reminded her of the glint in Pan Volya's eyes. Could Anatoli's request for help with the plague cure have anything to do with the feather that Pan Volya wanted?

For a moment she saw Valdim and Olena's silhouettes again, squared off against each other. Marisha thought of Valdim's request that she keep an eye out for Olena corresponding with Anatoli. She had thought that Valdim had been concerned about Baba Zima, but perhaps he was concerned for Olena instead.

And Valdim's confession about seeing colours–Marisha was not surprised he kept quiet about that. It was the kind of thing that could send whispers rippling around a person. Marisha wondered at Olena's extreme reaction to Valdim's description of her colours. To send her reeling like that–it must have meant something important to her.

Marisha's feet took her to the linen closet. She had thought that it may be a good place to perform the spell as Kiril's presence was usually a calming one. But she hesitated in the doorway. She was not sure if she should still go through with it after the evening's excitement. But Baba Zima was attending the banquet with the assistants, and surely Olena had snuck in there by now. Who knew when she would next get a moment alone?

She leaned against the doorframe, watching Kiril sleep. Olena's attempts at waking him with her tinctures had not been without effect. His hand twitched frequently now and his brow wrinkled as he dreamed. What did Kiril dream of? Was he as tormented as she was? She truly hoped not. To be trapped in one's dreams . . . a terrible sense of foreboding gripped her. She turned from the linen closet and went to the laundry room instead, all the while feeling like she was behaving in a very cowardly manner.

Pan Volya had said the spell was quite simple, she hoped he was right. She dug the vial from her pocket, dropped it onto the table, smoothed out the piece of paper with the incantation and read the instructions. She would light the circle of candles, add a few drops of whatever the bottle contained to water in a basin, say the incantation, and poof, her bad dreams would be banished.

Marisha unstoppered the bottle, her fingers trembling from nerves and excitement at trying out her first bit of koldunry. The drops dissolved one by one into the basin, turning the water cloudy and clear again. She took a deep breath and tried to mirror the way Baba Zima looked when she performed a spell: calm, far-seeing and confident. The words tripped on her tongue, but she made it through in the end. Marisha dropped the paper and looked into the basin. Pan Volya had said the water would show whether or not the spell had worked. But she only saw water. She leaned closer, her nose almost touching the surface. Her breath made ripples on the water, distorting her reflection into the swish of a red-and-yellow embroidered skirt.

Marisha sprung back from the basin, heart pounding, and knocked over one of the candles. She blew it out and blew out all the other ones for good measure. Her heart raced and she had a stitch in her side as though she had run from some awful danger. A door slam brought her to her senses. She hurried into the hallway.

'Who's there?' Baba Zima called. 'Olena? Confound the girl. If I did not know any better—' She stopped talking when she saw Marisha. 'What are you doing here? Where's Olena?'

'Oh, um.' Marisha thought for a moment. She could not tell Baba Zima where she had seen Olena, it felt wrong. 'Isn't the banquet still going on?' Marisha said, stalling for time.

'I felt a touch of indigestion,' Baba Zima said, wiggling her fingers. 'Now, where is Olena?'

At that moment Olena appeared in the hall behind Baba Zima. She froze.

'There you are,' Baba Zima said, turning around. 'Why weren't you at the banquet? Where were you?'

'I was working,' Olena said.

'Liar. Your workroom was empty. Now, where were you really?' Baba Zima looked angry. Marisha had never seen her look truly angry before, not at Olena. And Olena's mouth was open and her eyes wide, like a rabbit caught far from its den. Maybe that was why Marisha said what she said next.

'Olena was helping me.'

Both women turned to look at her, their expressions matching in disbelief.

'What?' Baba Zima said.

'I–I traded some linden sap for a spell, but I couldn't get it to work,' Marisha babbled. Damp dark earth, it was almost the truth.

'And you bought a spell, even though I had expressly said you wouldn't be allowed to practice koldunry for the first year of your contract?' Marisha bowed her head. She had forgotten. Her face grew hot. Baba Zima turned to Olena, 'And you were helping her?'

'I was going to perform the spell for her,' Olena said, her expression masterfully contrite.

'Not what it sounds like,' Baba Zima said. Her features finally relaxed, as though catching them in a transgression made their story more plausible. 'I'm disappointed you would encourage subterfuge.'

Olena shrugged. 'Better than letting her poison herself.'

'She may have learned a lesson if she were poisoned.' Baba Zima fixed her gaze on Marisha, who did her best to hunch her shoulders. 'I will dock you a week's pay and put you on laundry for the next month since you like being in the laundry room so much.'

Marisha suppressed a sigh. She told herself it could have been much worse.

'And as for you,' Baba Zima said to Olena, 'you will teach Marisha the spiritual arts.'

'But—'

'And I will test her. If she does not do well, I'll assume it's your fault.' Baba Zima swept out of the room, the Hands floating behind her.

Olena looked at Marisha, her eyes slitted. Marisha looked at the door. Tears stung her eyelids. She had put herself on the line for Olena and would not be thanked for it. Instead, she got punished, and even worse, she could not get the spell to work. Her nightmares. She would never escape them.

'Why did you do it?' Olena asked, her voice clipped. 'Did you want Baba Zima to force me to teach you sorcery?'

'Sure, that was my evil plan all along. I forgot to tell you, but I can read minds and see the future, so I knew exactly what Baba Zima would do from the very beginning.'

'Don't be impertinent with me. Did you think I would feel bound to owe you a favour?'

Marisha felt woozy all of a sudden. She realised this was the longest conversation she had had with Olena in almost a month. She thought she should want to yell at Olena for being so ungrateful, but she felt too crumpled to care. Like a dry leaf. Marisha tried to remember what it was like to feel peaceful. Rested. She thought for a moment of running to the cherry trees at the beginning of spring. The thin spring sun working hard to warm her face, the bark rough and cool under her hands, the cherries tart and delicious. That's what she wanted.

Marisha said, 'No. I don't want anything from you.' Her voice sounded tired even to herself. 'I don't know why I did it. You gave me no reason to.'

TWENTY-FOUR

Marisha stood in complete darkness. Last thing she remembered was the circle of candles, the ritual–panic rose up to choke her. Oh, damp dark earth, she had tried the spell a second time after leaving Olena in the laundry room. And now–she spun, looking wildly around her. She did not see anything, the darkness pressed from all sides. Marisha crouched on her heels and hugged her head. *Please don't let this be my dream.* After long moments her shallow breaths lengthened. She peeked out from behind her arms. It was still dark, but she saw something.

It was a spiral staircase, but it had no railing, it simply rose straight up from the ground and spiralled tightly around a column of air. She straightened, relief showering over her like snow from a trembling pine branch. She was dreaming, but it wasn't *that* dream.

She slapped herself. Her cheek stung, but still the staircase loomed ahead. Pinching got the same result. If nothing else, she could climb the staircase and throw herself off the edge, that would surely wake her up. But her stomach twisted at the idea. She bent down and touched the stair. The stone was rough and cold. So real.

Climbing a staircase that spiralled into pitch darkness without even the meagre protection of a railing was unnerving to say the least. She confirmed the existence of each successive tread with her toes before transferring her whole body to it. Not that she would die from a fall, since she was dreaming, but the sensation of both her mind and body teetering accompanied Marisha with every step. Finally, the absence of the next stair tread made her stumble. The staircase opened onto a wooden platform knotted over with vines. It was just a dream, she reminded herself as she leaned against the railing to catch her breath. But when she plucked a leaf off the vine coiling around the railing, it made the soft snap that green leaves make when they do not want to leave their stem. The place had a musty mildewy smell, like a room that had been unopened all winter. *Like the sanitorium*, Marisha could not help thinking to herself. Her shoulders tensed.

Marisha picked her way through the vines carefully. The wooden platform floor was rotten in places. Marisha swept her head from side to side and up and around, listening intently. Her heart beat very fast. Every creak made her body tense up more until she felt like her neck had retracted into her shoulders. Someone else was there, she could feel it.

She thought she heard something else underneath the creaking. It was very faint, but as she listened, she was sure–the faraway careening of a balalaika. The wind whistled and washed out the music. Marisha hoped she had imagined it, but when the wind died down, there it was again. Faint and plucky. Her chest constricted with terror.

'No!' she shouted out loud. The word cut into the dark space, much louder and harsher than the wind and the creaking of the platform.

'Who's there?'

The voice came from the middle of the platform, a few feet

away, where a huge hole gaped in the floor and a tree grew through it. A cherry tree, Marisha realised. It had no leaves, but the gnarl and twist of the branches were unmistakable. And the person who called out to her sat on one of the branches. Marisha stepped forward faster. She did not pay attention to the rotten floorboards, and her feet did not tear through anything.

It was Dima. Of all the people she had expected to see, her brother was the last of them. She felt shame at her surprise. For a moment, she had thought it was her father. She felt anxious–because she had not expected to see Dima here, she told herself.

Marisha did not think, she leapt. She landed nimbly and pulled herself across the shaky branch to her brother. He twisted around, his mouth open in surprise. Marisha braced herself against another branch so she could sit astride her perch. The rough bark bit her skin through her skirt.

'Hello, Dima,' she said, suddenly shy.

'Who are you? You're not one of them. No, your face–but you still could be, in disguise.' He scrambled further back on his branch.

'Dima, it's me, Marisha.'

'Maryonushka, what are you doing here?' She was surprised by how easily he accepted who she was. 'I didn't think they would try to get you too.'

'What are you talking about? Who's trying to get you?'

'Never mind. We'll hide here for now.' He looked proud of himself. 'They didn't see me get away.'

Marisha felt a confusing mix of love and guilt rise through her. 'Dima, where are you? I mean, when you're awake.'

Her brother frowned in confusion. 'Where is this place?' she asked when he did not answer. 'Have you been here before?'

'Oh yes. Many times.'

Marisha patted the branch, trying to get a better hold. 'Hey, this is one of the trees we used to climb as kids. When we hid from Pan Kazan.' Their tutor. Marisha couldn't draw straight lines and Dima had been a slow reader; they both hated geometry and hid whenever they had the chance. Looking back on it now, she knew they had been miserable children to teach.

'You're right,' Dima said, smiling as though he had recognised the tree as well. 'You're much older though.'

'So are you.'

'Yes, I guess I am.' His eyebrows rose. 'Are you all right? You look a little sick.'

Marisha slumped. She took a closer look at Dima. He too had signs of strain: lines around his mouth where there used to be none, white threads in his light brown hair. He was only twenty-four years old, he shouldn't have any. The usual laugh lines around his eyes looked deeper, like worry lines. She wondered if they were real or a reflection of how he saw himself.

'Dima, do you remember that scar Papa had on his wrist?'

'Sure.'

'Do you know where it came from?'

'Papa said something about upsetting a leshi.' He smiled. His face looked so different when he smiled. 'But I doubt that was it.'

She smiled in return and said, 'Nothing about a koldun? Or a feather?'

'No. Lots of other stories. Remember how he could make a coin appear from between your toes?'

'Yes.' Marisha struggled to keep her smile from slipping. It was painful to remember. Their father would tickle her and eventually let her pull the coin from between his fingers. It had been magic to her.

'Dima,' she started carefully. She was not sure how to broach the subject. Marisha was not even sure she was truly talking to her brother. But she had to ask. She did not remember if the letter had been in her pocket before, but she pulled it out now. 'Do you remember sending this to me?'

She showed it to Dima. He grabbed a corner, but she did not let him take it from her. He scanned the first lines and snatched his hand back, shooting her a look of mingled accusation and hurt, as though the paper had been woven from nettles and she had known it.

'Why did you send this?' she asked. 'Why didn't you come to me in person? Did you really leave to rebuild our fortune after the mine collapsed? Or did you give up?' She did not mean to raise her voice.

'I'm sorry,' he said. 'I was ashamed.'

'Ashamed? Of what, of our parents? Why didn't you at least tell me where you went?'

'I didn't want you to know.' Dima spoke to his knees instead of her.

'But why?' Marisha wanted to shake him.

'I wanted you to think well of me. To at least remember me well.'

Dread rolled over Marisha. 'What did you do?'

His shoulders slumped even further. 'It was not the mine collapse that ruined us.'

She gripped the branch so tightly the bark cut into her hands. 'What do you mean? What happened?'

'I–I have a little problem. After I gained my majority and took charge of the mine, I felt bold without Papa or Dyadya Vanya and I had such rich friends. They did what they wanted! They said the plague could end us, so why wait until we were old to spend the money? They didn't care and I didn't want to care either.'

'Boys from school?' Marisha asked evenly, trying not to let her anger show. There had been similar girls at her preparatory, girls who inspired envy and cultivated followings. Girls who were mean to those who did not have as much as them. And Marisha had known she could never aspire to be in their circle, not that she wanted to. But it seemed like her brother had not thought the same.

'No. I met them after. Spending the money . . . I know it sounds stupid now, but it made me feel invincible, like I needn't be afraid . . . The fortune seemed endless and the plague was only a few years away. And the mine collapsed . . . I can't believe it dried up so fast.'

Their father had not been born a boyar, he had made his fortune on his own. In fact, it was only because he showed such incredible and rapid success at such a young age that Marisha's grandfather consented for her parents to marry. Even so, it had been quite the scandal. But despite all the care Dima had seen their father put into building his business, he had liquidated it in only three years. Marisha gripped the bark harder to stop herself from shoving Dima out of the tree.

'How could you do something like that?'

This was her big brother, the one who had shielded her from her aunt's accusations that her birth had made their mother weaker and more susceptible to the plague, the one who had taken the blame when they were caught stealing sweets from the kitchen, the one who she had clung to after their father had fallen asleep to the plague. He had said she could count on him. She had believed him.

He shook and hugged his knees closer. Was he crying? He had no right to cry when he had abandoned her and run away. Marisha remembered her aunt and uncle's pity mixed with revulsion when they took her in. She had thought it was due to their fear of her drawing the evil eye with her fate to be victim of the ensuing plague, but maybe it was also because of what Dima had done.

'So, you spent so much of Papa's money that we were ruined when the mine collapsed. And you ran away? Where are you now?'

'It's worse. You're mad at me, but I haven't even told you the worst part. I racked up debt. Horrible debt. I fell in love and she—' he looked down '—she loved beautiful things. I wanted to make her happy and show her parents I was the kind of husband they wanted for their daughter. And my so-called friends–once they knew I had nothing left, they acted as if they didn't know me.' His face twisted in bitterness. 'I was in Severny, all alone, the house was gone, and it still wasn't enough. The only thing left was the fund for our parents, and you. And I may have sunk low, but I would have died before I let the creditors take our parents' beds in the sanitorium or throw you out of preparatory school.' He smiled. 'I think I left you enough for one or two courting seasons.'

Marisha did not want to let him know it would have almost been enough, except no one had wanted her with two plague-struck parents.

'What did you do?' she whispered.

'I did the only thing I could think to do.' He pulled back his sleeve to show the red thread encircling his wrist. 'I indentured myself.'

Marisha shrunk back with horror. 'No, Dima, you didn't!'

'I did. I didn't have a choice.'

'Of course you had a choice, you could have gone to Vanya and tried to find a different way to pay off your debt. You could have even gone on that senseless voyage to the Spice Islands. You did not need to sell yourself.'

How was this situation even possible? Yes, serfdom still happened in some of the backwater places of Chernozemlya, but it was mostly abolished. And it certainly did not happen in the city; no one needed a slave when one could pay a servant a pittance for the same job without incurring a heavy tax. How did Dima even get the idea?

He smiled strangely. 'There was one bidder. And the upfront price was more than enough to cover my debts and the sanitorium care for our parents and leave a bit over for you. I had not expected to get so much.'

'Who?' Marisha said, her voice hoarse. 'Who did you indenture yourself to?'

'I can't say.'

'This is a dream, you can say anything you want.'

He shook his head. 'I can't.'

A few months ago, she would have thought her brother was being pig-headed. Now she thought someone had demanded the spirits keep his silence. He patted her hand. 'Don't worry Maryonushka, it will all be all right. In a year I'll be free, and I'll have made all the money back to boot.'

His words made the back of her neck crawl. 'How?' she said. 'You've only been indentured three years, that can't be enough to make back what you owe.'

'Well,' he looked away from her again. He seemed reluctant to tell her. 'I've agreed to something to shorten the contract.'

'What is it?' She had a horrible feeling she knew what it might be, but she hoped it was not.

'I agreed to be part of a spell that will protect my master from the plague.'

Marisha gripped his arm, her fingernails dug into his skin.

He yelped.

'You agreed to be a shield for the plague?' Her mind raced to recall what Baba Zima had told her about the spell. 'If your master is fated for the sleeping plague, it will fall on you instead? And you agreed to this?'

'It's not sure it will happen,' His eyes shone with the hope it would pass him by. 'And if it doesn't, I'll be free after only one more year, and I can face you again.'

'You're gambling with your life,' Marisha said.

'I gambled away everything else. My life was all I had left.'

She closed her eyes against the tears pooling at the lids. 'Maryonushka,' he said, putting an arm around her shoulder, 'I don't feel very attached to it. I am quite worthless. And I must try to make up for my wrongs.' He smiled, that irresistible smile that made him look both innocent and mischievous at once. 'Besides, with Mama catching the plague, and Papa afterwards, I always figured I would be the next one to fall asleep.'

'No!' Marisha shouted and gripped Dima by the shoulders. They almost fell out of the tree. 'I'm the one who's supposed to be next! Me! First the mother, then the father, then the daughter, *then* the son. I'm next, not you!'

Her heart raced. She was next. That's what her relatives had always implied with their whispers and forked fingers. And in this moment, she realised that knowing she would fall asleep this cycle, thereby giving Dima more time to live, had always been a great comfort to her.

He gave her a sad smile. 'No, Maryonushka. I'll be next. It's all I have left to give you.'

'Who's your master?' Marisha shouted. Dima shook his head. She reached over and gripped his shoulder. She did not care about falling out of the tree. 'Who is it? Tell me!'

Dima only shook his head. He looked down. 'Strange,' he said. 'There's people dancing. A festival. I do love festivals,' he said with a sigh of longing.

The spiral staircase was gone. Dancers wearing peasant costumes and masks whirled away among the enormous roots of the tree. The lilting notes of the balalaika wafted through. Terror clawed at Marisha's chest.

The tree swayed. Marisha almost fell but Dima steadied her in time. She looked down. A crowd of dancers had gathered around the tree. Some tried to climb up. One man in a green kaftan and whiskered mask knelt to give his partner a boost.

'I think they want us to come down,' Dima said, seemingly unperturbed by their change in surroundings. 'A festival.' He smiled. 'It will be fun.'

'No.' Marisha shook her head, keeping her grip on Dima's arm. 'We can't. It's not safe. Don't leave me.'

He drew her into a hug. He smelled like wind-ruffled leaves and sour cherry preserves. For a moment she felt like a little girl again, safe and calm, like everything would be all right. But that awful music.

'Dima,' she wailed, 'you promised you'd take care of me. You promised.'

But he wasn't really there. She was dreaming. She was alone.

'Don't worry,' he said, smiling in a soft way that broke her heart, 'I'll catch you.'

He let go and jumped from the tree.

Marisha screamed. She peered down, but she could not spot him among the other dancers, and leaned so far over she lost her balance. She clung to the branch, palms scraped raw by the bark, her fingertips aching, their grip weakening. And the branch slipped from her grasp.

Marisha slammed into the ground. Something grabbed her ankle in a vicelike grip, her hands scraped against dirt. The beaked man flipped her over and pinned her wrists against the ground with his talons.

Wake up! This was the point she would wake, she remembered now, but the beaked man grazed a talon down her side and it left a line of fire like a red hot poker. She screamed. Why wouldn't she wake?

She knew what came next. The beaked man slammed a talon-like hand to her throat, pinning her to the ground. She clawed at the pressure on her throat but it wouldn't budge. His eyes were deep, colourless pools. Burning. And he bent his neck impossibly far back so the beak pointed straight up into the air.

He brought his head crashing down.

Pain exploded inside her. She screamed. Through the pain she heard her breastbone crack as loudly as a tree branch breaking and she could feel his beak there, lodged below her breastbone. He pulled his head out–she saw through swimming haze that he had blood and gore dripping from his face and she had the sick realisation it was hers. He opened his beak and cawed and brought it back down.

TWENTY-FIVE

he screams continued, they were her own. She writhed but something pinned her down. She pressed her fist into her breastbone, it was there, she could breathe, but she could still feel his beak spearing through, pinning her to the floor—

'Marisha, for goodness sake, be quiet.' Someone shook her. 'Wake up, you're awake.'

Marisha opened her eyes. The light from the candle was much too bright. Olena's face swam into view, her red birthmark looking like a sinister mask. Marisha turned her face away.

'What happened?'

'I dreamed,' Marisha choked out, 'and I remember.' The details of her dream were so vivid: the smells, the colours, the vice-like grip of the beaked man's talon on her ankle—

'What did you dream?'

Marisha shook her head.

'Tell me.'

Marisha would not accede to Olena's demands, she could not tell her, not about the dancers, not about the beaked man, not about the hole he had gouged in her body. Oh, damp dark earth–she could feel it again, his beak lodged below her broken breastbone, pain burning through her stomach like acid, the flesh dripping off of his beaked mask, it was her own flesh—

Marisha vomited. The splattering sound shut Olena up. Marisha spat away the acrid taste in her mouth.

A moment later a cool hand smoothed her hair back and mopped her face with a cold wet rag. It dulled the jagged echo of her mangled chest, somehow. 'Marisha,' Olena said again, her voice soft but insistent, her hand moving to Marisha's shoulder. 'This room. Tell me something you see, something you touch.'

'This room?'

'Yes. What do you see?'

The room swam into focus. 'The wall.'

'What is it made of?'

'Plaster. White plaster.'

'Good. What else?'

'I see you. The candle. Flickering light.' Marisha breathed in deeply. She thought she could feel it whistle through the hole in her chest. But she was solid. 'I smell . . . my sick. And pine. Sharp and sweet. And dried flower. Marigold, I think. And the floor is hard. I'm sitting on the floor.' She breathed in deeply again. Olena did not interrupt her, nor did she take her hand off her shoulder. Marisha was glad of it. It felt like an anchor.

'Good. That's good.'

Marisha took more shuddering breaths until she felt like she could almost hear the rustling of pine branches instead of blood rushing through her ears.

'What were you trying to do?'

Marisha buried her head in her knees. 'I was trying to cast a spell for dreamless sleep.'

'I see.'

Olena lifted her hand from Marisha's shoulder. Marisha did not raise her head but could hear Olena's light footsteps.

'Marigold,' Olena muttered, 'You should have used lavender. Marigold wakens, lavender weightens. And—' Marisha heard the smoothing of crinkled paper '—this is the incantation you used?'

Marisha made a muffled noise of assent. Paper crumpled. Olena must have thought the incantation was terrible.

Marisha finally raised her head and met Olena's gaze. She saw restrained concern and curiosity. 'What could have frightened you so much?'

Olena's gaze had a glint behind her concern. She would not stop trying to find out, even if she stopped asking. Marisha pressed her fist to her sternum.

'I was attacked by a monster. And–I fell,' Marisha said. She had almost forgotten about that. Her conversation with Dima seemed like a lifetime ago. Her heartbeat hammered again, thinking about seeing Dima. He had made himself a shield for the plague. She had to find him!

'You fell?' Olena's voice brought her back to the room.

'Out of a cherry tree.'

'It must have been quite a fall.'

'It was.' Marisha paused and closed her eyes. She heard Olena's firm tread as she moved about. The sound of a bucket being shifted. Olena must have been cleaning up Marisha's mess on the floor. She was too ashamed to open her eyes. Something cool touched her shoulder and she started. It was a glass of water. She took it from Olena with a murmured thank you. Tears spilled down her cheeks. Damp dark earth, of course she would have to start crying now.

'How long have you been here?' Marisha asked.

'Not too long. I had not seen you after . . . earlier.' Olena lowered her gaze for a moment. 'And I thought I would look for you. I did not expect to find you back in the laundry room. Though I do suppose you spend a lot of time here.'

Marisha did not react.

'I went to the linen closet first.'

It took Marisha a moment to recognise their code-word for Kiril. She sat up straight. 'Olena!'

Olena grinned. And Marisha could not help smiling back though it felt ungainly. She finished her glass of water.

'Who gave you this potion?'

Marisha shook her head. 'A koldun. Remember? I said I traded it for linden sap.'

'I thought you were making that up. If you had trouble sleeping, you should have come to me. Or Baba Zima.'

'I didn't want to ask her. I thought I might give Kiril away.'

'Overcautious–but commendable impulse. Why didn't you come to me?'

'I didn't think you would help me.'

Olena's nostrils flared. 'You think I would let you needlessly suffer?'

'You haven't given me much reason to think otherwise.'

Olena's birthmark flushed purple. She tilted her head and looked at the floor, her mouth pressed into a line. She grabbed the vial and shoved it at Marisha's face. 'So, you picked this instead? After all this time here, how could you have been so stupid?'

'He didn't have a reason not to help me—'

'Apparently, you're wrong. Do you really think this was an accident? That spell you were given–it increased your perception of your dreaming self. And for some reason, it also didn't allow you to wake up. I tried waking you for *minutes* before I could. I even tried eyebright and ammoniac, neither worked.' The distress in Olena's voice made Marisha look up. The parts of Olena's face not covered by her birthmark were extremely pale.

'I'm sorry,' Marisha said.

Olena snorted. 'I'm sure you are–now.'

Marisha only then noticed the ingredients scattered over the usually pristine bench, most with lids and ties still open. Olena had lectured her time and time again about the importance of closing jars to prevent wastage or accidents. The golden powder strewn across the floor signalled to Marisha how dire the situation had really been.

'What did you end up using?'

'The birch bark and saffron infusion. I had to beg the spirits for it to work. That was the last of my ginseng too.' Olena shook her head and a muscle twitched in her neck. 'Don't you remember that marigold causes the body to stiffen? I must have told you hundreds of times.' Marisha did not answer. Olena tossed her hair back and exhaled loudly. 'You know Baba Zima has many enemies.'

'Like Anatoli.'

'Anatoli's just one. There are many more who want nothing more than to learn her secrets.'

Marisha straightened. 'And what better way to get at them than through her assistant? Except, through her apprentice.'

'Well, I'm not as stupid as you, to take a potion from a strange koldun.'

'No? So, you're saying you've done nothing reckless? *Nothing* that could be construed as against Baba Zima's best interests?' Marisha silently dared Olena to think she only referred to kidnapping Kiril.

Olena's eyes flashed. 'I know what I'm doing. So, did this koldun want anything besides the linden sap?'

Marisha sighed. She might as well tell Olena. Besides, it may be related to what Anatoli had requested of her. 'He wanted to know if Baba Zima had a feather. Black steel, about as long as a forearm. I said I hadn't seen it.'

Olena wrinkled her nose. 'A feather of black steel,' she mused, 'I haven't heard of that.' But if that was true, what did Anatoli want?

'Apparently if one touches it, they get a scar on their wrist.'

Olena frowned even further. 'That's quite a large consequence. Golgolin's feathers don't produce anything like that–just a bit of transparency around the edges.' Marisha's eyebrows shot up. Olena did not notice. 'But feathers can be extremely potent links. Just look at what Golgolin's can do.'

'The koldun said the feather could help contain the plague.'

'Really?' Olena's eyes lit up at the mention of her favourite topic. 'Hmm. There are stories of course, about kolduni who acquired objects with abilities to influence the plague. Mostly about charms, amulets of sorts–I don't remember any about feathers. The mark though . . . Baba Elizaveta told me a story about a koldun who had a chertenok's sigil stamped on his wrist. She said he had developed such an affinity for the plague he could elect victims in the following cycle.'

'That's terrible,' Marisha said, 'Why aren't you more concerned about this?'

Olena snorted. 'Baba Elizaveta is full of these stories. If hearsay were a currency, kolduni would be richer than ten princes and she would have the bulk of the wealth.'

Marisha thought of Olena bent over her workbench, more inclined to work alone or look in a book than ask someone a question. 'Maybe you haven't heard hearsay from the right people.'

Olena raised an eyebrow. 'Who was this koldun?'

'Said his name was Pan Volya. Middling height, black well-groomed whiskers past the chin streaked with silver. Cold eyes.' She tried to internalise Olena's scepticism of Baba Elizaveta's stories, but all she could see in her mind was the scar on her father's wrist. And he fell victim to the plague. Though the strange koldun, Pan Volya, had the same scar and remained awake. One did not cause the other. But her father had the same scar as Pan Volya, something else connected them. Should she tell Olena?

'I don't think I know him. Though his name sounds familiar,' Olena frowned and bowed her head for a long moment, then she exclaimed, 'Aha! That ridiculous apprentice! The one with the pen. I think he said his master's name was Pan Volya. That's a bit of a problem.'

'Why?'

'He doesn't like me. No matter. You'll point out this Pan Volya to me tomorrow?'

'Yes.' Marisha pressed a fist to her sternum. 'Olena,' she said. 'My father . . .'

'What about your father?'

'I think he had that scar on his wrist. The one that Pan Volya had. From touching the feather.'

'You think or you know?'

'I know.' It felt good to say, and it felt even better that Olena was taking her seriously.

'So, your father used this feather? But how? And why?'

Marisha shrugged. 'I don't know. I didn't ask.'

Olena said, 'That's quite extraordinary. And you said you had no koldunry in your history.'

'I don't!' Marisha said. But now she was not so sure. If her father had that mark on his wrist, then it meant that he touched the feather, maybe even used it for . . . what? 'So you don't think this black feather has anything to do with the plague?'

'Well, your father—' Olena frowned.

Marisha knew what she was thinking, that Marisha's father had fallen to the plague and had become a deep sleeper. Marisha said, 'Pan Volya had the same scar and is not touched by the plague.'

'True. Still, we can't rule anything out of course, but I haven't come across anything concrete in my research. Though the fact that your father has the same mark . . . That is quite the coincidence.'

'I thought coincidences were signposts from the spirits,' Marisha said, sarcastically. Coincidences did not exist in reasonable philosophy. She missed that way of thinking.

Olena ignored Marisha's comment. 'And Pan Volya thought Baba Zima had it? And that it had something to do with preventing the plague?'

'He said Baba Serafima had acquired it from him.'

'Hm. Baba Serafima again. Baba Zima said Baba Serafima took all her notes with her when she left. But, I do wonder . . .' Olena frowned, deep in thought.

Marisha thought of Pan Volya's surprise that she didn't know about Baba Serafima's sudden flight. 'Do kolduni usually disappear like Baba Serafima did?'

'Kolduni often do strange things after letting go of their bolshina. Baba Zima says that holding on to it is a huge burden, especially if the bolshina encompasses an authority over a particularly powerful house or domain: you have to be fit in both body and spirit and it's an active, daily struggle. And when you can't hold it anymore, passing it on is imperative.' Olena paused. 'But I don't see how holding on to it would grow so wearisome when the ability to *know* becomes stronger with age.'

'Maybe it's something you can only understand once you experience it.'

'I suppose. In any case, even after they pass a house's bolshina to another, kolduni can elect to stay in the household. Since they don't have authority over the day-to-day running of things, they can devote themselves to more esoteric pursuits. But many kolduni elect to leave. I can only imagine watching an apprentice take over what used to be yours cannot be easy. But still, to leave without ever coming back . . . there must have been something very important that Baba Serafima wanted to do.'

'Baba Zima doesn't talk about it?'

'No. I think she misses her very much and is upset she hasn't come back. She hasn't even written any letters.'

Marisha thought of Dima and how she hadn't heard from him in five years. 'I would be worried something had happened to her.'

'Baba Zima isn't worried, I don't think, maybe because Baba Serafima is so powerful. She's just hurt.'

They both fell into silence for a while. Olena broke it. 'You said you've had trouble sleeping. Have you dreamt like this before?'

Marisha shook her head. She did remember sensations from her past nightmares, warm blue and yellow, someone who felt like Kiril clasping her hand. And a terror so familiar. But beyond that, she remembered nothing. 'I have been having terrible nightmares. But I can't remember the others. I wonder . . . do you think it has something to do with kidnapping Kiril?'

'Why would you think that? Did you see Kiril in your dream?'

'Not this one. But I just have this feeling.' Marisha shrugged to cover her shivering. 'I felt something, when I crossed the threshold to the sanitorium. Something cold.'

'Why didn't you say something? I told you the threshold is

the surest way to the other world.' Olena said.

'I thought the cold was normal! It didn't seem like a big deal at the time. I mean, the threshold looked cold and dark . . .'

'Damp earth preserve me against the pig-headed. Something happened when you crossed the threshold to the sanitorium. We will do a cleansing ritual. Besides, this house creates a nexus between the other world and the damp earth, and the mind is more open during sleep which makes it easy prey for malignant spirits. You've only been here for a short while; it stands to reason you'd be vulnerable.'

Relief washed over Marisha. Olena would help her. Her dreams did not have any significant portent. But still something did not sit right with her, she felt it, like a heaviness in her belly from a lump of congealed kasha. 'I–saw my brother. We talked.'

Olena had a strange look on her face. Guarded. Careful. Marisha wondered if Olena felt any remorse about reading her letter from Dima.

Olena asked, 'Had you been thinking about him?'

Marisha looked down. 'Yes. We haven't talked in many years. I'd actually hoped . . . that I could find him. He went on this voyage to the Spice Islands.' Marisha let out a small chuckle and shook her head. 'But you knew that already.'

Olena frowned. 'And where is he now?'

'I don't know,' Marisha hugged her knees to her chest. The sense of urgency that had overcome her in her dream washed over her again. She needed to find him. Dima, indentured, a shield for the plague. It's not real, Marisha tried to tell herself. It's just a dream.

'I can help you find him,' Olena said.

'Really?'

Olena looked surprised and miffed at her surprise. 'Of course.

Finding a missing person, especially one you're so closely related to, is child's play. Just a little matter of blood.'

'Right,' Marisha said, unable to keep the bitterness from her voice. A little matter of blood. Marisha said, 'Do you think it's possible I actually talked to him?'

Olena nodded her head slowly, 'Yes.' She traced the outline of her birthmark on her cheek, 'Though dream-walking, roving your spirit to the dreams of others or even to the other world itself, takes a lot of skill. Years and years of practice.'

'Yes, we've all seen how shoddy my skills are.'

Sharp pain blossomed from her ear. 'Ow!' Olena had pinched it. 'What did you do that for?'

'You were feeling sorry for yourself. Stop.'

'That's no reason to pinch me!'

'You successfully cast a very difficult incantation; it was very stupid and ill-advised, but you still did it. And only with the indirect training you've received–I wasn't joking earlier this evening when I said it was very dangerous. And yet you still tried, even though Baba Zima alluded to the possibility of you poisoning yourself. Brave. Reckless.'

Olena looked at her, her eyes slitted in exasperation. But Marisha thought she detected something in Olena's expression bordering on respect. Marisha shook her head. If racing straight into danger from pure desperation was what it took to gain Olena's respect, it did not seem worth it.

'Maybe you did dream-walk into your brother's dream. But you probably didn't, unless you've been working on focusing your thoughts and awareness of your dream-self while awake. Your dream was more likely a result of Pan Volya's potion designed to twist your recent thoughts and fears.'

'Huh.' That did make sense to Marisha. Though she had been

surprised to see him, Dima was never far from her mind. 'And the beaked man had black feathers. Maybe because Pan Volya had just asked me about a giant black feather, I had thought about it and . . . conjured it?'

'I'm guessing that you had been thinking a lot about monsters lately. I'm surprised the bogotir Grisha did not make an appearance.'

Marisha shivered. She wished the hero had. But just her luck, she got skewered instead. Marisha's entire body felt heavy all of a sudden. Olena did not think she had actually talked to Dima, which was a relief. If that was so, then Marisha had made up Dima indenturing himself. But what if she was wrong? What if Dima really had made himself a shield for the plague? The squeezing returned to her chest. Dima could be in danger.

Olena said, 'I'll make you a potion to help you sleep.'

'Oh. Thank you.' Marisha breathed in deeply and let her breath out slowly to dispel the feeling of an iron band clenching her chest. She would find Dima. Olena said she would help. They would find him, and everything would be all right.

'And next time you want to experiment I'd rather you come to me before you burn a hole through your forehead.'

'Like *you* never did something like this when you were at my stage.'

'My, my, is it possible that Marisha the sceptic wants to learn koldunry?'

'Just mix me the damn potion.'

'No. You'll watch me do it so you'll learn its components. Consider this your first real lesson.'

'Fine.'

She watched intently as Olena sprinkled then mashed herbs together in the mortar in her special one-handed way. She did it so quickly that Marisha had to concentrate hard to see the proportions.

'You don't actually need an incantation: sleep is something your body wants to do naturally.'

'And I won't dream?'

'No. You will take it, won't you?'

'Of course.'

'Drink. Two sips to start with.'

'You want to watch me drink?'

'Yes.'

'Why?'

Olena smiled in a pained way. 'No. I don't. I just know . . . if I knew I could talk to my brother, even if it were only in my dreams, I would not stop at the opportunity. Even if it became a nightmare.'

Marisha's eyes widened. Olena looked at Marisha, and for the first time, Marisha felt no distance of contempt between them. She tipped the bowl back and swallowed the bitter liquid.

TWENTY-SIX

Olena had been looking forward to the last day of the krug, the blessing of the water from the Chistaya spring and the Marazovla Eve celebration that would leave them bleary-eyed the following day. She walked beside Baba Zima, Dunya and Anka-ny following close behind. Valdim walked with them. Olena made sure not to look anywhere near him.

Marisha had pleaded to be excused due to illness. Baba Zima had frowned but did not force her to come. Olena had stayed silent. She knew Baba Zima was very disappointed by the lack of dedication this act showed. Guilt wrinkled Olena's brow as she remembered her remark about teaching Marisha a lesson by letting her poison herself, and finding her hours later, poisoned. And especially after Marisha had unbiddenly helped her hide her absence from Baba Zima. Olena was still not sure why Marisha had done it. She snorted. Nothing was free in this life. And yet, Marisha had helped her. Olena bit the inside of her lip. Her chest felt tight.

She realised she had paused her stride and walked faster to catch up. The girl was a fool. She should have come to her for help with her nightmares long ago. Although, Olena should have noticed something was wrong. Why hadn't she? Even Valdim had noticed. Heat rose to her face as she remembered how she had dismissed Valdim's concerns for Marisha. It was an uncomfortable thought, that Marisha had been stricken with such a misfortune for weeks and Olena had not noticed. They had not been speaking much, yes, but she had seen Marisha every day. She ought to have noticed, she was to hold the house's bolshina after all. How could she be a powerful koldunya if she did not even notice her assistant was suffering?

And yet Marisha had proven herself much tougher than Olena had thought. She had to hand it to her, Marisha's attempt had been most impressive: to have the mettle to cast that spell by herself and succeed... Olena smiled to herself. Marisha might be annoying and self-righteous at times, but she was no coward.

And maybe that was what still bothered her about it. Marisha was brave or foolhardy enough to breathe the fumes from that potion, but the distress in her body, the way it had contorted–the pain in her eyes. Marisha said it was from falling after the monster attacked her, but Olena knew it wasn't. Would talking to Fedya have made Olena react the same way? Her heart hitched to think of her little brother... his impish smile, his fast footfalls as he ran through the door. He always ran to talk to her before everyone else. Olena smiled sadly at the memory.

'What are you smiling at?' Baba Zima asked.

Olena's smile turned brittle. 'I'm looking forward to the ceremony, I hope we get some strong water out of it. The lovely weather helps.'

'Hmph,' Baba Zima said, 'I suppose the company is nice too. For the most part. Of course, you may not agree with me.'

Olena suppressed a sigh. Baba Zima had been making a lot of jabs lately about her and Valdim snipping at each other. Maybe if Baba Zima had stuck with them at the demonstration fair, she might have caught that moment where Valdim had made her laugh. But no, Valdim had made it clear the previous evening with his spying that he had simply been ingratiating himself with her for some purpose of his own. 'I don't think we've been that bad. Who knows, at this rate we may be best friends in a few decades.'

'I don't think that's something to joke about.'

Olena cocked her head at Baba Zima. 'Not something to joke about? That's a first. I thought my sense of humour was one of your favourite things about me.'

Baba Zima's expression stayed impassive. 'Some things are too serious for you to make light of. You do wish to follow me, yes? Inherit the poker from me one day?'

Olena breathed in sharply. 'Of course I do, Matrionka. I'm working all the time to be worthy of your bolshina. It's all I want.'

'Is it? Work harder to show me so. You will have to make a choice, my dear. You are talented and ruthless enough to succeed. However, I let you know now I will not suffer my bolshina to pass to a fool.'

Olena's chest felt constricted by an iron band. 'All this talk of fools and warnings because of some bickering? I didn't realise you took what we say so seriously. Are you having this conversation with him as well?'

'Of course not. I don't give a mustard grain's eye about him. It's your loyalty I care about. Your self-control.'

Olena was confused. 'But, Baba Zima, of course you care about him. I know you do.'

Baba Zima blanched. 'What are you talking about? I don't care at all! I never did!' Her nostrils flared as wide as a horse's. She hissed, 'Why are you looking at me like I have the head of a toad and the ears of a rabbit?'

'Matrionka,' Olena said carefully, 'I'm simply surprised to hear you speak of your son that way.'

Baba Zima's eyebrows shot to her forehead, 'My son? Did you think—' Her eyes flitted up and she laughed so hard she doubled over. Olena did not join her. 'Oh, oh my dear Olena, my little buttered blin, did you really think I was talking of Valdim?'

'Well, yes. Who else would you be talking about?' Olena said, suddenly knowing exactly who else she would be talking about.

'Oh, you sly little fox. Innocent as a fledgling sparrow, are you? Now, you may be thinking I'm exaggerating or being unfair, but I'm not. You will take heed of my experience and my word. I am your mistress, and while I turn a blind eye to many things you do, this is not something you can simply stuff into a closet.' Olena repressed a sharp inhalation. She had been so careful, she had put the strongest concealment spells on the workroom. Could Baba Zima's words simply be a coincidence? 'You will not correspond with Anatoli.'

How did Baba Zima know? Olena's vision contracted, blood rushed in her ears. She felt like her mistress had walked in on her in the oven room, the poker not hanging by the oven door as it ought to, but mid-swing in her hand.

'But, Matrionka,' Olena sputtered. At least Baba Zima had said 'correspond,' which meant that she did not know that Olena and Anatoli had met. Olena shuddered at the thought of Baba Zima finding *that* out. But Baba Zima knew that Olena had sent Anatoli a letter a few days ago. How could Olena have been so careless?

'No. I have said what I needed to. That's all.'

'Does it . . . have something to do with what happened yesterday?' The wall of fire keeping Baba Zima from leaving. The flaming hand coming for her and her terrified expression. When

Olena asked about it yesterday, she had expressed concern for her mistress's well-being. Baba Zima had brushed her off, saying that she was fine, and that it was surely the work of some capricious spirit. But her mouth had been pressed in a brittle line and she stood staring at the wall.

'Yesterday? You mean the triumph of my demonstration? Why would that have anything to do with this?

So, Baba Zima was going to pretend that it had gone off without a hitch. Olena deliberated whether it was worth pressing her on it and decided against it. 'Then why now?' She said evenly, not betraying the importance of the question, 'Don't you trust me?'

'I trust you and now you must trust me. I forbid it. That's all you need to know.'

Baba Zima's syllables were clipped and her nostrils flared. Olena knew pushing was useless. She felt better for a moment that Baba Zima had said that she trusted her–their relationship was not broken. But for Baba Zima to forbid something . . . Olena struggled for a moment but couldn't help it. 'But what if he really wants to help?'

Baba Zima raised an eyebrow. 'Is that what he said now? He's lying.'

'But what if you're wrong?' Olena said it so softly she barely heard her own voice.

'Olena, enough! I will not tolerate such backtalk from you! You will not correspond with Anatoli, and that's final.'

Olena almost tripped. Baba Zima had never once spoken to her this way, never once forbidden her anything like this. When Olena accidentally burned a hole in the floor because she mixed some solvents she ought not to, Baba Zima reprimanded her, yes, but she did not forbid her from touching them again. Olena met her mistress's gaze. Baba Zima was furious, but there was something underneath that. Fear? And maybe even guilt? Olena dipped her head tersely to indicate she understood, and Baba Zima let out a little huff and began talking again at a normal volume as though the conversation had never happened. Olena gave automatic answers, but her mind was occupied. What was Baba Zima scared of? And why now?

The attack during Baba Zima's demonstration, that was the only answer. It was simple: Baba Zima thought Anatoli was responsible. But he was right: he had been by her side during Baba Zima's unannounced demonstration and even Olena had not known when Baba Zima was planning her display. Most of all, she believed Anatoli when he said he would not want to jeopardise the possibility of collaboration by attacking her mistress.

But she could say none of that to her mistress because she could not tell her about meeting Anatoli. Olena wanted to look back at Valdim but kept her gaze ahead. He had said he would not tell Baba Zima, but would he have done so anyways? He had no right! But if he had talked to her–a more reasonable part of Olena's mind said–Baba Zima would never act on it, she would keep the information to herself and wait to catch Olena in the act. Or maybe this was another test, a test in obedience. Baba Zima always thought of new ways to bend Olena, like the time she told Olena to talk down angry supplicants after she handed out the wrong tinctures. Olena had always suspected Baba Zima had mixed them up on purpose. Was she now doing the same thing?

Olena slowed until she was walking with Valdim. 'Did you say anything to her?'

'No,' he answered, 'But if I stumbled upon your illicit meeting, then just think what else she may have stumbled upon. You're not as good at subterfuge as you think.'

But he knew nothing about the sleeping person in the linen closet. 'Why wouldn't you tell her?' Olena said. 'You don't gain anything by staying silent, especially if you think she is in danger.'

He barked out a laugh, 'Oh, Olena. If there's one thing that she can do, it's take care of herself. Look. You know you were my mother's second attempt at an apprentice, right?'

Olena crossed her arms. 'Yes. Baba Zima said that she took someone on. But that they didn't last more than a few weeks.'

'Yes. She drove her to leave.' He looked at her. 'I didn't like the new girl, but I hadn't enjoyed watching it happen either. I knew that my mother had a cruel streak. But that was my first time truly seeing it. And then you came and I thought you would go the same. But you didn't.'

'What's your point?'

'Remember that time, before I left to study with the luthier, she asked you to grind madder root? You didn't know which storeroom to get it from and you were using an older root. I knew where the fresher ones were and I left it there for you.'

Olena's eyes widened, 'That was you? I thought the house was helping me.' It was hard not to show how crestfallen she was. That was the first instance that she remembered where the house had clearly helped her. And now she learned that it hadn't been the house at all, but Valdim.

Valdim smiled wryly at her reaction. 'Don't worry, that's the only time I did that. My mother pulled me aside and told me not to do it again. She said you wouldn't thank me for my help, which, judging by your expression, she was right about.' Valdim paused his gaze turning to the slim columns of birch trees. 'She said that I didn't understand what was needed to prepare you to hold the house's bolshina. And I shouldn't interfere.' He shook his head and put his hands in his pockets. 'Well, I'm not interfering.'

Olena turned and stared at him. She had no idea that he had tried to help. He had always stayed away from her. They'd had moments where Olena thought that maybe Valdim wanted to be her friend, like when they were cleaning up the mess after the disaster with the pineapple. But then he drew away, always more interested in violins, always aloof. Always resenting her presence. Or so she assumed.

'And last night, that was you not interfering?'

He flashed her a smile, 'I didn't interrupt your meeting, did I?' Then his expression became more serious. 'I still wondered though, whenever I returned to the house, whether you'd be there. But you always were.'

'Much to your disappointment.'

The corner of his mouth raised, then fell. 'I told you what I know about Anatoli. But I didn't say anything to my mother. Nor will I. The rest is up to you.'

They reached the edge of the stream. Olena felt relieved, as though she needed an excuse to pull away from Valdim. He was adding another layer of muddle to her already muddled thoughts. Her past and present seemed turned around: ten years ago Valdim had tried to help her complete one of Baba Zima's tasks, and today he would keep her meeting with Anatoli a secret despite his loud misgivings. Today, Valdim seemed to trust Olena more than Baba Zima did.

I still wondered though, whenever I returned, whether you'd be there.

That was the crux of their relationship–who was he to her? Competitor or conspirator? She thought of stumbling into that room with the skulls, how neither of them wanted to show the other how scared they were, how she had tingled with excitement at sharing the discovery. She had felt less scared because he had been there, though she would never admit it. And then he had left the house, he had built a life for himself in a way that she had not: separate and independent from Baba Zima. And she'd be lying if she said she didn't admire that he'd managed. Separate and independent from Baba Zima was something she would never be, even when she inherited the house, she still would be connected to her mistress. And still there was always that grain of competition for Baba Zima's attention, that assessment in his gaze whenever he returned to the house: you're still here. Before now, she had always thought that he'd been disappointed when she'd survived another year with his mother. But had she got it wrong?

Did Valdim actually want her to succeed?

And had she perhaps wanted to show him that she could? She had always seen him as the prodigal son, the one who returned and effortlessly had so much that Olena worked hard at: an unshakable relationship with Baba Zima and the house. He had kept to himself, but, perhaps she had done the same? And then Baba Zima had told him not to interfere, and then Baba Zima had sent him away to learn luthiering. How much had she judged him for what had been Baba Zima's decisions?

Olena didn't know what to think. She couldn't think about him, not right now, not when more important problems required her thought. The water ran in little gulleys over large dark boulders, cutting a clear channel through the snow. They followed the banks of the stream until it widened into a pool. The surface looked calm, but Olena knew it was deceptive. The current ran swiftly at this spot.

The kolduni dipped their hands and vessels into the water and chanted. Baba Zima had carried the two empty pails in the crooks of her elbows. They would all help fill the pails, handful by handful of water, until they were filled close to the brim. While Olena would murmur her blessing, Baba Zima would chant loud and clear. Up and down the long pool were other clusters of kolduni, some with apothecaries of their own, many still apprentices or assistants. The sounds of chanting and the water streaming from hand to pail were soothing, but Olena had trouble joining the mass murmur. She forgot where she was in the chant and mumbled so no one could hear before picking up at another point.

As she sank further into the rhythm of the chant, her mind drifted away from the confusion that every recent interaction with Valdim seemed to bring and back to the circle of thoughts she had been thinking for the past hour: if her dissection of the shield spell proved to be unsuccessful, then working with Anatoli might be her best lead for curing the plague. Yet how could Olena trust someone who Baba Zima did not let into the house, surely for good reason?

But why wouldn't Baba Zima explain her reasoning to Olena?

That was a fruitless question, one that Olena had asked herself many times. The fact that Baba Zima had stated to her apprentice clearly that she might not always share the reasons for her actions did not lessen the frustration. In fact, Baba Zima had made her intentions clear towards Olena in their very first conversation.

Olena's mind went over it often. It had happened twelve years ago, soon after the winter festival. After days of being locked in her room, Papa finally opened it, and a tall and foreboding woman strode in. Olena remembered being struck by her ridiculous pink hat with three peacock feathers stuck in it. And then—

She must have cursed him. Everyone said I was a fool to keep her, that I would pay for it one day. And now—Mama buried her head in her hands, heaved, and looked at Olena. *Oh how I wish I had listened.*

Olena still flinched from the words' memory.

She did not remember exactly what her parents had said to turn her out, nor did she remember the walk with Baba Zima through the village. She had felt detached, numb, floating: her ties with her family and village had been severed. And there was one odd thought amidst the haze of numb fear and grief, that she had never walked this way, past the well and now past the crooked pine, without knowing that she could turn around and go home.

Then her gaze snagged on orange. Olena followed Baba Zima into the orange house, down corridors and somehow ended up in a large and warm, spacious room. A plate flew in through the door. It was carried by two red gloves. Olena's eyes had widened. But she hadn't been afraid. She was still too numb for that. She only remembered being struck by the oddness of it.

'Sit, girl.' Baba Zima pointed to a chair at the table next to the warm oven. Olena did as she was told. Baba Zima pointed at the food. 'Eat.'

Olena lifted the fork to her mouth. She managed to get a couple of bites down of a mushroom dumpling. But it was hard to swallow the gluey mass even though the mushroom dumpling was thick with herbs and sour cream. She put her fork down.

'That's it?' Baba Zima said. 'You must be hungry, you look as skinny as a cat that's been locked out for the winter.'

Olena looked at the oven door. The outline glowed from the smouldering coals behind it. Baba Zima said, 'If you're done eating, we can talk. Your life is going to be very different now. I'm sure you have many questions for me.'

Olena still did not answer. She still did not look at the koldunya. A chair scraped and Baba Zima sighed. 'It's as you wish, girl. But I don't always give full answers to questions, and if you'll stay with me for a while, you'll have many. You get five questions tonight. And just this once, I'll answer them as honestly as I can.'

Olena moved her head slightly and dared to peek at the koldunya. The woman was sitting in a squishy, comfortable chair. Her feet were crossed and resting on the ledge in front of the oven. Olena opened her mouth. 'Why five?'

'One for each of the four earth's corners and one for the spirits below. You have four remaining.'

Olena sat up straight. 'Who are you?' Olena asked, looking squarely at the koldunya.

'I am Baba Zima: koldunya, mistress of this house. I'm one of the ones who *know*.'

Olena waited but Baba Zima did not say anything else. She asked, 'Why did you bring me here?'

'To be my apprentice,' Baba Zima said with complete seriousness. Olena's eyes widened but she bit her tongue before she asked, 'really?' Baba Zima seemed satisfied that Olena remained silent for she added, 'I will work you very hard, but I will also teach you many secrets and magic. And, assuming you still want it by then, you will have my house when I am done with it.'

Olena looked around the room. The candlelight didn't quite reach the corners. It was warm near the oven, but the house felt like a vast uncharted sea, overwhelming to her senses. It seemed to Olena quite a big promise to make. She said, 'But you don't even know me.'

Baba Zima chuckled, 'I do know you, though not in the way you think.' She paused. 'You have talent, but one cannot hold this house with talent alone. You needs intent. You needs to want this house, and the power that comes with it, with every fibre of your being.' She paused. 'I think you're the kind of person who could have such an intent. Whether or not you actually cursed your brother and whether or not it was on purpose, people notice you. There's power there.'

'I didn't curse him,' Olena said. But she knew by the way that Baba Zima held her gaze impassively that the koldunya knew that Olena was not completely sure. Olena looked away. No one had ever thought that it was a good thing that people noticed her. Olena wished that people didn't, that they didn't treat her differently. Maybe if they did, she would still be home. Her eyes filled with tears as she thought of her brother. The last time she saw him he'd been lying on the bed, struggling to sit up. He couldn't move his legs. Olena asked, her voice low. 'Can you heal Fedya?'

'I'm sorry,' Baba Zima said. 'There are certain things that we cannot ask the spirits to do. I did what I could for him. But I can do no more.' Baba Zima stood up. 'You are tired, I will show you where you sleep.'

'Wait, I get one more question!'

Baba Zima turned around. 'Ask,' she said.

Olena did not know how to put into words the feelings that roiled through her chest. She blurted out, 'Were my parents sad to let me go with you?'

Baba Zima, slowly, shook her head. 'They were afraid of you. They wanted you to go.' She paused, looking at Olena, her eyes glittering. 'I will not be afraid of you, little one. I cannot promise to always be kind, nor can I even promise to always be fair. I know I can be difficult. I can be taken to sudden whims and I know that's not easy to live with. I may ask you to do things that you think are pointless, stupid, and unfair. I'll always have a reason for it, though whether I share those reasons,' she barked out a laugh, 'that's up to me. But know that I'll be working you constantly to become the koldunya you'll need to be to hold this house's bolshina. Resourceful, self-reliant, with a will of iron. It will be a hard path, little one. You will have to want it, every single day.' Baba Zima paused, 'But if you do, if you want to stay and do the work, then I promise you three things.' She raised three fingers, one by one, 'I will never push you beyond what I think you're capable of. I will never treat you like anything less than what you are. And, so long as you want it, so long as you do the work–I will never ask you to leave. This house will be your home.'

The ceremony ended. Olena straightened her back. Baba Zima shooed Dunya and Anka-ny forward. Valdim reached for the pails, but Baba Zima stopped him. It was the koldunya's task to carry them.

Olena thought that Valdim's gaze sought her out but she avoided it. As an afterthought, Olena bent back down and scooped her numb fingers into the water. She murmured, 'May this water grant me the clarity to see with my mind as I do with my eyes.'

She poured the water onto her face, making certain to splash her eyelids. The cold made her shudder. But it felt good, the single note of blinding pain cut through her indecision. To what? She did not know. But she felt as though the clouds whirling inside her head lifted for a moment.

Olena blinked the water from her eyes and rubbed her nose. Dunya and Anka-ny were long gone, Valdim with them. Baba Zima was only a few steps away, her back bent, hands hovering over the pail's handles.

Olena did not know why touching things with her hands caused Baba Zima so much pain. In the house, it seemed unnatural to see Baba Zima without the Hands hovering by her shoulders, except in front of the supplicants because she did not want to show weakness. The only things she sometimes handled herself were her teacups, and even those she grasped by her fingertips. And the poker of course, but that went without saying. No koldunya would ever let anyone else hold the symbol of her bolshina–not even servants from the other world. No matter how it may pain her.

But of course, the Hands could not fly more than thirty feet from the house. Watching her mistress set her mouth and steel herself against the task caused a wave of affection and admiration to rise in Olena. Her mistress was so strong. Olena often wondered if Baba Zima had felt a similarity between their conditions: Olena missing a hand and Baba Zima unable to handle anything without pain. She wondered if growing up that way had been as difficult for Baba Zima as it had been for Olena. She wondered whether Baba Zima's family had ever shied away from her as though she were the plague itself. It was certainly one of the reasons Baba Zima offered to take Olena in after her brother's accident: a child with a terrible accusation levelled against her as her only proof of talent.

And Baba Zima had never treated her like anything less. Sometimes Olena had despaired at that enforced independence, especially when she was younger. In those dark moments, Olena resented Baba Zima for relying on the Hands so much when she was allowed no help, but she knew now it had been the right decision. Baba Zima had earned the privilege of commanding the Hands when she had earned the bolshina from Baba Serafima. And when Olena's turn came, she would know she had earned what she was given.

She knew Baba Zima loved her. Relied on her. Baba Zima

didn't need to say it for it to be true. Maybe she now wanted to rein Olena in a bit too much for her own taste, but Baba Zima had made her what she was and had given her the chance to try. Wasn't that enough?

Olena stepped forward to her mistress. She gestured to take the pails. Baba Zima hesitated. It really ought to be the mistress's task, the possessor of the house's bolshina. They both knew it. Baba Zima scrutinised Olena a moment, then stepped back without a word of thanks. The pails were heavy and Olena walked with one grasped by the handle, the other dangled from the crook of her little arm's elbow. The ground was slippery and the weight of the pails strained her right side more than her left, but she walked next to Baba Zima without spilling a drop. They walked in silence. Her shoulders and back screamed and the handles had surely cut the circulation off from her fingers and elbow by the time they reached the clearing and the house. Olena set the pails down on the threshold without slopping any water over the brim. She swung her arms and rolled her shoulders.

The Hands took it from there, whisking the pails away to the cellar where the strongest water was kept. 'Thank you,' Baba Zima said. Olena nodded. Baba Zima smoothed back a thick strand of Olena's hair; her fingers lingered on her cheek.

'I won't disappoint you,' Olena said, the words escaping her lips.

Baba Zima raised an eyebrow. 'I should hope not. You've never disappointed me. Why start now?'

Olena nodded, affection welling up in her chest. She did not need Anatoli, he had nothing to add about the shield spell anyway, just more speculation about where the house could be hiding a source of the water of death. But without the water of life that Anatoli claimed he could provide, searching for the water of death was useless. She entered the house, keen to warm her extremities before returning to the krug.

As she opened the door, she paused for a moment before entering, remembering Anatoli's earnest expression when he had said, *Olena, what is more important here–a twenty-year-old rivalry, or the chance to cure the plague forever?*

Anatoli was wrong. It was not a twenty-year old rivalry that was impeding their partnership. Baba Zima's trust in Olena was at stake. This was why it was important that she make the shield spell work as a cure: she did not want to find out what she would choose if Anatoli became her only option.

TWENTY-SEVEN

One of the Hands floated in on Marisha sitting in the library at a table covered in maps of Severny. It poked her on the shoulder. She swatted it away, still focused on studying the map. Her fingertip tapped the northern corner of Prakov street and Korisha street. Dima was there. Marisha felt slightly ashamed of how easy it had been to locate him using koldunry, only the work of a few minutes. Of course, it had helped that Olena had made good on her offer of assistance. Marisha had not expected the apprentice to go back on her word, but she had been surprised that Olena had kept her promise only the day after she had made it.

Olena had instructed Marisha to wrap a knife handle with yarn and dip it into a bowl of water, into which had dropped some of Marisha's blood. She then told to swing the knife over the map of Chernozemlya, from to south, east to west. Marisha was worried about rops of water on the map, but the knife seemed to ll she had to do, Olena said, was concentrate her point of the knife. Point to Dima. And the swi maller and smaller until the knife had settled everny. Marisha was not sure what was mo hat Olena's ritual had worked or that Dima y this whole time.

A minute or two later, Marisha knew that not only was Dima in Severny, but he was at the corner of Prakov and Korisha.

She still couldn't believe it. It had only been a few hours, but she was tempted to try the ritual again, just to see if it would work if she did it alone. Just to make sure it was real.

The Hand interrupted her reverie by tapping her on the shoulder. It wouldn't leave when swatted, and tugged a lock of her hair when she wouldn't turn around. Marisha turned and rubbed her scalp. The Hand did not pay attention to her glare, it hovered and very casually crooked its forefinger. Marisha huffed. The Hand floated down the corridor and Marisha followed it, still rubbing her head.

'You wanted me?' Marisha peeked around the door of the receiving room. Baba Zima sat while the other Hand stirred a spoonful of strawberry jam into her tea.

'Come in.' Baba Zima waved Marisha forward. Marisha side-stepped the Hand and it slammed the door shut. The noise made Marisha jump.

'So,' Baba Zima said, peering at her in a way that made Marisha feel small, even though she stood while Baba Zima sat. 'How are you feeling? Much better, I hope.'

Marish[...]osed her mouth. Baba Zima had never before asked her ho[...]was feeling, or really shown any consideration for her wellbei[...]. She had expected to be reprimanded for missing the bles[...]he waters that morning, but this consideration made h[...]ore nervous. 'Much better,' Marisha said cautiously.

'Good. Please, sit,' [...]said.

Marisha clamped he[...]t while Baba Zima slurped her tea.

'I'm going to tell you a[...]fima told me. There

was once a sparrow about to lay her eggs. Now, this sparrow had lost her chicks to a hawk every year, and had vowed to herself that this year she would keep her offspring safe. As the sparrow was quite small and had no wicked claws, she knew she could not fight the hawk head on: her best chance was to hide the nest. So, she built it on the uppermost branch of a poplar tree, and the tree grew on the tip of a mountain, and the mountain was ringed by a desolate plain, and the plain dipped off an island into the ocean. No hawks flew for miles around and the sparrow was content. Unfortunately, she had been so intent on hiding her nest that she built it shoddily and forgot to account for the weight of her eggs. Her chicks hatched and one day, while she flew far to find food, one of the chicks peeked its head out of the nest and flapped its wings. The chick took its first good look at the world and the nest, which balanced on the branch of a poplar tree on the tip of a mountain on a lonesome island, fell to the ground.'

Baba Zima paused as though to allow Marisha time to think about the story. Marisha arranged her face in a mildly puzzled expression.

'So why did the nest fall?' Baba Zima asked.

'Um. The mother built her nest badly?'

'But why?'

Marisha shrugged. 'She focused too hard on hiding from the hawk.'

'Exactly. So intent on protecting against one danger, she completely forgot about another.' Baba Zima paused again and fixed Marisha with her sharp and beady eyes. 'It has been three months.'

'Ah.' Her quarterly review. Marisha wiped her suddenly sweaty palms on her skirt.

'I know, easy to forget with the excitement of the krug. But you're good at forgetting things, aren't you? Such as coming to the blessings of the water this morning.'

Marisha bit the inside of her lip.

Baba Zima said, 'How do you think your performance has been?'

'Um. Good. I think Olena's happy with my performance.'

'You think so, do you?'

'Yes,' Marisha said staunchly.

'You're a hard worker, Marisha. I will not deny it. But you lack a certain . . . How can I put it . . .'

'Koldunic quality?' Marisha could not keep the bitter sarcasm from her voice.

'Exactly.'

Of course Baba Zima liked those words. She had used them at Marisha's interview three months ago. Marisha thought if she could tell Baba Zima about performing Pan Volya's ritual, the starukha would eat her words about koldunic quality. Except she knew Baba Zima did not refer to her ability, but to her attitude.

'But you hired me despite it.'

'Yes. And now I'm starting to wonder if I was mistaken.'

Marisha's throat constricted. She couldn't be dismissed, not when finding Dima was more important than ever. Baba Zima studied Marisha as if she were a faulty incantation she wished to fix. 'You're close to Olena.'

'It's my job to help her.'

'Yes. But she helps you. She usually does not form such bonds with the assistants, but I suppose you're special. You are *her* assistant after all.' Baba Zima smiled bitterly. 'But your contract is with me.' She paused to sip. 'I know Olena is colluding with Anatoli. You know it too, don't you?'

Marisha did not know where to look. Baba Zima barked a

mirthless laugh. 'Of course you know. But hear this and hear it well: no good can come of this. Anatoli is jealous, but he cannot take what I have earned.'

'Why don't you explain this to Olena?'

'Of course I have. And she has promised to stop working with him. But... I don't know if she will keep it.' She shot Marisha a look that made her feel like a fish on a hook.

'Can't you,' Marisha's voice was croaky, 'can't you keep an eye out on her, you know, with your koldunry?'

'Ha!' Baba Zima threw her head back. 'Don't you think Olena has taken necessary precautions? Don't you think I would have taught her to ward herself against such possibilities?'

'I would have thought you would keep some options.'

'My little sugared blin, that's what I have you for.'

Marisha turned cold. 'Me?'

'Of course.'

'No.' Marisha had told herself she would not become a pawn in their games.

'Won't you?' Baba Zima repeated, fixing her with beady eyes. 'What if I made it worth your while? What if I promised to pay you your full year's salary when you find out what Olena plans to do with Anatoli.'

Marisha felt as though a snowball had slipped down her back. Her whole year's salary? She could start a new life, and Dima could too.

'And if I refuse?'

Baba Zima shrugged. 'I'll assume you're not serious about this position.' She raised her eyebrows slightly, as if to say no more words were necessary.

'Fine,' Marisha said. 'I'll spy on Olena.' Her stomach felt a little sick saying it. Especially after Olena had helped her this morning. She could not believe she was risking their new intimacy this way. Then she had an idea. 'But only if my brother can come to visit us for a time.'

'Your brother? Why in the damp dark earth would I allow that?'

'I haven't seen him in years. I miss him.'

'And you think he'll benefit from the protection of this house.'

Marisha did not answer. She often considered whether the house's protection was real, weighing the long history of a plagueless household against possibility and exaggeration. All her rational arguments paled against the true koldunry she had witnessed. Besides, if Marisha brought Dima into the house, even if the house's protection didn't hold, at least they would be together.

'Where is your brother?'

'Severny.' She could not believe she could now say it with such certainty.

'We are heading to Severny after the krug so Valdim can return. Fine. If you tell me what Olena is up to before we get there, I will pay you, say, a quarter of your salary, and we can invite your brother for a short visit. No more than three days.'

'Three quarters of my salary and three months.'

'A third and three weeks. And his room and board will be docked from your salary. This is not a guesthouse!'

Marisha took a deep breath and nodded. Three weeks was short, but if Olena could hide Kiril in her workroom surely Marisha could find a way to hide Dima. But she first needed to get Dima into the house.

'Good.' Baba Zima smiled. 'And as a show of good faith—' She rummaged into her pockets and pulled out a small drawstring purse. 'Your salary for your first month.' The fact that Baba

Zima had the bag prepared made Marisha feel worse. And the image of her father came unbidden to her mind, urging her not to enter in a bargain with a koldun. *But I know what the terms are*, she told herself, arguing against the memory of her father's sad and serious gaze. Still, the knot in her stomach remained.

'And, I have something that may help you.' Baba Zima sent the Hands swooping to the chest of drawers behind her. One Hand opened the drawer with a spotted leopard carved into it, ducked inside, and dropped a vial into Marisha's palm. 'As long as you stand in shadow, you will be invisible.'

'Does it work in dark corners too?' Marisha didn't even try to soften her tone.

Baba Zima grinned. Her teeth were stained yellow from her incessant tea-drinking. 'This will hide you much better than a dark corner, you will see.'

After explaining to Marisha how to use it, Baba Zima shooed her out, one of the Hands pushing the small of her back for emphasis. Marisha's skin crawled. The transaction felt wrong to her. But Olena herself had said action sprang from necessity. Besides, Olena had pried into her things before, didn't that mean she deserved to be spied on? The logic was flawed, Marisha knew it. But she stuck with it.

TWENTY-EIGHT

The next day, after the ashes of the Marazovla dolls had cooled and the clearing's occupants had recovered from a night of dancing and singing around the bonfire, the giant tent covered in small mirrors was struck down and packed into a trunk for the following year. Kolduni took to their mortars and covered wagons, or travelling houses if they were lucky. Though none of the travelling houses that Marisha had seen were anywhere near as magnificent as Baba Zima's orange chicken-legged house.

Olena was in a bad mood. She had spent the last afternoon of the krug trying to track down Pan Volya, but when she found the apprentice with the still-broken stylus, his master turned out to be altogether different from the koldun that Marisha had encountered, though they shared a name. And Olena was unable to find anyone else who had heard of another Pan Volya. Marisha and Olena had scoured the faces at the bonfire, but he was nowhere to be found.

As the chicken-legged house rose to its feet and began lumbering between the pines and birches, Marisha sat by the window in Olena's workroom, enjoying a quiet moment after tending to Kiril.

'Look at the this!' Olena thrust a piece of paper between

Marisha's face and the window. "Something about Pan Volya's name sounded familiar, and not just because of that idiot apprentice."

Marisha took the proffered page.

Esteemed Pan Volya,

I have considered your request, but I cannot fulfil it at this time. Your accusation is presumptuous. I have not seen your missing talisman, nor do I know how you think it may have come into my possession. The shield spell is the best defence I have against the plague, but it is not the only one. This house has deep waters, some that you couldn't fathom, some that keep out the unwanted sort, and some that welcome only death–if you come seeking. I do not recommend that you do.

Yours,
Baba Serafima

Marisha looked up from the page to Olena, her heart pattering in excitement. 'You think it's the same Pan Volya?'

'Yes! And the missing talisman must be this black feather of his.'

Of course, Marisha thought as she scanned the letter once again. 'But she says she knows nothing about it.'

'She could be lying.'

'Ah.' Marisha looked at the piece of paper again. 'She mentions the shield spell, and another defence against the plague. Do you think it has to do with Pan Volya's feather?'

'No.' Olena looked away. She was not telling Marisha everything. 'But this is fascinating. Pan Volya knew Baba Serafima, and his black feather went missing. And somehow, your father is involved.'

'But Baba Zima hasn't touched the feather, she has no scar.' The hairs rose on Marisha's neck. She didn't like the idea that her father got in the middle of Pan Volya and Baba Serafima. She didn't like the idea that he had anything to do with something so powerful as an object which Pan Volya claimed had any bearing on the sleeping plague.

Olena disappeared to talk to Baba Zima. Marisha went down to the oven room for a cup of tea. Anka-ny sat at the table: a book, paper, and her new bottle of long-lasting ink opened in front of her. Marisha took a chair by one of the large windows, looking out at the pine trees brushing against the house as it began its journey. The woods were too thick for the house to ski at this point, but it was moving fast: either the house or Baba Zima were eager to get underway, or perhaps get away from the krug.

She enjoyed the companionable silence of sitting near Anka-ny without either of them feeling the need to talk. Marisha was suddenly struck by how incredible it was that she had got so used to living in the skiing house that she didn't notice the house rocking as it walked. Marisha took a moment to feel the movement and imagine the awe of witnessing the house walking by, the giant chicken feet flattening the forest underbrush and leaving stag-sized three-toed prints in its wake. The tea and the warm glow of marvelling at her circumstances left her feeling calm and satisfied in a way that she hadn't for such a long time.

Olena returned to claim her attention a few minutes later. Marisha left her cup in the oven room. 'I asked Baba Zima. She said that Baba Serafima had no scar on her wrist.'

'Did you tell her about the black feather?'

'Yes. She says she hasn't heard anything about it. Not that that rules out all possibilities. Still, in her letter, Baba Serafima mentions the shield spell and water, but denies the feather . . .' Olena looked up, a slight frown on her face.

Marisha said, 'You didn't tell Baba Zima about my father, right?'

Olena shook her head. 'No.'

'Thanks.' Marisha did not like the idea of Baba Zima knowing how koldunry had touched her father, it felt too much like something the koldunya would use against her. Though she did not know how.

'Do you still have the potion? The one that Pan Volya gave you?'

Marisha rummaged around in her pockets and produced the potion. She held it out to Olena, who motioned for her to set it on the floor.

'What are you doing?' Marisha asked as Olena grabbed a stick from the corner and traced it around the potion in a circle several times, then reversed directions.

'Dowsing rod,' Olena answered. 'Pan Volya made this potion. The rod will point to anything else that Pan Volya touched. If the feather is in the house, this will lead us to it.'

Marisha waited with bated breath, but when Olena tugged the dowsing rod from the circle, nothing happened. Olena swung it around several times, before stopping and looking at the rod with a frown. Disappointment plummeted into Marisha's stomach. 'Isn't it working?'

'It is,' Olena said. 'The rod is still attracted to the potion. And even faintly to you.' She demonstrated how the rod gave a sharp tug when she waved it in their direction. 'You used the potion. It must still be inside your body.'

'Great,' Marisha grimaced. Hopefully it wouldn't linger. Luckily, Olena's sleeping draught seemed to be counteracting any remaining effect.

Olena sighed and lowered her arm. 'The feather isn't in the house. Maybe Baba Serafima wasn't lying after all.'

'Then why did Pan Volya seem convinced that she had it?'

Olena shrugged. 'Who knows. I'll try some other way. But the dowsing rod is quite foolproof in my experience.'

Marisha tried not to show how disappointed she was. 'So, the feather's a dead end.'

'Maybe.' Olena frowned. 'I don't like how this koldun attacked you. I didn't tell Baba Zima about it either, but I really don't like it. I think it's worth trying to find out everything we can about Pan Volya.'

Olena's new protectiveness made guilt prickle at Marisha, as she thought of her agreement to spy on Olena. A few days ago, she never would have expected that Olena would pull her out of her nightmare or help her find Dima. She never would have expected for them to be *friends*. Marisha studied the look of determination on Olena's face. So long as Olena was focused on the shield spell and Pan Volya, she would forget about Anatoli and whatever she had planned with him.

A WEEK AFTER they left the krug it seemed like everything was back to normal. They toured villages in the vicinity of Severny and peddled Baba Zima's salves and incantations as they had for the previous months. But the house-wide lassitude that lasted a few days after the krug gave way to an eerie alertness that reminded Marisha of the way the forest felt when the birds were too quiet.

The household gathered around the table for dinner. The house had meandered through pools and streams, and the Hands baked freshly caught fish into delicious pies that dripped butter like tears. Marisha chewed a steaming mouthful and forced herself to wait to swallow before chasing it with a bite of tart cucumber pickles. She smiled. Her appetite had returned. For the past week she had used the sleeping potion Olena had given her and slept through the night. She did not feel completely rested, but she felt much less grey, as though snow had melted from her mind. She felt as though she recognised herself.

Golgolin flapped into the dining room as they finished dinner. It squeaked and dropped a letter onto Baba Zima's lap before flapping over to Olena. She cuddled the guinea pig-fowl and smoothed its wings with her hand while it snuffled joyfully into her neck. Olena flashed a look of triumph at Valdim, though he was careful not to pay attention. Marisha thought Olena sat in a spot better aligned with the guinea pig-fowl's initial trajectory, but she was not about to butt in on their competition over who Golgolin loved most.

'Kchort!' Baba Zima banged on the table and upset her tea. Everyone looked up from their plates. Dunya dropped her fork with a clatter that made Valdim wince.

'What is it?' Dunya asked.

'Quiet, I'm still reading.' The Hands poured Baba Zima more tea as she reread the letter. 'Oh, well this puts us in a nice pickle indeed.'

'Does it now?' Olena said, still stroking the guinea pig-fowl's furry head.

'Yes. If I asked you to guess, you would never figure it out.'

'Don't ask,' Valdim said, 'Put us out of our misery.'

Olena put her hand out for the letter. Golgolin slipped from its perch and flapped away to Valdim. Baba Zima handed her the letter and gave Olena a moment to scan it before she said, 'There are reports of the plague in Forny Oblast.'

Everyone let out a collective gasp.

'But it's six months early!' Dunya exclaimed.

'So it is,' Baba Zima said with a touch of grimness.

Marisha's breath caught in her chest. 'How many?' she asked softly.

'Two hundred,' Olena answered.

Marisha pressed her mouth shut and sat back in her seat, crossing her arms.

'How is that even possible?' Anka-ny asked.

'Maybe all the collective efforts to get rid of the plague are making it stronger,' Baba Zima said.

'But if it's getting stronger . . .' Dunya gripped her fork so tightly her fingers turned red.

'Don't worry yourself, you silly girl, you know very well that no one in this house can be touched by the plague.' Baba Zima said the last to Olena who nodded, her eyes still scanning the lines.

'I want you to stay for longer,' Baba Zima said to Valdim. 'We will still go to Severny and stay there for a few weeks, but you will conduct your business from this house.'

Marisha tried to keep herself from reacting to Baba Zima's mention of going to Severny. They would be there in a week or two at most and she would fetch Dima. Surely he would not be in this early wave of victims. She had to put her cup down and place her hands in her lap to keep her fingers from trembling. If Dima caught the plague, if she could not bring him to the house's safety, it would all be for nothing.

She remembered how scared she had been during the last

plague year, almost ten years ago. The fear was formless, permeating everything. Dima and her father had told her again and again she would not fall asleep. While her brother had said it with an air of mild reassurance, her father had said it with grave certainty, as though he actually believed it. But she could never forget that her mother had fallen to the plague ten years prior. Marisha spoke to her sleeping mother more frequently as the plague drew close. She whispered her fears and asked for protection. The sleeping woman never twitched, her mouth stayed partly open, her skin dry and cool, her eyes closed. Marisha had wished her own lashes were as long and dark as her mother's. She had wished her mother's hand would squeeze hers back.

When Dima had come to her and said their father would not wake, she looked at him dumbstruck. Her mind pressed back on Dima's words like a door that opened the wrong way. She had been spared, but Papa! The koldun with the cold eyes had said Papa had drawn the evil eye by stating so boldly that the plague would not touch his children because his wife had already been claimed. Or maybe, Marisha thought, it was her own fault for asking for her mother's protection for herself and not for her father.

She remembered how the koldun's icy gaze had shifted from her father to her, and he looked so angry. She had had the terrible feeling that he wanted to hit her or drag her away, kicking and screaming. And he might have, had Dima not come to stand next to her and ask him to leave. He was just thirteen, his voice was thin, but she remembered how strong his stance was and how protected she had felt. Marisha was momentarily warmed by the memory of her brother standing next to her as solid as an oak door. In that moment, he had protected her. Now it was her turn. She would find him and keep him safe.

'We will need to do a lot more work. People will be frantic.' Baba Zima did not look as gleeful as she normally did when speaking of the plague preparations. Her brow crinkled with worry.

'But how can the plague be six months early?' Anka-ny asked. Marisha had been wondering the same thing. 'I thought it had come exactly every ten years since the beginning.'

Baba Zima nodded. 'Olena, any thoughts?'

Olena put the letter down. 'The plague outbreaks have only been recorded with such precision for the last, oh, hundred and fifty years. Maybe the ten-year cycle was a fluke.'

'It would be a fine time to have a cure,' Baba Zima said softly. Almost gently.

Olena shook her head. 'It would be nice. But I'm getting nowhere with the shield spell.'

'You'll get there. You said you would, so you will. Remember, you said you wouldn't disappoint me.'

Olena sat up straighter. She fixed Baba Zima a long stare before nodding.

'Besides,' Baba Zima said, 'we'll want your cure to stir the pot, not slip soundlessly into the broth. Think of this as the drama before the great reveal.'

Olena smiled slightly. 'It would not do to forego theatrics.'

'That is part of the job,' Baba Zima said.

Marisha felt sickened by what they said. She knew she should not take Baba Zima's strange sense of humour seriously, but to be so callous sounded like a challenge to the evil eye.

A small gasp came from Anka-ny.

'Anka-ny, what is it?' Dunya said. Everyone leaned over the table in alarm.

Anka-ny thrust out the letter to Dunya, her face contorted

with emotion. She said, the words barely intelligible, 'My sister.'

Dunya read the letter quickly. She said softly. 'Anka-ny's sister has fallen asleep to the plague.'

Marisha glanced up at the rest of the table. Olena looked horrified, Baba Zima impassive.

Baba Zima said, 'Anka-ny, such a terrible misfortune. I will ask the spirits if they can lend some relief to your family.'

At her voice, Anka-ny took several deep shuddering breaths and seemed to calm. 'We're not too far from my village? Will you–will you take me home?' She looked the koldunya in the eye. 'No other *theatrics* are necessary.'

Olena looked cowed and ashamed. Baba Zima's expression didn't change. 'Very well,' she said. 'I will direct the house to change course. It's in Drevost, isn't it?' At Anka-ny's nod, Baba Zima got up from the table. 'We should be there by morning.'

The pair of Hands that customarily floated at Baba Zima's shoulders lingered as the koldunya left the table. One of the ivory gloves held a teacup while the other poured in tea from the samovar. They brought it over to Anka-ny. When she didn't take it, they set it down in front of her and flew out of the room, after the koldunya.

OLENA LOOKED UP as Marisha walked into her workroom. She was feeling through a stack of papers. 'Honestly, you must have organised these so terribly on purpose, so that I would have to rely on you!' Olena leaned forward and pinned a stack of papers with her stump before it could slide off the table.

'What little organisation I have is much better than chaos, which was your system before I got here.'

'And yet, I never seemed to misplace my notes before then.'

Marisha opened a drawer and handed Olena her notes.

Olena shook her head and set the pages flat on the desk. 'Marisha. I have to ask you something.' She raised her finger and traced the outline of her birthmark. She closed her hand as though to stop the gesture. 'I need your help again. It's to do with the cure. And it's—'

'Breaking the rules?'

Olena licked her lips. 'Yes.'

'I'll help.'

Olena's eyes narrowed. 'You're a lot more eager than last time.'

'Things have changed.' Marisha thought of Anka-ny shuddering over her letter. What if she had received a similar letter for Dima? She did not want to try imagining what Anka-ny must be feeling.

'Hm. So you don't think I'm about to propose something reckless and stupid again?'

Marisha smirked. 'My standard for what constitutes reckless behaviour is one of the things that has changed.'

The corner of Olena's mouth raised in response.

Marisha said, 'What do you want to do?'

'I need to decide something, since the plague has already started.'

Marisha waited.

'I have heard there is a stash of the water of death hidden in the house and I want to find it.'

'Water of death?' Marisha raised her eyebrows. 'As in the water of death that fanatics believe exists somewhere in some puddle in some hamlet deep in the black woods?'

'Yes, that water of death, as in the water of death that when mixed with the water of life can cure any ills.'

Marisha tried to keep the disbelief from creeping on her face. Her aunt had once received a pilgrim in tattered clothes who said he searched for the water of death for the glory of Chernozemlya. Though her aunt was rapt by the man's story, she still made him sleep in the barn.

Olena was not fooled by Marisha's expression. 'What? You're telling me that after everything you've seen you did not think the water of death was real? And here I thought you were learning.' Olena's slight smile dropped. 'You've seen the progress we've made. Kiril is showing signs of stirring from the tinctures. But the physical koldunry isn't enough, we need a powerful spiritual anchor to loosen the plague's grip, and I was hoping the shield spell would be the key, but I can't figure it out. But maybe the waters of death could work instead.'

'And if it *really* exists why has no one tried it on the plague before?'

Olena grimaced. 'The waters do exist but they're from the other world–I must have told you hundreds of times that it's nearly impossible to bring anything back from there. I don't think anyone thought it existed up on the earth–not anyone serious anyway.' Olena must not have considered the pilgrim fanatics searching for mythical fountains as serious. 'But I received good information that there is some in this house.' Ah, so that was what Anatoli had told her.

'Wouldn't Baba Zima know about it? Why not ask her?'

'She doesn't know everything about this house, not by a long stretch. Besides, the water of death may have enough spiritual power to redirect the plague's attention by itself, but if it doesn't, we would also need the water of life, and in that case—' Olena looked to the side.

'She'll ask questions?'

Olena did not answer but began tracing the outline of her scarlet cheek with a finger.

'Well?' Marisha said.

'Well, what?' Olena stood tall and returned Marisha's direct gaze.

'If we find this water of death–then what? Don't we still need the water of life for it to work?'

'We have to see if we can find it first.' Olena's mouth was set.

Marisha shook her head. 'If these waters of life and death are so powerful and would be such a great cure to the plague, what do you need to decide?'

'Whether there is any other option. I still think that modifying the shield spell would work.' Olena sighed and lowered her hand from her face. 'But now with the plague come early, it feels like we're running out of time.'

'What about Pan Volya's black feather?'

'It's not in the house.' Marisha knew that Olena was probably right. Olena had tried other methods of locating the feather after the dowsing rod hadn't work, but nothing came up. Still, something that surely existed, if only because how deeply Pan Volya seemed to desire it, seemed more obtainable to Marisha than the stuff of legends. Obviously, Olena did not agree.

Marisha hesitated. She wanted to probe more. Olena was obviously conflicted about whether to follow Anatoli's suggestion, but Marisha did not want to push too much in case Olena became suspicious.

'I'll help you. But remember I'm taking a day off when we reach Severny.'

Olena's frown cleared as she remembered. 'That's right. To find your brother.'

Marisha nodded and looked down. She had told Olena of her plan to find Dima but not that Baba Zima had said she could bring him into the house–that is, if Marisha told her about Olena's agenda.

'Where do we need to look for the water of death?'

'There are many hidden places within the house, but,' Olena frowned, 'I'm worried that it would be somewhere that only Baba Zima has access to. If it comes to it, we can steal her keys.'

Marisha frowned. She pictured running down a corridor, the keys clutched tightly to her chest and the ivory Hands flying behind her like kestrels closing in on their prey, fingers outstretched.

'But it hasn't come to that yet. There are many places in the house that are neglected. I would like to examine the water stores, I believe there are rooms with barrels of water that have not been opened for a while–some because they need time to mature, others because they contain water that is not powerful enough. But I could imagine that a powerful source of water may be hiding amongst them, maybe even the water of death.'

'Right,' Marisha said. 'Shall we start looking? I'll find some chalk–we could mark the barrels as we examine them.'

Olena's brow relaxed. 'Thank you.' And Marisha knew the apprentice did not only refer to getting the chalk. Then Olena's expression darkened. 'This goes without saying–don't tell anyone about this.'

Marisha's palms suddenly felt clammy. She made an overcompensatory eye-roll. 'It's written in my contract that I must keep secrets.'

Olena looked at Marisha, and a small smile curved her lips. Marisha was happy that she had not told Baba Zima about seeing Olena with Anatoli. But she also felt a frisson of unease. If she helped Olena now and without informing Baba Zima, well, the koldunya might not let her bring Dima under the house's protection. But at the same time, the thought of tattling on Olena when she smiled at her with gratitude sickened Marisha. She could not shake the feeling she was like a fly caught in a spider web, so tangled she could not see the wheel-spoke structure. But she did not need to tell Baba Zima anything yet. And besides, Marisha really wanted to find out more about what Olena planned.

TWENTY-NINE

he next morning, Marisha's exhaustion from prying open one hundred and eighty-six barrels of water was swallowed by the general malaise of the house. The house slowed to a stop as they reached Drevost. The household gathered by the door to wish Anka-ny well. She and Dunya had hugged for a long time, and Dunya stood slumped by the door after her friend left.

'Dunya,' Marisha took a step forward, her hand raised slightly. Dunya straightened and turned. She walked past Marisha, either ignoring or not seeing her outstretched hand.

Marisha bit her lip. Since kidnapping Kiril, Marisha spent so much time with him and Olena, that she did not pay the other two assistants much mind. It had not seemed like a problem because Dunya and Anka-ny were always together. But now Dunya would be lonely. She thought of how kind Dunya had been when Marisha first arrived at the house. She crossed her arms, her stomach feeling heavy. She resolved to be more kind to Dunya.

'What are you doing?' Baba Zima, startling Marisha out of her thoughts. 'Loitering? Olena's giving you too little to do.'

Marisha jumped, not having heard Baba Zima approach. 'I—sorry, I should go—'

'You should indeed. Deciding whether or not to follow Anka-ny?' Baba Zima had a cruel smile on her lips. 'If you have so little to do, I have a task for you. The roof shingles are positively crusted with moss. I want them to gleam, do you hear?'

Baba Zima swept away and took a moment to look back at the dumbfounded Marisha. 'Oh, and if I feel even one twitch of complaint from the house, I will have the Hands dump you in a snowdrift while the house is skiing downhill. Understood?'

Marisha groaned. What a stupid task for her to do! The house's shingles needed regular cleaning, but the Hands were usually the ones to do it as they could get underneath the gutters much more easily than any assistant. Baba Zima was taking out her irritation on her, and for what? For Anka-ny abandoning them? For the plague coming early? For Marisha not yet producing any useful information? And how did Baba Zima think Marisha could gather anything useful if she was cleaning the roof instead of sticking with Olena? Now Olena would look for the water of death without her.

Marisha stomped up the stairs, pausing on the third floor to grab a harness and cleaning supplies. As she put her arms through the harness, she thought back on the first time she had gone up to the house's roof. Perhaps two weeks after she joined the household, the house had rubbed itself against a pine tree, sending lunch careening off the table. Baba Zima was angry at the neglect of her house's comfort and had sent all three assistants along with the Hands to clean and varnish the shingles. Though it had been hard work, Marisha had found it exhilarating to be so high up. The wood had shivered under her fingers as she knocked off a particularly large piece of moss that had been lodged between two shingles. She had patted the roof as though the house were enjoying the demossing. Marisha's memory of her surprising affection for the house mollified her frustration somewhat as she crammed herself, the varnish and the small flat spade up the rickety stairs to the trapdoor which opened up to the roof.

It was shockingly cold, but mercifully calm. Marisha snapped her harness onto the shoulder-high rope that hung taught between the house's two chimneys. The roof sloped in front of her like a mountain. She sighed at the futility of the task, and so she was very surprised and not at all unpleased at seeing Valdim a bit further down the line, crouched down and chisel in hand.

Marisha yelled out to Valdim and walked over, holding onto the rope with one hand and carefully placing her feet. The house skied smoothly, but Marisha felt like she was on the edge of tumbling the whole time. 'What are you doing out here?' Marisha yelled.

Valdim stood up. He wore a harness but did not hold onto the rope. 'I thought the house might need some seeing to, given everyone's poor mood. It can be sensitive, I think.' He sat down and invited Marisha to sit next to him, chisel already moving to scrape another shingle. 'This was my favourite chore when I was little.'

'You're very strange.'

Valdim let out a little chuckle, 'I suppose that's true.'

'It's very peaceful up here,' Marisha said, looking out at the white-and-brown landscape. She was reluctant to let go of the safety line and sit. 'A little scary, but peaceful.' She opened her hand and swayed for a moment before sitting down. It was the openness, the lack of cocooning structure, she decided, that made walking on the roof feel so much more unsafe than climbing a tree.

'You're done with the violin then,' Marisha said.

'No, not yet.'

Marisha turned to Valdim, noticing his frown. He stopped scraping the shingle and looked out to the white clouds that blanketed the pale spring sun.

'I wouldn't begrudge your help, but why aren't you holed away in your workshop? Don't you have to deliver the violin when we get to Severny?'

'Hmm. Well.' He ran a hand through his hair so that it stuck up on one side. 'I'm having a bit of trouble with that commission.' He shook his head. 'I don't think I can finish it.'

'What do you mean?'

'The commission came anonymously. I found an envelope on my doorstep which contained an unsigned letter and a sizable advance. That's usually not how I operate. I like to talk to the patron, learn about their style of playing, see their colours.'

'See their colours?'

'Yes, I mean, their musical preferences. It's a music term.' Valdim waved his arm as though his meaning were obvious, but the movement was abrupt. 'It's . . . difficult for me to craft an instrument if I can't suit the player. Like trying to find a house without being given an address.'

'So why did you take the commission?'

He looked away. 'I could not afford to turn it down. I can't even afford an apprentice at the moment. And since it's only me, it really does have to be quality over quantity. So, I really didn't have a choice, I had to take this commission.'

Marisha finally put two and two together. 'You're visiting Baba Zima because you need a place to stay!'

Valdim rounded his shoulders. 'A bit embarrassing. But yes.'

'But does it need to be perfect? I mean, whoever it is . . . will they really be able to tell the difference?'

'I would know,' he said. He was too smug for her taste.

'Well, there's nothing to be done, is there? Just sit in that nice hole you dug for yourself.'

'You don't understand.'

She snorted. 'Obviously.'

He muttered, 'I should go,' and stood up.

Marisha stared out at the snow, listening to the smooth whisper of Valdim's harness ring sliding down the rope and the clack of the trapdoor. She and Valdim usually got on so well. She had the sudden urge to throw her spade off the roof. Why had she got mad? She snorted. It all came back to what Baba Zima had said about her not having the right koldunic quality. Marisha may not have the right passion, but at least she took action instead of wasting time reaching for the treetops like Valdim—or Olena. She wondered if Olena's search for a cure to the plague was as unattainable as Valdim's search for perfection in his craft. If she really believed Olena's quest was so unattainable, maybe she should simply tell Baba Zima about Olena's plans. At least then she would get something out of her time in the house.

Later that day, Marisha had still not come to a decision. Instead of looking for Olena to help her with the search for the water of death, she went to the backroom to visit Kiril. He looked exactly the same. She approached her stool to the bed and whispered an apology for being so neglectful of him these past days. A feeling of peace washed over her, despite her heightened anxiety at the reports of the plague and Baba Zima's demands to report on Olena. She let her hand lay on the coverlet, inches away from his.

She wished to ask him what he thought about during that precious time in the evening when the day slowed. She wished to know if he liked sour cherry preserves or sugar in his tea.

'I like the preserves,' she whispered, 'at least two spoonfuls.'

She smoothed his hair back. She couldn't help herself. She thought of her parents asleep in their beds, and wished she had a memory of them awake together. With sunlight and laughter. She wished fervently that she had known Kiril before he caught the plague. She promised herself that she would drag Dima past Baba Zima and lock him in one of the cupboards if it would keep him safe.

'What are you doing here?'

Marisha jumped, startled. She had not heard Olena enter. She was embarrassed at being caught at Kiril's side. 'I was just sitting. Thinking.'

'Oh.' Olena stood there for a moment longer. 'Well, I didn't find anything on the fourth-floor right-wing corridors. We should try the other side.' Olena did not leave the doorway. She looked around the closet. 'Were you trying a tincture of your own?'

'What? No. I haven't tried anything yet.'

'You should. I saw you mixing some things together the other day. You must have some ideas after all this time.'

'Um. Maybe. But I wasn't doing anything like that now. I was thinking of my parents.' She looked back at Kiril in the bed. 'I wish I could talk to them. Do you—' Marisha stopped herself from asking whether Olena wished she could talk to her parents.

Olena pressed her mouth into a line for a moment before speaking again. 'Brooding won't accomplish anything. The only thing you can do is work on the cure. And when we find it, I promise the next people we will wake after Kiril will be your parents.'

Marisha gasped. 'Olena! Thank you.' Even though Marisha only ever half believed they would find the cure, Marisha knew Olena believed whole-heartedly and was touched by the gesture.

After evening fell, their brief conversation stuck in Marisha's mind like a burr as she rifled through Olena's notes. She knew she was doing wrong, but she began to feel frantic. She did not want to betray Olena by telling Baba Zima her actual plans, but she needed to find something, anything, to satisfy the koldunya. Anything to get Dima into the house. But she did not uncover anything beyond some more notes on the Nightingale the Robber story.

On the last page, Olena had written in her spiky script:

Shield spell deflects plague onto another person. Improved shield spell would deflect plague without needing another person to capture the plague's attention and become a deep sleeper. But how?

Pan Volya's feather supposedly can help contain the plague. M's father and Pan Volya have scar on wrist from feather. Grisha had sigil on his arm which protects against Nightingale. But M's father had the feather and is a deep sleeper, so feather does not lead to shield! What is feather for?

Then underneath Olena had written *scar*, *sigil*, and *shield* at three points of a triangle with thick lines in between them, as though Olena had repeatedly chased the words with her pencil. And in big letters underneath that was *BLACK FEATHER* boxed by lines, with an arrow to the right leading to *Nightingale?*

So, Olena was not as disinterested in Pan Volya and his mysterious black feather as Marisha had thought. They had come to the same conclusion. The feather could not protect against the plague since her father had become a deep sleeper. But Marisha had made no connection with the Nightingale the Robber story. It was true, the bogotir Grisha that slayed Nightingale the

Robber did have a sigil on his arm that protected him from the monster's deadly cry, but the connection with the feather was tenuous at best since Olena had said one could be marked by any number of powerful objects.

But Marisha stared at the arrow between *feather* and *Nightingale,* feeling sick. She pressed her fist to her sternum, doing her best not to think of the beaked man. Olena had seen a connection that Marisha had been unconsciously attempting to dismiss: between Nightingale the Robber and the black feather of Pan Volya's description, to the monster of her nightmare. Marisha swallowed the helpless feeling of being hunted. She set the notes back in their place while turning over Olena's question in her mind: What was the feather for?

She rummaged through the rest of the workroom, unsure of what she would find. She came upon a package at the bottom of a chest, wrapped in tissue paper. It held a beautiful green veil: layers of soft sage-green silk with gold beading on the edges and a gold band. She shook it out and three feathers fell. She recognised them as Golgolin's. She quickly wrapped everything up and put it back the way she found it. This was far beyond spying for Baba Zima; this was true prying. At least she had given Olena's possessions more consideration than Olena had given hers.

Much later than it should have been, Marisha stumbled up the attic stairs into bed. She watched the wet snow fall for a while and thought to herself that spring must be coming. She wondered how the house would travel from village to village without snow and skis in the summer. Probably by running. That would surely make Dunya feel quite nauseous. She hoped she would not get nauseous herself. Then she hoped Dima would still be awake come summer to enjoy it.

MARISHA STOOD AT the centre of a large room. She wore a strangely familiar wine-red dress with sickbed-yellow embroidery and ribbons twined through her overlong braids. Her heart raced. She must be dreaming, but how? She groaned. Her exhaustion had been so great she forgot Olena's potion.

Dancing people in outlandish clothes and masks surrounded her. She took deep breaths and scanned her surroundings. A woman in a midnight-blue dress picked over with silver thread sat on a dais, absorbed in conversation with a man in an orange kaftan with a black collar. A man with an olive-green cape and black whiskers streaked in white stood next to them. She suppressed a yelp and forced herself to look again: his height seemed wrong, but she could not see his eyes through the helmet-like green mask. Her heart calmed as she convinced herself he was not Pan Volya. Out of the corner of her eye, she saw someone in a blue kaftan approach her. He wore a blue-and-yellow feathered mask. She smiled despite his visible agitation. He felt familiar.

'You should not have come back here, it's all changed. You must have noticed up there.' He spoke to her like he knew her. The feeling of familiarity hung frustratingly out of reach, as though it would float away if she lifted her arms to catch it.

'What do you mean?' she asked. 'What's changed?'

'He promised to bring her what she wants, so she's already started everything. And if they find you here–you won't be safe from *him* anymore. Not after last time. You've damaged your protection.' Marisha pressed her hands to her sternum as though to stopper a hole in her chest. 'You must leave.'

He looked around and danced her to an opening along the wall. They ducked through it and the music died to a hum. They stood in an alcove. Three other couples paid Marisha and her partner no attention. One girl with mussed rusi blonde curls in a purple peacock dress was crying. Marisha's partner in the blue kaftan steered her towards a door in between two pillars of the alcove. He tried the handle, but it would not budge. He gestured for her to try and when she turned it, the door clicked open.

Trees lined a path beyond the doorway, trees that sparkled strangely in the moonlight, like they were made of diamond.

'Come with me,' she said and tugged at his sleeve.

'I cannot pass through.' He tapped his mask with a finger.

Marisha studied him for a minute, trying to remember something. Her eyes swept downwards from the edges of his blue feathered mask to his full lips. He had a scar on his chin, shaped like a horseshoe.

Her heart soared. 'Kiril! It's you! Why didn't you tell me?'

He smiled slightly. 'It's embarrassing to say, but I don't remember who I am. But I'm glad you recognise me. I hoped you would.'

'Is there nothing I can do?'

'Don't stop keeping watch over me. It keeps me safe.'

'Safe–from *him?*

He nodded. 'And don't come back here again. His mask is fusing already, and she's lengthened his tether.' He pushed her through the door.

'But—'

'You have to go.'

Marisha braced herself against the door to keep him from closing it. 'I will get you out of here. I promise.'

'Don't make promises you can't keep.'

'I promise.'

He stared at her for a moment as though struggling to say

something, then his mouth slackened and he reeled back. 'Run!'

He shoved her out the door. The dark lady in the midnight-blue dress clamped a hand around Kiril's arm. The movement threw the dark lady's sleeve back and Marisha glimpsed two interconnected whorls of raised skin on the back of her wrist. She winked at Marisha.

The beaked man exploded from the doorway and spread a cloak that looked like wings. The black feathers had filled in since the last time she saw him and glossed neatly away from his beak to his neck, covering what previously had been scales and fledgling down. Marisha fled.

MARISHA WOKE UP in the attic room drenched in sweat. She lay there for a long time listening to her heart hammer, before forcing herself to get out of bed and go downstairs. She intended to prepare tea but stood in front of the oven, immobile, lost in thought. She remembered so much of her dream, almost as vividly as the dream from the krug. The Hands rudely brought her up to earth by shoving her aside with a tray of sour cabbage and mushroom dumplings. She swatted at one and dodged its retaliatory floury handprint. It was a close call; she had forgot her apron. Marisha grumbled all the way through the unnecessary trip up the stairs and cursed Baba Zima for being so cruel as to put the assistants in the attic. She found her apron immediately and was almost out the doorway when she noticed something odd.

Anka-ny had left her pallet neatly made when she had left the house, the heavy woollen blankets properly tucked at the corners and wrinkle free. The blankets on Marisha's own pallet were thrown over half-heartedly. But Dunya was still in bed.

If the Hands had put the rolls in the oven, it was past six-thirty. Marisha would not begrudge Dunya some well-deserved extra sleep, but Baba Zima became snippy when they were late to the breakfast table.

Marisha crouched down and put a hand on Dunya's shoulder. Nothing. She shook it. The girl did not react. She had a horrible thought and felt for Dunya's heartbeat in her neck. Marisha sighed with relief at the slow but strong pulse . . . but why wasn't she waking up?

Marisha reeled back. No, it was impossible.

The house was warded against it, no one had ever caught the plague here. But she clapped loudly next to Dunya's ears, shook her until her own teeth rattled, put a bottle of Dunya's favourite strong rose oil under her nose. Finally, Marisha resorted to the ammonia.

Nothing.

Only a faint but steady heartbeat. The slow rise and fall of her breath.

The room spun. If Dunya had caught the plague, none of them were safe.

THIRTY

aba Zima stood, mouth open, eyebrows almost to her hairline. She pushed past Marisha and ran up the stairs, her footsteps audible from the oven room. Olena started to follow but Baba Zima told her sharply to stay put. She came back down fifteen minutes later, her mouth a grim line, her eyes wide with fear.

'It's the plague,' she said, her syllables short and clipped.

'But how—' Olena started.

'I don't know,' Baba Zima said. 'I will have to see to the wards. Do not disturb me.'

She pulled her keys from her belt and grabbed the poker from next to the oven on the way out. The Hands followed a few paces behind her. Marisha, Olena, and Valdim sat by the oven in silence. They were all that were left in the house, that were awake, anyways.

'I should go back to my violin,' Valdim said. His gaze flitted over to the other two, but neither of them said anything. He walked slowly to the door and paused in the doorway. 'Let me know if there is anything I can do to help.'

Marisha and Olena barely said anything to each other all day. They sat at opposite ends of the workroom or went about their chores, each wrapped in their own thoughts. The air felt as thick as linden oil. A few chords of music wafted down the stairs, but they stopped almost as suddenly as they started, as though Valdim's bow had broken mid-stroke.

Marisha felt completely helpless, for herself, for Baba Zima, for Olena and Valdim. Poor Dunya. Marisha scrunched her face at the thought of Dunya passing her last wakeful day doing pointless chores. And Dima–she had felt so hopeful that she could bring him into the house, into safety. She had even found out where he was! But now . . . She shook her head. And underneath the disappointment, dark fear weighed at the pit of her stomach. She was not safe. She could not escape.

And Baba Zima had been so certain that the house would protect them from the plague. She had said the house was not of this world, that it would protect their inhabitants. So long as they cared for the house, so long as the mistress's hold on the bolshina was strong, the house would take care of them. What had happened? Marisha had noticed how the house responded to Dunya: the floorboards never creaked when she walked, the doors never slammed around her, the air was never cold when she was in a room. Why would the house let Dunya fall asleep when it kept the others safe?

For some reason Marisha's thoughts were pulled back to her dream: Kiril's warning about the beaked man, how he had told her to run. She kept replaying the dark lady's wink at her, as though she knew a secret. And the whorl on her wrist–the same as the one Marisha's father and Pan Volya had. Marisha's stomach twisted into a knot.

'Olena?' Marisha could not say anything more.

'What is it?' Olena stopped her pacing back and forth for a moment to look at Marisha.

Marisha took a deep breath. Then held it. 'Would you like

some tea?'

'Oh. No thanks.' And Olena resumed her pacing.

Marisha stood for a moment longer, then left the workshop and went down to the oven room. She shook her head at herself and bit the inside of her lower lip. What could she have said? *I've been having nightmares again.* But the complaint sounded feeble and childish, even in her own mind. The dark lady having the same mark on her wrist as her father and Pan Volya was not proof of anything except Marisha's own anxiety, and her guilty thoughts about her father's sleeping state. The dream was only a product of that horrible potion's lingering effects and her fears. And her wishes. How else could she explain Kiril rescuing her? She stood still for a moment, the memory of dancing with Kiril rising through her, making her feel uncomfortably warm. She shook herself and tended to the samovar.

The coals glowed red in the oven. The day Baba Zima forgot to stoke it would be the day the sky fell on her head. Baba Zima would probably appreciate being brought tea, and Marisha wanted to be useful. Instead of drinking the first cup, Marisha filled a teapot with hot water from the samovar and carried it over to the receiving room where she thought Baba Zima sat in silent contemplation. But as she approached the door, she heard Baba Zima and Valdim's voices. Marisha hesitated, then set the teapot more comfortably in her arms. She stepped closer so she could listen better.

'How can the wards be weakened?' Valdim's voice was very loud in his agitation. He was pacing. His footfalls were much softer than Olena's. 'Is there the possibility they've been tampered with?'

'That possibility always exists.' Baba Zima sounded as calculating as always, but her voice lacked its humorous edge. She sounded tired.

'You are worried,' he said.

'More than worried,' she answered. 'Baffled.' She huffed. 'I've let Olena play for far too long–I think it's my turn.'

The sentence was punctuated by soft slurping. So, Marisha had not needed to bring Baba Zima tea after all.

'You think you can find a cure?'

'Hmm? For what? The plague? No, this has nothing to do with it. This is about her, trying to undermine my powers. I should have known she would try to come back.'

'She? Who are you talking about?'

The pacing stopped. Wood against wood scraped softly, the creak of a chair settling to bear its load.

'It does not matter, Valdim. But . . . do you remember, my son, that Anatoli and I were not the only apprentices of Baba Serafima? She had another one.'

'She did? Who?'

'Olga.'

'You don't speak of her.'

'I know. I've done my best not to,' she sighed, 'Valdim, there are things I should tell you, things that I should say, just in case—'

'What are you talking about? The plague may be getting stronger, but . . . you're the most powerful koldunya in all of Chernozemlya.'

'Your faith in my abilities has been misplaced before, my son.' She paused and Marisha could almost feel the weight of past conversations settle out of the air onto them. Baba Zima's voice lightened, 'But I'm afraid I may be only a chicken pretending to be a duck, clucking on the edge of the lake about to wet my feet for the first time. We shall see.'

'You're not a chicken or a duck. You're an albatross.'

'Ah, you are sweet. What did I ever do to deserve such a good son as you?'

Valdim said, 'Switch to eating out of wooden bowls so my skin wouldn't crawl?'

'I am a poor mother by those standards.'

'No, I didn't mean—' A heel scraped against wood. 'Would it . . . can I help you in any way? With my sight?'

'Thank you for offering. No, I do not think so. What I must do, I must do alone.'

'I wish—' He cut himself off.

'I have wishes too, you know.'

'You wish that I could have been a koldun.' Marisha could almost hear the bowing of his head.

'I wish I could give you the peace you crave. Sometimes I do wonder if studying koldunry might have made things easier—'

'I tried,' Valdim said stiffly.

'You did not try very hard. And I did not push you.'

'No. You gave me wooden spoons and violins.'

'It's what you said you wanted.'

A long pause passed unpunctuated by shuffling feet or drumming fingers. Valdim said, 'You were talking about the other apprentice, Olga.'

'So, I was. But it's not important now, I'll tell you about her when I get back.'

'Get back? Where are you going?'

'On a trip. It's time I take matters into my own hands. So to speak. Olena will be so pleased to have the run of the house. Temporarily of course.'

The chairs squeaked against the floor. Marisha rushed away from the door as quietly as she could and hurried back to the oven room. She mixed hot water into the black tea when Baba

Zima and Valdim walked in.

'Ah, I was bringing you tea,' Marisha said.

'How thoughtful. Took what I said about proving your devotion to heart, didn't you?'

Marisha did not answer but she could feel Baba Zima's gaze burning a hole into the back of her head.

'Where's Olena?' Baba Zima asked. Marisha shrugged and Baba Zima sent one of her Hands flying. It returned with Olena in its wake. A bag dangled from her stump and she carried a sheaf of paper in her hand.

'I've strengthened the wards,' Baba Zima announced.

'Already?' Olena sat down at the table and divested herself of her trappings.

Baba Zima waved a hand in the air. 'I did not redo them, simply strengthened them. Though a great load of good that will do.' She frowned at her teacup. 'I must leave for a few days,' she said.

Marisha acted surprised.

Baba Zima put a Hand out to forestall Olena from talking. It hovered, finger almost on her lips, an inch from her face. Baba Zima continued, 'I will leave Olena in charge. Temporarily. You will *not* have access to my poker.'

'And the oven?' Marisha asked.

Baba Zima waved the question away. 'I will only be gone a few days. I will leave enough coal to keep it burning. If not, there's always the stove.' Marisha looked in the corner where the small, pitiful stove stood. Its current use was as a surface for the Hands to pile dishes on.

Baba Zima said to Valdim, 'You are still set on going to Severny tomorrow?'

'Yes.'

'I suppose with Dunya asleep, there's no reason for you not to go.' Dry humour and bitterness laced Baba Zima's voice.

'Once I've delivered my commission, I'll return to the house. I'll probably be back before you will.'

Baba Zima did not ask Marisha if she still planned to go to Severny. Marisha did not know herself. Yesterday she had almost been looking forward to going. Even though the thought of seeing Dima again for the first time in so long made her palms sweat, she would have been bringing him good news. But now that Dunya was asleep . . . was there any point? A part of her asserted that she could still go to see him. She could find out if he had actually indentured himself. Her skin crawled. She almost did not want to know.

A traitorous small voice said even though she did not have a year's salary from Baba Zima, she did have a month's worth. A hefty amount. She could not escape the plague by staying in the house, nor could the house save Dima. But she could take the money, find her brother, and run. But where to? Was there a place beyond Chernozemlya safe from the plague? She did not think so.

Olena's voice interrupted her musings. 'You don't need any of us to come with you?'

'No.' Baba Zima said. 'I must go alone.'

'But if it's for the plague—'

'You will continue to work on your cure here. And it goes without saying, no one but us enters this house. So good news, you will not need to receive supplicants. I know how much they annoy you, Olena.'

None of them said anything.

Baba Zima let out a short chuckle. 'One would almost think that you will miss me. I'm only leaving for a few days. No need to act like this is my funeral.'

Baba Zima called Marisha into the receiving room soon after, but Marisha had nothing to say to her about Olena's plans. Why should she? The house could not protect Dima at all, now. It would not protect her either. And Marisha resented Baba Zima for putting her in this difficult position with Olena. Marisha wavered for a moment as she reminded herself that Baba Zima might have a good reason to fear Anatoli–it could not be for nothing that she had asked Marisha to spy for her. Besides, maybe Olena was wrong, maybe Baba Zima did know something about the water of death that Anatoli did not. But she pictured the hurt and betrayal on Olena's face if Baba Zima waltzed into her work room to ask about the water of death. It made Marisha squirm just imagining it. The koldunya only narrowed her eyes and made a great show of putting a large purse back into one of her pink-and-blue striped skirt pockets. But still, Marisha said nothing. There was nothing for her to say.

The feeling of restlessness remained. Marisha went to Kiril's bedside. She told him the new developments, that Dunya slept upstairs and Baba Zima planned a mysterious trip. She told him she was scared and she hoped she could still find Dima, even though it was too late to offer any measure of safety. She even told him of the conversation she overheard between Baba Zima and Valdim, and speculated about who Olga was. Marisha wished she had been able to see if Baba Zima's face had reflected the note of sadness Marisha had heard in the koldunya's voice. It made Marisha think Olga was not dead, but forcefully forgotten.

Marisha did not want to leave the peace she found by Kiril's side, but the pressures of the day intruded. They would arrive in Severny the next day and she would have to decide whether to go or stay.

The door to the linen closet swung open and Olena burst

through. Golgolin perched on her shoulder like an enormous furry parrot.

Olena declared, 'Oh good, you're here. Of course, what happened to Dunya is terrible. But one good thing did come out of Baba Zima leaving me in charge.' Olena unhooked the keys dangling at her belt and jangled them in front of Marisha.

'Baba Zima's keys,' Marisha said, feeling relieved. 'We don't need to steal them after all.'

'No. Must be a sign from the spirits that the time is right.' Olena's eyes glittered. 'We'll find the water of death. Tonight.'

THIRTY-ONE

Olena asked Marisha to help her chant softly in front of a locked door. It was partially hidden by the back stair, but Marisha had noticed it before because it had no doorknob but two keyholes: one near the top of the door and one at the bottom.

Olena produced the ring of keys from her pocket. 'Here, help me with this.' She handed Marisha a small, tarnished key. Marisha put her candle down and stepped onto the stool they had brought, and she fit the key into the keyhole at the top of the door. It went in smoothly. She tried to turn it but nothing happened.

'We have to do it together,' Olena said. She crouched and fit a key in the lower keyhole. A cynical part of Marisha's mind wondered if this was the only reason why Olena had asked for her help.

The door opened with a smooth click and they descended the stairs in a quick patter. Marisha's heart pounded in excitement. The stairway opened on a long corridor with doors lining each side. The corridor had a heavy silence that reminded Marisha of the sanitorium, except that the edge of sadness and neglect she had felt there was replaced with a prickling sensation that behind the doors lay sleeping things that were best left sleeping. They stopped before the first door and pulled it open.

The first two rooms had only cobwebs to decorate them. The third room contained only chairs, each unique: one tall, narrow and wooden with taloned feet, one squat and upholstered in a faded raspberry velvet. Marisha wondered if they would find a room that contained only tables.

The next room contained what at first glance appeared like pieces of fence leaning against the wall. When Marisha raised her candle in the doorway, it was clear that the fenceposts were not made of wood, but of long bones, and they were tipped with human skulls.

Olena stepped into the room, and the eyes in the human skulls glowed. Marisha stepped back further into the hall. 'I can't believe it,' Olena said. 'It's been here all this time!'

'What?' Marisha said. 'Did you need skulls for something?' Her voice came out squeakier than she had meant it to.

'No.' Olena replied, poking her head back out the door. She cradled a skull in the crook of her stump. 'I found this room with Valdim years ago! We were scared shitless.'

Marisha noted Olena's broad grin. The light from Marisha's candle reflecting off the bones of Olena's teeth as it did the skull's. 'I didn't realise you and Valdim played together.'

'We didn't,' Olena said. 'It was just the one time.' She looked back in the room. 'I remember it being much scarier. He'll never believe it.'

Marisha was suddenly curious about Olena and Valdim's childhood. 'Why didn't you play together? You're the same age. You grew up together.'

'Not really,' Olena said, stepping back into the room to return the skull. 'He left to study his violins only a few months after I arrived and he only came back about once a year after that.

So, not many occasions to play together.'

'Hm,' Marisha replied, thinking about them yelling at each other in the clearing at the krug. 'For some reason, I imagined the two of you butted heads as children.'

'I did break one of his violins,' Olena looked down. 'But it was an accident.'

'But nothing beyond that?'

Olena shook her head. Marisha said, 'Doesn't sound that bad.'

Olena tilted her chin to the side. 'No. I guess it doesn't.' She peeked one last time into the room with the skulls, then closed the door.

Through the opposite door, they found a pool of a molten silvery metal sunk into the floor. It took up almost the entirety of the room, with only a small edge wide enough to walk around it.

'It isn't water,' Marisha said. 'Right?' She knew she shouldn't take appearances for granted.

'No,' Olena said, but she stepped closer to the pool's edge. Marisha did the same and when she looked into the pool, she saw her own reflection, but instead of looking back at her, it was turned towards Olena with an expression of surprise on her face. Her reflection was saying something to Olena's.

'Did you see that?' She hissed at Olena, the strangeness of the phenomenon making her whisper. 'It's us, but not.'

'I see,' Olena said, frowning. They both looked back at the pool, and instead of seeing them crouched over it, Olena's reflection mumbled something to Marisha, looked to the right and got to her feet, Marisha's reflection doing the same a moment later.

'Where are we going?' Olena said and got up.

Marisha stood up too and saw her reflection walking around the pool's edge, her candle held high and angled towards it, her eyes searching to the right and in the pool, as though she were chasing something. Marisha and Olena followed their reflections' movements and began searching for whatever their doubles were looking for. Then Marisha saw Olena's strange reflection freeze, mouth open and eyes gazing into the middle distance. Her own reflection stopped walking as well. Their reflections leaned into each other and began talking. Marisha stopped and came to the same realisation as Olena turned to her and said, 'It's us a few seconds from now!'

They both peered back into the pool, their silvery future selves for a moment a mirror of the present, still and focused, absorbing the strange image. Then Marisha saw her reflection peer closer into the pool. Marisha did the same, lifting her candle higher, bending closer, her reflection also getting bigger, searching–then her eyes widened and Olena's reflection grabbed her reflection's arm and they scrambled back and disappeared from the metallic pool. Marisha stood stunned, a sense of foreboding gripping her. Then the pool rippled from the centre and sent metallic waves to the edge, as though something had disturbed the surface from underneath. Olena grabbed her arm and they both ran from the room and slammed the door behind them.

'What was that?' Marisha said, gasping.

'Scrying mirror. Must be the one that killed Baba Helga a hundred and fifty years ago. Extremely dangerous.' Olena said, panting.

Instead of being discouraged, Olena took it as a sign that they were on the right path.

The next door did not open, and none of Baba Zima's keys worked on it. Olena reluctantly left it, saying that they would need to return to it if they did not find the water behind the other doors.

The door after that opened outwards and revealed an empty room with what appeared to be a basin at the centre. Before stepping inside, Olena crouched down. Marisha looked as well and saw that a number of branches were placed upon the threshold.

Marisha said, 'Rowanberry,' as though they were back in Olena's workroom surrounded by packets of herbs to identify.

'Yes,' Olena said, 'And what is it for?'

Marisha crouched down next to her. The branches adorned with bunches of bright red berries had been placed carefully across the doorway in a small heap to make a low barrier. Who had placed the rowan branches there? Was it Baba Zima, or an older koldunya? The rowanberries looked fresh, but perhaps the koldunry itself preserved them. She said, 'Rowan is sharp and placed across the entry threshold, it can protect against malevolent spirits from entering a house.'

'Or a room, in this case,' Olena said. She stayed crouched for a few more moments, her fingers hovering over the rowan as though feeling for any boundaries. Then she straightened and stepped over the threshold.

'Come,' she said, 'It's not us it's guarding against.'

Seeing that Olena stepped over the rowan branches without any ill effect, Marisha followed suit. And though nothing happened, she felt even more the intruder than when they had used Baba Zima's keys to enter this forbidden hallway.

Olena approached the basin and gestured for Marisha to come closer with the candle. Marisha looked around, noting that indeed, the room was empty except for the basin. This basin was much smaller than the silver pool, only the size of a birdbath. She angled the candle behind her to throw better light onto the basin. It had rough granite walls, and a round lip level with her elbow. It reminded Marisha of a mortar. Olena motioned for her to bring the candle closer. The light did not reflect off the surface. But that could not be right. Marisha lowered her face cautiously to get a closer look. Her breath ruffled its surface, and ripples hit the sides, changing the level where the mortar walls dissolved into nothing. Definitely water. But water that gave no reflection.

'I think this is it,' Olena whispered so loudly it bordered on a squeak.

Marisha found her excitement infectious. 'It's certainly strange.' She leaned closer.

'Don't touch it! You could lose a finger.' Olena pulled her back, her fingernails digging in Marisha's shoulder.

'I wasn't going to!' Marisha rubbed her shoulder while Olena examined the strange substance.

'I can't believe it,' she said, 'Anatoli was right.'

'Anatoli?' Marisha was unsurprised.

'Oh. Yes.' Olena pointedly did not look at her.

'So, he's the one who told you about the water of death?' Marisha thought it a safe assumption to come to on her own.

'Yes.' Olena turned to Marisha. 'Don't you know what this means? Marisha, we can cure the plague! Your parents! We can wake them.'

Her words made Marisha's chest freeze in painful longing. 'That's wonderful, Olena, but aren't you forgetting something? The water of life?'

'Don't worry about that.' And she shifted again away from Marisha, gaze locked on the basin.

'Olena, where will you find the water of life?'

Olena still looked away from Marisha. 'Anatoli has some. And if this works, we'll be written into history.'

Marisha did not answer. She felt hot and cold all over. She

should be as happy as Olena, happier even, at the possibility of waking her parents. But she felt hollow. Olena interpreted Marisha's silence as awe and did not question it when they left the corridor and locked the door behind them. But the feeling accompanied her to bed and for the first time in a long while, fear of what could happen while awake, not asleep, kept her open-eyed.

THE HOUSE HAD been approaching Severny all night. It skied through fields still barren with frost and past little clusters of wooden dachas. By morning they traversed a forest so thick with pine that it would be impossible to know the greatest city in Chernozemlya was close by. Marisha stood by a window, marvelling at their speed and how the house never knocked into tree trunks or got scratched by branches. The trees must somehow jump out of the house's way. Marisha felt almost certain she would notice if the house squeezed in between the trunks.

She recognised Olena's firm tread up the stairs. 'I can't believe you're leaving,' Olena shook her head. 'Especially now! We're so close to finding a cure.'

Marisha tried to keep the wall of guilt at bay. She was not purposefully abandoning Olena, but she needed to talk to Dima, now more than ever. She had woken up with a feeling of absolute clarity. If she was honest with herself, she felt more guilty about abandoning Kiril. Her promise to herself that she would never leave him had even surfaced in her unguarded dream a few nights ago. Olena, on the other hand, was more than capable of taking care of herself.

'I'll only be gone for two days, three at the most.'

'But must you leave now?' The pleading quality to Olena's

voice surprised Marisha.

'Who knows when we'll next be in Severny.' Marisha could not explain the sense of urgency she felt. What if she was too late and Dima had already fallen asleep? Again, she reminded herself her dream was just that; she had not actually talked to Dima, he was not actually indentured. But Marisha felt uneasy, and not only about Dima.

'Olena,' Marisha hesitated. She remembered the joy that had shined from Olena's eyes last night when they had found the water of death. It was joy bordering on zealousness, which at once scared her and made her wonder whether any intervention would matter. But she had to say something. 'Are you sure about this?'

'About what?'

'About trusting Anatoli–Baba Zima told you not to talk to him. Don't you think she has her reasons?'

Olena snorted. 'You mean old arguments and petty grievances?'

'It's more than a petty grievance, Olena. I'm sure Baba Zima has held lots of grudges, but this is the only person she has forbidden you contact. And the water of death, doesn't it seem too easy, too convenient to you that Anatoli knew it was here?'

'He lived in this house too and Baba Serafima told him things she did not tell Baba Zima.'

'But why? If she left the house to Baba Zima, how could she not tell her?'

Olena shrugged. 'I don't know. But I wouldn't be surprised if some pettiness were involved. And Anatoli might not have been entirely truthful about how he came to the information about the water of death.'

'And doesn't that bother you?'

'No.'

Marisha took a deep breath. 'I don't think you should work with Anatoli. It's a mistake.'

Marisha's words hung in silence for a moment. Olena let out a small puff of air. 'Your concerns are noted.'

Marisha waited to see if Olena would say more. When she didn't, Marisha said, 'But you'll work with him anyway.'

'I don't see why not. It seems that I am the only person who sees that a cure is more important than pride or old squabbles.'

'More important than pride? Olena, you are the proudest person in this house. If Baba Zima's pride could fill a teacup yours would overflow the laundry tub.'

'I think that's an exaggeration.' Olena smirked. Marisha did not let her frown soften. 'It's the only way,' Olena said in a reasonable tone. 'Don't you want to find the cure? Just think, we could wake your parents. And Kiril! Don't you want to talk to him?'

Marisha wished she could cool the blush she knew spread on her cheeks. 'Of course I do. But something about this feels wrong.'

'You're saying that because of Baba Zima's attitude.' Olena shook her head and frowned. 'I'm surprised this is where you draw the line. Breaking into the sanitorium was fine, as was kidnapping. Experimenting on a plague victim for months–no problem. But working with someone who gives you a wrong feeling, someone who may hold the key to the cure, and that's too far. Care to explain the logic?'

'He feels wrong. You just can't sense it because he's been buttering you up. Telling you exactly what you want to hear.'

Olena bristled. 'Oh, is that so? And yet his help has led to us finding the water of death.'

'The water of life and death can't be the only way to find a cure, you've been working for months—'

'With no results! You know that!' For a moment Olena's confident expression crumpled.

'So, you're giving up?'

'Dunya is asleep! Baba Zima is scared! There are no other options.'

'There have to be!'

'Do you have any brilliant ideas? No, I didn't think so. You don't take risks, you don't make leaps. You'll always be a mediocre koldunya at best, and it's not because you're starting late, it's because you don't have the dedication to do what's necessary.'

Marisha could not stop the wince from crossing her face. Olena's insult settled at the bottom of her belly and spread like a fire upwards through her chest. Her breath came quickly and she drew her arms away from her side, fingers splayed. She took a step forward and met Olena's gaze straight on. 'I may not be a great koldunya as you so well put it, but by your own definition, neither are you. You are acting out of desperation and fear, not dedication. Even I, from my perch well below Olena the Great, can see that nothing good can come of this.'

Olena's birthmark flushed purple. 'What do you care, you'll be running after your brother, remember? And what good will finding him do? It won't keep him safe from the plague! It won't wake your parents.'

'What good will it do? It will allow me to talk to him for the first time in five years! It would let me know–don't pretend for even one second that if you had the opportunity to tell *your* brother all the things gnawing at your soul you wouldn't go in a heartbeat. Even if it meant delaying your glory at finding a cure. Probably even if it meant never finding a cure at all. But that option is gone, isn't it?'

Olena did not speak. She sagged and put her hand out to the wall for support. The lightning Marisha had felt coursing between her fingertips evaporated. She wished she could swallow back her words. She had never expected to see Olena look that way, with a trembling lip like she was about to cry. And Marisha had caused it. 'I'm sorry,' Marisha said, 'I didn't mean–look, I don't know what happened there–but it was out of line.'

Olena took a shaky breath and looked at the floor. 'I will manage fine. And Dunya will soon be awake; she can do your work for a few days.'

'But Olena, I still want to help—'

'It doesn't sound like you do. It does not sound like the cure is a priority for you.'

'I will be gone for a day! Two at most! You really can't wait that long?'

'How do you not understand how urgent this is?'

'Is it that it's urgent or is it that Baba Zima will be back at any moment and you don't want to be caught doing something you know is wrong?'

The house shuddered to a stop, throwing Marisha and Olena forward. It felt strange to be still, dizzying. Marisha reached a hand to the wall for support.

'This is where we leave you. I hope—' Olena stopped herself from saying something. She bit her lip. 'I hope it's worth it.'

'Olena, promise you'll wait for me to come back before meeting him!'

But Olena walked away without another word. Marisha cursed the woman's stubbornness. She wavered for a moment. Should she leave now that Olena promised to do something rash? She wondered again why Olena wanted to be *the one* to find the cure. Then she thought guiltily that if she had told Baba Zima what she knew before the koldunya had left, then maybe this could have been prevented. She let out a long exhale through her nose. No. Spying on Olena was wrong, and no amount of good it could have done would have changed that.

She had to go see Dima; she owed it to herself. She would be lying if she said Olena's insults hadn't stung. Part of her wanted to leave Olena to her fate, to let her make this big mistake and deal with the consequences alone. She would deserve it. But Kiril, and now Dunya . . . the idea of leaving them did not sit well with Marisha at all.

She stood still for so long that her neck was stiff when Valdim came upstairs and called out to her, 'Are you ready?'

Valdim had traded his large sawdust-covered shirt for a tailored white linen one. He wore a clean kaftan and his ironed trousers folded neatly into his boots. His beard was trimmed into an actual shape and his face was free from smudges.

'Sorry for staring, I hardly recognised you.'

He set down an oblong wooden case and bowed. 'I must look the part at times.'

She forced a smile and pointed to the case. 'You finished the violin?'

'Yes,' Valdim said. 'It was hard, and it's nowhere near perfect, but I think I like it that way.' He smiled at Marisha briefly, and Marisha felt the acknowledgement of their difference in opinion. 'Its tone has something else. A more . . . spontaneous strength.'

Marisha smiled genuinely. 'I'm glad.' Then the words burst from her mouth, 'Valdim, I don't know if I should go. I'm worried Olena will do something stupid.'

He snorted. 'That particular danger is always present. She's not your responsibility, Marisha. If she wants to play mistress of the house, let her.'

Marisha lapsed into frowning silence. It was only when they stepped into the cart that she realised Valdim was just as taciturn as she was.

'And what's bothering you?' Marisha asked.

'Oh, you know,' Valdim waved in the house's direction. He seemed unwilling to say more. Marisha understood his mood and turned to watch the trees go by. She told herself that Valdim was right, that Olena was responsible and had made up her own mind and there was nothing she could do. But the view of the orange house swallowed by the white-and-grey landscape left Marisha with a terrible feeling she should return and grab it.

THIRTY-TWO

Olena was alone. She swung the keys around her finger. When Baba Zima had given them to her, she had sardonically told her not to burn the house down while she was gone.

At least she had Golgolin. The guinea pig-fowl sat perched on her shoulder as she walked around the house. It was peaceful in a way. She no longer felt the oppressive presence of the others, though their memories lingered. She was tempted to perform a cleansing ritual but instead went to the door of the locked hall with the Hands standing in for Marisha to turn the top key. See, she did not need Marisha. Her stomach clenched at the thought of her assistant. If Marisha wanted to go, good riddance. She had made her priorities clear. And as for Valdim . . . Why had she sought him out?

She replayed their encounter in her mind one more time.

Not long after arguing with Marisha, she had found herself before Valdim's door. Olena had not known why, but she knocked. He had been surprised to see her, as surprised as she had been by his neat appearance.

She said, 'You do perform after all.'

'Yes. You sound disappointed.'

'On the contrary. It's what I expected from you.'

'Aren't you in a charming mood today.' He turned to let her come in. A half-open trunk stood to one side of the room. He was still packing. 'I would've expected you to be more thrilled that you've been made temporary mistress of the house. So close to what you've always wanted.'

'Well, if those aren't the most half-hearted congratulations ever offered, I'll eat my mortar. I'll need to scourge this room to stop the evil eye from sticking.'

'I've never wished you ill, Olena.'

She snorted. 'Not out loud.'

His voice crackled with impatience, 'What do you want? You've avoided me ever since the krug and now you seek me out. Why?'

'I–I don't know.' She faltered. Why was she there? He was right, she had avoided him. There were several times when she had heard his footsteps approaching and she would pause in whatever room she was in to make sure he had walked well past the door before opening it. She could not explain her behaviour, except that after the krug and his stunt with the mouse and his keeping quiet about Anatoli, she felt like the ground had been pulled from beneath her feet. Even though he had rejected a life of koldunry and managed to escape Baba Zima's pull in a way that Olena never would, she had thought he had only always viewed her as a rival for his mother's affections. But now, everything felt different.

Olena suddenly found that she wanted him as an ally. If he decided he had to reveal her secret to Baba Zima at the last minute, Olena sensed she would be devastated. And she wouldn't only be devastated that Baba Zima would know she had been untrustworthy, no–it was that *he* would tell, that was the part that would make her crumple up inside.

And she didn't know how to feel about that. Valdim's eyes were trained on her, his brow crinkled. She hated his shiny boots even more than the sawdust-covered ones.

Valdim repeated, 'You don't know why you're here.' He crossed his arms. 'For the pleasure of lording my mother's keys over me, perhaps.'

Heat rose to her face. 'You can't stand the thought of me having the bolshina, can you? Too bad.'

'You do not have the bolshina. You have the keys for a few days, nothing more.'

'And you're bitter about it. Ha! Maybe that's why you're leaving.'

He slammed the trunk's lid shut. Olena tried not to flinch at the loud crack. He said, 'I'm leaving because I have a living to make! But of course, you can't conceive of a reason that doesn't involve you. Because you think your problems are so vast that those of others can't compare. What about Marisha? She's the best friend you've ever had, but is she going to Severny with your blessing? You don't care, Olena. And maybe if you did, you wouldn't be stuck in this house all alone.'

She had wanted to hit a nerve and had succeeded. But she had not expected him to shout at her. She kept her voice even to show him who was really in control. Her jaw clenched with the effort. 'I happen to like being alone.'

'Then why are you talking to me?' Valdim shook his head. 'You're lying to yourself. You live in a dreamworld, Olena.'

Olena felt as though her breath had been stolen out of her chest. She closed her open mouth. 'I should leave you to pack up your wood shavings.'

He gave her a look so scathing she took a step back. He side-stepped her and opened the door. 'Please. Leave. I hope you're happy in this big empty house. It's all you've ever wanted.'

OLENA PAUSED BY the room with the mirror of molten silver on the way to examine the water of death. It was an unnecessary risk, now that she knew that the creature that killed Baba Helga lurked underneath the surface. But she was drawn to the room and sat by the pool, her candle casting enough light to see herself clearly in the silvery surface. She both did and did not want to scry the future; she both did and did not want to know what choice she would make. But all she saw when she looked in the mirror was her own frowning face, looking back. Her reflection raised a hand and brought it near the surface, almost touching it, and so did she, following her reflection's lead in a strange game.

She could not remember the last time she had scrutinised her own reflection. The pool had a silver sheen to it, making her look otherworldly, a glowing moonchild. It was strange, with the delay between her and the reflection's minute movements, she felt as though she looked at a whole other person. The reflected Olena smiled wryly at her. Olena wondered what it would be like to talk to another one of herself. They probably wouldn't stand each other. The thought brought a sad smile to her lips. Her reflection was now turning her head and holding the pose so that Olena could only see half her face. Olena leaned in fascinated. The two sides of her face looked so different. In one of them, she was a red and purple demon, all rage, all fire. But when her reflection turned her face, she could barely see her birthmark, just a little red creeping over the bridge of her nose and chin. She looked almost demure. Almost beautiful.

What would it have been like to be that woman, the one without the terrible birthmark? Maybe that woman would not have had the strength to be a koldunya. Maybe that woman would not be standing in the basement of a chicken-legged house, with only a guinea pig-fowl and her reflection for company.

In truth, she was not as resolved to reach out to Anatoli as she had told Marisha. But if the waters of life and death worked... Her imagination ran away with her. She saw herself being crowned by the Grand Prince for finding a cure to the plague. Baba Zima would hug her, crying, and hand her the poker, telling her she was prouder than words could say. Marisha, her eyes glowing with tears, begged forgiveness for having doubted her.

And her family. The Grand Prince would find them all: her parents, grandparents, aunts, uncles and cousins, and they would be forced to acknowledge she was not born cursed. They would say she was a blessing. They would bring Fedya and maybe they would admit what had happened to him was not her fault. Maybe he would forgive her.

She tore her mind away from her fantasy and thought of her recent letter from Anatoli. He had been all niceties. She had expected him to ask to come into the house, so they could mix the water of death and life together. But instead, he had suggested they meet and mix the waters outside the house. She had been prepared to refuse him entrance and had not been sure what to say at the unexpected proposal.

Olena put her hand in her pocket and drew out the double-walled glass vial that she had found in Serafima's trunk. It fit so nicely in her hand and when she squeezed it, it felt like squeezing an egg–surprisingly unbreakable. Baba Zima had said that her mistress had used it to call her destiny. Was Olena shying away from calling her own?

Marisha's misgivings about Anatoli echoed in her mind.

Yes, Baba Zima had explicitly forbidden her to contact Anatoli. Of course, at the time, the plague had not broken out early and cursed so many. It had not overcome the house's protection and struck Dunya. Surely now, since the situation was drastic enough that Baba Zima left the house, it was drastic enough to work with Anatoli.

Olena had promised she would let no one enter the house. She had promised she would not see Anatoli. But she had laboured so long to find the cure. She wanted it more than she wanted anything else. Her irrefutable proof she was not cursed.

'All right,' Olena said to the silver pool's surface, her reflection already standing up and leaving. 'I'll do it.'

THIRTY-THREE

arisha entered Severny with only the clothes on her back, a heavy purse, a folded letter, and a pocketful of potions. The cart had dropped Valdim off at a boarding house first and because she did not want even the driver to know her true destination, she asked him to drop her at the public sanitorium. The huge spire was visible from almost everywhere in the city. It was usually very quiet, but today a knot of people clamoured before long sheets of paper tacked to the sanitorium wall and covered with columns of tiny writing: the names of those who had already fallen asleep to the plague unnaturally early.

So many, she thought, and a chill rose up her spine. The cart driver was long gone, she turned away from the sanitorium and walked towards Korisha Street. The city hadn't changed much since she last left it. Except the streets were emptier, more businesses were boarded up. Marisha walked faster. A cat slunk into the shadows as she turned the corner to Korisha street. A single house, small and gated, stood there. She noted that it seemed better kept than the neighbouring houses: the gate was free of dry rot and the step was swept clean of ice. Her blood pounded in her ears. Maybe it would be Dima to open the gate. But what if it wasn't? She rang the bell. For an instant, she would rather dash down the street than know if Dima was in the house.

When the gate opened, an old maid with a pear-shaped face, wearing a black dress and a starched yellow cap stood waiting. 'The master koldun is not taking supplicants anymore.'

Marisha stuck a hand out to keep the gate open. 'My good woman, I'm obviously not a supplicant,' she said in her best imitation of Baba Zima's tone. 'I'm a colleague.'

The woman gave her a dubious look but stopped trying to shut the gate. 'You?'

Marisha was pleased she had never bothered to remove the krug amulet from her pocket. She showed it. The old maid's scowl of suspicion dropped to a business-like haughty frown and she opened the gate wider.

Marisha followed the maid up a short cobblestone path and through the front door. She fiddled with her shawl as she had seen Baba Zima do many times. The maid waited impatiently. Marisha let her wait. When she was done, she said, 'Take me to your master.'

The maid blew the air out of her cheeks and took Marisha to a room with the table and chairs of a receiving room. She left to get the master. This receiving room was very different from the one in Baba Zima's house. One wall was completely lined with shelved bottles. The bottles on one shelf held various liquids. The next two had ones that contained tight rolls of paper. Incantations. Marisha walked over to examine them, in the hope that the distraction would help calm her beating heart.

The middle shelf was a mishmash of objects laid out in an ordered hodgepodge. There were lacquered boxes, a flowerpot, a round mirror, rolled-up embroidery. Her gaze arrested on a palm-sized wedge of glass. Somehow, even among the haphazardly lined objects, it seemed the odd one out, maybe because of its irregular edges or because it distorted the blue-green colour of the glass bottle it leaned against to a light grey. How very strange.

Marisha picked it up and almost promptly dropped it. Her fingers, as she saw them through the piece of glass, swirled with a particular shade of burgundy veined with a particular shade of sickbed yellow. Her stomach seized with recognition and her fingers curled tighter until the blunt edges of the glass bit into her palm. Her dress in her latest dream had been these shades exactly, that rich burgundy wool with that awful yellow embroidery. Her breath came in sharp pants.

'Miss,' the maid was back, 'the master will see you.' She looked disapprovingly at Marisha's double-handed hold on the glass. A man stood behind her. Marisha's eyes widened.

The maid tilted her head towards Marisha. 'The young lady who says she's a colleague.' Marisha did not miss the maid's dubious tone.

Pan Volya clapped his hands together. 'Of course, I know the young lady. Welcome, welcome.' The maid's jaw slackened and she left the room, glancing back at Marisha.

Pan Volya smiled at her and gestured at a chair, inviting her to sit. Pan Volya, the koldun with the cold eyes who had asked about a black steel feather. The one who had given her the potion he said would calm her sleep, but that had almost killed her instead. She masked her surprise with a polite smile and murmured her greeting.

He said, 'I had not thought to see you again, so shortly after our last encounter.'

Marisha found her voice back. 'No, I do not suppose you would have expected to ever see me again at all.'

'But what–oh, the potion, yes, I am terribly embarrassed

about my error. By the time I realised, the krug was over and we were long separated. But obviously you are skilled enough to have caught the mistake yourself. Marigold, what had possessed me? But no harm done. You do forgive me, don't you?'

Marisha forced her mouth into a smile. 'I should not think to hold a grudge for a lapse like that. I have made such small mistakes myself. As you said, no harm done.'

Marisha turned around to put the glass back on the shelf. She took a deep breath. He had surprised her, but she needed to recover her calm. The location spell had pointed to this house so Dima must be here. Where was he? She wrestled the anger that wanted to claw its way up her throat. She would gain nothing by lashing out. And besides, fear curled around her anger. This man had poisoned her without scruple and she was now in his house. At his mercy. She had nothing to defend herself with, only Baba Zima's shadow potion. A poor weapon. Her fingertips tingled with adrenaline. She dropped her hands from the shelf to her side and settled into an expression of amused disinterest borrowed from Baba Zima.

She sat down in the offered chair. 'A very interesting object,' Marisha said, glancing back at the glass, as a way to start the conversation in a safe spot.

'It is, isn't it?' the koldun replied. 'I don't think I've ever seen anyone pick this one up before. Though it is one of the most precious objects in my collection, very important for my research. I am curious, what drew you to it?'

Marisha lifted an eyebrow and smiled with the corner of her mouth. 'Perhaps I will tell you. But I was hoping I you could answer a question of my own, first.'

'Ah. Of course. I almost forgot I did not invite you here. Have you come to tell me news of the feather? No? Then please, tell me how I may be of service.'

Marisha swallowed. 'I am looking for someone. A Dimitri Elyasevich Galinov. I was told I might find him here.'

'I see. And may I ask why?'

'I'm sure you can imagine Baba Zima taught me ways of locating things.'

'Quite. But I meant, why do you wish to see him?'

She had not prepared for this particular lie and panic flashed through her. She did not want to reveal that Dima was her brother. Besides, she had introduced herself to Pan Volya as Dunya. The lie formed in her mind as quickly as a snowball rolling downhill. 'One of the other assistants–Marisha. She asked me to find him. He's her brother. She's plague stricken.'

The koldun's eyebrows rose. 'Really? But how–how unfortunate.' He must have known about Baba Zima's house shielding its inhabitants from the plague. He suppressed his surprise quickly; his eyes remained cold, his expression unreadable. She hoped he believed her.

'Yes. Baba Zima is distraught. To have one of her assistants fall asleep . . .' Marisha sighed. She remembered Baba Zima saying a good lie was built like a plum, it contained a pit of truth. 'It's affecting us all. After reports that the plague started, Marisha made me promise that I would find her brother in case she fell asleep. It's strange, she had this conviction that she would be struck, even though no one in Baba Zima's house has ever been touched by the plague. Isn't that strange?'

As Marisha spoke, the koldun's face relaxed. Did he believe her? 'Sometimes what people fear comes to pass and it's easy to think that one caused the other.'

'And you don't think this is the case?'

'I didn't say that.' Pan Volya paused meditatively.

Marisha let some of her impatience show through. 'So, may I talk to her brother?'

He contemplated her for a moment and nodded. 'You may. Though you won't get an answer.'

No! Little dots swam before her eyes. She didn't want to ask, she didn't want to know. But she had to. She put her hands on the armrests to keep herself from clasping them. 'Why is that?'

'He too was struck by the plague.'

She was too late! Marisha gripped the armrests, pushing back to keep herself from collapsing. She focused only on keeping her face blank while her mind raced. Yes, part of her had expected this, but it did not mean she was prepared to hear it. Her brother! She knew she needed to stop the wave of grief that threatened to overcome her: she couldn't think about him, but he was all she could think about. Dima making faces at Pan Kazan behind his back to make her laugh, Dima jumping with glee at finding the largest, most perfect mushroom and putting it in her basket, even Dima's gentle smile in her dream when he promised he would catch her when she jumped from the branch. But he hadn't. And now, he was asleep to the plague. She tried to breathe. She needed to think about something, anything else.

'The glass, how does it work?' she choked out.

'The glass?' Pan Volya wrinkled his brow in confusion.

'Yes. When I looked at my hand, I saw colours.'

'Ah, yes. Fascinating, isn't it? Some believe they are a physical attribute, like brown hair, or green eyes. Others believe that they are a piece of a person's soul.'

His words reminded her of what she had overheard Valdim say to Olena about seeing colours around people. But the thought blew away like a feather in a gale. Her mind was like a hurricane and in the eye of the storm was Dima.

'You are distraught,' Pan Volya noted, his voice more curious than sympathetic.

'Yes,' Marisha breathed out, 'yes, I was hoping–I was hoping I could do this one thing for her. But I cannot even do that. What terrible, terrible luck. For them both to fall asleep. I'm sorry for my display, Marisha was . . . dear to me.' She took a deep breath, reminding herself that she was in this koldun's house and he had tried to poison her. She couldn't show such weakness. And Dima was here. She clung to her fear of Pan Volya and took another deep breath. But she barely knew what she was saying. 'They must have done something terrible to offend the spirits, for both of them to fall asleep.'

He sniffed. 'Not as unusual as you might expect. Sometimes the plague has ways of choosing its victims.'

'No. It can't.' Marisha thought back to all those tedious days squinting at slanted Old Slavonic script with Olena. 'There was no pattern. We looked but we didn't find any.'

'Perhaps you were not looking in the right place. Remember I've conducted my own research as well, and let's just say that if your friend had reason to believe she was marked for the plague, it's probably because she knew of . . . extenuating circumstances. You must not be so distraught. It was her fate. She knew it.'

The hairs rose on the back of Marisha's neck. 'You're just trying to make me feel better.'

'Well, yes. But that doesn't mean I'm not telling the truth.'

She wanted to probe more, to ask if it had been Dima's fate to fall asleep to the plague too. Pan Volya smiled politely but his eyes remained hard, glittering ice chips. Fear jolted down her spine. He had not openly threatened her, but she did not want to stay in his house a moment longer than necessary.

'Well. I made a promise to speak to her brother, and I will

keep that promise.' She stood up. Her legs felt shaky, but she did not lean on the chair.

'Ah. A true friend. Very well, I will take you to him.' He stood up and gestured deeper into the house.

'He's not in a sanitorium?' She pictured for a moment a room without a window. A box.

'We're still arranging transfer. There's a long waitlist. Besides, he's certainly more comfortable here.'

Marisha silently disagreed. He beckoned her to follow. She did not notice what doors she traversed nor the colour of the walls. Her tread felt ungainly, as though she wore buckets instead of shoes. She stopped when he opened a door and paused in the doorway, not willing to come inside any further. The overly sweet and rotting smell of sickbed-yellow roses filled the air. Over Pan Volya's shoulder she saw a bed in the room, and a body in the bed.

'As you can see, any conversation will be one-sided.'

She swallowed and took several steps forward. Her throat felt strangled and she pushed the words out. 'But he can listen.'

At the periphery of her vision, she saw Pan Volya give her a slight bow. She forced herself to acknowledge his bow with a nod as he left the room.

The door's click made her jump. And her gaze focused on Dima's face. His skin looked waxy: sleep smoothed out the lines around his mouth that he had had in her dream. She collapsed next to the bed. Seeing Dima, recognising him despite not seeing him in years, shattered her composure like a rock thrown at a weak layer of ice.

She wept and wept. Even though she knew she did not have much time to be alone with him, she couldn't help herself. She grabbed his hand. He did not squeeze back. And the tears blurred her vision so she couldn't even see him, just feel his hand in hers. Her whole body shook as she tried to suppress any noise. She tried to stop, but she couldn't: she had finally found her brother, but she had been too late. She was powerless, utterly useless.

Olena, curse her, had been right. Finding Dima didn't do anything. Her only accomplishment was soaking his sheets with tears. He did not even know she was there! Marisha should have tried harder to find the cure. If Anatoli really was the only way forward, how could she have flinched away from it? She had not even had the strength to see that through. She should not have left Olena. She should not have left the house. If only to avoid sitting here–if only to avoid knowing she was the only person in her family still awake.

She imagined her parents, asleep in their beds in the sanitorium. She tried to picture her mother's face, but she couldn't. All she could imagine was her prostrate form, like Dima's, her chest rising and falling, like Dima's. As though they were dead. Except they weren't. And the hope of their living breath made it worse, like the hope of a fish yanking away on a line as it was reeled in slowly. She had been so close to them when she and Olena were in the sanitorium to kidnap Kiril, but she had felt relieved when she did not see them. Relieved! How shameful.

'I'm sorry,' she whispered. 'Dima, I'm so sorry. I should have tried harder.'

She wanted to say more, but she couldn't. She didn't think he would hear, and she didn't want to listen to her own words.

The wetness of her tears on Dima's hand quieted her. She leaned her head back and took a deep breath, then another. She looked at her brother. Her swollen eyelids made her eyes feel big. For a moment, she was silent and empty. The sallow colour of the sickbed roses on the bedside table drew her eye. How she hated them. And she held her breath, remembering something.

She reached across Dima's sleeping form and pushed up his right sleeve. And there, around his wrist, was tied an acorn on a red thread, just as it had been in her dream. Her fingers paused, touching the symbol of an indentured servant, and drew back as though it burned.

Dima was indentured to Pan Volya. And now he was asleep.

Her nightmare had come true.

THIRTY-FOUR

arisha knew her eyes were red and puffy. She dabbed them with a corner of Dima's bedsheet, gave her whole body a shake, huffed and threw her shoulders back. She looked at Dima's sleeping form one last time before leaving the room. Her grief was tamped down and a cool, empty feeling of reckoning spread through her. Olena had said that she hadn't truly spoken to her brother, that she hadn't dream-walked, but Olena was wrong. Somehow, her dreams were real.

But what about the rest of it? What about the beaked man and seeing Kiril in the dance hall? Was that real too?

Marisha's feet led her back to the receiving room and she silently stepped inside. She had so many questions, but how to find out more from Pan Volya without rousing his suspicions?

He got up from his chair when she entered. 'Ah, so. You told the young man everything you wished?'

Her face felt smooth, as though she wore a mask. She slipped into the persona of the koldunya's assistant easily, gratefully. 'Yes. I . . . felt a little silly doing it. But I feel better now. Thank you.'

'Well, if there's nothing else, I am very busy and while it was a pleasure—'

'I'm curious. You said the glass helps you with your research–

about what happens to a deep sleeper when they wake, is that correct? How?'

'Yes, that is my primary interest.' She had asked the right question. His determination to hurry her out the door was mollified. 'It is my theory that the colours of sleepers shown by the glass are changed. Muted. As though they are preyed upon—'

'Preyed upon?' Marisha repeated softly.

'—yes, preyed upon. And some of their vitality, some of their soul, is drained away. Of course, to know for sure, one would have to record the hue before and after a person falls to the plague, a difficult task. Though, not impossible with a little help from luck.'

Was Dima nothing more than a test subject for him to experiment on? She thought of Kiril and tamped down the anger and shame rising in her throat.

Pan Volya studied Marisha. 'You don't like my wording.'

Did he think she was acting strangely? Her heartbeat sped up. 'No, it's just—' Her mind raced. She couldn't let on that she was nervous. She couldn't let him know she was Dima's sister. She reached for the back of the chair that she had sat in, realising that she was still standing and she should probably sit, lest he see her ankles wobble. 'When you said, "preyed upon", it made me think of—' the beaked man '—Nightingale the Robber.'

'Oh?' Pan Volya looked at her with polite interest. 'Who's that?'

'Oh, he's–just a man who made a pact with a demon to learn the language of birds, it's from this story I read in one of the histories that Olena–Baba Zima's apprentice–dug up.' Marisha knew she was babbling but did not care. At that moment, speaking felt less poisonous than thinking. 'Olena was mad at me for almost overlooking it. She thought it might have something to do with the plague.' She forced herself to stop and smile. She made no sense at all. She ought to leave.

Pan Volya smirked, 'According to some, she may not be so far from the truth.'

'What?' Marisha exclaimed. Her attention snapped back together, like shards of glass impossibly pressing back into a single pane. 'You think that Nightingale the Robber caused the plague?'

Pan Volya waved his hand, 'No, not your Nightingale the Robber, not exactly . . . but there is a similar story . . .' He shook his head. 'The language of birds–why do all such stories start with that?' He paused. 'There's an Ivan the Fool story, one that's not well known. Indulge me, if you'd be so kind. A long time ago, a young boy wanted to learn the language of birds so badly he agreed to steal a treasure for a man who promised to teach it to him. Ivan stole the treasure, but unfortunately, the treasure belonged to a roc–a magpie as big as a bear that eats cattle for breakfast. The roc offered to let Ivan live if he promised to find and return the treasure. But the roc had one caveat: it demanded a piece of Ivan's spirit to demonstrate his goodwill. Ivan agreed to the roc's bargain. After all, he had not really noticed his spirit for all the short years of his life, so why should he notice a missing piece now? However, I'm sure you can imagine . . . he did notice.

'The world was dull. Ivan now knew the language of birds, but he was annoyed by everything that used to bring him joy, even birdsong. He searched for many years, only to find the roc's treasure was lost at sea. Ivan was desperate. If he couldn't trade for his spirit, he would steal it back.

'After a year and a day of wandering, Ivan reached the bird's nest in the other world. The roc found him rummaging through his possessions and gleefully told Ivan that the piece of his spirit was gone. Just as Ivan had lost the roc's treasure, now the roc had let the splinter of spirit go up to the earth. He said the splinter would endlessly latch on to other people in search for its missing whole. Ivan's boiling anger made him strong and quick, and he killed the great magpie. He stole the roc's eyes, ears, and beak for himself and vowed to do whatever it would take to make his spirit whole again. And since then, the sleeping plague has struck Chernozemlya every ten years.'

'What? How?'

Pan Volya shrugged. 'It's a story. The mechanical details are thin.' He leaned forward and said, 'But, if the plague-bringer truly had lost a piece of his spirit in a bargain and has been searching for it ever since, it makes a pretty story for my glass. Perhaps the glass could reveal that extra sliver of spirit in someone, perhaps not.'

'But you think that the plague bringer is this Ivan the Fool? That he traded off a piece of his soul?' And there it was, another terrible bargain. A tingle went up Marisha's spine. 'And what does it have to do with Nightingale the Robber?'

'Well, it has some pleasing similarities with your story about Nightingale the Robber, doesn't it? Stories don't tell all the truth. But still, both have protagonists wishing to learn the language of birds, both have a bargain gone wrong, and both end with a monster.'

'But the sleeping plague . . . there was no mention of the sleeping plague in Nightingale the Robber.' Marisha said, though her mind immediately went to the line about the monster being *a plague upon Kul*. She said, 'And in the story, the bogotir Grisha slays him. He . . . he had a sigil that protected him.'

'A sigil you say?' Pan Volya's mouth quirked into a knowing smile. 'Stories remain stories. Still, when you compare them, you can uncover the pit of truth–if you're lucky. Did your version of the Nightingale the Robber story say that the monster had black feathers of steel?'

Marisha's throat was dry. She cleared it and said, 'You mean like the feather that you asked about?'

Pan Volya's smile became fixed, as though it was only held up by the corners. 'Yes. That one.'

The realisation settled to the pit of Marisha's stomach. If her dream about Dima was real, then why not the one of the beaked man?

She thought back to her dream right before Dunya fell asleep to the plague. It had all happened so fast, but she remembered how the beaked man's black feathers had winked in the light when he spread his wings. They were as long as her arm . . . maybe they were a bit like steel? If what Pan Volya said was true, then did that mean she had somehow walked into the dreams of the plague-bringer himself?

Marisha asked, 'But why so many plague victims if this Ivan the Fool is just looking for one person with that piece of his spirit?'

'Perhaps the piece flits from person to person constantly. Or perhaps the plague-bringer has trouble recognising it.'

She paused, mulling it over. 'But if that's the case, why would you think Marisha was fated to fall asleep?'

'Dunya, while I can understand your distress about your friend, I'm afraid there's nothing more I can say on that account. I merely sought to comfort you.'

His cold eyes flashed his lie. She wanted to demand he tell her if the black feather he wanted came from the beaked man, demand he say how Dima had become his indentured servant, for it couldn't be a coincidence. But at the hardness of his gaze, her anger twisted into a knot of fear. She had to leave. But would she really leave her brother to his care?

She had no choice. 'Thank you,' she said. It was ridiculously easy to say those words. She hated herself for it. 'Your theories are fascinating.'

'Not at all. It is always gratifying to have a willing listener.'

He contemplated her for a second too long and Marisha had the terrifying thought he would not let her leave. But he turned and gestured to the door. She rose to her feet, her heart still hammering in her throat, and walked with him out of the receiving room, away from the hall where Dima was hidden. He opened the front door for her and the cold air dispelled the smell of dried skullcap and cloves.

'You seem to be a person with surprisingly hidden depths, Miss Dunya. I do hope I will see you again. Soon.'

The corners of his mouth were upturned into a smile, but his eyes were stony. She would leave Dima to those eyes. In her mind she saw her brother laid out on the bed as Kiril was laid out on a table. And the koldun performing all sorts of experiments on him, his hands less gentle than Olena's.

'No,' Marisha said. But she was already out the door. She turned in time to see Pan Volya give her a slight bow. And the door closed, not quite a slam, but it shut with finality all the same.

She stood in front of the door for a moment, then she walked until she had turned the corner, and as soon as she left the house's view, she ran.

She ran until a stitch in her side forced her to slow to a walk and she began to torture herself with a grim set of facts. Dima was asleep and indentured to Pan Volya, the koldun who had poisoned her, the one who had the same mark her father had on his wrist, the mark caused by a black, steely feather that might belong to the beaked man. Pan Volya thought Ivan the Fool-

Nightingale the Robber–the beaked man–caused the plague.

A large building loomed in front of her. Her feet had brought her back to the public sanitorium, with the walls plastered in their long sheets of paper listing names. A crier read the names out to a crowd. Anxiety and despair bubbled off of the gathered people. She leaned against the grey sanitorium wall and closed her eyes. She touched the sanitorium but was not yet inside it. How strangely appropriate. It was only a matter of time.

Dima was indentured to Pan Volya and asleep from the plague. How was that possible? Pan Volya was connected to her father through this black feather, it seemed like too great of a coincidence, it couldn't be coincidence, coincidence didn't exist–Baba Zima surged out of her memory, the feather in her purple turban bobbing as she said: *coincidence is what those silly philosophers use to describe patterns they can't explain.* But how to explain it?

Then she remembered. The koldun with the cold eyes, the one who had come ten years ago after Papa had fallen asleep to the plague. He had looked at her with such loathing and Dima had stood in front of her and had told him to leave. It was Pan Volya.

She sank against the sanitorium wall. Part of her wanted to return to his home right away and demand an explanation. Had he sought Dima out? And why? The lines that connected them all made her head spin. It hadn't been a coincidence. And Pan Volya had been unsurprised to hear that she–Marisha–had fallen asleep to the plague.

And yet, she was still awake. She could still do something.

She pushed away from the sanitorium and walked again; she did not know where. She had to return to the orange house and tell Olena about Pan Volya. She had to tell her that she had somehow dream-walked and her dreams of the beaked man were real. But Olena had dismissed her misgivings about Anatoli. Would she dismiss this too?

A wave of helplessness and anger washed over her. Olena should have believed her about Anatoli, she should have listened. What had Valdim said? That the man's colours were wrong. Marisha wondered what she would see if she looked at Anatoli through Pan Volya's glass.

Marisha stopped walking as suddenly as if she had met a glass wall. Pan Volya had said that the colours in the glass might be a piece of a person's soul. Baba Zima thought Valdim could see the colours of people's souls. The pieces fell into place like a waterfall.

The colours. Orange and black spikes, like Valdim had said. The maskless man who hung by the dark lady in her dream wore an orange kaftan and a black spiky colour. And now, she was almost certain of why Anatoli had looked so familiar to her when she first saw him: he was the same man.

Her mind went to her last memory of the dream she had before Dunya fell asleep to the plague, the dark lady flashed her wrist with the scar that her father and Pan Volya shared. Somehow, they were all part of the same web. And now Anatoli was involved too.

One thing was certain: if Anatoli really was the dark lady's companion, he was up to no good.

Olena was in danger. Marisha had to get back to the house.

THIRTY-FIVE

arisha sat by the oven in Valdim's boarding house. Olena had agreed to pick her and Valdim up tomorrow, but by then it would be too late. Marisha reasoned that Baba Zima must have arranged some kind of secret, magical way for Valdim to get back to the house. She only needed to convince him of the urgency of returning. It had taken a silver kopek to let her sit at an establishment for men only, though she had to endure the disapproving look of the matrona peering at her from the kitchen. The old lady had insisted on keeping the door open.

'Marisha . . . ah there you are. It's a pleasure to see you, but you're coming at an inopportune time.'

'I apologise, but it's urgent.' She noticed the oblong wooden case polished and shining by the light of the oven. 'You must be on your way to make the delivery.'

He smiled in assent. 'Actually, the mysterious personage already picked it up. I was hoping to meet him, I'd never received a commission anonymously before. But alas.' He shrugged, palms open. 'I'm on my way to meet a potential patron, someone who will actually pay me a wage, not a single commission. Can you believe it?' His eyes shined.

'Valdim, I need to talk to you. Somewhere private.'

Valdim tugged at his shirt collar. He caught the eye of the matrona who scowled. But Marisha's coin held and the matrona let Marisha follow Valdim up to his room.

'It's not that I don't want to talk to you,' Valdim said, 'but the matrona gives me a discounted rate. I doubt I'll get to keep it now.'

'I'm sorry. But this is very important.'

Valdim stopped fidgeting and focused on her the same way she imagined he focused on a piece of spruce ready for planing. 'I'm listening.'

'I'm not sure where to begin.' She took a deep breath. 'A few months ago, I started having these dreams.' And she described how her nightmares left her heaving from fear even though she could not remember them. She told him about Kiril and how she and Olena had hidden him and how she had seen him in her dream before Dunya fell asleep.

'The beaked man was so terrifying I forgot everything else. But another man spoke with the dark lady. He wore a beige shirt and an orange-and-black kaftan with spikes at the collar.'

Valdim, who had stayed motionless with his gaze fixed on Marisha throughout her entire story, twitched at her description. Marisha paused. 'Does that mean anything to you?'

Valdim shook his head.

Marisha took a deep breath and held his gaze. 'I saw you arguing with Olena in the clearing that night at the krug.'

Valdim inhaled sharply. 'You did? Why? Were you spying for my mother?'

'No! I was coming back from getting my sleep potion and I saw Olena go in the woods with Anatoli . . . so I stayed. I was curious.'

'I see.' Valdim bent his head for a while. 'So, you heard us yelling.'

'Yes, and something you said, about the colours—' Valdim raised his head and gave Marisha a hurt and accusatory look. Marisha did not allow herself to wilt. 'You said you see colours when you look at people. What do you see for me?'

She pulled a newly acquired long and wide wooden box from her bag. It had cost a good chunk of her three-month salary. She opened it and handed it to him. He looked at the long rows of sewing thread, dyed all different shades of the rainbow.

'I don't want to play this game.'

'This is important.'

'There are not enough shades.'

'This is the biggest box they had. Just pick the closest one.'

Valdim looked her in the eye and Marisha held her own, willing him to understand how important this was. His gaze flicked between her and the thread in the box, his eyes scanning the rows. Finally, he picked out two spools, one of burgundy, and one of pale yellow.

'These aren't it exactly, but they're close.'

Marisha nodded, not trusting her own voice. She took a deep breath. 'I think Anatoli is the maskless man in my dream.'

'Why do you say that?'

'Because he looked familiar. And I think I know why. You picked the closest colours to what my skirt is when I am in the dance hall. That means if the maskless man wore these,' she picked out the closest shades of orange, beige and black, 'he really is Anatoli.'

Valdim stared at the spools of thread she had handed to him. 'I don't know what to think.'

'But I do. For the first time, I feel *certain* of something. And Kiril was there too, I'm certain of that.'

'So, you think, the dream, the dancers—'

'I'm seeing the sleepers.'

'But Anatoli is not asleep.'

'Neither am I. But he did not have a mask either.'

'It doesn't make any sense.'

'I know, but Valdim, what if I'm right? What if right now Olena is inviting someone into your mother's house who is colluding with the beaked man and the dark lady? The beaked man is the plague bringer, Valdim.' Marisha knew she sounded crazy, but she felt with every fibre of her being she was right.

'You really believe this?'

'I think I've known deep down from the beginning, ever since we kidnapped Kiril. I picked him. He must have . . . pulled me in somehow. I know Olena said it takes skill to dream-walk to the other world, but I think the connection with Kiril must have done it.' She paused. 'He protected me from the beaked man as long as he could.' She must have sounded like she was raving. 'I'm not making this up.'

He looked into the distance. 'I don't believe you are. But are you sure?'

'Yes. You said his colours are wrong.'

He got up from the chair. 'But even if you're right, what does he want? And what could it have to do with Olena?'

'Anatoli told Olena he needs her help to cure the plague and that there's water of death hidden somewhere in the house. We found it the night before I left. But he wouldn't want to cure the plague: he's benefitting from it, he must be, he's friends with the dark lady and the beaked man.' Marisha started to pace. 'Maybe he can use it to put even more people asleep.'

Valdim groaned and sunk his face into his hands. 'That stupid, idiot—'

'What?'

'She'll invite him into the house.'

'She wouldn't.'

'My mother has forbidden him from entering the house, but she made Olena mistress. She will invite him into the house to try to wake Dunya with the mixture of the waters of life and death. And he'll try to steal the house.'

Marisha contemplated what Valdim said. It made sense, of course Anatoli would want to steal the house. Baba Zima had always harped on his jealousy.

She shook herself. 'We need to get back to the house before it's too late.'

'This is not your problem. This is my mother and her twisted feuds.' Valdim ran a hand through his hair. 'You don't need to go back.'

Marisha looked at the plaster wall, not really seeing it. *Run*, Kiril had told her. And she had. She had run away from the beaked man and left Kiril to the dark lady. And what if she had found Dima awake, what then? Revisiting her fantasy of escaping Chernozemlya with Dima felt like lacing up a shoe that no longer fit.

'Everyone I love most is asleep to the plague. I need to help them. Besides, I'd still have my nightmares without the sleeping potion. Leaving won't change that.' She closed her eyes at the thought that Kiril's request for her to stay nearby was justified. That her presence had actually afforded him some protection. What if something terrible had happened to him because she had left the house? 'I need to know how Anatoli is linked to the plague.'

He looked at the violin case in the corner. 'This was to be my big chance. A wealthy patron . . .'

Marisha did not say anything.

He sighed. 'I'll come.' His voice was heavy. 'Of course I'll come. How can I not?'

'Good.'

The silence grew for a moment, then she said, 'Do you have a way of returning? I assumed Baba Zima would have arranged something for you fancier than a cart.'

Valdim shook his head. 'I have ways of contacting my mother, but they take time.'

Marisha's heart sank. So much for the easy way. 'Maybe the matrona can find a neighbour to take us back to Halitso?' It had taken them almost two hours to get from the orange house to Severny, but they had stopped for lunch along the way. Surely they could go faster now.

'No,' Valdim said, 'Olena would not keep the house still. Not in the state of mind she's in. It's not there anymore.'

Panic began to rise up Marisha's throat. 'But it has to still be there. We have to get back.'

'It's not,' Valdim said. He opened up the latch to his violin case. 'There's one other way.' He reached his finger under the plush velvet lining and pulled out a slim leather-bound book. And from one of the pages, a feather.

Marisha's mouth fell open. She said, 'You have one of Golgolin's feathers?'

'Yes, I have a few hidden. I don't actually know how to use them to open doors, I took them because I wanted to have a piece of Golgolin too.' He fixed his gaze on Marisha. 'But you said you used one to kidnap your plague victim.'

'Yes, but Olena performed the spell, I watched.' Marisha had not thought she would actually need to use Golgolin's feather. 'Shouldn't we check if the house is still there, just in case?'

'No,' Valdim said. 'I'm sure.'

Marisha bit her lip. He was probably right. For all their bickering, sometimes Marisha thought Valdim understood Olena better than anyone.

He said, 'You've been assisting Olena for months, you've trained for this.'

Marisha met his eyes and nodded. She was not about to let on how nervous she was. While she had performed incantations before, it was never in front of another person.

'I need a door,' she said a little too loudly. Valdim pointed to the closet. Marisha stood in front of it, her fist pressed to her sternum as though to slow her heartbeat.

'I need water–and blood. To forge a link. I think your blood would be stronger, you have stronger ties to the house.'

Valdim rummaged through his pack for his canteen and knife. He pricked the back of his hand and held it out to Marisha. She let the crimson drop well into the soft silver down at the base of the feather. Marisha faced the door. She needed an incantation. A few months ago, if someone had told her she would desperately be trying to think of a good incantation to open a door to a chicken-legged house leagues away using a guinea pig-fowl's feather, she would have laughed and laughed. As it was, she let out a small snort at the absurdity.

She looked sideways at Valdim then spoke as soft as she dared. 'Spirits of air and spirits of water, may you guide this feather to its true home whether it be over hill, over snow . . . wherever it may be. And please, bring me there safe as well. This I humbly beg.'

Nothing happened. She stood frozen, the feather touching the doorknob, trembling in her grip. She felt Valdim shift behind her.

'Everything all right?'

'Of course,' Marisha said, trying to play the part of the confident koldunya, but inside she panicked.

Marisha gripped the tough quill at the base of the feather. She had successfully performed the spell Pan Volya had given her as well as the location spell to find Dima. She could do this too. She clenched her eyes shut and thought about the chicken-legged house, a large orange blotch against the snow, skiing across the perfectly white landscape. When she opened her eyes, she still held the feather in her hand.

No! How could it not have worked? This was supposed to be simple. She had seen Olena do it: the feather melted into the keyhole before her eyes. Marisha clenched her fist tighter around the quill until it began to crumple.

They would never reach the house in time. She really was a mediocre koldunya at best. Tears gathered in the corner of her eyes; she took a deep breath. *Spirits, I may not be your favourite, but if you care at all about Olena, you'll make this work.* And a plea lifted through her, the desire that the wish itself be enough, even though she sensed deep down that asking would not make a difference to the outcome.

Marisha felt rather than saw the feather cling to the keyhole, dissolve, and infuse the brass doorknob with silver. Valdim clutched her arm and cheered. Her whole body thrummed and she leaned against the handle, no longer even worrying whether the door would open to the right place or not. She knew it would.

She pulled the door open, and a deep abyss yawned between their room and the next. Marisha moved back to take a running leap and was glad she did; the threshold was wider than last time, her heel had not quite landed. Valdim followed, his eyes betraying no surprise at the threshold, as if leaping over a gaping abyss were an everyday occurrence. The threshold was so wide that the boarding house's closet door was too far away to shut.

She and Valdim exchanged a glance. He said, 'I can try to get to it.'

'It should close on its own.' They had locked the door to his boarding house room from the inside. It would be a good long while before the matrona returned to check on Valdim, and hopefully the closet door would swing shut before then.

Marisha looked around. The door had opened off of the back hallway into the chicken-legged house's oven room. The large, domed oven loomed to her right. The fire crackled merrily, casting a warm glow on the blue-painted tiles. The poker was not hanging in its familiar place as Baba Zima had taken it with her. The window opposite her was framed by the hideous pink-and-green paisley curtains. Marisha smiled. She had never been so happy to see those curtains before.

She took a moment to brush her hand against the windowsill and was surprised to feel warm, solid oak beneath her fingers. Only a few short months ago, she had gripped the windowsill as the house ran, her feet firmly planted and arms braced against the dizzy foreboding that the house may tip her out of the open window. She did not feel that way anymore. 'Thank you,' she whispered, noting that the wood was silky smooth. A warm pulse went through her fingertips, and she could smell the comforting aroma of baking bread, even though it was much past the time for the Hands to be using the oven for cooking. Perhaps the house was accepting her–glad, even, that she had returned. Whatever it was, an answering fondness spread through Marisha's chest like melting butter.

A breeze rustled the curtains. She opened them. The house was still and surrounded by pine trees. Had Olena already met with Anatoli? Marisha hurried from the window, hoping they were not too late.

THIRTY-SIX

arisha and Valdim split up to look for Olena. Marisha checked on Kiril first and was relieved to find him as she had left him, asleep and unharmed. She climbed the stairs as fast as she could and found Dunya in the attic, still asleep as well. Marisha raced back down, trying her best to be quiet. The front door clicked open and shut. She tiptoed out of the oven room and peeked around the doorframe. It was Olena, alone. Relief flooded Marisha. She made a small noise, but Olena did not notice. Olena walked slowly, concentrating on not spilling the contents of her flask.

Marisha whispered, 'Olena.' No reaction. She tried again, louder.

Olena jumped back. The liquid in her flask sloshed. 'Firehounds and hellhorses, Marisha, what in the damp dark earth are you doing here?' She breathed in and out, her birthmark flushed to deep crimson. 'Look at what you almost made me do.'

Marisha rushed forward. 'Doesn't matter, Olena—'

'Yes, it does, and what are you doing here? I thought you left. Have you been hiding here all this time?' She looked furious and a tinge embarrassed.

'No, I haven't. I came back.'

Olena stared at her, her jaw slack. 'How could you have come back? We're leagues away from where we dropped you.'

Marisha waved her hand in dismissal at Olena's question. 'Olena, are you meeting Anatoli?'

'So what if I am?'

Marisha's heart sank. 'Don't meet with him, you can't trust him, he's lied to you; he says he wants to help with the cure, but he really wants to get into the house.'

Olena's eyebrows shot up her forehead. 'What? Why do you say that?'

'I will explain, but it's a long story. You have to trust me.'

Olena shook her head. She frowned. 'I would not be stupid enough to invite him in. He's standing outside. We mixed the waters and I'm giving it to Kiril, and he'll be cured.'

'What? No, Anatoli's doing something—'

'Doing what? He's waiting outside. He doesn't want to hurt me, he wants to help. Move out of the way.'

'No.'

'*No*?'

'Olena, something's wrong. How do you even know it's the water of life? Do you even know what it looks like? Or did you just take his word for it?'

'Of course it is. What else would it be? Why would he even be here if it wasn't to cure the plague? He can't come into the house.'

'You know something's wrong or you wouldn't be trying to convince yourself it's all right. Olena, Kiril's life is at stake. Will you really give him that mixture without being completely sure of what it is?'

Olena did not answer, but she did not move either. Her birthmark purpled. 'I don't–but–it has to be the water of life,' she said finally, 'What else could it be?'

'I don't know.'

'I do.' Anatoli stepped forward through the corridor, his eyes glittering. Her hypothesis, now confirmed, sank to the bottom of Marisha's stomach like a granite mortar.

Olena, eyes wide and mouth slack in surprise, glanced between the flask and Anatoli. 'What are you doing here? You shouldn't be able to come in!'

Anatoli chuckled softly and advanced into the oven room, neatly sidestepping both women. 'It's been so long since I've been here, but it all looks the same. Except for the curtains, they're a lot more horrible.'

Olena set the flask down on the table with a thump. 'So, this isn't a cure? All of this, for what? To make a fool out of me?' Olena's jaw clenched. A muscle in the corner of her mouth twitched.

'Of course not, that was never my objective. But it was easy, you were so . . . eager.'

'Leave, now!' Olena spat the words out.

'My dear Olena, I don't see you carrying the poker. No. You were mistress enough to hand me the charm. Zima had barred me from the house using water. All I needed was a sip to be allowed back in."

Olena looked down at the flask of water on the table, and let out a barely audible gasp.

Anatoli smiled smugly. 'That's right. You brought it to me, Olena, without even testing its properties. Thank you.'

Marisha glanced to Olena. The apprentice slumped at the table, her face pale.

'I must say, your hospitality is a bit lacking. I should take that up with Zima. Where is she, by the way?' He peered about. 'I have an appointment with her, a bit of an old argument to settle–and it's high time she settled it fair and square.' His face twisted from his pleasant mask into something ugly.

'She's not here,' Marisha said, backing away. Where was Valdim? She hoped he was using his private method of contacting Baba Zima.

'Get out, now!' Olena said. She put her hand in her pocket.

Anatoli ignored her. He took a step forward, his gaze fixed on Olena, and reached for the bag on his shoulder. She took a step back, almost at the wall. Anatoli advanced again. Olena whipped her hand out of her pocket and flung something at him that turned into flames. He dodged most of them, but the edge of his kaftan's hem sparked and he stamped it out. Olena yelled and the brown kitchen Hands burst forth from the door to the hall and rushed for Anatoli's throat. Yes! They would force him back out of the house. But Anatoli put his own hands up and the Hands stopped, gloved fingers inches from his throat.

'Enough,' he said. And the Hands floated to his shoulders, pointing outwards.

He smirked at Olena, 'You are not the true mistress of this house, my dear. And they—' he tilted his head at the Hands '—know the difference.'

The pair of brown kitchen Hands split and each grabbed Marisha and Olena by the wrist. Marisha pulled and pulled but the Hand had an iron grip. Baba Zima's ivory pair whizzed through the door to aid the kitchen Hands and together they pinned Marisha and Olena against the wall opposite the oven and Anatoli. Marisha's heartbeat roared in her ears. They were trapped.

A litany of curses fell from Olena's lips. Anatoli ignored them. He pulled something out of his sac. It was such an unlikely object that even Olena paused in her cursing. A very recognisable violin.

'You're Valdim's anonymous patron?' Marisha exclaimed.

Olena stopped struggling, lost for words.

'Yes. You see, musical koldunry has become something of a specialty of mine. Music from an ordinary but gifted player has the power to compel emotions from the listener, but, with a strong enough link, I can take it one step further.'

And he raised the violin to his chin and touched the bow to its strings. The strings glowed red as though they burned. Anatoli stomped his foot in time with the strange tune, and Marisha thought she heard an echo. The echo grew louder. With each stamp of Anatoli's foot, the oven door answered with a resounding knock. And he began to sing, but his words were drowned out by the stamping and knocking which only grew louder and louder. Marisha and Olena shared a single, terrified glance.

The oven door burst open and out onto the floor rolled an ash-covered Valdim.

He groaned and rolled to his knees, clutching a heavy iron adze in one fist. But before he could even try swinging it, the ivory Hands released their holds on Marisha and Olena's wrists and twisted his arms around his back. Olena yelled for Anatoli to stop and beat her fist against the wall, but the Hands did not release any of their prisoners. When Anatoli took out a knife, Marisha let out a strangled cry.

'You must allow me to compliment you on the quality of your work, really, it's exquisite.' Anatoli slashed the knife against Valdim's arm. He yelled. Marisha's panic eased slightly when Anatoli put the knife away. He wiped the violin bow on the blood dripping from Valdim's sleeve.

'Thank you for that,' Anatoli said, and the ivory Hands wrestled Valdim to the ground. Anatoli played the violin with the bloody bow and stomped his foot on the floor, same as before. Valdim screamed as though in pain. But this time no answering knock sounded on the oven door.

Anatoli looked at Valdim and snarled, 'How are you doing that? You answered the call, and so should Zima–blood magic is one of the strongest magics there is.'

Valdim did not answer. As soon as Anatoli stopped playing, Valdim resumed his struggle to fight off the Hands. The floor was smeared with his blood. Anatoli said, 'Fine. Zima refuses to answer, it's no more than a setback. There are other ways to create a link than with kin's blood.' His gaze flicked to the two women in the circle.

'You,' he said, and the brown Hand pinning Marisha's wrist to the wall dragged her forward instead.

Marisha's breath came in short gasps. She did not think she could have stood were it not for the Hand holding her up.

'How to use you to create a link . . .' he said, tapping his lip with a finger. He frowned. 'Now tell me, where is Zima?'

'I don't know.'

'I find it hard to believe you don't have the tiniest, slightest, sliver of an idea.'

Marisha shook. 'I don't know.'

'Leave her alone,' Valdim shouted, his voice muffled.

'Quiet!' Anatoli growled.

Olena's voice drifted over. 'Anatoli. Let me go. Marisha doesn't know anything. Why would she? Talk to me instead.' Olena's voice was even and her expression carefully collected, as though the kitchen Hand pinning her stump to the wall was a mere inconvenience and not a betrayal of her authority. But Marisha saw her fingers flex.

'Oh Olena, nothing fazes you, does it? Do you know, you remind me of—' He glanced at Marisha again, and his eyes widened. He started laughing. 'Oh, that's too much! I've seen you there, haven't I?' And he kept on laughing.

'What do you mean?' Marisha said, hairs rising on the back of her neck.

Anatoli quieted his laughter. 'Oh, oh, nothing of consequence, at least–not right this very moment. Now–I will ask again, and you had better give me a real answer this time, where is Zima?' He reached to the table and grabbed a teacup, smashed it half away, and drew the sharp edge close to her cheek.

'How dare you,' said a booming voice from the doorway. 'That's my porcelain! Put the cup down, you ingrate!'

The brown Hand dropped Marisha's arm and zoomed straight to Baba Zima's side. A thud signalled that the ivory Hands holding Valdim dropped as well and joined their counterparts at Baba Zima's other shoulder. She advanced into the room, slowly, the poker drawn in front of her like a sword, the Hands pointing outwards at her shoulders like birds of prey. Her eyes flashed as she took in the scene.

'Olena, I leave for two days. And this is what I come back to?' Olena sagged against the wall, rubbing her stump where the Hand had held it. Baba Zima's gaze moved to Valdim. 'And you? If you're still here, why did we bother making a stop in Severny?' Then she simply looked at Marisha and shook her head.

Baba Zima turned to Anatoli, 'I think it's time I ended you. You have been nothing but a splinter in my thumb, ever since Serafima brought you in.'

'Ah yes, Serafima, the root of the problem. So you've always thought. But Zima, maybe you should think of the real reason why you live in a house that is not truly yours, have an apprentice that is not truly loyal, and a son that is not truly your blood.'

The colour drained from Baba Zima's face. 'You are nothing, Anatoli. I won! I am the mistress. The bolshina is mine!'

Anatoli's face twisted. 'You lie! Everything you have is built on injustice!'

The Hands lunged at Anatoli but he swatted them off. He ran to the cupboard and hurled teacup after teacup at the Hands. They smashed to bits on the wall.

'Enough!' Baba Zima thundered and Anatoli paused mid-throw, the two pairs of Hands restraining him as he leaned forward on one leg, his arm wound back. It would have been comical had his face not been contorted in a snarl of pure loathing. His gaze flitted to something behind Marisha and his expression transformed for a split second into one of triumph. He met Marisha's gaze as though they were complicit. He winked.

'It's over,' Baba Zima said, breathing heavily. Her arms were limp by her sides.

'No,' Anatoli said quietly, 'it's not.' He yelled three words and the Hands let him go. He sprang forth and tried to wrench the poker from Baba Zima. He screamed as smoke burst forth and the smell of burning flesh permeated the air.

They both gripped the poker. Baba Zima's hands were closer towards the middle, but Anatoli was stronger and had the element of surprise. He seemed to be pushing Baba Zima in a particular direction.

'No!' Marisha screamed when she realised his intention. But by the time she rushed forward to stop him, it was too late.

Anatoli pushed the poker and Baba Zima to the side-door of the oven room, to the doorway of the Severny boarding house that Marisha and Valdim had left open, the threshold gaping between the two locations, solid as a bridge of feathers. He shouted to Baba Zima, 'It's time to meet your maker.' He pushed her with the poker up to the threshold, and they teetered on the edge. In a slow arc, they fell through.

The door shut.

THIRTY-SEVEN

Silence hung heavy in the oven room for a long moment. Marisha finally broke it.

'The door,' she said, her voice strangled, 'we left the door open. I'm so sorry. We should have tried to close it.' She leaned against the wall for support.

Valdim was huddled on the floor, using his hand to staunch the still-bleeding cut on his arm. Olena crouched next to him and tore away a strip from the bottom of her skirt with a piece of the sharp porcelain pieces that littered the floor. She set the flower-lined shard down and gathered the fabric in her hand. He helped her anchor the strip as she wrapped it around his arm.

Olena rose and began walking around the room. She picked up the largest chunks of porcelain and piled them in the crook of her stump.

'How did you open the door?' Olena asked, sounding only half-interested in the answer.

Valdim's eyes were closed, he leaned his head back against the wall. Marisha said, 'I used one of the feathers. From Golgolin. Valdim had it.'

Olena's gaze snapped on Valdim. He sat up straighter. 'What are you going to do?' came Valdim's demand. 'You need to get her back. You got us into this mess.'

'Our door did not help,' Marisha cut in.

'Fine. We helped,' he conceded, and he turned back to Olena, 'but it would not have mattered had you not invited Anatoli. So, how are you fixing it?'

'Just give me a minute for pity's sake.'

'No! You don't deserve a minute! Right now, that graveyard-dirt eater is torturing my mother!'

Marisha shared a glance with Olena. She knew they recognised Anatoli's strong implication that Valdim was not Baba Zima's son by blood. And Valdim must have seen what they thought for he slumped back down.

'I'll think of something,' Olena said. But her voice was weary.

Marisha looked at the wall, keeping Olena and Valdim in the periphery of her vision. She nudged a lump of coal with her foot. Coal was scattered all over the floor, as though the house had spat up in revolt through the oven door. A mass of it still burned red hot in the oven, but how long would the fire last without a mistress to stoke it? Marisha swept up the coal. Then she walked over to the oven and closed its door.

She said, 'I know where Anatoli took Baba Zima.'

'Where?' Olena said. Marisha shared a look with Valdim. He gave her a nod of encouragement.

Marisha took a deep breath. This was it. Even though she had already convinced Valdim her dreams were real, even after seeing Dima indentured and asleep and even with Anatoli's amazed recognition of her, she struggled to put any breath behind the words her mouth formed.

'To my dream.'

Olena wrinkled her nose. 'What are you talking about?'

Marisha told Olena everything: her confused impressions of her early dreams, seeing Olena in the woods with Anatoli and her argument with Valdim. She even told Olena about Pan Volya's assertion that she was fated to fall asleep to the plague. The only thing she kept to herself was her joy in dancing with Kiril. Olena stood still and listened while staring at the wall.

'So, you were right,' Olena said softly. She raised a finger to the edge of her birthmark and traced it along her cheek. 'I should have enquired more about Pan Volya and his black feather. Not the water of death. Not the shield spell.'

'You were right about Nightingale the Robber being important. His story was related to the Ivan the Fool story.'

'But everything else . . . you may have held the key to the plague the whole time.' Olena laughed softly, and it sounded like she exerted a lot of effort to keep it soft. 'And you had no idea–none–that you were falling into the plague bringer's domain.'

'No.'

'But you said you remembered your dream, the one right before Dunya fell asleep. And you did not suspect then?'

'No,' Marisha said, unable to keep the irritation out of her voice. 'I thought it was an echo from Pan Volya's potion, since I forgot to take the sleeping potion. You said yourself dreamwalking takes too much skill for me to have done.'

'But why didn't you tell me about it? Surely you must have thought it was important.'

Marisha's rage flared. 'Why should I have? When have you ever given me any indication that you valued my opinion? You made it very clear that I was following your plan, your rules and that I was to contribute nothing. You dismissed my misgivings about Anatoli. Why should I have thought that you would care about me having another nightmare?'

Olena stood there with her mouth open. 'I thought–but I asked for your opinion. I asked if you had ideas, if you wanted to try out a tincture of your own.'

'And Anatoli?'

Olena's expression twisted between a smile and a grimace. 'I told you to come to me if the potion stopped working. I told you it was important.'

'But not as important as finding the cure.' Cold air seemed to blow on Marisha's neck. The truth of it was that she had closed her eyes against the possibility. 'And I was scared. I didn't want to think about the dream and what it meant. I didn't want to think what the consequences might be. I just wanted it to be a nightmare I could banish. I'm sorry.'

Olena sighed. 'Don't be. You're right, I did not treat you as I ought to have. If you did not feel that you could come to me with this, it's my fault. I knew something was wrong, but I didn't ask. And I should have.' Olena's gaze flicked to Valdim and her mouth slackened for a moment before her black eyes focused back on Marisha. She stepped forward, raised her hand to Marisha's shoulder. 'I'm sorry.' Her shoulders heaved with her inhale. 'Besides, if I had not forced you to choose Kiril in the first place—'

'No.' Marisha shook her head. 'I mean, that's definitely part of it. But it's more than that. My father is involved somehow. I... I wonder if he made a bargain with Pan Volya. And if it involved the beaked man's feather.' Marisha thought of her father, making a coin appear from between her toes, the whorl of raised skin visible from under his sleeve as he walked the coin across his knuckles. He had touched the feather, the scar on his wrist was proof. Pan Volya's cold eyes flashed in her mind. How did her father fit into all of this?

'I don't know. But I'm learning I'm too quick at dismissing possibilities.' Olena took a deep breath, 'And I'm sorry about ignoring you. About Anatoli.' Olena's birthmark flushed. 'That was wrong of me. It's just . . .' She turned her head. 'I thought . . . I don't know what I thought.'

She tipped her head back and closed her eyes. Even though Olena couldn't explain, Marisha could understand. She remembered the way Anatoli had spoken to Olena, as someone to respect. As an equal. Marisha slipped an arm around Olena's shoulder and squeezed. 'You must think me a terrible fool.' Olena avoided looking at Valdim.

Marisha said nothing and pinched Olena's ear.

Olena clapped her hand to her head. 'Ow! What did you do that for?'

'You were feeling sorry for yourself. Stop.'

Olena rubbed her ear but had a small smile for hearing her own words parroted back to her.

'Great, now that all the blame for our situation has properly been squabbled over,' Valdim said, 'we need to get my mother back. How are we getting into Marisha's dream?'

Olena's smile broadened. Marisha detected some of her old twinkle, the look she had when she brainstormed. 'There are several possibilities. First, we could perform a dream-walking spell on Marisha.'

'But wouldn't Marisha be asleep?' Valdim interjected. 'Isn't that inconvenient?'

Olena nodded slowly. 'Yes, but more importantly, Anatoli brought Baba Zima to the other world both in body and spirit. So, we will have to go in body and spirit as well.'

Marisha said, 'I thought going to the other world in body is dangerous.'

'It is. It would probably mean a year off our lives. Maybe more depending on how long we stay. And kolduni who go intending to bring something back, well, they rarely return.' She took a deep breath. 'But we would be bringing back Baba Zima. Since she does not belong to the other world, the consequences should not be so dire. Nevertheless, you don't need to go if you think the risk is too great.'

Valdim said, 'I'm coming with you.'

Olena's expression was carefully blank. She looked at Marisha. Marisha took a deep breath and let it out slowly.

'I will come too,' she said.

'Good,' Olena said, 'We—'

'But I'm also bringing my family and Kiril back up to the earth with us. And Dunya too.'

Olena stared at Marisha. 'Didn't you just hear what I said about bringing things back?'

'They're not things, and they don't belong there any more than Baba Zima does. I'll help find Baba Zima first, but I'm getting my family. And don't you think we owe Dunya and Kiril?' The set of Olena's mouth was stony. 'Most sleepers wake up from the plague, how is this any different?' Marisha was reminded of what Pan Volya had told her about the trouble with deep sleepers waking. He had said the awoken might be drained of their vitality altogether, or at best they might be so changed they would neither recognise themselves nor their loved ones. He had sounded as though he spoke from experience. She shook the thought from her mind and focused on Olena. 'And I know if your brother were stricken you would want to do the same.'

Olena met Marisha's gaze for a long moment and nodded. She said, 'So be it. And I suppose we do owe Dunya and Kiril. But first things first, we have to get there. To go through the threshold, we need to know exactly where we are going in order to get to the correct part of the other world. You'll have to guide us.'

Marisha's eyebrows shot up. 'Me?'

'Of course you. You're the only one who knows where it is, we can't *go* there without you. You came here using the feather. How would this be different? And I'll help you.' She said the last with a pained smile.

Marisha nodded slowly.

'And how will we come back?' Valdim asked.

Olena said, 'We can use Golgolin's feather, I think.'

'Maybe we should bring Golgolin,' Marisha suggested.

Olena and Valdim said *no* at the same time. Marisha rolled her eyes at how protective they were of that animal. Olena added, 'Let's take the feathers. One there, and one back. It should be enough.'

Valdim nodded, though his expression was grim. He walked over to the violin that Anatoli had dropped on the floor and picked it up along with the still-bloody bow.

'I need to gather a few things,' Olena said. She briskly walked out of the receiving room.

Marisha followed her for a few steps but paused. Valdim held the violin in a fist at the neck and kept staring at it as Olena's footfalls disappeared. Marisha knew she should say something, he had offered to listen so often. She took a deep breath. 'Valdim, are you all right?'

Marisha hovered in the doorway, biting her lip. Finally, Valdim spoke. 'He said music compels emotions.'

'That reminds me of something you said. That music is the language of the soul.' She tried a joke. 'If that's so I don't think mine liked what Anatoli had to say.'

Valdim set the violin down. 'I can't believe he controlled me with something I built. It's perverse! You know what the worst part is? This was one of my favourite pieces in the end. It was so difficult to create without any direction from the client's colours, so I think I poured myself into it instead.' He ran a finger down the glossy wood, smearing a drop of blood. 'But it still was not enough to summon my—' He drew in a sharp breath and looked at the violin like he wanted to smash it.

'Valdim, I'm sorry.'

'It doesn't matter.' But the bitterness in his tone told her otherwise. He said, 'You spend your whole life thinking one thing, thinking you know why you cannot do as you wish. But at least when you know that, you know who you are. Now I know nothing.'

'I thought I knew who I was too,' Marisha said, thinking about how she would have never imagined koldunry was anything more than mummery, or that she would be rescuing Dima instead of the other way around. 'But I was wrong. Or maybe I have changed. Either way, I'm glad. Maybe being confused about who you are is better than being wrong.'

He stared at the violin. The silence stretched. He touched the bloody bow to the strings at an angle, but held it so perfectly still, the bow did not tremble.

FIFTEEN MINUTES LATER, they stood in front of the oven-room door. Olena raised an eyebrow at Valdim slinging the strap of the violin case on his shoulder but did not comment.

'No, dearest,' Olena peeled Golgolin off her shoulder, 'you can't come with us. It's much too dangerous for a guinea pigfowl.' Golgolin flapped to the oven and curled up on the blue-and-white mantel, snuffling loudly as he settled.

'Are you ready?' she asked Marisha.

Marisha nodded. She focused on the door, taking calming

breaths. They linked hands. Olena's palm was moist. She was scared, Marisha realised. Somehow this made Marisha feel better. She gave the other woman's hand a small squeeze, and Olena looked at her in surprise. Her steel concentration dropped for a moment in silent acknowledgement, and the mask went up again.

Marisha picked up the feather in her other hand. She did not doubt this time. In fact, she did not really think. She simply brushed the feather to the knob and thought of Kiril. She felt a mix of excitement that she would finally meet him, dull terror of plunging into her dream on purpose, and relief that one way or another, it would be over. She would never have to dream of going to the room with the trapped dancers again.

The feather melted into the door. Marisha pushed it open. They could not see the other side, the threshold was so wide. Marisha grabbed Valdim's hand so they were all linked through her.

'Let's jump on three,' Olena said. And they counted, *one, two, three*, and jumped. They stepped slightly out of sync, but after a small jerk in Marisha's arms they fell, darkness and air swirling around them. Marisha could not think, her screams were lost in the air whipping her face. She only concentrated on gripping Olena and Valdim's hands–their hands in hers were the only parts of her body that felt real. The fear of what would happen when they hit the ground consumed everything else.

THIRTY-EIGHT

arisha woke up in a heap on the ground. She raised her head. Soft rustling sounds and light groans came from beside her. She instinctively rolled away before she remembered Olena and Valdim. She stopped mid-roll and flopped on her back.

At least this place had some light, unlike that place of pitch-black panic before she had spotted the stairs to Dima's tree. Though it was not sunlight, but a fog-like dusky glow. She got up to her elbows. They were outside, definitely not in the dance hall. She touched her skirt and felt the familiar, rough swirls of the yellow embroidery and breathed a sigh of relief. She patted the ground next to her feet. Dry grass. Not even the squishiness of recent spring snow melt that usually lasted until the end of May. Someone groaned nearby. Valdim rubbed his arm and twisted around slowly. Olena struggled to her feet.

Marisha rose as well and squinted. Large shapes rose from the ground ahead. Trees. And next to her feet lay a dirt path. She felt relieved at the other world's lack of subtlety and stepped onto the path. A snort of exasperation came from behind her. Marisha turned and stifled a laugh. Olena examined her two long black braids as though they were snakes.

'I like it.' Valdim grinned at Olena's obvious discomfort.

'I don't know why you didn't get braids as well.' Olena snapped.

'I'm missing out terribly.' Valdim wore an ankle-length kaftan in light brown, though it was difficult to be sure of the colour in the grey light.

Olena tried taking a step forward but stumbled. 'How are you supposed to walk in this stupid skirt?'

Marisha said, 'I don't think the skirt is for walking, but for dancing.'

'Cows will fart pirozhkis before I dance. Are we in the right place?' Olena's question cut through Marisha's badly suppressed laughter.

'I think so, yes. The clothes are right. But I usually appear in the room with the dancers. Maybe things are a bit different since we're here in body.' Marisha sobered at remembering the danger of their physical presence.

'Shall we?' Valdim gestured to the path.

For a few moments the only sounds were Olena's mutters of exasperation as she tried to tug the metal circlet out of her hair. Dark shapes loomed along the path–trees, most likely, but everything remained difficult to see. Marisha hoped they approached the village square or the dacha or wherever the dance hall actually was. She had never entered it, even in the dream with Dima: the dancers had simply appeared.

'Oh.' Marisha stopped.

The clouds parted and a full moon shone silvery, throwing the entire landscape into dramatic relief. Marisha barely noticed the large dark shape of the dacha ahead, for the moonlight reflected sharply off the trees that lined the path. A breeze ruffled the leaves, making them shimmer. Marisha reached up and broke off the closest leaf on the branch with a snap. The stem was cold beneath her fingers and brittle, as though it had been a dead leaf laying on the ground. But when Marisha applied some small pressure to crumble the leaf's edges, they did not bend. The light shone partly through, except at the leaf's veins which the moonlight painted in silver brushstrokes so fine they could have been applied with a single hair. It was a beautiful dead thing of glass and silver.

'Look,' Valdim said, his voice full of wonder as he proffered a leaf that reflected the moon in a warm flash like it was plated in gold. 'This is incredible,' he said, examining a twig still attached to the tree. It bent with the suppleness of its green and living counterpart.

They walked down the path at a slower pace, pausing to examine the trees despite their haste to rescue Baba Zima. An enormous dacha loomed ahead, the size of one the Grand Prince might build. It was studded with a different light than that of the moon: warm and yellow and rich. In front of the dacha were three tiers of courtyards with fountains and steps leading to each one. Marisha felt drawn forward by the beauty of the scene. A few notes of the balalaika wafted their way. Marisha stopped.

'What's wrong?' Valdim asked.

'The music.' Marisha knew she shouldn't alarm her companions with her fear that the music signalled the beaked man's proximity, lying in wait. 'It's nothing.' She focused on her mission. Rescue Baba Zima and wake her family, Kiril and Dunya.

As they approached the courtyard, they started to pick out silhouettes of people milling around. The sound of laughter wove with the mazurka tune. And suddenly, Marisha realised what had been niggling her about their appearance.

'They'll notice us,' Marisha said, stopping.

Olena said, 'I'm sure they're having too much of a good time to notice us.'

'No,' Marisha said, 'we don't have masks.' She touched her own face and it felt exposed. She did not know why the masks were important, but she felt instinctively that they would blend in much better if they had them.

'That can't be helped,' Olena said, 'unless we borrow their masks.'

Marisha shook her head. 'It won't work.' Kiril had said he could not take his mask off. 'We really ought to go unnoticed for as long as possible. It's really important.'

'Maybe we can transform a piece of our skirts,' Olena mused.

'With koldunry?'

'Yes. Baba Zima said koldunry works differently in the other world. That it's easier. Bigger. Feats like making the Hands or giving a house chicken legs are still possible here. I suppose . . . since the spirits are closer . . .' Olena frowned slightly and looked unsure of how to work this bigger, easier sorcery.

'I have an idea,' Valdim said.

He darted back a few steps where a small path split from the main one and wound its way into a grove of trees. Marisha and Olena followed and found him standing next to a huge willow tree, holding a curved twig of beaten gold. 'I can make masks out of these.'

He beckoned Marisha forward and twisted long fronds around her head. He pulled a small knife from his violin case to cut them and they froze into shape. In no time, Valdim declared her mask done. Marisha walked to a stone bird bath to see her reflection. Two fronds crossed at the bridge of her nose and bent back across her forehead, framing her eyes. He had curled the excess into two spirals above her eyebrows, giving her face a heart-shape. And throughout, the golden leaves shimmered around the arterial stems anchoring the design.

Marisha heard Olena protesting from behind her. 'No,' she said, 'you make one for yourself first.'

'Think I need more practice?' Valdim said.

Marisha did not hear Olena's answer. She did not see why Olena would be this uncomfortable with a mask. Did she not want to be seen agreeing to hide her face? Maybe it had something to do with the green veil Marisha had found at the bottom of Olena's clothes chest.

Valdim fashioned a mask for himself that was a bit asymmetric, shaping the fronds around his face by feeling and cutting them so they stayed in place. He scrunched the leaves closer to the stem to keep them out of his eyes, and added a vine along the edge. The squarer shapes of the vine leaves contrasted with the spikiness of the willow. Marisha raised her eyebrows at the pleasing result, impressed with his artistic instinct. Valdim turned to Olena.

'Your turn,' he said.

Olena stepped forward, tossed her head and squared her hips as though she faced down a lake-dwelling snake demon. Valdim stared at Olena for a long moment and Olena stared back. Marisha tamped down the urge to clear her throat.

'Well?' Olena snapped, 'I thought you said you didn't need the practice.'

Valdim raised his eyebrows and shook his head slightly. He tugged Olena by the hand so she stood closer to the willow tree. He held a frond at her nose and cut. Many more cuts later and two tries ended discarded on the ground.

When the third followed them, Olena said, 'We can't stay here all year, Valdim. This is not one of your violins. It doesn't matter if it doesn't look good.'

He growled at her to be quiet and furiously stripped a frond of its leaves. The leaves fell at Olena's feet, fluttering like fallen butterfly wings.

It hit Marisha with the force of a charging bear: Valdim *liked* Olena. And–Marisha dared to glance at Olena. The woman's chin jutted out, resolute, her gaze pointedly staring out and not at Valdim. Yes. She must have feelings for him too. Though she would never admit it. Marisha took a few steps back and sank against a different diamond tree. How had she not noticed before?

Valdim had stripped a frond of many of its leaves and wrapped it around Olena's face in a simple V shape at the nose. But now he wove smaller pieces in and out. He cut a final frond and stopped, staring at his creation.

'Can you see?' he said. Olena finally looked at Valdim.

'Yes,' she said, her voice even, 'I can.'

He drew back.

Marisha breathed in sharply. Olena's mask was radiant, far more intricate than her own or Valdim's. It resembled a hawk's head, or a sunburst. If she had any doubts before . . . She forced a smile and said, 'You look beautiful.'

Olena stiffened. Marisha did not care if Olena thought she mocked her. Marisha meant it.

Olena thanked her but did not touch her mask or look at her reflection. Marisha fought back the urge to shake the woman's damn pride out of her body.

Couples milled about the path to the dacha without seeming to notice them. Marisha forced herself to focus on their surroundings instead of recalling all the interactions she'd witnessed between Olena and Valdim in light of her realisation. Valdim's stride lengthened as they approached the dacha.

Olena shivered and wrapped her shawl closer to her body. Marisha fell in step beside her.

'Are you all right?' Marisha asked in a low voice.

'Fine,' Olena said. 'A little cold.' Olena gave a little smile, but it looked sinister and sad without the rest of her face visible.

Marisha gestured at the couples milling about and said, 'It feels a bit like a festival. I think the last festival I went to my aunt pressed a third cousin to dance with me. I was dreading it, I hadn't seen him in ages. But, he didn't turn out to be that bad. Funny how time changes things, isn't it?' She hoped her prying was not too obvious.

'Are you asking me about my failed conquests at festivals?' The bitterness in Olena's voice sliced through Marisha's machinations.

'Uh, no. I was just . . .' Marisha trailed off.

They walked together in uncomfortable silence, passing through a circular courtyard with pillars lining its edge and an enormous diamond tree growing at its centre. Olena pressed her lips together and exhaled sharply through her nose. When she spoke it was in a quiet voice. 'I haven't been to a festival in twelve years. The last one I attended was in the village square, much less grand than this. I was not allowed to go, but I snuck in wearing my mother's veil. There were the most delicious cheese blintzes . . .' Olena's mouth relaxed and curved at the memory. She breathed in slowly as though she inhaled their sweet aroma. 'A boy, Misha, bought a cone of them for me.' She sighed deeply with such sadness.

Marisha waited a beat, then dared to ask, 'What happened?'

Olena didn't answer. They reached the enormous dacha. Valdim was still a ways away. Then Olena said. 'My little brother found us. He recognised the green veil. I had pretended to be sick, so he thought I was at home. I just didn't want to be *me* for once.' Olena chuckled softly. 'And once Fedya asked me what I was doing wearing Mama's veil, Misha knew it was me. And then, he wanted nothing to do with me. And, I got angry at Fedya.' She paused. 'I pushed him.'

Olena crumpled a little. She said, 'Everyone said I cursed him. If I had, I hadn't known it would be that easy.'

'Olena,' Marisha didn't know what to say. She tentatively put an arm around Olena's shoulders. 'I'm sorry. But whatever happened, it wasn't your fault—' Valdim caught up with them, saving Olena from having to answer her trite words. But what else could Marisha have said?

Valdim said he had looked for a door but had no luck. Olena stepped forward and scrutinised the wall for a door. They avoided the main entrance with light spilling out of it and went around the wall.

'There,' Marisha said, her hand already on the handle of a smaller, narrower door.

'Did you know it was here?' Valdim ran a hand through his hair, sticking it on ends. 'I could have sworn nothing was there.'

'No. Not exactly,' Marisha said. Her hand felt cold. 'I've never been here before.'

Marisha turned the handle and the warm, rich yellow light sprang out. They walked into a wide hall. She had to blink against the light of hundreds of candles, but as her eyes adjusted, she took in the details of the tall walls glossed in cream and powder blue. The mouldings on the floor and ceiling were gilded in gold paint. Their footsteps sounded strangely hollow on the floor made of wooden strips interlocking in a zig-zag patterns.

Valdim examined an elaborate candle holder on the wall carved out of glass to resemble a large glittering lily. Possibly grown in the garden of living jewels outside the dacha. His kaftan was the colour of freshly turned earth, edged in a soft, almost violet blue. Blue-and-white embroidery shimmered on the kaftan when he moved. Marisha looked down at the familiar, rich burgundy of her skirt swirled with sickbed yellow and glanced at Olena.

'Oh,' she said, 'your dress.'

Olena followed Marisha's gaze down to her own dress and her mouth puckered as though she had swallowed a salamander. It was made of sage green wool, with emerald and gold embroidery on the skirt. Silver swirled on her bodice, and her shawl was stunning translucent gold. Olena's green veil would have matched perfectly. Marisha remembered Valdim's description of Olena's colours and guessed at why he looked so satisfied.

'The red suits you,' Valdim said to Marisha.

'Now that we've sufficiently admired each other,' Olena said, 'should we not get to the problem at hand? We need to find them.'

'I think maybe Kiril would know.' Marisha swallowed, trying not to let her excitement and trepidation show. 'He's in the room with the dancers.' A wave of worry washed over her as she recalled the dark lady's wink in her last dream before she clamped a hand on Kiril's shoulder and tugged him away. She hoped fervently that his act of helping her had not caused him to come to harm.

She could hear the mazurka again. It sent a frisson up her spine and she looked to Valdim to see if he was affected by it as well.

'Let's go find him,' Olena said. 'Shall we?'

'Wait,' Marisha said, 'I need to tell you. It's important that we blend in. When we're in there, we have to dance. And more importantly, we can't say anything. If you speak, they'll notice you.' She said the last sentence as though it were an incantation and felt a bit ridiculous for it.

'What do you mean?' Valdim asked.

'The other dancers. They will not be kind.' Marisha was not sure the dancers would behave as they had in her dreams but didn't want to take that chance.

Marisha led them down the hall where the notes of the mazurka grew louder and richer. Vibrations travelled down the wooden floor, as though a herd of elk trampled to the music. Marisha put her fingers to her lips, reminding them of the necessary silence, pushed the door open and slid in.

Marisha breathed in sharply. The room was huge, larger than the hall of beds in the sanitorium, and packed with people. It was louder than in her dream, overfilled with swirling people and colours and scents. The perfume of hundreds of individuals was an almost physical blow: clouds of concentrated rose, heady jasmine and musk, and something earthy and spicy, maybe cinnamon, all clashed together but without even coming close to masking the salty, rancid smell of sweat.

How would she find Kiril in this mess?

She needed to stay calm and not let Olena and Valdim know of her concern. They were relying on her. Marisha stood on tiptoes, looking around the fray for any sign of sky blue and egg-yolk yellow. Smears of blue and yellow were everywhere, that was the problem. Two dancers, both women in teal silk, turned their heads in their direction.

She would have to go looking for Kiril. Immediately. She turned back to Valdim and Olena. Her stomach clenched at the thought of leaving them by themselves. But the beaked man–her friends would be safer without her. Marisha mimed walking and dancing and Olena's mouth puckered quizzically in response.

Marisha tried again. Valdim wiggled his hand in reply. Marisha rolled her eyes and whispered she would look for Kiril and they should dance so as not to draw attention to themselves. Olena looked at Marisha like she had suggested she drink the dirty laundry water.

Marisha raised her eyebrows. Olena huffed and rolled her eyes in response.

Marisha slipped away, revolving on the spot to avoid a brunette with a bronze mask and pink skirt cutting through the crowd. She smiled to herself. At least the dancers moved the same way they did in her dream.

She scanned the room while flitting her gaze back to Olena and Valdim every few seconds. Olena had drawn her shawl tighter around her body, covering her short arm completely. She looked straight ahead, not at Valdim. Marisha could feel Olena's discomfort as she began to sway self-consciously to the rhythm of the mazurka.

Marisha's amusement vanished when a dark blue man in a peacock mask jostled Olena. Olena pushed back with her shoulder. A woman in a lavender dress shot with pink and green embroidery tugged on Valdim's arm. Marisha had a vision of the crowd swallowing them. She could almost feel the hands on her arm, the tug of her hair, the bodies pressing in and cutting off air. Olena shoved the lavender lady back, but she returned and faced Olena head on as though sizing her up. Marisha rushed forward.

But before she reached them, Valdim grabbed Olena's hand. Olena looked as though she swallowed a shout when she noticed who touched her. She tugged but he didn't let go and rather pulled Olena closer to him. His hand went to her waist and Marisha could see the fingers curved and pressed into the fabric of her bodice.

Olena moved awkwardly, but Valdim's steps were smooth. Where had he learned to dance? Marisha could not reconcile his gliding confidence with his usual bumbling about the house, sawdust in his hair and wood polish on his clothes.

Marisha slowly revolved on the spot trying to focus on the people dancing by her. A man paused, his mask wolfish in chocolate brown, his kaftan red umber with grey sleeves. She ignored him, scanning the sea of colours for the particular flash of blue and yellow.

Someone touched her arm, purposefully stopping her.

She glanced back and went brittle with terror. The beaked man.

THIRTY-NINE

arisha barely even struggled against his iron grip. Her terror was so great she could not think, she could only feel her heart beating in her ears and his talons' vice-like grip dragging her along like a sack of barley. *No*, she thought wildly, *no, I will not!* And opened her mouth to scream but all that came out was a strangled squawk.

Her vision narrowed. A flash of green slippers, the edge of a mirror, the door slammed. The beaked man dragged her away from the dancers, but Marisha did not see where to. A more private spot for the evisceration? Bile burned at the back of her throat and spots danced before her eyes. The beaked man's breath was warm on her neck. Her ears roared and her vision shut.

When she opened her eyes again she saw nothing. She thrashed around and sensation rushed back to her limbs with the prickling pain of needles. Marisha pinched her eyes closed. She opened them when the pain subsided.

It was cold and smelled musty. Her legs were heavy. She stretched her hands to her ankles and felt cold metal. Chains. At least her arms were free. She pushed herself up in a more comfortable seated position and wiggled her toes. She took a deep breath, and the drumming in her ears faded. Being chained in an unknown part of the dacha would make escaping a lot more difficult.

'Are you awake? Took your time about it.'

Marisha squinted. She could see a dark shape shift nearby, but could not make out its features. But that voice was unmistakable. 'Baba Zima?'

'Of course.'

'We came to rescue you.'

'Well, you found me. When does the rescuing begin?' Baba Zima rattled her own leg chains. Then a pause. 'We? Please tell me you came alone.'

'I can't say I did. Olena and Valdim are here too.'

'No,' a long pause, a deep breath, 'that was extremely foolish. My poor dears. Now she'll have them all. What a bad brew this is.'

Marisha did not answer.

'Ah well,' Baba Zima said after a moment, 'it's nice to have company at any rate–even yours. But how did you get here? I did not think Olena knew of this place.'

'She didn't. I did.'

'Well now I *am* surprised.'

Marisha took a long deep breath through her nostrils. 'Why are you here?'

'Oh, I suppose to be kept in discomfort until my captors have the good will to return.'

'No, I mean why did Anatoli bring you here? And how?'

'Remember, I'm the one who asks the questions, not the other way around.'

'Baba Zima, must I remind you of the events of the past hours? Are you even mistress of the house anymore?'

Baba Zima drew in a sharp breath. 'They'll have to kill me to stop me.' Her voice was gritty, but Marisha could hear the pain behind it.

'I hope it doesn't come to that. In the meantime, please. Answer my questions. You owe it to me. You have not been a very good mistress.'

'I have not?'

'You know you have not.'

Baba Zima shifted to sit straighter and grumbled, 'Fine.' She breathed rather heavily. 'I suppose Anatoli brought me here because he's allied with *her*. But I thought she was gone. Or I hoped she was. But during my demonstration at the krug, she reached out to me from the fire. What is that old adage? About playing with fire. All you get from kicking an ember is burned toes. Ha! You certainly get more than that when stepping into the Marazovla bonfire–especially when someone in the spirit world holds a grudge.'

'And who is *she*?'

'Serafima Vladimirovna Nasieva.'

'Serafima?' Marisha had been half expecting Baba Zima to say Olga, Serafima's other apprentice.

'Yes. My former mistress. Surely you paid enough attention to know that.'

'I thought you said she chose you over Anatoli as her successor, and he never forgave you for it.'

'That's right.'

Marisha hesitated. 'But if she picked you over him, why would you assume that Anatoli is allied with her?'

Baba Zima exhaled loudly. 'Maybe it happened a bit differently from that.'

Marisha let the silence go on for long seconds before prodding, none too gently, 'So . . . what really happened?'

Baba Zima was silent for so long that Marisha thought she had become wilfully deaf. She was about to prod again when Baba Zima finally said, 'I took it.'

'What do you mean? Took what?'

'The bolshina. It was mine. I had been her apprentice the longest, she had always favoured me; I was her natural successor. And how could she do otherwise–pick him over me? After what he did to Olga? That stinking skulking viper, he seduced his way into her secrets, and he abandoned her. I didn't think my matrionka could be taken by him as well. But she let Olga leave.' Baba Zima paused, closing her mouth as though it would dam the flood of her past. She pressed her lips together tightly then said. 'He broke Olga's heart. I didn't realise she was pregnant until later. But she left and I couldn't let Anatoli be victorious over me.'

'So you . . . took it?'

'If I had not, he would have. As though he would submit to Baba Serafima's test. Pah.'

'I'm still not exactly sure what you mean.'

'Baba Serafima was cruel. She enjoyed toying with us, played little games to test our devotion. Be kind with a kiss one day and snide with a slap the next. It was disconcerting, never to know where one stood with her.'

'Sounds familiar,' Marisha muttered.

'Ha! You think I'm bad? She–you have no idea. None. Flirting with him and looking at me, as though daring me to say something. And after poor Olga left, Baba Serafima didn't even say anything, not one word. That snake Anatoli stayed. And she wouldn't stop dropping hints about the test, about how difficult it would be. Hinting only one of us would be left alive. One day she would announce she'd forego the test and hand the bolshina to me; the next day, she'd say she thought he would win. But when she started looking at him that way, that's when I knew I had to act.'

'But what do you mean? What did you do?'

'The poker, you stupid girl. I took the poker.'

The poker. Marisha had halfway thought that Baba Zima's strict prohibition on stoking the oven was another of her idiosyncrasies. True, Anatoli had held on to the poker, but Marisha had assumed he had only done it so that he could pull Baba Zima into the threshold. 'That's it? You just . . . took the poker? But how?'

'With my hands.'

Marisha snorted, remembering how she had brandished the poker at Valdim without becoming mistress of the house. 'If that's all it takes, how come Anatoli didn't take it first?'

'Hmph. Ignorant girl.'

'And whose fault is that!'

'I told you enough. You have not even been with me for a full year. But even if I had not explicitly explained how the bolshina passes, you ought to have been able to figure out that it's not so simple as grasping the poker. You need intent. Intent, always intent! That's all koldunry really is. Unless the bolshina is given to you, you need to take it. And taking it has consequences.'

'Like what?'

'Haven't you ever wondered why I avoid touching things with my bare hands?' Marisha could hear the sad smile in Baba Zima's voice.

'Um. Yes. But I assumed it was a . . . quirk.'

'Something I adopted by choice? No. Rather, one of the consequences of taking the bolshina by force. Touching things . . . burns me. Except for hot things themselves, ironically enough.'

'What about people?' Marisha asked.

'They burn, but not as badly as with cold things. Touching you would be unpleasant, but bearable. But if I touch this chain with bare hands—' The chain rattled.

Marisha tried to imagine the sensation of grabbing something, an ordinary object like a book or a mortar, and having it burn her fingers. Her stomach twisted. 'Is that why you take your tea scalding hot?'

'Yes. The teacups don't hurt as much.'

She sounded so forlorn that Marisha actually felt sorry for her. 'And you knew it would happen that way?'

'Not exactly. You hear terrible tales among kolduni, of apprentices driven mad in their attempts to steal the bolshina from their masters. Of finding an apprentice in the morning, hand outstretched, dead cold.'

'I don't understand. If the cost was so high, if you knew you could go mad, even die, why do it? How could it be worth it?'

'Of course it was worth it! The bolshina was all I ever wanted! I had been working my whole life to get it, I could not let it slip away. The mere chance she would pass me over and give it to Anatoli–unthinkable! But don't even try to understand, you never will. That was always the problem with you, you never did want it enough. I tried to tell you, from the very beginning.'

'Why hire me? Why take me as an assistant if you knew I would fail?'

Baba Zima paused. 'I did not want to give Olena a rival. I vowed I never would.'

'But you forced me to spy on her. You pitted me against her!'

'But you were never a threat. You were useful, or, you should have been. And I made it so easy for you, I even agreed to that nonsense request of yours to bring your brother into the house.

Although why you would want to see him after what he did to you, I don't know. But I promised it to you, and you still failed. We would not be here now if you'd told me what she planned.'

Marisha's breath froze. 'How did you know what Dima did to me?'

'That letter of yours.'

'*You* read my letter?'

'Yes. Don't sound so affronted. I had let you into my house. It was my right to know who you were and what you were hiding.'

'No, it wasn't! And why did you leave the letter out on my bed like that? I thought—' She clamped her mouth shut. Obviously, Baba Zima had no idea what seeds of discord she had planted in Marisha's mind against Olena.

'I surely instructed the Hands to put your items back.'

Marisha shot Baba Zima a venomous look. 'I don't believe you. And why should I? All you've ever done is seek to manipulate everyone in your house. Secrets and lies, yes, I remember those from your contract. But at what cost? You blame me for not telling you what Olena planned, but didn't it occur to you that if you had explained to her *why* you wanted her to stay away from Anatoli, she would have listened? Your secrets choked you in the end, Baba Zima!'

Marisha breathed in deeply, once, twice. Silence settled over the chamber once again.

Baba Zima said, 'And here I had thought you were so transparent. I'll admit, I did underestimate you. How funny that we repeat the mistakes of our elders. Baba Serafima underestimated me, I underestimated you. Of course, not to the same deleterious result. But still. One must amuse oneself somehow.'

Baba Zima paused. The only sound was her heavy breathing.

Marisha said, 'But you did it in the end. Steal the bolshina.'

'Yes.' Baba Zima inhaled sharply but continued to speak, 'Reluctantly, I did. You see, after Anatoli drove Olga away, I fantasised about taking the bolshina. And punishing him. Of course, it was just a thought, a fancy, but when Baba Serafima and Anatoli became closer, I made an actual plan. I would drug my mistress, then take the poker as she slept. She would never see it coming. Or so I thought.

'I put the sleeping draught in our tea and I drank the antidote myself. And when I came down to the oven room to see if she was still asleep–Serafima still kept the old-fashioned tradition of sleeping on top of the oven–I had not even truly decided whether I would go through with it. But she was not asleep, she knew it was me who doctored her tea. And so, I had no choice. I grabbed it. Serafima lunged for it too, scrambling off the oven. But the oven door was open and when I turned away, I must have elbowed her and she fell into it and . . . gone. She simply . . . disappeared'

'So she did not underestimate you in the end. Not really. She knew what you were up to.'

'I suppose. But I don't think she thought I would really take the poker. Even though I had turned my skill against her, she never thought I actually would do it.'

'You never really meant to take it,' a low and musical female voice said. 'I should have remembered how a cornered cat strikes the hand of its master.'

Marisha jumped at the voice. She had not heard anyone come in. Her heart beat wildly as light flooded the room. Marisha could finally see Baba Zima sitting nearby on the floor. Her dress was rich purple satin embroidered in white-and-red thread, but it was creased and smudged. Her face and neck were flushed and sweat sheened on her skin. She wore no mask.

Marisha immediately recognised the woman who walked in as the dark lady. Her dress was of a deep midnight blue with patterns of leaves and thorns in silver thread. Her mask covered her eyes and glittered with diamonds, a beautiful complement to her dark blonde hair streaked with white. Despite the age her hair revealed, the dark lady radiated power and strength, carrying herself in a regal way that Marisha imagined the princess did. She was accompanied only by Anatoli, who wore his familiar black-and-orange zigzagged cape and spiky collar. Marisha breathed easier. She knew, rationally, that this woman must be as dangerous as the beaked man, but she did not inspire terror in her heart like he did, just grim apprehension.

'My dear Zima, it has been far too long.' Serafima's voice was soft and taunting. Anatoli did not say anything, just grinned. 'I can't believe it took you so long to visit after banishing me here all those years ago. One might call such an oversight . . . rude. And speaking of rude,' Serafima turned her gaze to Marisha, 'I do not believe we have been formerly introduced. You look familiar, how vexing.'

'She's been here before,' Anatoli said.

'Has she now?' Serafima tilted her face towards Marisha. Marisha wished she could see the expression in Serafima's eyes behind the glittering mask.

Anatoli said, 'But she's of little consequence. Just one of Zima's new hires.'

Serafima answered softly, 'He would not be so interested in her if she were of little consequence.'

Marisha's stomach knotted. They must be referring to the beaked man. Serafima addressed her, 'Why is he so interested in you?'

'I don't know,' Marisha said dully. Serafima leaned in closer, causing Marisha to notice how the light smoothly oiled down a long black feather hanging from her belt on a chain.

'The feather, at your belt—'

Serafima's hand shot to her hip. 'Pretty, isn't it?'

'Did it give you the scar on your wrist?'

Serafima let out a breathy laugh and said, 'My, Zima, whatever have you been teaching your minions?'

'I did not teach her this.' Baba Zima looked at Marisha as though she had never seen her before.

Serafima turned back to Marisha. 'How curious.'

Baba Zima said to Serafima, 'How is it that you're here? I've been looking for you—'

'To make sure I'd never return? Don't lie, Zima. You were never very good at it. As to how I got here–your assistant appears more intuitive than you are.' Serafima touched the feather at her belt. 'I had recently acquired this odd feather and had it on my person when you banished me to the other world.' A muscle in her jaw twitched. 'I found myself here. A happy coincidence, is it not?'

Marisha knew it was no coincidence. The feather must have pulled Serafima to its owner–the beaked man. It was a link to him, like Pan Volya had insinuated. Serafima's soft voice commanded the room. 'The monster–he scared me. I spent a long time trying to leave. I did not understand how I was able to survive. A bodied person can't *be* in the other world for long, but I survived, unchanged. For years. Eventually, I realised I was stealing some of the vitality that he took from his victims. Enough to sustain me. Not enough to leave.' She pressed her lips together, then her mouth relaxed into a small smile. 'Feathers truly are potent links. Almost twenty years had passed according to Anatoli. That was quite a long time to be searching for one's vanished matrona. But to me, it felt much shorter. Once I understood how to use this feather as a link to the monster, I tried to take more of what he stole from his victims. But it still wasn't enough. Not when there weren't any new ones yet. Don't feel bad for him, he got something in return. He did recover from his moult faster this time around.' Marisha thought of how the beaked man's fledgling feathers had filled in between the first and last time she saw him. She shuddered.

Serafima's smile broadened, 'More food for him means more fuel for me.' She turned to Baba Zima. 'I imagine the early arrival of the plague must have given you quite a fright.'

Marisha looked away from the droop in Baba Zima's neck. She remembered how Kiril had told her that the beaked man's tether was lengthening–Serafima must be the one holding the reins. Marisha asked, 'Did you set the beaked man on Dunya?'

Serafima frowned. 'Who's Dunya?' She looked at Anatoli who shrugged in response.

Marisha exhaled and said, 'You can't elect plague victims.'

'No. This Dunya was a friend of yours, I presume?' Serafima's smile was indulgent, a cat playing with her food. Her cold gaze reminded Marisha of Pan Volya's. 'My dear, I barely kept him from devouring you on sight.' She touched the black feather swaying slightly at her waist. 'No. I can protect a few souls from him, but that is the extent of my control. Though, I have never really tried to direct his efforts. His mind is very different, I'd have to get close enough to ask, which is tricky. You see, he only approaches people to feed. Besides, he does not like me.' Her smile broadened. 'He does seem to like you.' She turned to Baba Zima, 'Maybe you know why your assistant has piqued the plague-bringer's fancy?'

'I don't know.' Baba Zima's lips pressed tightly together. The sweat on her neck formed beads.

'Of course you don't. You were always so oblivious to everything not immediately concerning you.'

'I remember.' Anatoli snapped his fingers, interrupting Serafima. 'Dunya. One of Zima's assistants.'

Serafima let out a booming laugh. 'No! One of your assistants fell asleep to the plague? And while she was in the house? Ha! That's leagues better than the plague coming early–you must have been frightened witless. Oh, my dear Zima, how could you fail to realise your control was slipping?'

Baba Zima gave Serafima a scathing look. 'I suspected you might be interfering. I just didn't realise you'd stooped so low.' Baba Zima glanced pointedly at Anatoli.

'Is that how Anatoli breezed past your wards? Quite careless of you, Zima. I would have thought your paranoia to be much more extensive.'

'I had decided to put my trust in my apprentice, something you would know nothing about.'

'But you did not trust your little apprentice enough. Did not want history to repeat itself. Poor thing.'

'That's not at all–Anatoli, little snake–how could you choose him?'

Anatoli sneered. 'I was better than you, Zima. As I would have proven to you had you not cheated.'

Serafima held up a hand and Anatoli fell silent. The shadowy light made the whorled scar on Serafima's wrist seem darker and uglier than Marisha remembered it being on her father's. 'Might I remind you, Zima, that I did not choose him. Don't you remember what I told you that night you betrayed me? You were your own downfall: you doubted whether you would prevail against him. And in that, you showed yourself weak. Even when you thought you took my bolshina, it was never really yours. How else could the house have failed to protect your assistant? How else could Anatoli have so easily controlled the Hands?'

'The water—'

'No. It was because I had given him permission: because you were never the true mistress of the house, you never fully took the bolshina away from me, you left a piece of it behind. And that's why I could use Anatoli to get you here.' Anatoli frowned slightly at her words but did not counter them. Serafima took a step closer. 'But you, Zima. You disappointed me. You could have had everything.' Baba Zima flinched as though the words were physical blows.

Serafima paused. 'I'll be interested to meet this Olena of yours. Unless your training has ruined her completely, she might make a suitable replacement for when I return up to the earth.'

Baba Zima hissed. 'No, she is loyal to me.'

'Is she now? Even when she finds out why you picked her as an apprentice?'

Baba Zima's skin blanched visibly. 'What do you mean?'

'Oh yes,' Serafima said, 'I know you well and I have observed your apprentice and her myriad . . . talents. I know why you would have thought her a safe choice. Do you think she will still be yours when I tell her?'

Baba Zima pressed her lips together so tightly they were almost invisible. She spat out, 'You know nothing. And if you think I could have picked my apprentice based on so shallow a reason, you misjudged me.'

Marisha felt a mix of curiosity and disgust. What was Serafima talking about?

Serafima said, 'Maybe we should continue this conversation in a more pleasant locale. I do believe I have given my ally enough time to find your apprentice and wayward son. How very obliging of them to come to me.' Serafima turned to Marisha. 'Unfortunately, this is where our acquaintance ends. I had to be very stern about him bringing you here alive, first.'

Marisha did not trust herself to speak. She placed her hands on her knees to quell the trembling. It did not work.

Serafima crouched and unlocked Baba Zima's chains. Anatoli swooped down and lifted her up. Baba Zima groaned.

'Now, now, Zima. Perk up. You still have that test to take. It is what, twenty-one years overdue? Anatoli is positively champing at the bit. And your apprentice and son will be there to witness it, isn't that nice.' Anatoli dragged Baba Zima to the doorway.

Marisha panicked. They could not be leaving her alone like this. Not with the beaked man coming. 'Wait,' she said.

Baba Zima twisted back towards Marisha. 'Don't leave the girl, it's not right. She has no part in this.'

'Even you don't really believe that, do you, Zima?' Serafima turned to address Marisha. 'I do not leave you here lightly–I am so very curious about why he wants you so much. But he must be kept happy. Besides, I have been waiting for so long to deal with my apprentice, and simply, I'm running out of time. So . . .' she shrugged and turned and led Anatoli and Baba Zima out.

'No,' Marisha croaked, 'don't leave me.' But her words were lost in the clang of the door.

FORTY

arisha drew her head to her knees and sobbed. She had failed to rescue anyone. She had even brought Olena and Valdim with her to this hell, all to the benefit of Serafima. And now she was about to die.

She wished with all her might she could wake up, but clench her eyes tight as she could, she did not. Her sobs quieted. She felt a curious numbness settle in, an odd sense of relief; she could stop fighting. She breathed. Each breath was a gift, another moment she lived. Marisha wailed, softly at first but then with all her might so her voice echoed and filled the empty chamber. She did not want to die.

The door swung open. Numbness flooded away and a familiar terror replaced it. *This is it,* she thought to herself wildly, *I am about to die.* She balled the chains in her hands, intending to use them to bludgeon her attacker if she could.

But the man that entered was not the black-swathed giant. Marisha could not comprehend at first. Her heart leapt at thinking it was Kiril, but while he wore a blue kaftan with yellow trim, his mask was not Kiril's band of feathers across the eyes. The blue and yellow feathers spread from his nose over his cheeks and forehead down to his neck.

The bird-faced stranger rushed towards her and set his lamp

down near Marisha's feet. He produced a key. She drew back. 'Who are you?'

He sat back on his heels. 'It's me. Marisha–don't you recognise me?' He touched his cheek.

She recognised Kiril's voice from her dream. Relief made Marisha feel faint. 'Sorry, your mask is different than I remember.'

'It's grown,' he said. Marisha looked closer and saw that the feathers covering his face sprouted directly from his skin. She felt sickened and shrank away. The key turned and he removed the chains on her ankle. He pulled her to her feet. She leaned against the wall, turning her ankles to make them work again. The pins and needles felt almost good. She was still alive. Kiril had come for her.

'How did you know I was here?' she asked as she followed him out of the room. 'And how did you have the key?'

'It was on a nail inside the door,' he said, closing his hand on hers and pulling her along a narrow hallway. 'She doesn't need to hide the keys, since we can't leave the zal sumerek, the room where we dance. Not while the mazurka plays.'

Marisha tugged him to a stop. 'If you can't leave the zal sumerek, how are you here?' The torchlight reflected smoothly off the feathers covering his cheek and neck. 'Kiril, what happened to your mask?' She reached out a hand to touch his cheek. The feathers were silky and rigid.

'He took more.'

'Of what?'

'Me.'

Her fingers froze. 'Did this happen because I left you?'

Kiril's lips and eyelids were the only feather-free spots on his face. 'It's not your fault.'

Marisha shrank her fingers back. She breathed in quickly through her nose, trying to calm the yammering of her heartbeat. She should have stayed in the house. It was all he had asked her to do. He said he'd be protected if she stayed.

'I'm sorry I left. I–I didn't think my dreams were real. I thought I was delusional to believe such a silly fantasy.'

'Marisha, I don't blame you. I wouldn't have believed the zal sumerek was a real place either.'

Marisha smiled sadly. He had misunderstood what kind of fantasy she referred to. But she was not about to correct him. 'Still, I should not have left. I'm sorry.'

'You protected me long enough for the plague-bringer to return with new souls. He lost interest in me. Eventually. As did Serafima. I was lucky.'

'I–I'm glad to hear it.' She took a deep breath. 'And the new souls, they're all in the zal sumerek?'

'Yes.'

'But how does he bring them there?'

'I'm not sure. I remember when he first brought me here, his wings were full, but as he kept bringing back more souls to the dacha, more feathers were lost and his wings became scraggly. He brings the souls here and he—' Kiril pressed his lips together. 'He consumes. When his feathers are gone and he can't return to the earth, the souls are able to leave. At least, those not in the zal sumerek.'

'But he kept you, and others. Why?'

'I don't know. I think he likes watching us dance.' The corner of his mouth raised, ruffling the yellow feathers on his cheek. 'Maybe he's lonely.'

Marisha thought back to how Ivan the Fool in Pan Volya's story wanted to be reunited with that little piece of his spirit that flitted from person to person no matter what the cost. Could he be motivated by anything else?

Marisha closed her eyes. 'Kiril, I came here to bring back Baba Zima, but also to get you out. And my family.'

'You can't. I can't leave with my mask on.'

Was it even a mask anymore? Marisha asked, 'How do you take it off?'

'I don't know. I thought leaving the zal sumerek would do it, but—' He shook his head. 'Maybe only the plague-bringer can remove it.'

Marisha grimaced and said, 'I wonder if Serafima could use his feather to force him to let the trapped souls go.' Serafima had said the feather did not allow much control over the beaked man, but Marisha doubted the koldunya had tried to use it for the purpose of freeing his victims. 'I don't suppose there are any more of the beaked man's feathers lying around?'

'No. He never loses them here. Some say they got lost in the threshold between the dark earth and the other world. I don't know how Serafima got her hands on one.'

Marisha remembered how Pan Volya's jaw had tightened when he had told her at their first meeting that Baba Serafima had acquired a feather from him. He must not have given it up willingly. Marisha sighed and said, 'I guess the only option is to take it from her and get it to Olena.'

He shook his head. 'It's much too big a risk.'

'What other choice do I have?'

'You could leave. You still have one of the guinea pig-fowl's feathers, don't you?'

'Yes, but–how do you know?'

'You told me.'

'No, I didn't.'

'Yes, when you said goodbye to me before jumping into the threshold.'

Marisha was confused, until she remembered how she had visited Kiril in the linen closet one last time. Her face grew hot. While on some level she had hoped he could hear her, she never imagined he actually would. She had not censored herself at all. 'Oh. I would not have blathered on and on all those times if I thought you could hear me. I hope it was not too tiresome for you.' Her cheeks grew even warmer. She was glad her mask hid her face.

'No,' he said quietly, 'I wish I could have answered.'

The warm light of the hallway sheened off the yellow feathers on his temple and jaw. They had been like this before, when she had dreamed so vividly after forgetting to take Olena's sleeping potion: him rushing her out, her escaping with nothing but a promise. A promise she later broke.

She took a deep breath. 'I'm not going. Not yet. I have to stop Serafima. She has my friends. And if I can take the feather from her, maybe I can make the beaked man let you go. Everyone could leave.'

'And how do you propose to defeat her?'

'I'm not sure. It doesn't make sense to me that Serafima would go through all this trouble to get Anatoli to bring Baba Zima here for revenge. And, she said it was a nice surprise for Anatoli to have brought Baba Zima . . . Hmm. She said she wants to return up to the earth. But oh, she has Olena and Valdim captive, she could take one of Golgolin's feathers from them and use it to leave.'

'She can't. She has been here too long. It won't be enough. She uses all she can get from the plague bringer to sustain her body, she could never siphon off enough power from him to leave. Already he has claimed many victims, and she is still here.'

Marisha reeled with sudden realisation. Anatoli had pulled the poker along with Baba Zima into the threshold. 'But now Serafima not only has the beaked man's feather, but the poker too.'

'What?'

'Anatoli brought Baba Zima to Serafima, but he also brought her the poker. I think the poker must have been what Serafima asked Anatoli to bring her, not Baba Zima. If Serafima takes the bolshina from Baba Zima, maybe it would be enough power for her to strengthen her link to the beaked man and drain more of his victims' vitality. Or—' She looked at Kiril, wishing she could decipher his expression behind the feathers. 'Maybe she could use the bolshina to bolster the beaked man and help him claim more victims for her to drain. And she could use that power to get back up to the earth.'

'It would be disastrous,' Kiril said, 'It would take hundreds of thousands of souls. Maybe enough to decimate half Chernozemlya. My family—' he swallowed.

Marisha realised with a pang that she had not thought much about the people that Kiril had left behind. She had only spared a thought about his hypothetical wife on the night she had kidnapped him. It was almost as though he had existed only for Marisha, in the linen closet and in her dreams. How self-centred and small-minded she was.

She swallowed, not wanting to think of what came next. 'We must stop them.'

'But how?'

'The poker. And the feather. I must steal them. Serafima would never suspect that I could.' Marisha supposed she had not suffered any consequences herself for brandishing the poker at Valdim because she had not wanted to steal the bolshina. This time would be different. She clenched her teeth, thinking of Baba Zima being unable to hold anything without burning. It was a price Marisha was willing to pay. 'Do you think the other souls would help?'

'We can't leave the zal sumerek, not when the musicians play. Don't you remember? I told you often enough.'

Marisha frowned, 'I only remember seeing you the night that Dunya fell asleep to the plague, when you distracted the beaked man so I could leave.' Marisha grew hot, remembering how the dark lady–Serafima–had clamped her hand on Kiril's wrist, and the beaked man's caw had sounded like a roar. 'How many times have I visited you?'

'Around thirty times. Thirty-seven to be exact.'

'You kept count.'

She couldn't read Kiril's facial expression as he nodded. She said, 'I only remember the last one clearly. But I remember some vague impressions. I knew that I saw you, those were the only good part of my dreams.'

'I knew that it caused you pain. But I couldn't help hoping that you would come.'

Heat rose through Marisha's body and she was very aware of Kiril next to her. She wished they were in the zal sumerek so she could have the excuse of dancing to touch him.

She told herself to focus on the problem at hand, and then realised something she should have as soon as Kiril rescued her from the dungeon. 'You said that you couldn't leave the zal sumerek when the mazurka played. How is it that you're here?'

He looked slantwise at her. 'I'm not sure. I just knew. I could feel you, like you were at the other end of a tether. I felt your distress somehow. And,' he shrugged. 'I can't explain it. I was just able to leave.'

'The end of a tether?' She wrinkled her nose in distaste. 'Damp dark earth, kidnapping you had much bigger consequences than I imagined.'

Kiril's mouth curved in a smile. She had whispered to him all her thoughts. Which he remembered. It made her squirm, as did the idea he could feel her distress. Could he feel her other feelings too? Her heart beat faster. She hoped he didn't know. 'Thank you, for coming. You saved me. Again.'

He squeezed her hand. Marisha smiled–she couldn't help it. But she remembered the danger at hand.

'We have to go,' Marisha said. But she could not ask him to come with her; she had already failed to keep him safe once. 'Since you can move freely, maybe you can stop the musicians in the zal sumerek from playing? Then the other souls might be able to leave. I'll get the poker.'

'No, I'm coming with you.'

Marisha shook her head. 'If you can stop the musicians and open the doors, maybe the others would help.' And he would be safer there than with her.

'And the plague-bringer? He still wants you.'

Marisha bit the inside of her lip. She was resolute. 'It can't be helped. Even if I left here without the poker, well, I would probably end up back down here anyways. I need to do this,' she said to herself as much as to Kiril. 'If I don't, I will never be rid of him.'

'If you are sure, I trust you.'

Marisha wrinkled her nose. She was not sure she deserved Kiril's trust. She asked, 'Where do you think Serafima is?'

'In the courtyard. The plague-bringer surely captured your friends. Once he brings them to her, he will be free to return to your cell. And once that happens . . .'

'As Baba Zima would say: the stew is spilled,' Marisha finished. 'Fine. We must go as quickly as possible. The only element we have is surprise. That and—' she fished inside her pocket '—my shadow potion.' She was glad her paranoia at being discovered spying on Olena had made her keep it with her at all times. 'Don't worry, I didn't make it; Baba Zima gave it to me. So, it actually works.'

'I remember,' Kiril said, smiling faintly. Marisha forgot she had already told him everything. He grabbed her hand and led her down hallway after hallway, cutting corners so quickly she stumbled into more than one wall. She focused on the warm grip of his hand in hers, the smooth shine of the blue and yellow feathers on the back of his neck, the sure sound of his footfalls.

Kiril paused before a door. He mouthed, 'In there.' They retraced their steps around the corner. 'I will do my utmost to get the other souls and bring them here as quickly as possible. And I hope that, once this is done, we'll see each other again. Zal sumerek or not.' A note in his voice gave Marisha pause. She was very aware they still held hands.

'I'd rather it not be in the zal sumerek.'

Kiril's smile made the feathers on his cheek bristle. 'Me too.'

Marisha let go of his hand and unstoppered the bottle, then poured a drop on the tip of her finger. She breathed in deeply several times, reaching for peace and resolve, which, strangely enough, were quite easy for her to find this time.

She murmured, 'Hide me, dark shadows, from preying hearts and preying sight. Wrap me, deep shadows, in safe corners and safe night. Shield me, warm shadows, from cold intentions and cold light.'

Not bad, she was getting the hang of these incantations. She placed the drop in the hollow of her neck and watched the inky shadow blossom until it covered her dress and body. The spell worked much faster than her attempts with Golgolin's feather had. She raised her hands. They were practically invisible. She could only see her own shadow against the wall. Olena must have been right about koldunry being bigger and easier in the other world. But Marisha liked to think her skill had improved a little too.

Kiril's mouth opened in surprise. Damn the dark earth, this was her last chance. She leaned forward and kissed him. Feathers tickled her nose, but her mask protected most of her face. He seemed too surprised to respond. After all, he could not have seen the kiss coming in her shadow state, but he leaned in and kissed her back with a ferocity that she had only imagined in her deepest fantasies. He pulled her closer, so her body was flush against his. One arm wrapped below her shoulder, and the other pressed in the small of her back, pinning her against him. He felt wonderfully solid. She touched her fingers to his velvety neck and along the point where it thickened into bristly quills where his hair should have been–except for this one feather-free line that ran down the centre of his skull. She pressed on it, her fingertips sensing that if she could rub at it, right at the edge, she could pry and it would peel off—

He pulled away. 'You can't take off my mask,' he said.

'I know, I was just—' She was not sure what she had meant to do.

'If you had tried, it would kill me.'

Marisha breathed in sharply. Yes, he had said he could not take it off, but she had not felt deep down how serious it was. His arms were still around her, loosely.

Kiril leaned forward and, maybe by lucky accident, brushed her lips with his. She thought she would gladly volunteer to stay in the zal sumerek with him if everyone else could leave. She thought she was very silly.

Time for her to go.

'You must,' he said as though he knew her thoughts. And his circle of arms fell away. She was glad he could not see her face.

Marisha breathed in shakily and said, 'Goodbye, Kiril.'

'Goodbye, Marisha.'

His whisper echoed in her mind as she crossed the final threshold.

FORTY-ONE

he door led outside to an open circular courtyard, fresh air buoying Marisha's spirit after leaving Kiril behind. Her eye was immediately drawn to the enormous diamond tree growing at the centre; its branches spread out and up and its roots tore the elaborate mosaic floor. Half of the courtyard was enclosed by the dacha wall while the other half opened up to the gardens. Marisha slipped into the courtyard, the door closing soundlessly behind her. She pressed her back against the dacha wall. Her vision was partially obscured by columns that stood a few feet away from the wall, lining the courtyard's enormous circular mosaic. Marisha squinted and could parse out trees glittering behind the dark columns on the other side of the courtyard. The moon was unnaturally bright, but the crisscrossing shadows of the tree and columns would provide her with plenty of hiding spots. She began her slow creep forward.

The enormous diamond tree made the courtyard appear smaller than it was. She walked slowly, keeping close to the wall. A murmur up ahead echoed between the dacha and pillars. Marisha followed the curve of the wall until she came upon two figures standing at a pillar, arguing. She recognised their voices.

'Surely I'm hearing wrong.' Anatoli's low voice shook. 'I did not bring you the poker for you to spare her.'

'If you thought you could take the bolshina by stealing the poker without suffering Zima's fate or worse, you would have never brought me either of them. But don't look so down.' Serafima's voice, on the other hand, was light and filmy, as though they talked of goldfish and not her old apprentice. 'Think of this as your chance to prove your superiority. You begged for it all those years ago.'

'But it's pointless now.'

'Oh, no, I think not.'

'Believe me, there are better revenges.' Anatoli sounded very bitter.

'Oh? Such as your failed design to poach her charming apprentice?'

'They were not failed, it was by those designs that I got to Zima in the first place. You could have never got the poker without me.'

'Oh, my dear Anatoli, don't think for a second you had any control over what has happened. You performed your end of our bargain admirably, and I'm impressed you had the presence of mind to jump into that open threshold. But you would have failed had I not given you permission to command the Hands.'

'I almost didn't need it.'

'Yes. The violin should have made an excellent link to subdue Zima. I also enjoyed the delicious detail of getting her son to craft it for you. But it didn't work. I'm sensing a pattern.'

Anatoli growled, 'It should have worked! I had no reason to believe he was not her son by blood.' He made a slashing motion with his hand. 'No matter. In the end, *I'm* the one who found *you*. I came to you.'

'You did. Accidentally, but it can't be overlooked. Which

is why I'm giving you the opportunity to best Zima. And don't worry, you'll get your due. If you defeat her, she'll be broken. And if you don't, *I* will break her.'

Marisha looked away from the arguing pair and saw two figures standing against the trunk of the diamond tree in the centre of the courtyard. She crept through two columns, away from the relative safety of the dacha's outer walls. The courtyard was a bit smaller than the Severny square next to the sanitorium. The tree was in the middle, perhaps forty paces away. But it felt like a terrible distance with no cover in between the tree and the columns that lined the edge of the courtyard. Luckily, the moon was at an angle that cast the tree's shadow almost to the edge of the columns where Marisha stood. If she could make it to the tree's shadow, she should be safe. Marisha spared one more glance at the arguing pair and crept out. She paused for a moment, standing in the crisp shadow of the tree's leaves and branches on the ground and feeling very exposed. But Serafima and Anatoli did not turn to her. She stepped forward carefully and needed to remind herself to breathe as she followed the shadow of one of the main tree branches back to the trunk.

Olena and Valdim were bound to the trunk of the tree with diamond vines. Marisha did not see Baba Zima. She had to be careful of where she stepped; the tree's roots sprawled out and tore the blue and white mosaic. One step, and another, and she was finally close enough to reach out and touch Olena. Marisha thought something looked strange about them and realised they were no longer wearing their masks. Marisha glanced back. Serafima and Anatoli strolled to the tree.

She whispered in Olena's ear, 'It's me.'

Olena jerked her neck but did not make a sound beyond a muffled squeak.

Marisha said, 'Where's the poker? Does she have it on her or did she leave it somewhere?'

'I don't know. Are you all right?'

'I'm fine, I'm wearing the shadow potion.'

'What? When did you brew a shadow potion?'

'I didn't, Baba Zima gave it to me.'

'When—'

'It doesn't matter.' Now was not the time for more confessions. 'She's going to make Baba Zima and Anatoli fight.' Marisha pulled on the vines but they wouldn't budge. 'I can't loosen these vines.'

'Of course not, they're diamond, you nitwit.'

'Shh. We need to get the poker fast, or–steal the feather.'

'And you know where it is?'

'On her belt.'

Olena snorted. 'Well, that's convenient.'

'Do you have a better idea?'

'I'll find out where the poker is. And delay the duel as much as possible.'

Serafima and Anatoli were too close for Marisha to answer. Olena flitted her eyes back to the approaching pair with ferocious intensity.

They looked like they would pass her by. Olena shot out, 'What's the test?'

Serafima ignored her and gestured for Anatoli to stand by. She flicked her wrist and vines twisted from a bundle on the ground and Baba Zima was thrust out, trussed like a chicken. Marisha's eyes widened: the vines responded to Serafima like the Hands did to Baba Zima. What else could Serafima control in this world? Marisha's dread mounted as she reminded herself that not only was koldunry easier here, but Serafima had had a long time in this world to practise.

'There you are,' Serafima said, clapping her hands together. 'And now.' She motioned Anatoli to step forward. He did, his mouth twisted in an ugly expression, fists balled at his thighs.

'I said, what's the test?' Olena repeated loudly.

But again, Serafima ignored her. Marisha could tell by the set of Olena's mouth that she found it infuriating.

Marisha hoped the poker was hidden somewhere nearby. Though Marisha knew where the beaked man's feather was, the prospect of stealing something off Serafima's waist was terrifying.

Marisha tried scanning the courtyard but the diamond tree sprawled both outwards and upwards. Of course it did, it was a cherry tree, Marisha realised. She lay a hand on the diamond trunk. It was hard and dark, but the light slanted off the bark's rough planes as though the diamond encased a living tree in a shell.

'If there's a competition for the bolshina, I want to join.' Olena shouted.

It seemed Olena had finally hit upon something that would engage Serafima. The masked koldunya raised an eyebrow. 'Is that some opportunism I hear?'

'No one gets anywhere without ambition.'

'Or ruthlessness,' Serafima commented. 'It's admirable in a koldunya, but no. This competition is not for you. But maybe upon the conclusion, we can come to some sort of agreement.' Serafima grinned wolfishly at Olena. 'I understand that you wish to help your mistress. It's sweet that you're still loyal to her, after all the lies she's been feeding you.'

'What lies?'

'What do you think, Zima?' Serafima mock-addressed her

old apprentice, who was bound by vines ten paces away from Anatoli. 'Shall we tell her?'

'I don't know what you're talking about,' Baba Zima answered, her tone scathing.

'No? I suppose you've told so many falsehoods that you are unsure to which I am referring. But what I want to discuss in particular is the reason why you decided to hire this fiery young lady as your apprentice so many years ago.' Baba Zima pursed her lips. Serafima turned to Olena. 'Any ideas?'

'She recognised my talent,' Olena said staunchly.

Serafima let out a booming laugh, too large to come from such a small woman. 'Of course you're talented. I know it, Anatoli does too. What about you,' she turned to Valdim who was bound and gagged by the diamond vines, 'you've recognised this woman's talents. It's one of the roots of your attraction. But I digress. We were discussing why Zima hired dear Olena all those years ago. Back then your talent could have only been unknowable.'

Olena swallowed. 'No. I proved it.'

'Oh? How so.'

'I . . . caused a tree to fall.'

'Ah, I see. Unfortunately, that's not enough to explain it. I'm sure Zima had already come across hundreds of suitable young girls, oh yes, she would only take girls: unfair I know, but,' Serafima nodded at Anatoli, 'I'm afraid you soured her to the charms of male apprentices. But she did not consider any of them. Not seriously, anyways. And why is that? I imagine that my dear apprentice had made the decision not to train anyone at all, that is, until she met the lovely Olena. Now, we have determined it wasn't Olena's incredible raw talent that attracted her, nor pity for her precarious familial situation. You did have a precarious familial situation, didn't you, dear?'

Olena's jaw was clenched so tightly Marisha could see the muscles in her neck.

Serafima smiled. 'Of course you did.'

'Enough horseshit, Serafima!' Baba Zima cried out in a guttural voice. Her face was crimson.

Serafima turned to her and raised her hands. The diamond vines swayed and wrapped themselves around Baba Zima's mouth, gagging her. 'If you address me with disrespect, my apprentice, you lose the privilege of speaking.'

Marisha wanted to tell Olena it was not worth it, but she did not move. She knew she ought to be looking for the poker, but she hadn't crept far from the trunk. Her gaze was latched on Serafima.

Serafima turned back to Olena. 'My former apprentice did not act from pity. Olena, care to guess what could have moved her? No? Then let's get started.'

'She knew I'd be grateful,' Olena said through gritted teeth. Her cheeks burned so that the left and right sides of her face almost matched.

'Oh, you mean because you're a disfigured cripple? No.'

Marisha breathed in so loudly she worried Serafima had heard it. Olena's expression did not move save the corner of her mouth, which twitched.

Serafima smiled and said, 'Quite simply dear, Zima picked you because she thought you lacked the necessary strength of body to steal the bolshina from her. If I remember correctly, Zima needed both her hands to wrest it away from me that night. Isn't that so?'

Serafima turned to Baba Zima who had gone white and sagged. The diamond vines gagging her loosened and fell to her feet. She breathed heavily, her eyes wide. She said nothing.

Olena's eyes bulged. 'Matrionka, is it true? Is that really why you took me in?'

Baba Zima shook her head, her gaze far away.

'Look at me!' Olena shouted, the cry ripped from her throat.

Baba Zima's head jerked. 'My dear girl, I took you because you were my heart's own child. Yes, maybe once or twice, I thought–but that's not why. There was something inside you, something I recognised. You know it to be true. Don't let her poison you–us.'

Olena took deep breaths, her body heaving with each one.

'I'm sorry, dear,' Serafima said, and Marisha was surprised to hear a trace of actual sadness in her voice. 'The truth is, Zima took you in because she thought you would never pose a threat to her. And you deserve better.'

Silence hung heavy for a moment and in that silence, Marisha knew Olena could not delay the duel any longer. She watched, unseen, a few paces away from the tree as Serafima uncorked a bottle and poured a drop onto the ground. The vines restraining Baba Zima, Olena and Valdim loosened and fell as though withered.

'Serafima,' Baba Zima called out, her voice harsh, 'I renounce you. You can make me fight Anatoli, but I am yours no longer. I admired you, I feared you, I loved you–I wanted to be you. And what does that say about me?' She shook her head slightly and looked down before riveting her gaze back on her former mistress. 'You are nothing but your twisting vines. If lies were water, your mouth would have filled an ocean.'

Serafima tilted her chin. 'You've built your house on an ocean of lies, Zima. But now, its coming apart.'

Anatoli stepped forward a pace. Baba Zima tottered and matched it. Serafima held her hands up, stopping them.

Baba Zima hissed, 'We will see.'

FORTY-TWO

natoli broke off one of his collar's black spikes and threw it at Baba Zima. It transformed into a flaming spear, hurtling towards her throat. But with a quick flash of her wrist, Baba Zima tore the tortoiseshell comb out of her hair and threw it. It landed a few feet before her and a tight stand of trees sprang up and blocked the spear. Marisha stood, transfixed. Anatoli shredded a long skein of silk from his vest which became a river. Baba Zima kicked off her shoe and clambered into it, floating on a boat-sized clog.

Marisha scrambled up the first branch of the diamond cherry tree to get out of the river's way. Baba Zima tore a button off her sleeve which grew into a large flat boulder. It landed on the source of the river, blocking it off. When she stepped out of the boat-like shoe, it shrank back down to its normal size. Before Anatoli could react, she threw another button that grew into a boulder and almost flattened him. And another. Marisha craned her neck to watch, mouth open.

'Imbecile,' Serafima said, and rolled up her sleeves. Sounds of shouting came from the edge of the courtyard and Serafima looked towards the dacha. Marisha followed her gaze and saw the figures pouring through the door. Kiril must have been successful at freeing the dancers from the zal sumerek! Hope surged through her, but then Serafima drew a circle into the air with her finger and the mazurka started up again as loud as though a troupe of musicians played in the garden beyond the courtyard columns. The outpouring of people stopped and they stood frozen behind the columns as though they had encountered a glass wall that blocked them from stepping into the courtyard. Marisha's shoulders sagged and she leaned her head against the tree trunk. The dancers would not be able to help. At least Kiril would be safely out of the way.

Serafima positioned herself next to Anatoli, only a few paces from the tree trunk, who still dodged Baba Zima's buttons-turned-boulders. She pointed at Baba Zima.

Marisha tugged at a knot of diamond cherries overhead and threw a handful at Serafima, but her aim was poor, and the diamonds regrettably stayed diamond and cherry-sized. Olena, who had been watching the scene limply, screamed. Valdim ran and collided into Serafima, throwing her off. They clutched the ground as a rope of flame skimmed the air where their heads had been. Valdim rolled away in the cover of the flames.

Marisha jumped down from the branch and ran to Olena. 'Looking for the poker will take too long. The feather–we have to get it.'

Olena shook her head, her face contorted. She glanced at Baba Zima, 'I can't.' And squared off her stance against Anatoli.

Anatoli threw his other bootlace which transformed into a twin of the flaming snake. Baba Zima fended it off with her shawl. It turned into a net of watery seaweed, but her throw barely caught the snake. She bent over to catch her breath.

Marisha steeled herself. She was the one still hidden by the shadow potion. 'I'll get it.' And she left, but not before catching Olena's look of disbelief.

Anatoli shouted something and threw a handful of plaster shards. A storm of birds erupted from the plaster and flew straight at Baba Zima. She grabbed a handful of earth from between the diamond tree roots and blew. It became a swarm of bees and collided with the birds.

But the birds bore down and Baba Zima sagged against one of the boulders. Serafima looked upon her struggling apprentice with a righteous glint in her eyes. Her smile became impossibly wide.

A single violin note sliced through the air like a blade. The courtyard's occupants froze as though drawing a collective breath. The single note ended and cascaded into a lively and unpredictable tune that drowned the infernal mazurka. A musician in a brown and blue kaftan stamped his foot and played the violin as if the very devil had possessed him. Valdim. The music trilled in Marisha's bones and the crushing hopelessness of the situation lifted for a moment. Marisha walked a straight line towards Serafima.

The dancers which had been contained to the courtyard's edge by Serafima's conjured mazurka broke through the line of columns at the edge of the dacha and poured into the courtyard. They looked around, jerking their limbs like puppets with long strings. Some of them shouted angrily and began to converge onto Anatoli. Some of them even advanced upon Serafima. Marisha dodged the dancers, keeping unconscious time with Valdim's tune. She was close enough to see Serafima flinch. For the first time, she looked frightened. The black feather on Serafima's belt swung rather than fluttered. Marisha reached her hand out. Her fingers trembled.

'Enough,' Serafima yelled and she threw something up in the air. The dancers shifted back as though repelled. The poker, she'd had it all along. The poker flew like a loosed arrow and collided with the diamond tree, shaking it so hard that leaves fell. Marisha squinted. A few seconds later, the fallen diamond leaves swarmed and hurtled straight at Baba Zima, their sharp edges like knives. Baba Zima pulled at her dress, but she had no more buttons left.

'No!' Olena cried and threw something at Baba Zima, then bent over double, clutching her side as though she had a stitch. It was a button, obvious as it retained its shape though it grew to an enormous size. It hurtled through the air, stopping between Baba Zima and the deadly leaves like a shield. The leaves peppered themselves into the giant button.

At that moment, Marisha darted her hand as quick as she could to Serafima's waist. Her fingertips grabbed the steel feather, and with that touch came a jumble of images that tripped into her mind one after the other.

Her mind seemed split: in one half, she was aware she had been touching the feather for only an instant, but in the other, the instant stretched for seconds and minutes as images whirred through her mind in a steady stream, like falling grains of sand. The part of her mind aware of her grip on the feather was surprised, panicked even, but the part of her mind watching the images was calm.

An image stopped and sharpened. Marisha fell into it. She stood in a room with a large window overlooking a vast frozen lake. Right before her, a small basin bubbled black water. Marisha bent forward and until her nose almost touched it. A basin of black water that absorbed all light. Marisha dreamily touched the water with one finger, and her dress's colour and the sensation in her hand drained out of her. She stumbled back, realising with a panic that she could no longer feel her legs. Suddenly, an invisible force grabbed the fabric of her dress at her collarbone and yanked her. She flew, insubstantial and ghostly, down a corridor. She flew past open doors, the invisible Hand pulling her forward. It pulled her past so many doors and corridors that they became a dizzying blur and the part of her mind that was conscious of being in the other world almost dropped the feather. Marisha finally thought that she recognised doors and familiar paisley curtains, and she realised that they were on the first floor of Baba Zima's chicken-legged house.

Almost as soon as she made that realisation, the invisible Hand pulling her along took a hard right through a corridor and slowed. Marisha should have been thrown to the ground, but instead she floated, still insubstantial from having touched the black water. She was in front of a huge frame of solid oak. The door flung open and Marisha was pulled through.

A woman had opened the door, Baba Zima stood beside her. But Baba Zima was younger, her hair raven black instead of streaked with grey, her shawl a muted brown. But more than anything else, her youth was marked by the way that uncertainty rimmed her eyes and how she looked slighter and stooped without her mantle of power. Marisha did not recognise the other woman. She had bushy brown hair and reached a hand to the bundle clutched in Baba Zima's arms. A chubby hand reached out and clasped her finger. The bundle began to cry, a thin mewling sound.

Baba Zima's voice had not changed from her younger days. It crackled with anger and hurt. 'But what am I supposed to do with him? You can't waltz in here and say that you're too good to stay, but this baby is not. You can't simply ask me to raise your child for you.'

'And yet, that's what I'm doing.' The woman's gentle resolve ran in rivulets around the stone of Baba Zima's confused rejection. The koldunya looked down at the baby, frustration and despair building in her frown. 'Zima, I'm not well. I want to do what's best for him,' the woman's voice broke, 'And that's not staying with me.'

'If it's rubles you need, I can give you—'

'No. It's not. I need to start over. And I can't do that with him.'

'You knew I wouldn't say no. You knew that I'd feel guilty for what happened to you, for not leaving with you when you asked. Well . . . I'm not sorry!' Zima looked at the other woman fiercely. 'I'm not sorry for being the house's mistress now. It could be your home too if you weren't so stubbornly intent on punishing me.'

'Zima,' her voice was tired, 'this house can be my home no longer. That ended the day I walked out. But this little one–he could belong here. Please.' At that, her demeanour crumpled a little.

Baba Zima looked down at the bundle, her expression softening. 'So, this is it then. You came to drop off this child, and then off you go. And I suppose you'll not return?'

'Not now.' But the look in her eyes said, *not ever.*

'Why do you wish to be alone when we could be together?' Tears ran down Baba Zima's cheeks.

'I'm sorry Zima. I wish things were different. You know, I tried to return using Golgolin's feather, but I wasn't able to open the door. Not until I intended to leave Valdim with you.'

'Is that his name then?' Zima looked down at the sleeping bundle.

'Yes,' A smile broke on the woman's face. She had to be Olga. 'This is hard for me too, Zima. So very, very hard. But I know it's the right thing to do.'

'What do you want to me to tell him? About this? About

you?' The look on Baba Zima's face was heartbreaking.

Olga shook her head. 'You will be his mother. This house will be his home.' She spoke the words like they were a covenant.

Marisha had one last glimpse of the tears shining on Baba Zima's face before the Hand yanked her forward. She was still as insubstantial as a dust mote and the corridor swirled around her. Then, the invisible Hand let her go, as though it had only now brought her to its intended destination. Once her dizziness had subsided, she recognised that she was floating in Baba Zima's receiving room. Given what she had just seen, she expected to see Baba Zima, perhaps alone with baby Valdim, except Baba Zima did not sit in the taloned chair. Though the image was washed of colour, Marisha recognised Baba Serafima. She was unmasked, her gaze relaxed and focused on the person sitting before her. She held her chin in her hand, her white-streaked dark blonde hair combed back into a simple chignon, her clothes ordinary and drab compared with the finery of the midnight-blue dress embroidered in silver.

Marisha's father sat opposite her.

At seeing her father, all thought of Baba Zima, Olga, and Valdim fled her mind. She remembered him always perfectly groomed, his shirt white and ironed, his fingernails clean. He often said half of respectability was in appearances. But here he had let his maxim fall by the wayside. His long whiskers were uncombed, his jacket was stained and his right trouser leg was stuffed into his sock.

'Baba Serafima,' Marisha's father said, bowing his head, 'I couldn't get what you asked, but I brought something as valuable, I swear. Now, please. Help me.'

'Let's see,' Serafima said. Marisha's father drew out a long black feather from inside his coat. Marisha started, part of her mind aware she touched that very feather, but the other part seeing it in her father's hand. 'Wait,' he said. 'When I touched it—' he revealed the inside of his wrist with the whorled scar on it.

The part of Marisha's mind that was aware she was touching the feather knew that she now had a scar on the inside of her wrist mirroring her father's.

Serafima picked a handkerchief from off her desk and used it to take the feather from him and scrutinised it, frowning slightly. 'I can't imagine what manner of creature this belongs to.'

Marisha's father said nothing, but Marisha saw how he gripped his cap between his knees with both hands as though it were an anchor. Serafima said, 'While I'm a little . . . disappointed . . . It seems quite unique. And feathers can command great influence.' She glanced pointedly at his wrist and wrapped the handkerchief more securely around the feather before pocketing it. 'It is adequate payment.' At her words, Marisha's father's hands relaxed.

Serafima reached into her pocket for a vial of clear liquid. She set it on the table.

Marisha's father picked it up and studied it. 'This will keep my son safe?'

'Yes. You will fall asleep instead, I can assure you. And the shield spell will last beyond this coming cycle. Your son will be safe from the plague for all his life.'

He took a deep breath: half relief, half resignation.

Serafima drummed a finger on the table and stared at Marisha's father until he fidgeted. She said, 'Your wife came to see me while you were gone. Did you know she was pregnant?'

'Yes. At least, I suspected.' He smiled. A jolt ran through the part of Marisha's mind that was not focused on keeping contact with the feather. Her mother must have been pregnant with her.

'Then you'll know why she came to see me.' Serafima pushed a second vial towards him.

'What's this?'

'Don't you understand? In exchange for his aid, Pan Volya demanded the soul of your child for the plague. As I've told you, I cannot break the terms of your bargain, but with this shield spell, the plague will claim your soul instead of your son's. But your unborn child will still be at risk.'

'And so . . . my Tanya. She'll have to pay as well.' He raised a finger to his face and ruffled and smoothed one eyebrow, back and forth. 'I can't shield them both?'

'No. That's not how it works.' Marisha was surprised to see pity in Serafima's gaze.

Her father was silent in stunned disbelief, then he banged his hand flat against the table. 'Pan Volya! He did this.'

The pity in Serafima's expression evaporated. 'You agreed to his bargain. And he kept his end. You got what you wanted.'

'I was young and in love. I only thought of marrying Tanya, I could not think of the future–and I thought if I were rich and with her, it would be worth the price no matter what he asked for someday. I did not know what I agreed to.'

'All the more fool you were.'

But before he could answer, Marisha was thrown back from Serafima and the image left her mind.

Her hand was empty.

'You!' Serafima roared. Serafima could see her. The shadow potion must have worn off. Marisha scrambled back. 'How did you do that?' Serafima's mouth was slightly open with confusion. 'Who are you, really?'

'My father–he's the one who gave you the beaked man's feather?' Marisha asked.

Serafima's mouth opened even further. '*That* was your father?'

She was silent for a moment then her head tipped back. She laughed and laughed.

'My dear girl, I understand now why the plague-bringer cares so much.' Serafima put a hand on her chest and caught her breath. She said, 'Your father stole his feather from that koldun, Pan Volya, as payment for my services. A shield spell for the plague is no small thing. I didn't have time to investigate the nature of the feather, Zima stole what was mine only a few weeks later.' She shook her head. 'Your father handed me the one thing I could have used to truly make a difference to his fate, but neither of us knew it. When the spirits laugh at us, they laugh well.'

'But, I don't understand.' Marisha said. 'My father needed a shield spell to protect Dima?'

'Your father made a bargain with that koldun, Pan Volya, for a change of luck that allowed him to marry a girl well above his social station. And he could not get out of his end of the bargain–his child's soul for the plague–no matter how hard he tried. I helped him shoulder some of the responsibility. Unfortunately, I couldn't prevent it spilling over onto his wife.' Serafima's mouth tightened for a moment and her nostrils flared. Then she shrugged. 'It was her choice to marry him.'

Marisha gasped. 'But why would Pan Volya even want to claim Dima for the beaked man?'

'I can only think that Pan Volya used the feather as I did, to leech power from the plague-bringer. He must have thought a child's soul willingly given would yield even more.' She tilted her head. 'It's extraordinary. I found the plague-bringer to be most particular about his victims, but Pan Volya must have convinced him to go after your brother, somehow. I wonder how Pan Volya did it. Did the shield spells work?'

'Yes,' Marisha said softly. 'Both my parents are deep sleepers.'

Serafima's lips curved in a self-satisfied smile. 'Both your parents? So, I was right. Pan Volya did not mark your brother specifically, but only a child born of your father. And I helped your mother protect you, but here you are in the place she tried to keep you from.'

A loud cawing reverberated around the courtyard. Marisha's heart froze in fear. Serafima grinned. 'He seems angry about something.' Serafima wrapped her hand around the black feather at her belt. She did not do anything to stop Marisha from scrambling away.

FORTY-THREE

The claws of Serafima's accusation had gripped Olena's soul. Olena had wished Baba Zima had never come to her village, that someone else had tried to fix Fedya's spine, that she herself had been left to her parents' cold mercy as should have been her fate.

Olena wished Baba Zima would get what she deserved.

Then Serafima had hit the tree with the poker and the cloud of diamond leaves swarmed like bees and headed straight for Baba Zima's heart.

Olena had cried out and ripped a button from her sleeve and threw it. She had not been sure of what she did, all she felt was an intense hope and exhaustion overcome her, like she had sprinted through a snowdrift. The button did not become a boulder, but it did grow to enormous size and thickness and hurtled through the air, stopping between Baba Zima and the deadly leaves like a shield. The leaves peppered themselves into the enormous button, but it held them back. Elation ballooned inside her.

But Baba Zima collapsed, a dark stain growing on her purple dress.

Olena did not understand, she had stopped the attack.

But she could see the diamond leaf glittering on Baba Zima's breast. And with a click like a closing door, she understood.

The button's thread holes.

Olena staggered back, then ran towards the dacha's wall where Baba Zima lay near the columns at the edge of the courtyard, limbs splayed out. She could not be dead! Olena had not had the chance to tell her how angry she was with her.

Baba Zima had promised Olena would find her hard but fair. She had promised Olena would be respected, not coddled. She had promised Olena would always have a home. All lies. Olena's whole foundation, everything she was, everything she had believed, reduced to dust.

She felt like she was eleven again at the night of the festival: anger fading like Fedya's scream into a hangover of regret and fear. Misha was already gone, he had spat and ran when Fedya had revealed it was her under the veil. Olena had stood over the crumpled form of her brother next to the tree, confused that she could have pushed him so far. Scared for him, horrified with herself.

Silence, as Baba Zima had been silent when Serafima accused her of choosing Olena because of her bodily difference. Silent, as she herself had been all those years ago when she realised who she had destroyed.

But worse, so much worse. Or really just the same. That terrible, terrible realisation that she was alone and had failed. She had tried to save Baba Zima, but it had not made a difference, it only made her feel so . . . more. More outraged, more desperate, more cheated. And all the more so because Baba Zima was so *alive* in her mind, the snap and rolling timbre of her voice so perfectly ingrained that if Olena closed her eyes, she could be in her workroom and her mistress looking over her shoulder to inspect a concoction, telling her to quit trying to make the bitter melon brew taste better.

Chunks of columns littered the floor, coated with diamond dust. It was silent–Valdim had stopped playing. Some dancers jerkily ran for the shadows beyond the columns, while others were frozen like statues throughout the courtyard. Fear leapt into Olena's chest and squeezed her heart in two, finally smashing a dam that she had spent so long shoring up. Valdim, who saw things–*her*–so clearly, who was her counterpart, whose kindness she had overlooked, whose good opinion she somehow cared so much about. Everything had changed since he had come back to the house–suddenly it seemed clear to her why she kept hearing drifts of violin melodies late at night even though his workroom was no longer directly above hers.

She thought of her surprise and confusion when Valdim had taken her hand and pulled her into the mass of dancers. Her confusion was at the gesture, but also at her reaction–something in her stomach flipped and her chest felt tight, but not from revulsion. A deluge of thoughts had drowned her awareness–it was because he had a mask on, it was because they were in an unusual and trying situation, it was because she was nervous about dancing for the first time in twelve years–but she couldn't deny her own giddiness, the way she could feel his hand at her waist like a brand, how for a moment the urgency and fear for Baba Zima muted in the face of whatever *this* was.

She had been so wilfully blind. She could not lose him, too.

Cawing filled the air, startling Olena. She looked up, and a dark shape whistled over the columns and flew to the diamond tree. Was that—no! Someone in skirts scrambled up the branches. It was one of the dancers; it couldn't be Marisha. Marisha wore the shadow potion. Olena stood and started running toward the tree, but Serafima and Anatoli were suddenly in front of her, blocking her path.

'No,' Serafima said, and vines rose from the cracks in the floor and snaked around Olena's ankles. 'You stay here now.' Olena tugged but they would not budge. A cloud passed over the moon, extinguishing her view of the diamond tree and its occupants.

Serafima walked over to Baba Zima's body and stood still.

'So,' Serafima said, her voice soft but clear. 'It's over, my dear apprentice. And the bolshina is finally mine again.'

She ran her fingers down the length of the poker. Half of her mask was ripped off, revealing a hazel eye of surprising warmth, framed by long, dark blonde lashes. 'Something's wrong,' Serafima said. 'It's not all . . . pure.'

Serafima pointed at Anatoli with the poker. 'Is this your fault?' she shouted at him.

'I don't know what you're talking about,' he rasped.

'Do not deny it, you've held onto this, haven't you.'

'I wouldn't deny it,' Anatoli said, his voice more even. 'I did hold it. It's how I brought Zima here to you. As I said I would.'

'And I am very pleased you did Anatoli, very pleased.'

Anatoli bowed, but Olena could tell that he watched Serafima circle him like a rat might watch a circling cat.

'You promised, Serafima,' Anatoli said, his voice shaking.

'Ah yes. But what did I promise? I promised to share my revenge, I promised to share my triumph, I never promised to share my power. What makes *you* more worthy than Zima? You were just as conniving, as untrustworthy.'

'You made us so.'

Someone next to her breathed in sharply. Valdim stood mouth agape, eyes glued to his mother's prostrate form. Olena threw her arms around him. He was safe. He struggled limply but she held him. Tears wet her cheek. Olena clung to Valdim so hard she thought she would squeeze him in two.

A yell made Olena look up. Anatoli was splayed on the ground. He held his right arm up in the air. His hand was gone. His arm was stone until his elbow and his other hand turned granite. Serafima raised the poker high. Olena caught a glimpse of Anatoli's terrified eyes before she buried her face in Valdim's shoulder. It did not muffle the smash and Anatoli's wrenching wail of pain.

'Now, my dear apprentice, we're through. I have taken my due.' Serafima left Anatoli blubbering on the floor and turned to stroke the poker. But she frowned again. She cracked it against the mosaic. The tiles split, but it did not satisfy her.

'No,' she said, softly, and homed in on Olena and Valdim. 'It's still not pure,' Serafima said, 'someone else has laid claim to my bolshina.'

'No,' Olena said, 'I didn't, I never did.' She looked to Valdim, hoping he would believe her, he had to. 'I never did. I wouldn't. I respect her too much to even try, even out of curiosity. I wouldn't–I didn't.'

Olena still looked at Valdim, it was more important to convince him than Serafima; she needed him to know that for all she had done, she had never wanted to steal the bolshina from his mother.

He smiled slightly and smoothed her hair away from her forehead. 'I know you didn't,' he said softly, 'but I did.'

MARISHA PANICKED AT the beaked man's cawing. She started climbing the diamond tree before she even realised what she was doing.

Luckily, the diamond cherry tree was as knobby as its living counterpart, which made climbing easy. But the edges of the bark were razor-sharp. Her hand slipped and the bark cut her palm as easily as a letter opener.

Her limbs moved almost without her consent. She knew she should focus on escape, on the beaked man chasing her, but her mind froze on the feather's vision. Baba Zima and Olga. Valdim's father was Anatoli. Tears had streamed down Baba Zima's cheeks as she watched Olga in the doorway. Baba Zima had wanted Olga to stay. Marisha thought that she had never seen Baba Zima so unguarded, so human before. Was that the moment that everything had changed for her?

Marisha's mind turned towards what the feather had shown next, Baba Serafima and her father. Her father and his clever fingers, he had stolen it. He had pulled coins from between Marisha's toes and somehow, he had stolen the feather from Pan Volya. She squeezed her eyelids. Papa's voice rang in her mind, *Don't bargain with kolduni. You never know what you might be agreeing to.* His bargain with Pan Volya had taught him his hard-won advice—but how could he have agreed to something like that?

She thought of her parents' story, how it had always seemed like a fairy tale to her: her father catching her mother's eye when he was no more than a tailor's apprentice, and the spate of luck that made her father rich and her mother's father give him notice. But it had all been due to his bargain with Pan Volya. She struggled between pity and anger at her father's rash promise to the koldun.

And Pan Volya had followed her family. He had come when Papa had become a deep sleeper during the last plague year, ten years ago. But Mama and Papa falling asleep hadn't been enough, he had wanted Dima, perhaps because Dima who'd been promised to him as a plague victim. And since Pan Volya had lost the feather that allowed him some measure of control over the plague-bringer, he actually needed a shield for this current plague year. Perhaps seeking out Dima had allowed him to kill two birds with one stone: both obtaining a willing victim to serve as his shield for the plague, and obtaining what Papa owed him.

A crash nearly shook her from the branch. She twisted back. A large, dark shape settled down clumsily on one of the lower branches, reminding her of an overgrown vulture. Marisha's heart leapt in her throat and she scrambled onto another branch.

Marisha paid no more attention to how the branches sliced her hands with their diamond sharp edges. She cursed their un-wooden strength. What had possessed her to run from a flying monster by climbing a diamond tree? Even the skinny twigs would support his weight without snapping. The branches thinned and she rapidly ran out of purchase to climb. A vice clamped on her foot and tugged. She could not help it, she screamed, high-pitched and ear-splitting. Marisha instinctively held onto a handful of leaves, ignoring the edges biting into her fingers, but the beaked man was too strong. He pulled her down to a fork in the branches and slammed her against the trunk, knocking the breath out of her.

'Wait,' she choked out.

The beaked man did not answer, but his talon moved to Marisha's throat. He squeezed. Marisha clawed at it.

Something thudded, knocking into the beaked man and sending vibrations through the tree. His talon sprang open and the crushing weight lifted off Marisha's chest. She coughed, gasping air into her lungs. Someone had jumped into the tree and had pulled the beaked man off of her. Arms were wound around the the monster's neck, and he arched his back, spreading the tattered remains of his wings as he tried to throw off his assailant, but he overcorrected and threw his arms out. For a moment he teetered at an angle, and they both fell, a flash of black and mustard green cracking through the diamond branches.

Marisha scrambled to look down. Through the hole in the foliage that the falling pair had made, she could see the two stretched clearly on the ground, leaves littered around them like stars. The black one struggled to his feet while the yellow-and-green one jerked his knees feebly. His brown hair fell over his face, a bit too long. She recognised him instantly.

'No!' she cried out.

But the beaked man did not listen. He crawled over and raised his head, and brought it down with a dull, wet crack.

Dima jerked, impaled.

FORTY-FOUR

aldim had tried to take the bolshina from Baba Zima. Olena couldn't believe it. She squeaked out, 'You did what? Why?'

'Curious. Jealous. It was some time ago. I wanted to see . . . I thought I could make her love me.'

'But she does love you,' Olena said, indignant.

His shoulders drooped. 'I know she does. But I hoped if somehow I could figure out how it worked, then . . . I wanted her to love me the way she loved you.'

Olena looked away, tears blurring her vision.

'How sweet,' Serafima said. 'Excuse me for interrupting your lovers' spat, but my goodness, Olena, everyone does seem to be confessing to betraying you today. Either you instigate this sort of behaviour, or you have a terrible fortune.'

A shriek rang out from the other side of the courtyard. Marisha! Olena shared a panicked look with Valdim. Another shriek sounded, louder this time–a shriek of pain. The diamond vines around Olena's ankles released and she darted forward towards the tree, but Serafima grabbed her arm, wrenching her back. Olena tried to shake herself out of Serafima's grip, but Serafima pointed the poker at her. Olena stopped struggling. Her breath came in short wheezes and she bit her lip so hard she tasted blood. She looked to the diamond tree and the glittering grove beyond the ring of columns, silently begging the spirits to protect her friend.

'There's nothing you can do for her,' Serafima said, 'her own fate has made it so. But you needn't have that nasty end. I'm assured you are innocent, Olena. Once I get rid of this . . . baggage, you'll be free to start over, as *my* apprentice. Won't that be lovely?'

Olena's breath was rapid and shallow. Her gaze darted wildly around the courtyard, the diamond tree, the grove of golden willows beyond the columns. She hoped with every fibre of her being it had not been Marisha's scream. But she had recognised the sound, the same screams Marisha had made that horrible night at the krug when she would not wake up. She tried to swallow and scrunched her eyes shut, but the tears leaked out anyways.

Valdim stepped in front of Olena. How dare he try to protect her. Her heart was in her throat as she sidestepped him. No, she was alone. The overwhelming weight of loneliness pressed down on her for a moment, then lifted. If she was alone, she had nothing to lose, no one to care for. But in the back of her mind, that voice of inner truth said just because no one cared for her, did not mean she did not care for them.

Olena held her head high. It felt light. Her mask was gone, exposing her. But she remembered her true mask: her masking red mark.

'Behand him,' Serafima said softly.

'What?' Olena stepped away from Valdim.

'Remove his hands.'

'I'm not doing that,' Olena said.

'Remove his hands, or I will. And I'll take his head in the bargain.'

Serafima stepped forward. No, Olena could not lose Valdim

as well, but how could she cut off his hands–she could not do that either. She looked everywhere except for at him and at Serafima's beautiful face that shone with triumph.

'Hurry up, Olena. I need my bolshina pure, and you need to lay claim to your destiny, just as I reclaim my own. I've seen you, Olena–you have the intent that Zima did not. The bolshina needs a successor and I know you've wanted it, you've hungered for it.'

'No.' Olena shook her head vehemently.

'Even after your mistress and your lover have betrayed you? The power is all that's left for you.'

How did Serafima know the words of her own despair?

Olena looked into Serafima's eye and was reminded for a moment of sitting in front of the pool of molten silver, wondering what her life would be like if she had been born beautiful and whole.

'No,' Olena said, and repeated firmly, 'No. I did not want this. I didn't want it this badly.'

Serafima shrugged. 'Fine, your choice.'

And she raised the poker against Valdim. Olena threw herself in front of him but he pushed her away. Serafima whipped the poker down.

Golgolin collided against the poker in a ball of feathers and fur and hit the floor, letting out a feeble squawk. Golgolin! Where had he come from? Disbelief coursed through her as Valdim darted forward to scoop up the guinea pig-fowl. His wings were bent at a terrible angle. Olena felt like she saw him up above, through someone else's eyes.

'That insufferable abomination!' Serafima yelled, stamping her foot. 'It owes loyalty to *me*.'

Olena saw red. Serafima was an abomination. She herself was an abomination. But Golgolin? No. Serafima raised the poker again, but this time Olena was ready. She raised her hand and blocked. It slapped her hand nicely. Pain exploded across her palm. Serafima jerked the poker and Olena, surprised, let go. She held her searing hand against her chest.

'How dare you!' Serafima shrieked.

A cawing filled the air, sounding something between a murder of crows and bear's roar, causing Valdim to clap his hands to his ears and yell. Serafima hesitated and glanced at Valdim. It was enough. Olena gritted her teeth and closed her fist around the poker and pulled.

The pain burned through her, blinding her mind into a pure white scream. It hurt so much she could barely feel it anymore, in fact she could not feel anything. She heard shouting. And somewhere, she saw the smiling faces of her family. Her parents. Fedya. Baba Zima. So, they had forgiven her in the end. She smiled, the pain no match for the happiness blossoming out of her heart. She closed her eyes, the glowing faces of her brother and parents and matrionka dancing in a circle around her, whirling tighter and tighter until she collapsed in their fire.

MARISHA CLIMBED DOWN the trunk. Her heartbeat roared in her ears as she peeked around the tree. The beaked man was on his knees, bent over Dima, beak buried in his corpse. He was feeding. Marisha staggered and threw up. She stayed there, head bent, heaving. She would kill the beaked man for what he did. Kill him.

Marisha ran to the beaked man and shouted, 'Hey!'

He ignored her. She kicked him hard. He gargled and rasped and whipped around. His beak was so large it almost obscured the rest of his face. But his small eyes trained on her. 'That's my brother,' Marisha shouted. 'Stop!'

He opened up his beak and cawed. The sound sent chills up and down Marisha's spine. He fixed her with a beady eye. The anger that beat through her calmed slightly under his gaze as fear rose to replace it. Pan Volya said Ivan the Fool had stolen the roc's eyes and ears and beak, and there they were: his beak sharp and steely and dripping, his eyes colourless pupils without whites–but the feathers sprouting from the beaked man's face reminded her of Kiril, of the way his mask had fused with his head. Something dark stained the beaked man's collar. Dima's blood. Her rage surged above her terror.

'Leave him alone, you monster.' Marisha scooped down and hurled a handful of rubble at him.

He cawed again, the noise sounding more like a bear's roar than a bird call, and charged at her. She ran through the courtyard towards the outer edge of the columns and the grove of golden trees. A crash rattled her feet and Marisha dove for cover behind one of the columns. She heard a howl of pain coming from inside the courtyard, guttural and low. She inched her way around the column, hoping to see what happened on the other side of the courtyard, near the dacha.

She spotted the beaked man only two dozen feet from her. Her heart jumped in her throat. The beaked man paid the far-off shouts no attention. He stepped between the nearby frozen dancers, examining them carefully for what seemed like minutes. He toppled them over, one by one. Marisha breathed in and out slowly; her palms slipped on the stone column. She prayed to the spirits that he would not notice her.

The beaked man stopped at the next dancer. Marisha's stomach dropped. It was Kiril, frozen in a twist, his unseeing eyes facing away from the beaked man. The monster casually looked in her direction, as though he could sense her in her hiding place, and he looked back at Kiril, cocking his head. He leaned his head back, raising his beak to strike.

Marisha screamed and darted forward. The beaked man turned away and left Kiril without touching him, only to charge at her instead.

She ran back for the cover of the columns. She almost made it.

Marisha's wrist was caught in an iron grip that jerked her whole body back. The beaked man shoved her against the column. He raised a shiny talon and slammed it. She screamed as pain exploded through her hand and arm. He had pinned her hand to the stone with his talon, like an insect skewered to a piece of card. She squirmed around the pain, screaming to be let go.

The beaked man cocked his head at her.

'Who are you?' Marisha screamed. 'What do you want with me?'

He raised his head back.

'Stop! You took my parents. You took my brother.' The memory of Dima flat on the ground, a huge hole in his chest, made Marisha choke. 'You owe me the truth.'

She spoke to stall him, but he stopped, as though considering what she said.

'My father,' she repeated and lifted her other wrist to show the whorls raised on her skin from touching the black steel feather that Serafima wore on her belt. The beaked man hissed at the mark. 'He stole your feather from Pan Volya. Is that why you want me so badly? For revenge?'

The beaked man cocked his head, as though she had said something slightly puzzling. She thought she smelled something coppery, salty and astringent like preserved plums, and strangely, roses.

'At least, that's what I—' Marisha felt woozy, she put her free hand on her temple. It was sticky.

He opened his mouth to caw, but instead he gurgled, 'You're the last.'

Marisha opened her mouth, but her words were lost in the roar of her ears. Dots danced before her eyes.

'I'm the last,' she repeated. 'The last . . . of my family?' Marisha closed her eyes and saw the two vials of water Serafima shoved towards her father. One shield spell for him and one for Marisha's mother. But the beaked man still got Dima. Her brother threw away their father's protection when he agreed to be Pan Volya's shield. And now, her mother's sacrifice would be for nothing.

His beak smashed into the stone next to her head, she moved away just in time. He seemed to have got his beak stuck in a crack in the pillar. She twisted away as he scrabbled against it, but still he kept her arm pinned against the pillar.

The beaked man's cawing was muffled and furious, but Marisha thought she could still understand it. It reverberated in her bones. 'You're keeping it for me. Mine! Give it back!'

What could she have that was his? Pan Volya's story of Ivan the Fool. Nightingale the Robber. He sought a lost piece of his spirit and it flitted from person to person. But how could she have it?

'No,' she whispered, 'I don't have anything that belongs to you.'

His growl filled her ears. Her vision swam with coloured dots. This was it, she had nothing left. If only she could think of some spell. But no, she had no incantation, no potion in her pocket. She could do nothing.

A strange sort of calm suffused her, and she could almost see again: the silver light of the moon, the diamond tree, it all pulsed behind the beaked man as though his form was cut and pasted to it. Up close she could see the feathers tufting on his scaly skin. Her mind flashed to the feeling of that line that edged the feathers at the centre of Kiril's skull. She couldn't feel her fingers. Her mask slipped, covering her vision.

Memories jumbled through Marisha's mind: Olena's clammy grip as they jumped into the threshold, white-hot terror upon waking up from her dreams, wonder tingling at her spine when the house lurched to its chicken feet for the first time. The texture of the feathers on Kiril's cheek crushed against her own when they kissed. And the hope of the past hour that she could change her fate by facing it, now completely crumbled. She felt the waste of it all: her parents had sacrificed themselves to turn her fortune, Dima had too, and all for nothing.

She would see clearly. She would not shy away from it anymore. If he wanted to kill her, he would look her in the eye while he did it.

The monster reared his head back and roared.

Marisha reached her undamaged hand to the back of her head to unhook her mask. He noticed what she did and stopped, head cocked to the side, beak almost touching her nose. The moon's silver and cold light glinted off his beak's smooth surface. Her breath hitched. She fumbled with the catch, but after a moment the mask sprang free. She gripped it, the razor-sharp willow leaves bit into her fingers. His eyes glowed like coals.

He seemed transfixed by her face.

Slowly, without even realising the idea until she executed it, Marisha brought her hand, the one holding the mask, out and around and behind his head, as though to bring him closer. As though to push his head forward and press his beak into her skin. He did not move either, his eyes fixed on hers. Something flickered in them behind the cold hunger. Vulnerable. Even hopeful. Something begging her to understand and recognise, as though she were the only one that could.

Holding her breath, slowly, afraid to startle him, she slashed the sharp edge of her golden mask to the back of his head, on that feather-free line that ran down the centre.

The beaked man roared and clasped his talons to the sides of his head, releasing Marisha. She collapsed in a heap and edged away. Try as he might, he could not keep the black feathered mask from falling off his head.

At his caws of pain, the dancers sprang to life. They rushed forward and piled onto the beaked man. She caught a glimpse of the hole where his face ought to have been before he was swallowed by the crush of silk and velvet.

When they got up, he was gone.

FORTY-FIVE

Silence grew in the courtyard, but the figures did not freeze again. Instead, they looked at each other, surprise etched in their postures. Marisha's arm throbbed and bled. With her undamaged hand she picked up a diamond shard off the ground and used it to rip off a length of her skirt to wrap around her punctured arm. She repeated the ripping and wrapping, pulling the cloth tighter. Her arm throbbed less, the blood staunched for now. She lifted her head and her gaze focused on the glittering diamond tree.

Marisha ran through the courtyard, her eyes fixed on the yellow-and-green shape sprawled at the tree's roots. His torso was a bloody mess. She collapsed by Dima's side, grateful for the tears blurring her vision.

Time stopped. Unlike the first time she lost her brother, she felt no tide of rage nor grief. She felt nothing. A curious numbness. Perhaps logic would dictate that losing her brother once should make it easier to lose him a second time. But it didn't. It did nothing of the sort. After a while, she did not know how long, Marisha got up again. Thoughts of Olena and Valdim stabbed her mind, claiming her attention.

'I'll be back,' she whispered to Dima, and ran to the other side of the courtyard.

Marisha found Valdim at the columns near the door where she had entered the courtyard from the dacha. He was huddled on the floor next to the sprawling forms of Baba Zima and Olena. Olena was laid out, head pillowed on a piece of rubble. She held the poker in her hand. Baba Zima had a dark stain on her chest. Bile rose in Marisha's throat.

She crouched down next to Valdim. 'Marisha,' he said, his eyes glazed with confusion. 'You're hurt.'

Marisha nodded. Her hand throbbed horribly. 'Valdim, are they—'

'Olena's still alive,' he said, and his voice caught, 'but barely.' He took a deep breath. 'My mother—' He looked down.

'Baba Zima's dead?' Marisha said. She could not believe it. Baba Zima seemed like one of those women who could never be stopped. Baba Zima who had hired her in the first place, who had given her a chance. Marisha had never really liked her, and she had hated the koldunya's twisted games, but she had brought Marisha into her coterie. Without Baba Zima, Marisha would have never known what it was like to ski from town to town in a chicken-legged house.

Marisha looked at the wreckage before her. Three columns had collapsed and the floor was torn up. Anatoli sat nearby, feet bound, slumped in dejection. His arms looked strangely grey and brittle.

'Serafima?' Marisha asked. 'Where is she?'

'Gone,' Valdim said. 'When Olena took the poker, she disappeared.'

Marisha put a hand on Olena's forehead and exclaimed, 'She's burning up.'

'I know,' Valdim said, and more decisively, 'we need to get her back. Let's use the feather.'

'That would be a mistake,' Anatoli called from where he was bound.

'Shut up,' Valdim called back.

Anatoli motioned Marisha over with his head. Marisha glanced at Valdim. He was busy tucking his kaftan around Olena's form.

Marisha walked over to Anatoli and crouched down so her face was level with his. 'Well?'

Anatoli said, 'Her spirit is burning up. Taking her out of the other world will not make her better, she'll only burn faster. She needs to heal.' Marisha's heart started racing. Not Olena too. Not after Baba Zima–and Dima. She pressed her fist to her sternum. 'The fastest way would be with the waters of life and death. The water of life in particular.'

'The waters of life and death?' Marisha spat out. 'You mean how you tricked your way into the house?' But, Marisha remembered, the waters of life and death came from the other world! Marisha looked around the courtyard, as though to spot a fountain of the water of life in an overlooked corner.

Anatoli let out a small chuckle. 'It's not my fault that you were unable to find it. As my matrionka used to say, the house has hidden depths.' He paused, as though considering his own words. 'No need to strain your neck, there's none nearby. Luckily for you, I've a small vial of the water of life on my person.'

Marisha sat back on her heels. 'You said you didn't have any, it was all a ruse.'

'Of course I didn't show you the real thing.'

'Why are you telling me this?'

Anatoli jerked his chin in Valdim's direction. 'He won't let me live. I need a way out, and you have the guinea pig-fowl's feather.'

'I'm not giving it to you.'

'If you don't, Olena will die.' Anatoli said, his voice even but his gaze dead and far off.

But, if the water of life could bring Olena back from the brink of death, then maybe—

'And my brother?' Marisha asked. 'If the water of life can save Olena's spirit, could it save my brother's? He's one of the trapped sleepers, but the beaked man attacked him.'

Anatoli frowned. 'I don't see why not. The water of death knits the body while the water of life sparks the spirit. If your brother is a sleeper he's only here in spirit, so the water of life can revive him. But, be warned, there are hurts the water of life cannot erase, not without the water of death to repair them.'

'You mean, what the beaked man took from my brother's spirit . . .'

Anatoli nodded. Earlier that evening, Marisha had regretted that the water in the basin had not been the water of death because giving it to Anatoli had allowed him to enter the chicken-legged house. But now, Marisha regretted it even more. She could have used the water of death to heal Dima and the other deep sleepers so they were whole.

Then his brow wrinkled and he said, 'Now, wait, don't ask me about Zima. Only the waters of life and death used together can bring someone back in body and spirit. If you give her the water of life, her spirit will reanimate her body, but she will be unable to ascend to the dark earth.' Anatoli shrugged. 'You may wish you had left her be.'

Marisha bit her lip. At best Baba Zima would be trapped here . . . But the chance to say good-bye, to explain her actions to Olena and Valdim . . . What would Baba Zima have wanted?

Anatoli sighed impatiently. 'Olena doesn't have much time. What do you say?'

Marisha pretended to study his stone sleeve. 'In return for the water of life you want one of Golgolin's feathers.'

'And for you to convince the luthier to make me some hands.'

'What?'

'I want him to fashion me hands like he fashioned your masks. But don't tell him about the feather, that's between us.' Marisha studied Anatoli for an inkling of resemblance between him and Valdim. Did Anatoli have any idea that Valdim was his biological son?

Marisha said, 'I could go through your pockets and take it from you.'

Anatoli smiled grimly. 'I have many effects on my person, some of them are poison, only one is the water of life. Are you willing to take that risk?'

Marisha was not. She talked to Valdim and once she said that Anatoli was willing to save Olena in exchange for willow hands, he stopped arguing. Valdim requisitioned the help of a sleeper whose hands Anatoli said were of similar shape to his. He took the sleeper to the grove outside the courtyard. Marisha called for him to hurry.

She sat back down next to Olena. She should go back to Dima's body . . . but she kept recalling the beaked man feeding on him. She squeezed her eyes shut. She was so tired. And she kept hoping Kiril would appear, but when he didn't, she feared the worst.

A few minutes or maybe hours later, Valdim returned. He carried two golden hands in his arms. Even though they were hastily made and simple, they were beautiful. The fingers were fashioned from thick twigs knotted with willow leaf at the knuckles. Copper morning glory leaves with gold veins overlapped for the palm. Valdim dumped them in front of Anatoli.

'There,' he spat out.

Anatoli made a big show of examining them and said, 'They will do. Now, fasten them to my arms.'

Valdim looked around and pointed to the limp diamond vines at the base of one of the columns. Marisha kept the willow hand flush against Anatoli's stone stumps as Valdim twisted the vines and hooked the hands into place. He seemed completely absorbed by his work. Marisha wondered if he, like her, was only standing on the edge of hysteria. It seemed so strange, to see Valdim and Anatoli together, with Valdim looking at Anatoli with such hate and Anatoli responding with clear dislike. Marisha couldn't say anything about their connection, it wasn't her secret to tell. Just hold on for a little bit longer, she told herself. She tried her hardest to stop thinking she might see Dima alive again.

'There,' Valdim said, twisting the last vine into place. 'It's done. Now, Olena.'

Anatoli nodded. 'Yes, but I will only talk to Marisha. This is kolduni business. I'm sure you can understand.'

Valdim drew himself closer, his body tense and his hands in fists.

Marisha put a restraining hand on his shoulder. 'It's all right, I know what to do. Trust me.'

It took a moment, but Valdim nodded stiffly. He walked away, towards Olena.

Anatoli asked to see the feather. Marisha swallowed, but she had no choice. She showed him Golgolin's feather and placed it in one of his pockets. She told herself that it did not matter.

'You see that?' Anatoli said when she took a small vial with very thick glass walls from the instructed pocket. 'It's a special double-walled glass. The two vials are only touching at the neck.

There are six drops in that bottle, more than enough for me and Olena and your brother. Now, pour one drop out onto each of my hands. The water of death and the water of life would have given me my hands back, but the water of life alone should animate this stone and wire.'

'You want me to take care of you first?'

'Don't you want to make sure it works? Now. Go ahead. A drop onto the wrist, where it meets the stone arm.'

Marisha's hands trembled slightly as she unstoppered the vial. She tried to pretend it was a tincture of raspberry leaves and not a priceless cure. She carefully unstoppered the second inner vial, and tipped it. The neck of the inner bottle was so slim that the drop collected slowly. She dripped it, and it absorbed into the seam between the golden leaves and stone. They immediately sprang to life. Marisha only thought then maybe she ought to have bound him.

He met her eye. 'The other one.'

She swallowed and dripped once more. She jumped to her feet. He looked up at her with a crooked smile, 'Don't worry,' he said. 'I won't go back on my promise. I'm not so dishonourable.'

Marisha nodded. Then she remembered something. 'The sleepers, how will they leave?'

'Oh, that's easy,' he said carelessly, 'they have to remove their masks.'

'But Kiril said taking his mask off would kill him.'

'Not anymore. Now that the plague bringer doesn't hold them in thrall. Though some of them may have lasting damage.'

Marisha's face fell. 'And–the water of life. Could it, maybe help . . .'

Anatoli shook his head. 'The water of life revives. The water of death repairs. So, no. But, like the body, the spirit can heal. By forgetting. It's the easiest way.'

'They'll forget being here?'

'The sleepers who wake up after a year and a day, they don't remember this place. Why would it be any different for the deep sleepers?'

So Kiril would forget about her? *No one knows what will happen when deep sleepers awaken*, Pan Volya had said. She thought of Anka-ny's sister who fell into muteness and her aunt who lost all joy. 'There's nothing to be done for them?'

'They will be free of this place. That's not nothing.'

She took a deep breath and let it out slowly. 'Thank you, Anatoli.'

He shrugged. 'I wasn't doing *you* any favours.' And his gaze darted to Olena's supine form, where Valdim crouched next to it. Anatoli grimaced. Marisha wondered again if Anatoli had absolutely no inkling of how Valdim was related to him. Anatoli said, 'One drop, that's all she'll need. And remember what I said about reviving Zima.'

Marisha nodded and rushed to Olena. She had not even stoppered the bottle again but immediately crouched down beside her and poured a drop in the centre of her forehead. The drop absorbed into her skin like oil on cedar. Her shallow breath deepened and her expression relaxed. She murmured something. Valdim whooped and hugged Marisha. Marisha laughed, keeping the vial in her hand steady. He released her and knelt back besides Olena, smoothing her forehead.

Marisha's heart pounded. It had worked! She felt at once terribly relieved and terribly afraid. She ran back to the tree, to where Dima's body lay sprawled beneath it. She only peripherally noticed the dancers following her.

At least he did not look like Dima at all anymore. It made

it easier to crouch next to him and drop the water of life on the mass of flesh where his heart used to be. Marisha pressed her fist into her sternum, hoping. And the hole faded into substance. It was like watching a reflection on a disturbed pond stilling after a stone had been thrown at the centre. She had only a moment to see Dima's eyes flutter open before he shimmered and disappeared.

She pressed her hand on the stone tiles.

'His mask was off,' Kiril said. Marisha looked up. He stood at her side.

'So,' Marisha said, 'He left? To wake up?'

Kiril nodded. She felt relieved beyond measure.

She said, 'I'm so glad to see you, I was wondering where you were. I got worried.'

'Did you? Strange.' He frowned.

'Kiril, our bond–do you not feel it anymore?'

She held her breath in anticipation. When he shook his head, she was not sure how she was supposed to feel. Even though the idea that he was tethered to her had made her uncomfortable, she felt bereft now that it was gone. Would they have any connection without it?

'Kiril, it's possible that when you wake up, you may feel–different.' She closed her eyes. Pan Volya had said deep sleepers might wake so changed they'd be unrecognisable to themselves and their loved ones.

Kiril shook his head. 'Marisha, I have been here for ten years. I *am* different. You can't change that. Besides, why would you want to? You don't know what I was like ten years ago. But you know me now.'

She smiled sadly at thinking she might now never know him. She knew the zal sumerek version of him and the silent sleeper in the workroom who listened to all she had to say but never answered. She thought of Olena and Valdim dancing together, of the way he had tucked his kaftan around her sleeping form. They had the possibility of a future together. She closed her eyes, but tears ran down her cheeks anyway. It was entirely possible that without their emotional tether, she and Kiril shared nothing.

'Marisha, don't cry, I'll see you soon when I wake up.'

Marisha smiled through her tears. He did not know he would forget his time here–and her. But nothing could be done about it. 'Must you leave?'

'Yes. I feel the damp earth pulling me upwards. Fighting the urge is like wishing to stay in a dream when you've realised you're asleep.' His feathers began to fade at the edges.

Marisha said, 'You might be surprised to wake up in Olena's workroom.'

Kiril laughed. 'I think surprised is a grand understatement for what I will feel.'

Marisha tried to smile. 'Thank you, for coming for me. For not leaving me alone.' She blinked her eyes against the falling tears. He pulled her in close. She drew in a shuddering breath. She could not help it–she asked, 'Do you think you'll remember me?'

'Of course. How could I ever forget you?'

Marisha smiled. Kiril cupped her face and kissed her gently. But he seemed less solid somehow; the pressure of his lips was like a breath of air, not flesh. And he was gone.

FORTY-SIX

ll around her, the sleepers unhooked their masks and shimmered away. The space seemed large and empty. But a few feet to the left of the diamond tree, a green figure sat on a fallen branch. Marisha hurried over. Olena rose shakily to her feet with a cry of delight and the two women hugged each other.

'I was so worried,' Olena said, sobbing and clinging to Marisha. 'I thought–but what happened?'

'Let's talk about it later.'

Olena nodded and wiped her face. They settled back on the branch, Marisha on one side, Valdim on the other. Olena's hiccups quieted. They watched the last of the dancers disappear. When Marisha got up, neither Olena nor Valdim asked where she went, for which she was grateful. Meandering through the rubble, Marisha walked to where Baba Zima lay.

Marisha looked at the vial. Two drops left. She knew she did not have much time before Valdim and Olena joined her at Baba Zima's side. But still, she hesitated. Maybe under different circumstances she might have asked herself why she did not consult with Olena and Valdim, after all, they had a greater stake in whether or not she should revive Baba Zima. She raised the vial up, watching the thin layer of liquid glow as though it were light itself, then dripped one drop onto Baba Zima's forehead. Baba Zima's eyes opened and locked onto her face. Her eyelids flittered wildly with recognition and Marisha felt relief and apprehension.

'What happened,' Baba Zima said, 'Serafima—'

'She's gone. Olena took the poker.'

Baba Zima lay her head back down. 'Good.' She frowned. 'I feel strange.'

Marisha was not sure what to say. She wondered again if this was a good idea.

Baba Zima spoke again. 'So Valdim, and Olena?'

'Are fine.'

'And Anatoli?'

'He's gone. Off somewhere . . . Who knows.'

'Yes, well, he always was one to squirm away.' She paused. 'How did you revive me? I was gone . . . elsewhere. I know it.'

'The water of life. Anatoli gave it to me in exchange for freeing him, to help Olena.'

'Ha! And did he tell you that both the waters of life and death are necessary to revive someone truly dead?'

'He told me.'

'And yet you still chose to bring me back. Well, whatever's left of me. Why?'

Baba Zima looked down and saw the dark stain on her chest. She raised her fingers to it. Marisha recoiled in pity and horror and sprung to answer Baba Zima's question. 'I thought you might want a chance to explain.' Baba Zima's confession in the dungeon mingled with what the black feather had shown her, of Olga returning to the house and giving Valdim to Baba Zima's care. Of Olga's refusal to stay.

Baba Zima looked at her sharply. 'You know something you

ought not to. Don't deny it, you're an awful liar. Why I thought you'd be suitable as a koldunya's assistant is beyond me.' She paused, sucking in a deep, rattling breath. 'And when it's over? Am I to wander the other world for all eternity?'

Marisha shrugged. 'I suppose that's up to you. Serafima is still out there. And–I don't know if the beaked man is truly gone. It would make me feel better knowing you pursued them.'

'So, I'm to do your dirty work.' Baba Zima brooded for a moment, then said, 'Very well.'

Marisha steeled herself and turned. They walked the short distance around the tree to where Olena and Valdim sat on a fallen branch. They looked straight ahead, but on the branch between them, Olena and Valdim's hands were no more than a hairsbreadth apart.

The pair looked over. Their mouths fell open. Valdim rushed over and hugged his mother. She hugged him back and murmured, 'I am so proud of you.'

Olena looked at Marisha, an accusatory, questioning look. Marisha gave her a small nod. And Olena took a deep breath and faced her former mistress.

'It's true,' Olena said, her voice sharp, 'what she said. Wasn't it.'

Valdim let go of Baba Zima and shifted to stand beside Olena. The corner of Baba Zima's mouth lifted at the sight of them, and lowered at the hardness in Olena's face.

'In a way, yes. The same way the fears you whisper to yourself in the dead of the night are true–half-truths you would never acknowledge under the light of day. But that's the extent of it. It was never a conscious part of my choice.'

'Then what was?'

'Serafima was right, I had seen hundreds of girls, but I recognised *you* as my successor.'

'But why!'

'I recognised your pain, a mirror of my own.'

Olena clutched her stump. 'It's not painful, not like your hands.'

'Not that, you foolish child. You had hurt someone you loved, you had done the worst you could possibly do–I saw it in your eyes when your parents brought you to me after I tried to heal your brother's back. They asked me to be rid of your curse or to be rid of you.'

Olena recoiled as though the words were blows. Baba Zima continued, her eyes riveted on her former apprentice. 'I saw your pain, and I *knew* it. It's the same pain I had lived with for years after what I did to my mistress, the guilt eating away at me: I had robbed the person most dear to me, banished her to an unknown fate.'

Baba Zima's gaze darted around the courtyard and the rubble. She swallowed and took a deep breath. 'And for years I had sworn that I would never take an apprentice, that I would never give someone the opportunity to do to me as I had done to Baba Serafima. Then I saw you and your suffering: your mistakes, your strength. You endured through all of it, through the hardness of others, until that point–the point where you had destroyed what you valued most. And I thought, if I could give you a second chance, if I could help you find redemption, I could redeem myself.'

Olena wept silently. Baba Zima gathered her into her arms. 'I wanted to leave someone better than I was. I'm sorry if I was a hard mistress. I hadn't had a good example, but I think I succeeded. And I hoped to give you my blessing one day, when I passed my bolshina to you. It's a little late for that, but if you still want it . . .'

Olena nodded, tears still streaming. She bowed her head and Baba Zima clasped her hand and murmured streams of words flowed low under her voice.

Baba Zima turned to Valdim. 'My son.'

'Am I?'

'In all the ways that count.'

'Before you left you said that you had things to tell me. Was that one of them?'

'Yes. I wanted to tell you about Olga. She couldn't take care of you, but she hoped that you could find a home with me.' Baba Zima looked down and her eyes sparkled with tears. She drew him to the side and talked to him in a low voice.

Marisha settled a few feet away to give them more privacy. She was glad she had revived Baba Zima, this was worth it. But her mind lingered on Kiril. She wished she could have used the water of life to heal him instead. She wished, once again, that she and Olena had found the water of death after all. She thought of him, waking up in the workshop alone.

A shadow fell on her, then she felt Baba Zima's hand on her arm. Maybe it was knowing Baba Zima only existed in spirit, but the weight of it felt less, somehow.

Baba Zima said in a low voice, 'You're a puzzle to me, Marisha. It's clear you don't belong in this, not the way that I do, nor Olena, nor even Valdim. But–you have something else, and it's something we needed.'

'Perspective?'

Baba Zima laughed. 'Yes, maybe that's it. Wisdom beyond your years. Well, perhaps not far beyond your years, you are old for an assistant.'

'As you keep on reminding me.'

'Ha! Goodness, I will miss how easily you are ruffled. For what it's worth, I'm very glad for whatever temporary madness passed over me the day I thought to hire you.'

Marisha smiled, 'Me too.'

They stood silent for a moment. Baba Zima's gaze was fixed on Olena and Valdim, standing together. Olena's shy smile was visible for the whole world to see. Marisha's chest constricted at the joy that lighted on Baba Zima's face.

'It's a hard thing,' Baba Zima said, 'Carrying the bolshina. It helps to have people around you. I'm glad that I was much less alone than I could have been. There was a time, before Valdim, before Olena, when I felt very lonely. Luckily, Valdim came quickly.' Baba Zima smiled and shook her head. 'I was so angry at Olga, so angry. She returned only to dump her son on me, and when she left again she blamed the house. Ha! She said she had left, and it would no longer accept her. I see now that it was because she had made up her mind to leave. She's the one who closed the door. But she didn't have to.'

Marisha thought of Baba Zima standing at the front door holding Valdim in her arms, watching as Olga turned and left. It was the same door that Marisha had refused to let shut her out two decades later, though she had to rip her dress to follow Baba Zima inside.

'Why are you telling me this?'

'Just making conversation. You know all my secrets somehow, the least you could do is listen when I'm trying to tell you something.'

'All right, I'm listening.'

'I told you everything I wanted to, actually.'

Marisha rolled her eyes. They stood in silence for a few more seconds until Marisha couldn't stand it anymore. She said, 'Have you decided where you're going?'

'To hunt Serafima–eventually. There's a whole world here.' She said the last with a smile. 'You have given it to me.'

Baba Zima left them with the promise that this was not the last they would hear from her. They stood in silence for a long moment. Marisha's hands were in her pockets. She had checked the vial and one drop of water of life remained.

'We should go.' Valdim said.

'I know. It's only—' Olena gestured down at the guinea pig-fowl with bent wings and closed eyes. 'I don't know if he will make the journey back.' Olena bent her head and her shoulders trembled.

Marisha didn't hesitate. She knelt by the guinea pig-fowl and dropped the last drop of the water of life onto the little animal's fur. Golgolin blinked a beady eye and jerked into a seated position. He flapped directly into Olena's arms. Olena seemed lost for words. She hugged the guinea pig-fowl and drew Marisha into a hug, Golgolin squashed between them. He squawked in annoyance and flapped off to Valdim who hugged the creature in turn, to much continued squawking.

'But—' Olena looked at the bottle in Marisha's hand. 'There was more? I didn't–is there any left?'

Marisha shook her head. Olena sighed. 'I was hoping it still might work for a cure.'

'For the plague?' Marisha asked. Olena nodded. Marisha burst out into loud laughter that echoed around the courtyard. She doubled over and could not stop.

'What? What's so funny?'

Marisha quieted her deluge into a stream. Laughing hurt her chest, but it felt so good. Olena looked affronted and wore a decidedly Olena-ish frown of annoyance. It almost set Marisha off again.

'Nothing,' Marisha said, waving her uninjured hand before her face, 'It's just that, there isn't a plague anymore. Sorry Olena, but I believe I took care of it.'

Olena's comically perplexed expression made Marisha tremble with badly suppressed giggles. Olena said, 'You did what?'

'Can we talk about it later?'

Olena clamped her mouth shut, though it looked like it took some effort. Valdim waved at them by the door that led out of the courtyard, Golgolin perched on his shoulder. Olena melted Golgolin's final feather into the doorknob, they linked hands and leapt into the threshold.

FORTY-SEVEN

unya had only been asleep for a few days, but she found the idea so terrifying she demanded to be brought home to her parents immediately. Dunya had seemed surprised when Olena asked her if she needed more than a month of leave before she brought the house back to pick her up. Dunya shook her head *no*, one month would do nicely.

Anka-ny wrote to the house with the incredible news that her youngest sister, who had been in the early wave of plague victims, had awoken without any ill effects. She was also happy to take some more time to spend with her family.

Olena and Valdim tiptoed around each other, as though not wanting to startle their new relationship. But one morning, a few days later, Marisha woke up to a screechy noise, which apparently was Valdim teaching Olena to play the violin. He had built her a bow that fastened onto her stump. It sounded awful, but Olena was pleased and seemed to have taken it as appropriate amends for whatever offence Valdim had committed. Marisha happily teased Olena about her terrible playing to no end.

The house seemed empty without Baba Zima. The morning after they returned, Marisha set up an extra teacup on the table by accident. She left it there. For some reason, it made her feel a lot better.

When they arrived in Severny, Marisha headed to the sanitorium where her parents had slept. The orderly checked his book and told Marisha that her parents had been taken into care by one Dimitri Elyasevich Galinov. Marisha's face split into a smile. Dima was awake too! The wish to see them strummed through her body, but the longing almost immediately collapsed into guilty relief that they were gone.

Olena had asked Marisha if she needed more time in Severny, but she declined. She had said they needed to bring Kiril to his home before she could do anything else, which was partially true. But the real reason she wanted to leave Severny was that she was afraid of facing her family. She both wanted and did not want to talk to them. Not yet. She needed time to process what had happened and to figure out what she needed to say. The beaked man's feather had shown her things about her father that still stung. And Dima . . . the sanitorium's book was proof that he was alive, yes, but was he whole?

The state of Dima's spirit worried her like a loose tooth. Her thoughts constantly returned to Ivan the Fool from Pan Volya's story: how he had lost interest in the language of birds and was condemned to wander the world in search of his missing piece of spirit. She imagined Dima trying to understand what had happened, but not being able to remember why he felt the way he did. She wondered if her parents had fared better or worse. She wondered why she had not thought to look for her parents as the dancers trickled into the courtyard with the diamond tree.

And perhaps, if she was honest with herself, besides her fear of facing her family, she also needed to leave Severny to remove the temptation of returning to Pan Volya's house and confronting him. The koldun was too dangerous. Still, her mind buzzed with questions and she imagined a thousand ways that the conversation would go. They always seemed to culminate in rage at him for forcing her father into a bargain and indenturing Dima.

Pan Volya's possible explanations rang through her mind in her timberless inner voice: *Dima crossing my path was fate asserting itself. And Dima is very rich now because of it. You should be thanking me.*

Thanking you? My brother fell to the sleeping plague because of you! She could almost see the beaked man cracking Dima's ribs open. She pressed her fist to her sternum.

Her imaginary Pan Volya said simply: *Not because of me. Of course, I'm not innocent of the matter. But I did not force Dima into it. He knew the terms. He agreed. As did your father.*

Of course he would have said something like that. Of course it would have been impossible to reason with him.

And when the rage subsided, when she had spent enough time looking out the window at the pine branches brushing the house's wooden shingles with the gentleness of a mother running her fingers through her daughter's hair, another question bubbled up to the forefront of her mind: *How do you mark a soul for the beaked man?*

Pan Volya's voice answered her again: *Why do you ask?*

Did she really have to explain this to herself? *When I faced the beaked man, he spoke to me. He said, 'You're keeping it for me.' And I thought about that story you told me. About Nightingale the Robber–Ivan the Fool–looking for a piece of his spirit. It fits too neatly.*

And you think you have it?

Of course, she had considered it. That was the whole crux of the issue. *It's not important whether I have it or not. What's important is why the beaked man acted as though he knew I had it.*

Because, if he could have detected it himself, there would have been only one plague victim, not hundreds of thousands over the centuries.

And so? What do you think happened?

I think you marked the souls for the beaked man by telling him through the feather that they were carrying that missing piece of his spirit. I don't know why . . . maybe you were power-hungry or maybe you were simply curious. Marisha thought of how Pan Volya's eyes lit up when she asked him about the glass that could reveal a person's colours. How he leaned forward when he told her the story of Ivan the Fool. *For whatever reason, you told the beaked man that my father's child had his missing piece of spirit.*

She imagined Pan Volya cracking a lazy smile. *Yes. You're very clever. Except you're missing something. I would have expected the plague-bringer to target Dima, or at the very least, target both of you if I was so ambiguous with my suggestions. But no, the plague-bringer targeted you. He only returned for your brother during the next cycle when he realised that you were inaccessible due to your mother's shield spell.*

That's ridiculous.

And can you explain it any other way?

Her heart beat faster. Marisha remembered the recognition in the beaked man's eyes, the accusation. She pushed herself away from the window.

Marisha reminded herself that just because she could not explain the beaked man's actions in a way that satisfied her did not mean that a satisfactory explanation did not exist. It was not misfortune that had brought her to the beaked man. It was a consequence of Pan Volya's actions, and her father's. Cause and consequence. And that was that.

But she continued to think about fate in the days that followed. Her thoughts did not always turn to the off-putting idea that she carried a bit of the beaked man's spirit. She thought about the twist of circumstances that had led Baba Zima to hiring her. She thought about the even greater twist that had linked her to Serafima through her father, Baba Zima and Pan Volya. Perhaps cause and consequence was less like a chain and more like a web, with one tug of a thread cascading through the entire structure.

Through all the muddle, one thing remained clear to her: bringing Kiril home was the last step. And once that was done, her future dissolved into fog. Without fate, only possibility remained. But why did she feel like her path had not opened, but stopped?

As suspected, Kiril had not been overjoyed at waking up in the linen closet attached to Olena's workroom. Even though Marisha saw it as her mission to ensure his return home, she avoided seeing him. She could not bear to talk to Kiril as though he were a stranger. The day he was slated to leave, however, she knew she had to say goodbye, or she would regret it.

He sat in the receiving room, watching the landscape go by. The snow turned slushy. They would have to travel far north to find some remaining snow suitable for skiing.

'We'll be in Oblonsk soon,' Marisha said.

Kiril looked at her. Marisha hoped for a moment, but his gaze held no spark of recognition. 'Thank you,' he said carelessly.

Marisha almost left. But she forced herself to walk over to the window. She tried to smile. She almost couldn't recognise him without the feathers and wondered what it would be like to kiss him now. She felt very shy.

'It's remarkable, isn't it?' she said, 'These past months, I was so miserable here at times, I thought about leaving a lot. Then I'd look out the window and remember where I was.'

They both looked out the window for a long time. Though she faced outwards, she was very aware of the space Kiril occupied next to her.

'Ten years,' he said.

She looked at him curiously.

He repeated himself, 'Ten years. I've been asleep since I was sixteen. And now I find myself—' He shook his head. 'I can't sleep. I haven't slept since I've woken up.'

'Afraid?'

'Yes.'

'I understand what that's like,' Marisha said cautiously.

'You were a plague victim as well?'

'In a way.'

Kiril looked down. 'I know I should be grateful. I should be happy to be awake. But,' he shook his head, 'there are moments I think that I should have stayed asleep. That it would have been easier.' He took a deep breath. 'I apologise. I should not be burdening you like this. It's just . . . It feels easy to talk to you. Maybe it's because you took care of me. That's what Baba Olena said. That you took care of me.' He met her gaze for a moment.

Marisha opened and closed her mouth before simply saying, 'I did.'

'Thank you.' Kiril went back to looking out the window, a small frown on his face.

Marisha knew he was probably thinking about all the people he had left behind, his family and friends. Would they still know him? Would they be happy he returned from the half-dead? He had lost ten years of his life. He had been a teenager when he had fallen asleep, and now he was a grown man. She couldn't imagine what that must be like. And what it must be like for her mother, twenty years of her life lost as she slept. She now wished more than ever that she had talked to her parents and Dima immediately after returning from the other world. She wished she had given Kiril the drop of the water of life–even though she hated herself for wishing it.

Marisha racked her mind for something to say. 'What was your trade? You never did tell–I mean, I never knew.'

He gave her a puzzled look at her slip of the tongue but let it go. 'Farming. I was to take over the family land, but I guess my brother . . . we'll see.'

'I'm sorry.'

'Don't be. Farms always need extra hands. I wouldn't want to impose if I'm not needed. I have a feeling going back might be . . . a shock.'

'You could always try something new.'

He smiled sadly. 'Very true. A new path . . . who would have thought this would be my fate.' He turned and met her gaze with his. 'I think I will get ready, if we are almost there. Thank you for listening.'

Kiril left the windowsill. The road stretched flat through the countryside. They had left the forest and were now in the taiga. The tussock grass was a green almost as grey as the sky. The flatness stretched out as far as the eye could see, with only a few scraggly pines dotting the horizon like sparse teeth in a starukha's mouth. Mist obscured the horizon and Marisha was sure it rained somewhere. How incredible that such an open landscape could feel so terribly oppressive.

'May I say something?'

Marisha started. She thought Kiril had left. 'Yes?'

'There's something about you that's familiar. It's a bit infuriating actually. Like looking at something from out of the corner of the eye. When you try to catch it, it's gone.'

Marisha recalled all the maddening déjà vu the dreaming had induced in her. 'Like trying to pick up a handful of water.'

'There it is again! I think it's your voice.'

'Maybe it's because when you were asleep, I would talk to you.'

Kiril's frown smoothed. 'Ah, that must be it. I think you talked yourself into my dreams.'

'I did?'

'Yes, I think I dreamt of you. Except there was music.'

'And?' She should not dare to hope.

Kiril closed his eyes, his brows crinkled in concentration. 'That's all.'

'Ah,' Marisha forced a smile, 'I guess it's a good thing you don't remember what I said. It was mostly nonsense.'

'No. I don't think it was.' He studied her again for a long moment and said, 'If this house ever returns to Oblonsk, I hope you will visit.'

Marisha nodded. She wanted to say something to stop him from leaving, but she didn't know what.

He walked to the door.

'Wait,' Marisha said. 'I can make you a sleeping potion. Maybe it will help. I'm sorry I did not offer it before.'

After she prepared the potion, Marisha had an idea, 'Maybe I could write to you? To see how you get on.'

Kiril's mouth broke into a small smile. 'I would like that. Though I don't know how I would write back.'

Marisha smiled, thinking of Golgolin. 'We have ways to receive letters. That is, if you wanted to write.'

Kiril's smile broadened. Marisha remembered that feeling that she had had when she had said goodbye to him before entering the courtyard. She had felt that she would have been happy to stay with him in the other world if only everyone else could return.

But after Kiril left the house, whatever momentary elation Marisha had felt seeped out of her. She went back to looking out the window.

Later that day, Olena walked in and stood at the window beside Marisha. The Hands followed her, carrying the samovar between them. One of them handed Marisha a cup of tea. Marisha smiled at the painted pink-and-green mice along the porcelain rim. One of Baba Zima's favourites.

'Kiril left?' Marisha asked.

Olena nodded. She said, 'This really is a most dismal place.'

Marisha sighed and looked out. Only a handful of shabby houses in Oblonsk.

She said, 'But it's home for him.'

'Did he invite you to stay?'

Marisha snorted. 'He doesn't remember.'

'Ah. I still don't understand why you didn't want me to try whipping something up to jog his memory.'

Marisha shrugged. 'I did not think it would work.'

Olena sighed. 'You were right. It didn't work.'

'You tried?'

'Of course I tried. But I suppose the memories vanished with the beaked man. Whatever you did really finished him.'

Marisha shivered at the memory. Ever since they had returned, she had nightmares occasionally, but they had a different quality. Less real, less shimmery. The beaked man could only continue to torment her through her own mind.

'I still can't believe you solved it in the end.'

Marisha rolled her eyes. 'I told you, I didn't do it on purpose.

Nobody knows, it's not like I could take the credit anyway.' She hesitated. 'Are you upset that I did?'

'No, it just amuses me. For months I was the one obsessed with finding a cure, I risked everything for it, and you are the one who banishes the plague.' Olena shook her head. 'It's funny.' She hesitated. 'I know it doesn't count for much, but I'm very proud of you.'

Marisha giggled. 'My goodness, praise from the great Baba Olena, it really is like being thanked by the Grand Prince.'

'Oh, all right, mock me.'

Marisha smiled. 'It's probably a good thing no one knows I lifted the plague. Think of all the honours that would have been bestowed upon me, the fame. I think the envy might have made you melt.'

'You know what? I think I would have muddled through,' Olena said with as much dignity as possible, and grinned. 'But I'm glad I don't have to.'

'Olena,' Marisha said after a moment, 'I think I need to go home.' Wherever that was.

'Didn't you send your letters with Golgolin?'

'Of course I did. But I would like to visit Dima. And my parents.'

'Ah. I see.'

Olena squared her body away from Marisha to the window.

Marisha said, 'I need some time. To figure out what I want.'

'I don't understand. Are you telling me you want to leave?'

Marisha remembered Baba Zima squared off against Olga in the house's entryway. Baba Zima had said: *She's the one who closed the door. But she didn't have to.* Marisha sighed. This was a different situation. She turned to Olena. 'I think you need some time to figure out what it means to be mistress of this house.

And besides, you have Valdim. You need to figure out what you mean to each other as well.'

Olena blushed. 'Valdim is not important. I mean, he is, just not to this conversation. Marisha, I need you. I can't do this alone: I don't know how to be a mistress. I need your help. Please stay.'

Marisha took Olena's hand in hers. 'You need an apprentice who is passionate about the koldunic arts. That's not me.'

Olena frowned. 'So, you don't want to be a koldunya?'

Marisha said, 'I like being a koldunya. I like the challenge and the mystery of it. But I don't love it. Not like you do.'

'What do you love? Do you really want to go set up house for your brother? Do you want to get married?'

Marisha thought of her old ambitions to be a respectable married woman making her way into society. That now seemed so stifling to her she wanted to scream. 'No. I don't want that, not now anyways,' she said. 'Back then I was trying to run from Aunt Lyubov, and the plague, but now, I'm not so sure. Except I still want to run; not in the same way, not running from something but towards something. Explore.' She smiled at Olena. 'Maybe I'll take the trip to the Spice Islands that Dima said he would make.'

'You really are an idiot.'

Marisha frowned. 'Excuse me?'

'You say you want to explore and here you are sitting in a chicken-legged house that travels from village to village, from one side of the Chernozemlya to the other.'

'I know that—'

'Furthermore, Golgolin will surely moult sooner or later, and when he does, the whole other world will be open to us. And we'll have to track Serafima down–I don't believe she's dead–and Baba Zima surely can't do it on her own. And what about Anatoli, he still must be out there too.'

'That's true, but—'

'And I still think we should look for the water of death, it must be here somewhere. Who knows the cures we could make!'

Marisha opened her mouth to contradict Olena and then thought of the basin she had seen bubbling black water in her vision of the house while touching the black feather. She could not remember the dizzying sequence of hallways and stairs that had led her to the receiving room, but if it was there, then it could be found. 'Olena—'

'Well?'

Marisha did not know what to say. 'It will be years before Golgolin moults again.'

'But until then, there's the whole princedom to explore. Even beyond. You can't tell me you're not interested.'

Marisha could not help but smile. 'I suppose I should at least see my contract out. We can discuss again when it's done. And I still want to visit my parents.'

'Of course.' Olena nodded but ruined the solemnity with a little jump. 'I'm so glad you're staying.'

Marisha smiled back, her gaze arresting on the desolate grey landscape, which no longer seemed so desolate. Her scalp tingled. 'Me too.'

ACKNOWLEDGMENTS

TK

ABOUT THE AUTHOR

LAUREN WIESEBRON is a fantasy author, writing adventures for characters who don't yet know they need them. She grew up in France, developed incurable wanderlust, and became an itinerant academic studying sea creatures. When not writing, you can find her acquiring yarn and naming houseplants. She has also been known to pick up cats even when they don't want to be picked up.